WHAT PEOPLE ARE SAY

TIME KNOT

Time Knot is a fast-paced, time-slip novel, a sequel to Morison's debut, *Time Sphere*.

A most clever tale, unwrapping the notion that 'Gods created time that mankind could be free…to choose as their minds decided, ' *Time Knot* is a humorous, yet thought-provoking read.

The story opens with a prophecy:

'You must go both North and South. Find the fire before you find the ice. Trust the drum, it knows the dance of time. You are the dance and the dancer.'

And so it starts, the latest adventure of Rhory, The Red King, dodging bullets, arrows, and disbelief from his big sister, Juliette. Time-travelling to sixteenth century Sweden, where he embarks on crystal boat ride in turquoise waters, and sleigh-chases over a frozen lake, guided only by the yellow, crescent moon and the stars, Rhory leaves behind himself only footsteps in the snow.

Simultaneously, he 'lands' in modern-day Alexandria, at first, unaware of those on his trail.

"'BEWARE,' whispered the soundless voice. A voice older than Alexandria. A voice older than Egypt," denoting a slip back to Alexandria in the year 380 CE for Rhory (and a timely move for this book aimed at the YA market) offering up for the reader a rich, poetic insight into the legend of the true Goddess Isis.

Enriched by the scent of ancient sandalwood and the timeless Northern lights, this tale of alchemy stretches the imagination into what could be, and warns of the possible repercussions of misplaced personal possessions!

I'm already pondering the next instalment.

Helen Noble, author of *The 49th Day*

Time Knot is an excitingly non-stop adventure story, and Mr Morison has developed a literary style that brings the reader four-square into the exploits of the teenage protagonist Rhory as he pursues, and in turn is pursued, through time and space in his efforts to save the priceless wisdom of ancient Alexandria.

The book is a more than worthy successor to *Time Sphere* but it can most certainly be read alone.

Time Knot is aimed at a Young Adult market and it strikes exactly the right balance between fantasy and historical accuracy, neither condescending to the reader nor expecting too much of her either. Rhory encounters unexpected twists and turns in a dizzying helter skelter through time and space, and so will the reader. It is a lot of fun!

Philip Duke, author of *A Terrible Unrest*

M.C. Morison's *Time Sphere* left me anxious for the sequel. *Time Knot* is that sequel and it more than lives up to the action, mystery, and humor of the first book in the Timepathway Series. Rhory remains a lively and likeable hero and his adventures never fail to enthrall.

Jan Krause Greene, author of *I Call Myself Earth Girl*

The fast pace of this ingenious and skillfully woven story leads it's hero, Rhory, and the reader on an emotional roller coaster through time. A tale in which, Rhory, a modern day, somewhat naive, teenager is inextricably caught up in a battle between the forces of good and sinister perpetrators of evil. The action takes place concurrently in worlds as extreme as present day England, Alexandria in BC Egypt and the snow-covered countryside of sixteenth-century Sweden.

Time Knot is a fascinating, page-turner of an adventure aimed at the young adult, but equally enjoyable for anyone.

Veryan Williams-Wynn, author of *The Spirit Trap*

Time Knot

Time Knot

M.C. Morison

LODESTONE BOOKS

Winchester, UK
Washington, USA

First published by Lodestone Books, 2017
Lodestone Books is an imprint of John Hunt Publishing Ltd., Laurel House, Station Approach,
Alresford, Hants, SO24 9JH, UK
office1@jhpbooks.net
www.johnhuntpublishing.com

For distributor details and how to order please visit the 'Ordering' section on our website.

ISBN: 978 1 78535 490 8
978 1 78535 491 5 (ebook)
Library of Congress Control Number: 2016937656

A CIP catalogue record for this book is available from the British Library.

Design: Stuart Davies

Printed and bound by CPI Group (UK) Ltd, Croydon, CR0 4YY, UK

In honour of Hypatia,
and the wise women of all eras
who have kept the light of truth burning.

Acknowledgements

There are many to thank in the genesis of this story. Martha Lyn understands better than most the brilliance of the philosopher Hypatia and her grasp of the Mysteries, and shared her insights with me. The Fintry Trust made available to me a treasure trove of books, now long out of print, on the alchemist Paracelsus.

In Chania, our Writers' Group heard many parts of this story as we met over the last two years and their comments were invaluable. As always I am indebted to Marie Smith for her insights. Jussi Wendelin-Ottila and Riina Ilona Laamanen, who hale from snowy Scandinavia, helped me enormously with getting the snow and ice sequences in medieval Sweden believable.

The encouragement of my good friend and fellow author Philip Duke, who read through an early version of the manuscript, was most welcome.

Heather, my wife, patiently listened to most of this book being read as episodes were written, and her support and grasp of the intricacies of grammar are deeply appreciated.

Arlette Start kindly offered her services as a copy editor as did Jill Marrington. I am most grateful to you both for spotting so easily those things that hid themselves from my sight. Maria Moloney, my editor at John Hunt Publishing, also made invaluable suggestions about various crucial moments in the story.

This book rests on ideas seeded by the work of The Fintry Trust. I am grateful for all I have received from that source. I commend any who wish to explore the perennial philosophy behind this story to explore the treasure trove to be found at www.thefintrytrust.org.uk.

For more information about the background to this trilogy and the final volume of Rhory's adventures, please visit www.timepatheway.com

Return to the Well

England – about now

Juliette stepped in front of me, her arms wide apart, blocking my path.

"Rhory. No. You can't expect me to believe that. It defies science and it defies common sense. I don't know why you're saying these things."

Behind her the trees of Hammerford Park writhed and rustled in the chill wind. We stood facing each other midway between the bandstand and the old oak. Juliette is my favourite sister. Correction. Juliette is my only sister. Seventeen, brighter than a super-nova and prettier than your average celeb, she remained my older sister and thus terminally irritating.

I tried to explain for the umpteenth time: "But it's true. I can only tell you what I experienced. I wasn't going to share this with you because I knew you wouldn't get it. But you insisted. 'Tell me the truth,' you said. 'No, I'll understand,' you said. So I did. And you don't."

"Would you honestly expect any sane person to believe that under our stupid old bandstand there is an ancient temple?" She pointed at the structure with the green finger of her rainbow-coloured gloves. "And if it is there, which it isn't, but if it is there, that you're the only one who knows about it?"

Juliette turned to face the bandstand, as though expecting me to produce an old temple like a rabbit out of a hat. Her dark hair blew around her face and she pulled her multicoloured woolly hat lower.

"I never said I was the only one who knows about it. It's marked on an old map that Natasha and I found at the Town Hall, and I think that an ancient secret society—"

"You can stop right there." Jules spun back and poked me in

the chest. "Save me the ridiculousness of ancient secret societies. You've always had a vivid imagination. In many ways it's quite cute. But now you're going too far."

"Look, Jules, like it or not, there's a tunnel running from the old well in the Wild Wood." I pointed in the general direction beyond the swimming pool enclosure. "And it comes out into the temple. The temple then opens into the storage area under the bandstand. Jeez..." irritation buzzed through me, "...I walked it only a few weeks ago."

"Okay. The joke's gone on long enough. I don't even know why I've come with you." She thrust her hands into the pockets of her coat. "Frankly, you're making me complicit in your stupid fantasies. You'll be a laughing stock if you tell anyone else. Do you want that?"

"Bleeding heck, just come and look. It'll only take us a few minutes to get to the well, then you can see." I pulled on her arm. "It's quite possible to spot where the tunnel sets off near the metal rungs that go down towards the water. You can even go down and try it yourself."

My sister snorted at that suggestion. We set off in silence under a dark-grey and somewhat threatening sky.

Juliette looked up. "That's all I need. To get soaked while on a wild goose chase."

I glanced over towards the old oak. Its shape had definitely changed since the lightning struck, the night I found the temple. I'd pretty much avoided the park since then and had pretty much avoided thinking through all the implications. I hadn't shared that I'd travelled through time to a crucial moment in world history and prevented a human sacrifice. I hadn't even told Juliette that bit. I'd mentioned that I'd found an old temple beneath the bandstand and how this had helped me connect with the young Egyptian priestess.

A few minutes later we were by the fence that separated the path encircling Hammerford Park from the briars and brambles beyond. Dad had named this bit, with its years of old leaves and fallen branches, the Wild Wood. Last autumn, I'd climbed over with a mate and we'd found an old well hidden amongst the bushes.

The metal fence came up to my chin. I cupped my hands for Juliette's foot to help her climb over and then followed, landing with a crash on leaf-mould and old twigs. Juliette slipped off her small backpack. She extracted a powerful torch and one of Dad's paint-stained screwdrivers.

"So, where is it then?"

"Just over here."

I led the way in, and pulled back some ferns and a spiky branch from a hawthorn bush.

I looked in horror. The whole top of the well had changed. The wooden lid had entirely gone.

"Ha!" said Juliette. "Ha bloody ha. Now you're going to tell me you slipped through six inches of concrete! Just like some teenage priestess slipped through several thousand years of time."

"It wasn't like this ... I mean, just a few weeks ago. It had an old wooden top, held with a few rusty screws. Nat and I unscrewed it and—"

"Spare me, Rhory, spare me. Are you seriously going to tell me that someone just happens to have come along and sealed the top of the well since you went down it? I mean look around." She kicked at some leaves with her foot. "Can you see where a cement mixer sat? Can you see footprints from workmen? Just confess I've caught you in a lie and be man enough to admit it."

I felt sick and a little dizzy. The top of the well was completely sealed by concrete that looked like it had been there for months, if not years. I knelt down and poked around the edge of the brickwork. Something glinted. I eased it out from where it had been half buried. A long rusty screw, with its head partially sheared. The sheared part still sparkled with clean metal. This had to be the screw I'd broken when my cousin Natasha and I opened up the well-top some weeks earlier.

"Look, Jules..." I said. Then I stopped talking; I'd caught a glimpse of a man's face watching us through the fence, further round the path. Because I was kneeling, he hadn't seen that I could spot him.

"Can we help you?" I shouted. The face vanished.

Juliette swung round to me, the screwdriver in her hand.

"Who are you talking to?"

"Some guy's watching us."

"Yeah, okay, pull the other one, Rhory. No one in their right mind would be out in the park with a sky as dark as this." Juliette looked around, keeping tight hold of the screwdriver. "Come on, let's go. You've been caught out, my dear brother, admit it."

"No, I won't admit anything of the sort. You can ask Natasha. She was here, remember?"

Juliette just shook her head, and put the screwdriver in the backpack. I strode over and took it out again.

"Look. I'm going to prove it."

Vandalism

I crunched across to the metal railings and yanked myself over.

"Oh thanks very much," said Juliette, from the far side of the fence.

She went through the necessary contortions to put the backpack on. I checked up and down the path but couldn't see anyone. Perhaps I'd imagined the face? No. A man had been staring at us.

I ground my teeth and hunched my shoulders as I marched past the Hammerford Baths and up the slope towards the bandstand. I would show Juliette the trapdoor. It led down to the temple. In fact, if she had the courage, we would both go down and explore. I stopped and looked around. Juliette rounded the corner of the swimming pool enclosure about fifty metres behind me. The periphery of the park brooded in gloom, and if anyone was standing in the shadows I wouldn't be able to see them in the half light. I'd a distinct sense someone was watching us. A spot of rain glistened on the sleeve of my jacket. I pulled my scarf tighter around my neck to keep out the chill and marched towards the bandstand once more.

"Bloody hell, Rhory, you've vandalised it."

Juliette pointed at the old door to the storeroom beneath the bandstand. The wood around the lock had splintered where I'd forced it with the screwdriver.

"Look, Jules, just look. The lock on the door is brand new. Isn't it one coincidence too many that the door has a new lock and someone's capped the well, all within six or seven weeks of my using them?"

Juliette frowned: perhaps at the logic of my argument. More likely she disapproved of breaking into the storage room.

I scraped the door across the tarmac and held out my hand.

"Give me the torch and I'll show you the trap door."

Juliette opened up her backpack once more and drew out the torch. She looked towards the council offices where most of the windows were lit up. Then she surveyed the path beyond the swings and sandpit. We were alone, as far as we could see.

"Come on, let's be quick, I don't fancy coming up before a magistrate just because you can't tell fantasy from reality."

I ignored that jibe, switched on the torch and flashed the beam around inside. It looked all wrong. It smelt all wrong. Once more I felt like throwing up or smashing something precious. The floor had changed and the storage room reeked of adhesive. Someone had covered the whole area in thick linoleum, with a yellow and brown pattern. The deck chairs stood in neat piles over to the right. Straight ahead, where the trapdoor had been – the trapdoor I had used – the linoleum extended unbroken. Without a sharp knife there would be no way to get to the trapdoor, and without wrecking the whole floor there would be no way to find it.

I came out and kicked the door.

"Ouch."

Juliette took the torch and looked inside.

"We'd better get out of here before someone sees us." Juliette pushed the door back but it stuck six inches short of closing. "God, Rhory, you've bent the hinges." She giggled.

"I don't think so." I held the edge of the door, pulled upwards and kicked it closed at the same time. It slammed home; but splintered wood around the lock remained as evidence of our visit.

Juliette held my eyes for some moments, biting her bottom lip. She shrugged. "C'mon, Bro. We both need a cup of tea."

The man leaned against the wall of the office building at the corner of Suffolk Road. He'd followed the two youngsters back from the park. The kids hadn't spotted him this time. He reached into an inside pocket of his moss-green military-style coat and took out a bulky mobile phone. Across the road three girls came out of the newsagents and their indistinct voices carried over to him. The girls shared sweets as they dodged puddles reflecting the lit windows of the library. A slight drizzle left small glistening droplets on the man's cropped hair.

"Your intel was spot on," said the man into the phone. "They went to both the well and the bandstand at the time you specified." He listened for a moment and nodded. "The sister's a bit of all right." A squawk came from the speaker. "Okay, just sayin'. She's fit and I know where he lives. Do you want me to stiff the lad? It'd be easy to do now I know his house."

He concentrated on the answer, his forehead creased, and then closed down the phone. A car with dipped headlights approached Suffolk Road signalling to turn in. The man pulled up his collar and headed for the main road, keeping his face in the shadows.

Hospital Visit

"Will she die, Dad?" I asked, as we turned into the hospital car park.

"We all die, Rhory," my dad responded, "and she's had a good innings. But for the moment she's just quite ill, so we'll have to hope for the best."

We paid for a parking ticket, parked eventually and located the main entrance to the hospital. The lifts, with brainless graffiti, were off to the right.

"Aunt Bridget doesn't have a private room, but she's not on a big ward either. So there'll be other women in the room. Remember not to stare."

"Oh, Dad!" I responded, as the lift whisked us up towards the fourth floor. "She asked to see me though?"

"Yes. She made a point of it when she talked to Uncle Adam. He called and said she wanted to see both of us if we could make it."

We walked down a long corridor with wards on either side, looking for the correct room. An aroma, like that from our medical cabinet at home, wafted around. My right shoe squeaked each time I stepped on the rubberised floor. I stopped and looked in turn at the soles of both shoes. They appeared identical.

"Come on, Rhory, stop faffing around."

When we went in I thought Dad had made a mistake. I couldn't see Aunt Bridget. One woman sat up in bed watching the TV. She had on a bright pink top that clashed with her orange-coloured hair. One massive lady faced away from us. The third couldn't have been much older than Juliette and had her eyes closed with her iPod earphones blotting out the world. I looked more carefully at number four by the window. She looked back, her face gaunt, lined, and framed with grey hair that spilled all over her pillow. Above her, a bag of clear fluid connected to her thin arm through a plastic tube. She nodded.

"Hello, Bridget," said my dad. "We've brought the statutory grapes. I hope you like them."

"Well if I don't, Angus, the nurses certainly do." She smiled slightly. "And – " she pointed towards the teenage girl, with her head nodding in time to a silent beat – "I've friends here who eat all my extras." She caught my gaze. "Hello, Rhory. Good of you to come. I know visiting poorly relatives isn't the nicest way to spend your Sunday."

"Hello, Auntie," I mumbled, unsure how to talk to a sick great aunt. "How are you?" My gut tensed at the stupidity of my question.

Aunt Bridget smiled. "Oh you know, *comme ci, comme ça*. Now why don't you sit at the end of the bed … and Angus –" she extended a thin finger – "you take this chair after pulling the curtains around us a bit. Let's pretend at least that we have privacy."

Auntie and Dad caught up on family news. I stood up and peered through the metal frame window. Opposite, the white building needed a lick of paint over its rusty stains. In the quadrangle below people walked around in dressing gowns. Some smoked.

I reflected on what had happened the day before, and who it was who'd sealed off the old temple. I felt a complete prune having sworn I could show Juliette where the temple was and failing so miserably.

"You're in a dream, Rhory."

"Oh, sorry, Auntie." I looked around and couldn't see my dad anywhere.

"I sent your dad on an errand. Ciggies and another Sunday paper. I've already read this one from page one to page one hundred." She indicated the mangled heap of newspaper on the floor by the wall. She dropped her voice. "Rhory, basically I needed some time alone with you. Come, dear, sit down."

I nodded, not knowing quite what to say.

"Move a bit closer so I don't have to shout," she said, and I eased my way further up the bed. "That's better."

She leaned forward, grimacing and reaching out to touch my cheek with her finger. Her pale eyes held mine. "You're a good boy. A brave boy. I know much of what you've done, or rather ..." She cleared her throat, and taking a beige plastic beaker from the side cabinet, took a sip of water. "Or rather, I've seen what you've done."

She must have clocked my puzzlement.

"Rhory, as I approach my own death things that were once hidden have become clear." She smiled once more and nodded a few times. "You, more than most, will know that death is largely illusory. And you, now, must know that time operates quite differently from the way most people believe." She coughed and her eyes watered. I passed her the cup of water. "In my own way I've been able to follow parts of your adventure. Sometimes I've had vivid dreams and sometimes I've been on great voyages myself. My death, which is coming quite soon now, is only another part of the journey."

A sob rose up from nowhere and my eyes filled with tears.

"Now, Rhory, we don't have time for sentimentality. Listen carefully. You will go to my house and collect your ancestor's journal, the one I told you about. It will be okay for you to read it, now that you are underway, as it were. You may have to get parts translated because I guess you don't speak ancient Greek, even though you've been to ancient Greece." She chuckled at her own joke and started to cough again. I poured more water from a jug by the bed into the beaker. Dad's car keys lay on the bedside cabinet.

"Thanks, dear. Now, where was I? Oh yes. Look, we need to cut a few corners. I don't know if this will work but we'll see. Before your dad comes back."

She handed me the plastic cup and I placed it by the jug.

"Here, hold both of my hands," said my aunt.

She moved her left arm with care, holding the drip tube with her right hand to prevent it snagging on anything. She stretched out both her thin hands, with their veins and brown splodges. I held them in mine and felt the bones under the paper-thin skin.

"Close your eyes, Rhory, dear."

At first nothing happened at all. The faint noise from the iPod continued and a murmuring that might have been the TV on an imperfect mute. Outside a nurse called to a colleague. When the silence descended it fell like a thick soft blanket. I floated in a dark space, full of light that I couldn't see. I moved forward as though someone pulled my arms.

A fragrance, like one of Natasha's joss sticks, filled the air. Warm hands now held mine. The darkness shifted, and I looked into the clear blue eyes of a dark-haired woman. She sat in a large wooden chair and I stood just in front. Her blue cloak carried the embroidered device of a grey feather on her shoulder. Katesch: the Priestess of the Feather. I'd met her before when I'd slipped into Egypt of so long ago.

'Welcome back, Red King.' She smiled more with her eyes than her mouth. *'You've done well, but your initiation has only just started. Your faith will be tested. Remain resolute Rhor-Rhee. We all have to walk the Path alone. Such is the way of Thoth, which we have chosen.'*

I nodded. I'd no idea what she meant.

'You will come to know what these words mean. Ponder them deeply.'

I'd forgotten that Katesch didn't speak with her lips but with her mind; I could hear her thoughts and she could hear mine.

'Listen well.' Her eyes became a more intense blue and her hands quivered in mine. *'You must go both North and South. Find the Fire before you find the Ice. Trust the drum, it knows the Dance of Time. You are the Dance and the Dancer.'*

She watched me for an age and then drew a breath. The image

shattered like a dropped mirror, and I opened my eyes to find Aunt Bridget coughing and struggling to breathe.

I passed the cup to her but her hands were shaking so much she spilled most of the water on the bedspread. I wondered if I should call a nurse and started to get up. She caught my hand and shook her head. I poured more water and held the thin plastic cup to her lips. She managed a sip and nodded, once more bringing her breath under control.

"There's another thing, Rhory, one more message. I could hear it but it wasn't spoken. The priestess wanted to tell you to avoid the copper mirror. It holds great danger for you."

"I couldn't get an *Observer*," said Dad, appearing between the curtains. "They'd sold out, so I picked up *The Independent*. I hope that's okay." He handed them over, showing Aunt Bridget the cigarettes and matches hidden in one of the colour supplements.

She nodded and croaked a "Thank you, dear," and winked. "Now you'd better go. It's a long drive back to Hammerford and I expect Rhory has school tomorrow."

After the goodbyes, and another welling up of tears, I squeaked my way back down the long hospital corridor with Dad. When we reached the lift he patted his pockets and said, "Bother." I told him I'd seen his keys on the bedside table.

"You stay here, Rhory. Your shoe's breaking the sound barrier. I won't be a sec."

The Boy in Quickly Lane

We turned off the motorway at the sign for Chorley Wood, swapping six lanes of M25 madness for the tiny tree-lined lanes running through farmland. Dad had been quiet for most of the journey. He'd talked a bit about Aunt Bridget but otherwise had been deep in thought. A couple of times he'd sniffed and sighed.

The vision with the priestess Katesch filled my mind. *Go both North and South. Find the Fire before you find the Ice.* Her words reverberated, although I'd no idea what to make of them.

"She's a grand old bird, is Bridget," Dad said as we turned right into Quickly Lane. "She wants us to check that Jiminy is being fed okay, and to see to any mail that may have arrived." Dad tapped the driving wheel. "You know, there's something she wanted me to tell you." He flashed me a smile. "A senior moment I'm afraid, son ... comes to us all. But it will pop back into my mind, I'm sure."

Cars lined both sides of the road. Music blared nearby – the thump, thump of the bass rising above the noise of our engine. Dad drew up in the road a little way past Bridget's house. "You go in and look for Jiminy. Leave the door on the latch and I'll follow you when I've found a place to park. Seems someone's having a big party. I'll only be a few minutes. Hurry now, we don't want to be back too late for Mum."

I walked up the road and found the right number. I hovered by the garden gate, appreciating the music. It sounded African, perhaps West African. I love the music from that part of the world, especially the rhythms of the drums. I couldn't tell if the music was live, but I jiggled my fingers in time to the rippling beats. I can always remember beats once I've heard them.

Bridget's front garden, just into March, had a lot of colour. A boy nestled between two bushes gave me a start. He'd a grey face, hair and arms, and held a basin full of water. I smiled at my jumpiness when I remembered the birds taking a bath in his basin in the summer.

The key turned and the front door glided open easier than ours did at home. I fixed the latch so Dad could slip in, and put the house keys on the hall table. The door to Auntie's sitting room stood ajar, and I could see the Toby Jug on top of the piano. Beyond the piano, in the corner of the room, stood the cylindrical wooden drinks cabinet. Amazing what you can do with a commode. Bridget had shown me on my last visit where a secret drawer held our ancestor's journal. I'd collect that later. She'd tucked the key to the small lock in the Toby Jug.

I walked past the stairs and down the dim passageway to the kitchen at the back of the house. I scanned the room for Jiminy, Auntie's ginger and white longhaired cat. His food and water bowls both had food and water. He wasn't going to starve.

Outside, in the back garden, the music pounded away. The leaden sky lent a dull greyness to everything. I wandered along the central path, between flowerbeds full of tall blooms, calling for Jiminy. The huge tree at the back part of the garden swayed in the wind; I'd always enjoyed climbing trees, and this great spruce or whatever it was gave a grand view over the adjoining gardens. Auntie had screwed a metal rod about half a metre up the main trunk. It meant I could hoist myself to the lowest branch without too much difficulty. I would climb up, see if I could spot the cat, and wait for Dad.

In the middle of the tree, storm damage had thinned the main limbs. I had to stretch to climb and trust my weight on some pencil-thin minor branches. I positioned myself near the top and waited, enjoying the dusty resin-like smell. I'd climbed quite a bit higher than the window of the main bedroom and could almost see right into the loft window set into the roof. Dad walked past that window, so he must have parked really quickly. I hollered to him.

The figure moved back. It wasn't Dad at all. Someone else had entered the house: perhaps a burglar. The man approached the window, keeping to the side. He looked down into the garden and moments later, straight across at me. I'd seen him before. But where? He stepped back and vanished.

My heart pounded and I found it hard to breathe. I gripped a branch and reached into my inside pocket for my mobile. I struggled to switch it on, using just one hand. My fingers made sweaty marks on the screen. I looped my arm around the branch enabling me, just about, to use both hands on the phone. It slipped and fell. I kicked out with my foot and trapped the phone between my shoe and the trunk. I could feel it edging downwards. Freeing both hands I wobbled on the branch and squatted down, pinning the phone with my fingers. Bile stung my mouth as I punched 999.

"Hello," said a calm female voice, "what service do you require?"

"Police, I need the police, there is—"

"Just a moment I'll connect you."

A click and a long pause with no stupid music, and then a man asked, "What's your name and what address are you calling from?"

I gave both and explained that a burglar was actually in my aunt's house, robbing it as I spoke and could he please send a policeman, or maybe two, as the man was big.

"Yes, sir, there is a squad car on its way now. Where exactly are you, sir?"

I repeated the address.

"Yes, sir, I understand that, but where are you in the house? Can you lock the door?"

"I'm up a tree, the big tree in the back garden."

"This is not a joke is it, young man? There will be a lot of trouble for me and you if it's a joke, but, frankly, more trouble for you as we have your mobile number on our screen."

"No, it's not a joke. I'm up a tree looking for my auntie's cat.

She's in hospital and we, that's my dad and me, we—"

"Okay, son, I believe you, no one could make all that up. You and your dad just remain calm and the police will be with you in a jiffy."

At that point either he hung up or I lost the connection. The back door opened wider and the man stepped out. Only I recognised him now. I'd seen him when Juliette and I were examining the well in Hammerford Park. What on earth was he up to in Auntie's house?

He wore dark jeans and a dark-green coat with military-style shoulder thingies. He had a beret on his head angled over his cropped hair. He strode up the garden path towards the tree. He didn't look up at me, but fiddled with something dark. He stopped and his hands made a sliding motion. *Oh Jeez, oh God, he's got a gun …*

The branches of the tree gave me cover, though probably not from a bullet. I sat on a stout limb and pressed myself against the trunk. The man moved forward, looking up through the foliage. My brown leather jacket matched the dark-brown of the bark, and within the canopy of the fir tree I sat in relative dimness. Perhaps he wouldn't find me. In the distance I heard a police siren.

The man ducked under the lowest branches looking up, his face an indistinct blur. Then he fiddled with the gun as though screwing something onto it.

Up the Fir Tree

The music from the party changed and launched into a song I recognised. I pressed myself closer to the trunk, the rough bark biting into my face and sick fear radiating all through me. A branch cracked and the man below grunted. He was climbing.

Noise ripped through the upper branches and a cloud of tiny twigs and pine needles erupted and pattered down. Jeez-Louise, he's shot at me! I threw my phone straight down and heard it ricochet off something and then a grunt. I peered over. The man rubbed his face, his gun with its over-long barrel waving all over the place. Bull's eye!

He looked up, saw me looking down, saluted me with his gun barrel and offered a stiff grin. He'd climbed to where the branches thinned and he spread his legs between two insubstantial supports. His whole body swayed but his hand became steady. I watched mesmerised as the gun barrel became a single black dot.

The streak of white and ginger appearing from nowhere threw the man off his aim. He lost his footing as Jiminy, uttering a screeching yowl, used the man to descend the tree the easy way. The burglar fell through the lower branches and landed with an audible thump on the ground. The police siren joined the cat's screeching as it drew up near the house.

The man searched all over for his gun. Found it. Pointed it up at me. Pointed it down and fiddled with it. Blue flashing lights illumined the fascia boards of neighbours' houses.

A voice spoke over an intercom. Without looking back, the gunman sprinted away from the tree straight for the fence at the end of the garden. I heard a splash as he tried, and failed, to vault the shallow fishpond. I pivoted right round and could see him astride the wooden fence, which bucked back and forth under his weight. Then he'd gone. I climbed down and emerged from the cover of the tree just as my dad came out into the garden.

"Rhory!" he shouted.

"Stand right there, sir, if you don't mind," said the policeman.

Dad swung round. "What's happened, officer? Why are you here?"

"We're the law, sir, and we were called out about an incident. Now just stand still, sir, and I won't have to use this." The copper held out a truncheon.

"This is my aunt's house," said Dad, his voice much higher and a bit more quivery than usual.

I ran up at that point. "That's my dad," I said to the copper.

A second, older policeman came out into the back garden.

"So, is the burglar still in the house?"

"What burglar?" said my dad.

"Didn't you phone the police, sir?" asked the older of the two policemen.

"I did. I saw the man. He was up there." I pointed above my head to the attic bedroom. "And I was up there." I said, indicating the topmost part of the tree. It now reached sky high, disappearing into the murk of the overcast evening.

"Okay," said the older policeman, "search the house."

"No." I said. "He's gone now. It's all right. He ran past and went over the back fence."

"Did he harm you?" asked the younger man.

"No. No, not really."

I could see no point saying he'd shot at me with a gun fitted with a silencer. They wouldn't believe me. It would be like dealing with Juliette all over again.

Why on earth was this man following me and then trying to shoot me at the top of a tree? Even I found that hard to explain. But I knew it had to do with the people who wanted to stop me and the others. The people who wanted to control time for their own ends.

"Sarge," said a female voice from within the kitchen, "it does look like there's been a robbery. Someone's searched through this house methodically, starting at the top. All the drawers are open and stuffs on the floor." A young policewoman came out and offered us a "Good evening."

"Hmm," grunted the sergeant, "seems like you were lucky to be up the tree, young man. PC Templeton here will take a statement, and perhaps you, sir, can give a statement to PC Fleming." Dad nodded.

When PC Templeton had finished with me, I went back to the tree to rescue my phone. It lay by the base informing me I'd one text message. This proved to be from the police service saying I'd called them. The carpet of tiny twigs on the ground had saved both my phone and my would-be assassin's neck.

I slipped back into the house. Dad was still talking to the police in the dining room. I returned to the sitting room across the hall, and up-ended the Toby Jug. Nothing came out except one desiccated fly. I shook the jug but it held no key.

I flopped onto the settee feeling as though every elastic band in my body had snapped all at once. The commode loomed in the corner, with its hidden drawer locked. My ancestor's journal, that surely must explain what was happening to me, lay tucked away inside.

"Come on, Rhory, we need to go. I've spoken to your mum and explained we'll be quite late."

I levered myself out of the chair.

"Go to the bathroom and clean yourself up. You're absolutely filthy. I've no idea why you felt the need to climb the tree. Mind you –" Dad paused and scratched his head – "it stopped you confronting a professional burglar, which I expect is a good thing."

About three hours later we were nearly home. We'd stopped and had a quick fry-up at a Little Chef restaurant and told the girls at home to eat without us. A road sign said Hammerford four Miles.

"Ah. I've remembered," said Dad, grinning and nodding. "Yep, it always comes back in time. I've remembered what Aunt Bridget wanted me to tell you, though why, I've no idea. Can you explain why?"

"Explain what, Dad? You've not told me anything yet."

"Oh, right. Well, when I went back to get the keys, she told me various things. She said I was to say to you to look carefully at the boy in the front garden and that you would know what she meant. I think maybe her mind was beginning to wander at that point. Perhaps one of the neighbours has a little boy or something."

"Thanks, Dad. I'll think about that, see if I can work out what she meant."

I knew exactly what she meant. If my forgetful and dozy dad had told me before we went to Quickly Lane, I would've found the key which she'd obviously decided to hide outside. Bridget could also move through time a bit and maybe foresaw the robbery. She'd hidden the key in a less obvious place, under the statue in the front garden. If I'd found the key I could now have my ancestor's journal and might get more of a clue how to proceed and why people were trying to kill me.

"Can we go back to Auntie's house, Dad?"

"What? Why on earth would you want to go back? To climb more trees? Well, clearly not tonight." Dad paused and sighed.

"But if she doesn't make it out of hospital then some of us will have to go and tidy the house up, so there may be a chance."

A few minutes later Mum and Juliette were demanding all the details about my narrow squeak with the burglar.

The Bishop's Car

Rain splished and splattered on my brolly as I strode towards school. Dad had left early for a meeting and Mum drove Juliette as usual, as her school lay on the way to Mum's work. I drew the short straw and had to brave the elements. The knot hadn't left my stomach since yesterday. Someone had tried to kill me or at the very least use me for target practice. The same someone – the man in the dark-green coat – had followed Juliette and me to the well.

At breakfast Mum had asked if I was okay.

"Look, you're shaking," Juliette had said.

"I always shake a bit," I responded, "we all do on Mum's side of things. So do you for that matter, Jules."

"Yeah, but not like a leaf."

"You're a bit pale," said Mum. "Are you sure you wouldn't like to just stay at home, treasure? I'll call the school and tell them."

"No. I'm just tired after yesterday. I'll be okay. I can go to bed early tonight."

Now I regretted being quite so goody-two shoes. I could be curled up under the duvet watching TV on Juliette's new iPad. Instead my shoes had already let in a few gallons of water, and the bottoms of my trousers were damp. Cold rain blew straight into my face and every car that went past might carry an assassin.

What would've happened if I had told the police the truth? Would they have believed me? The older copper seemed nice enough, but PC Templeton had been keen to get a short statement and leave. She only wanted a description of the man, and where I'd seen him in the house. I doubted she would've wished to explore my thoughts about secret societies wanting to control the destinies of nations and the flow of time. She'd accepted he was a burglar, and that was good enough. Burglars burgle, they don't serve ancient gods. There is nowhere in the police manual for that type of person.

I stopped near the roundabout by Hammerford station. Puke rose right up the back of my throat. My heart raced and the streets around me spun slowly. I sat on the low wall of one of the houses that overlook the park. A car drew to a halt and the smoked window lowered. The driver beeped a couple of times on the horn. This is it. Now he'll shoot again. The back window lowered revealing a pale face with a mass of curly brown hair.

"Hey, Rhory, d'ya wanna lift?"

One of my classmates. Bishop.

I struggled up, feeling somewhat dizzy, and squidged over the wet grass to the car. Bishop's dad leaned across and opened the passenger door.

"Hi, Bishop. Hi, Mr… Oh sorry," I corrected myself. "Hello, Charles, hello, Mr Bishop. Hello…"

"Caroline," said Charles, "my sister."

"Hi, Caroline," I said to a girl similar to Charles, with longer brown hair, large brown doe eyes and full lips.

"Hello, Rhory," she said. "I know all about you, by the way."

"Oh. How? I didn't realise I was…" I trailed off, still too shaky for banter with a pretty girl. I fiddled with the umbrella, getting rainwater all over my hands.

"I'm a friend of Natasha's. She's told me all about you. I saw you in the school play last year. You were great as the cow."

She was winding me up.

"At least I didn't have to learn any lines."

"You all right?" said Mr Bishop. "You look about all in. I could run you home if you're ill, provided you don't live too far away."

"That's kind of you, Mr Bishop, but I need to go to school and I'll be fine." My stomach had settled somewhat and the reality of the risk to my life had receded a bit. When we left the car at Scrivener's School and crossed the road, Caroline lowered her window and waved with her her fingertips I felt sick all over again but this time I smiled.

As I entered the classroom, Calvin came over and said, "Hey, Brucie."

I nodded. I didn't like Calvin. His close-cropped hair and arched eyebrows, set in a narrow face, fitted his mean spirit.

He walked behind me as I made my way to my desk, the grin on the face of a couple of the other lads showing me he was mimicking my walk. I dropped my bag and turned. He reached up and swiped his arm around my neck, getting me into a headlock.

"Oh, bloody leave off, Calvin," I said.

He strengthened his grip and spots appeared in front of my eyes.

"Let go." I struggled to free myself and banged into a couple of desks.

"You're just a long streak of piss, Brucie, Brucie baby."

I felt queasy about hitting him or punching him in the tender parts. Being so much taller I would appear the aggressor if a teacher saw us fighting.

He let go.

"Settle down, settle down." Mr Hawksley strode into the room. He looked over to the desks and chairs all out of neat alignment. "Straighten those up, boys. I have to teach in here after assembly. This is the eight Blue classroom, isn't it?"

"Yes, sir," said one of those who had been happily watching Calvin throttle me. "Are you teaching us instead of Mr Twitford?"

"Yes. Instead of Mr Twighford," said Hawksley, correcting the way we pronounced the student teacher's name.

That night at tea, family Bruce discussed the Easter holidays.

"It falls early this year," said Dad, "so the snow should still be good."

"I want to ski in France," said Juliette. "I could do with polishing my French."

"The food's good there," said Mum. "Better than Croatia, that's for sure."

"I want to go where I can do freestyle jumping," I said.

"Any of the good French resorts have jumps," said Juliette, buttering the final crumpet.

I adored skiing and could do some passable acrobatics. I'd learned to back-flip the previous winter, and loved the sensation. Oddly, although I hated cross-country running, I really enjoyed cross-country skiing too. We'd done a lot of that in Norway in previous years. The steady rhythm of it and the silence of the forests appealed to me. Juliette preferred the thrill of fast downhill runs.

Dad offered to do more research on the internet, and we would decide tomorrow to make sure we booked in time.

"You're a bloody geek you are," Calvin said, his finger in Charles Bishop's face.

"Leave me alone, Calvin, you brainless moron," said Bishop, turning away.

"Who you calling names?"

Calvin shoved Bishop, who dropped the textbooks he was carrying onto the damp playground. Bishop didn't respond but bent down to pick up his books. Calvin used the sole of his foot to propel Bishop onto his face. As keen on fights as dogs are on bones, students of all years started forming a circle. Morning break meant boredom; this looked interesting.

Bishop stood up, looked at the mud and water on his trousers and a tear in his pocket and went for Calvin, fists flying. He landed a glancing blow. Calvin, his face contorting into a snarl, kneed Bishop in the groin and, as he stumbled, got him in a headlock. The circle of wide-eyed boys started chanting, "Fight.

Fight."

I'd had enough of Calvin's bullying ways and swung my arm around Calvin's neck.

"Let him go, Calvin," I snarled in his ear.

"That's enough," barked a voice. Dyer, the head prefect, had appeared from nowhere, the way prefects do. "We'll not have fights in the playground. Bruce, Calvin, Bishop, see me in the Prefects' Room. Now!"

Lucian

I had history with Dyer. I'd been instrumental in helping him catch a drug-pushing ring at the school in the Christmas Term. Nevertheless, I felt nervy as we waited in the dim corridor outside the Prefects' Room. The door opened and we were ushered in, the smell of stale sports kit wafting from the cupboard to our right.

"You were caught fair and square," said Dyer. "Any reason I shouldn't send you to the Old Man?"

Many reasons flitted through my mind, not least the inevitable letter sent home and a period of detention on a Saturday morning.

Pete Sheldon, one of Dyer's rugby-playing friends, cracked his knuckles one by one, looking at each of us in turn as he did so.

"A thousand lines each should do the trick," he suggested. "Something like 'I shall not be a prat and fight like that.'" He gave his index finger a final pull.

A blond-haired boy with a prefect's tie turned round from the table by the window. He held cards from a UNO game in his hand. He had the sort of good looks that would make George Clooney look lame. His blue eyes crinkled into a smile.

"Let's be creative," he said. "Let's have some fun. They can write a short essay, two sides of A4, at least 600 words, ending with the phrase *... and that's how a stick of rhubarb saved my life."*

The other prefects chortled and agreed.

As we headed back towards class, Calvin peeled off towards the loos.

"Thanks, mate," said Bishop. "Sorry to get you into this."

"No probs. By the way, who was the blond-haired prefect? Is he new?"

"Been around for a bit. Think he joined this year. He's caused quite a stir in the Girls' School, according to Caroline."

Juliette stared into the middle distance, smiling at something or other.

"What are you so pleased with yourself about?" I asked.

"Me? Oh nothing," she said, putting her tea down and stretching, cat-like. "Did the parents' division come up with ideas for the skiing holiday this Easter? I'd like to check out possibilities on the Internet."

"Dad's picking up some brochures today," said Mum. "We need to decide with reasonable alacrity, so we don't miss out."

My mum's English is always a little surprising, as she learnt it at school in Norway.

"Can I buy new ski pants, Mum? My old ones are far too small now," I said.

Mum's mouth tightened and she offered something halfway between a nod and a quiver of the head. "Let's get the booking first."

I stood up. "I don't have any homework tonight so I'm off to Bongo Bongo land." I didn't admit I had a damn fool essay to write for the Lucian git.

Up in the bedroom I sat cross-legged on the floor with the bongo drums nestled on my lap. I'd dashed off the punishment essay about a drummer who lost his sticks on the way to a gig, but who passed a patch of rhubarb. I put in plenty of long words and knew it would sound funny when we read it out in the prefects' room the next day.

I did a few riffs on the drums. Jester, my shadow and my cat, had followed me in and was contorting himself on my bed to clean distant parts of his anatomy. Juliette walked past my room and closed my door none too gently.

I thought back to the African music I'd heard at Aunt Bridget's house and started tapping out the main rhythms with my index fingers. I closed my eyes and let the beats flow from my memory, using the pads of my fingers to produce the staccato notes and the palm of my right hand on the bigger drum for the bass line. When I played I sensed coloured patterns swirling around and would use this to suggest changes in the rhythm. As I built towards a tympanic climax the doorbell rang.

I kept on playing, sure that Juliette would go or Mum, given that she was downstairs. The bell rang again. Sighing, I put down the bongos, tweaked Jester's outstretched back leg and thundered down the stairs. The door stuck worse than usual and I had to jerk it open.

The blond-haired boy smiled and nodded at me – the same blond boy who'd set the essay.

"Hello," he said. "I guess you're Rhory."

"Yes," I mumbled, feeling sort of lopsided in the presence of celebrity good looks.

"I'm Lucian," he said. "I must ask, was that you playing the drums?"

"Yes." I nodded inanely.

"You're good, Rhory. Really good."

"You could hear them down here?"

"Uh huh." He smiled, holding my eyes with his. "Anyway, it's good to meet you." He held out his hand and I shook it.

We stood looking at each other for a millisecond too long. He cleared his throat.

"Would it be all right if I came in, I would like to see—"

"God, Rhory, are you going to keep Lucian waiting on the doorstep?"

Juliette had made it halfway down the stairs. Her cheeks looked a little flushed and she'd acquired lipstick since having the crumpet earlier.

Lucian came in and the two of them went into our sitting room at the front of the house and closed the door. I meandered back to my bedroom wondering who on earth this boy was who knew both me and Jules, and whom as far as I could remember I hadn't seen before today.

An Invitation

"I feel really sad, although I didn't know her that well, I suppose," I said.

"She was a sort of bonus grandmother," said Natasha, my cousin.

I'd called her on my mobile when I learned that Aunt Bridget had died the previous night.

"Mum's been quite down. When she saw her in hospital she didn't think it was the final chapter."

I eased my way up the bed and sat cross-legged.

"Something happened when I saw her, Nat. Well, two things actually, well more..."

"Get on with it."

"Yes. Well, it's a little weird. Aunt Bridget sent Dad out of the hospital room and..." I told Natasha about my vision and the message the Egyptian priestess had given me. When I finished Natasha didn't respond for a while. I waited.

"You still there?" I asked.

"Yes. Yes ... I am. It's as though Aunt Bridget had a connection back to the past herself in some way. Do you think she, I don't know... Do you think she was actually the Egyptian priestess Ketchup?"

"Katesch," I said.

"Oh right, sorry. Do you think she was like a reincarnation of the priestess from ancient Egypt?"

"I don't know. Possibly. I think since she gave me the Time Sphere, and especially since I found the clues as to how to open it, and the objects surfaced in this moment of time." I scratched a tickle in my ear. "I think that sort of, you know, sort of opened a door for her too, if you know what I mean. She said something like that in the hospital."

"What do you think is meant by Fire and Ice?"

"I really have no idea. She also said about North and South, which is sort of opposite, isn't it? Unless you go to the Antarctic."

Again we sat in silence for a bit. Jester prowled around the room and then flopped on his side.

"What were the other things?"

"Other things?"

"The other things you said happened."

I cleared my throat. I'd told no one about the man who shot at me, not even Nick, my closest friend. I wondered if Natasha, who'd been through some adventures with me already and knew about the Society of Secrets, would believe me.

"When I got to Auntie's house, I went in alone. Dad was parking the car." I rubbed my chin. "But someone else was there," I said.

"Like a cleaner or something?"

"Not exactly. Like a burglar or something."

I explained how I'd climbed the tree and seen the man, and how I'd shouted and he'd come out with a gun and—

"You're pulling my leg, Rhory. You're seriously telling me someone tried to shoot you while you were up a tree?"

"That's what happened. Just as I told you. If it hadn't been for Auntie's cat jumping at him I don't think I would be talking to you now."

"Truly, Rho, you're not winding me up?"

"Honest, Nat. Honest. I've not told anyone else because I knew they wouldn't believe me." I explained how I'd seen the man before and how the police had arrived at exactly the right moment.

"God, Rhory, this is serious. Who on earth would want to kill you?" We both thought about that for a moment. "Aren't you scared?"

"Yes. I am. But there's not a lot I can do about it, is there?" I could feel a chilly worm of panic forming in a deep point in my stomach.

"Wow. We're going to the house this weekend to help pack up. Mum asked me if I wanted to go and I've said yes. Do you think this guy will attack us?"

"I don't think so. It's me he's following, and he was searching for either the Time Sphere or the journal my – or rather our – ancestor kept, that had a record of what had happened and what ... I don't know ... what would happen."

"Did he get it?"

"I don't think so. It's well hidden in her funny drinks cabinet, the cylindrical one in her sitting room. But someone had moved the key, so I couldn't get to it."

I told Natasha where the key was now hidden under the statue of the boy in the garden.

"If you get a chance this weekend, open up the drinks commode thingy and use the key to get the journal."

Natasha said that she would, and keep it safe until we met up.

"How do you feel about the Alexandria idea?"

"The what?" I asked.

"The idea of us going to Alexandria?"

"I've no idea what you're talking about, Nat."

"Aunt Aida phoned yesterday and invited me and you to go with her and Uncle Adam to Egypt this Easter. Uncle Adam will have work in Cairo, but we can stay with Auntie Aida and her parents in Alexandria."

"We're going skiing," I said.

"Oh," said Natasha. "I thought you would jump at the chance of going to Egypt."

I scratched my head, as tendrils of panic wandered up my legs. I hated making choices like this.

"I'm pretty sure Dad hasn't booked yet. In fact I know he hasn't because we've not decided where to go yet. I suppose ..."

"You should go, Rhory. We should both go. Egypt's hot. Don't you think that might have something to do with the fire you were told about?"

I continued scratching my head.

"Egypt is certainly South." A nervous chill ran right through me. My hand started shaking.

"I have a feeling," said Natasha. "A sort of intuition thing. You need to do this."

"I think so too, but it's getting kinda scary now. I'll need to clear it with Mum and Dad. Jules'll go ballistic."

We agreed I'd call her back once I'd found out if my parents knew anything about my Aunt Aida inviting me to go to Egypt.

"I don't know, Rhory," said Mum. "It's a sort of family thing us all going skiing together."

"You really would prefer hot, smelly Egypt to lovely cool alpine France?" said Juliette. "You must be an idiot. But then we knew that. And anyway, it's really dangerous, isn't it?"

"Rhory should make up his own mind. I spoke to Adam. His work takes him back and forth to Cairo all the time. He says Alexandria is abolutely fine. It's a generous offer, though I must say it's sort of come out of the blue," said Dad.

"Anyway," said Mum, "I'm sorry I didn't tell you last night, Rhory. Auntie Bridget's death sort of drove it from my mind. Now I made a few notes when Aida called ... let me see..." Mum rummaged around a small pile of papers near the phone. "Ah yes, here it is."

My aunt had invited Natasha and me to travel with her to Alexandria. The Egypt tourist board were paying for the trip for both of them. They could convert their two first-class seats into four ordinary seats. Mum took off her glasses and smiled at me. "So it won't cost you – that's us of course –" she grinned at Dad – "anything more than a bit of pocket money."

"You do what you like, Rhory. It'll be much more peaceful skiing without you," said Juliette. "Maybe now I could take a friend, Mum?"

"Do you really want to go, Rhory?" asked Dad. "Do you need

to sleep on it?"

"No. I do want to go." I said. "It'd be a sort of adventure. I've never actually been to Egypt."

Juliette gave me her 'I've caught you in a lie' look, but didn't say anything.

"Well, there's no accounting for tastes," said Mum, mangling her English a bit. "I'll call Aida. Saves me spending out on ski pants for another year, so it's a sort of win-win situation I guess."

The Girl in the Tower

"Are you going to the party?"

"Yes, Nick, I'm glad that you'll be there, it'll be good to have a friend."

"Actually, I'm not able to make it, mate. We have some sort of family do that night, and it's a three-line whip that I attend."

"Oh," I said, a little cloud of disappointment settling in my stomach.

We were standing in the school courtyard. It wasn't raining, but it was one of those days when the damp cold seemed to penetrate straight through my school jacket. I had my school bag wedged between my shoes. Nick rocked back and forth on his feet rubbing his hands together.

"Bloody ridiculous that we can't stay inside during break. It's flipping parky. Probably half the school will have pneumonia tomorrow."

"How do you know this Seb bloke, anyway?" I asked.

"Well, I don't really. We've met when I've played rugby against his school. He seems to have invited quite a few people from our class. He knows Bishop quite well, and I think that's why. Bishop used to go to the same school as Sebastian."

"It's really weird, you know, because Juliette's been invited to the same party. I mean, it's like the first grown-up party that I've ever been to and my sister'll be there as well."

We shuffled around a bit more and checked our watches to find that our purgatory in the freezing courtyard had at least five more minutes to run. I huffed on my hands and stuck them under my armpits.

"Oh, by the way, I'm going to Egypt."

"You're what?"

I explained my Aunt Aida's invitation.

"Personally, I would've chosen to go skiing," said Nick.

The bell rang and we entered the cosy warmth of the school, which now provided the opportunity to learn more French verbs.

Gloom was descending fast as I crossed the main road and entered the park on the way home from school. The sky above had the colour of cold porridge and looked about as attractive. The wind had picked up and my parka let in some of its damp coldness. I wanted to get home as quick as possible and strode in a bee-line over the damp grass. My shoes and the bottoms of my trousers turned a speckled green colour from grass cuttings. The bandstand appeared brighter than the dull grey light that struggled to illumine the rest of the park.

Thinking I saw someone moving inside, I stopped. It had to be a trick of the light. But as I turned to walk home I heard someone call from far away. I looked back at the bandstand. It now appeared as though someone had switched a light on, which was ridiculous, because it had no lights.

I made my way over and climbed up the steps. I could feel the damp wind on my back, but in front of me the air became warmer and drier. As I stepped inside, the sound of the wind dropped away. Once again someone called in the distance. I checked all around me, looking for anyone near the nursery school, or by the council offices, or over at the duck pond or the deserted swimming pool. I couldn't make out anybody. In some strange way the distant voice had come from within the bandstand itself. I leant my school bag against one of the pillars of the entrance.

After moving a few steps onto the bandstand stage area I closed my eyes and, holding my breath, listened inside. Something rustled.

"Bonjour."

I opened my eyes and stepped back quickly, bumping into a curtain and a hard wall. Sitting at a table in front of me was a girl, her hair gathered in a headdress. Her clothes were dark green and definitely not of now. Or last year. Or last century. She looked like a child left behind when her father saddled up to fight in the crusades.

She smiled and nodded. Once more she said, "*Bonjour.*" And then, "*Tu va bien?*"

With my hands pressed against the curtain and the wall I scanned the circular room. It was only a little bit bigger than the bandstand. Instead of the space through which I had entered, wooden doors filled a stone archway. Two windows let in sunlight, which illumined the tapestries covering the walls on the far side.

I said, "Who are you?"

She frowned, and slowly shook her head.

"*Tu es* Rhory!"

Then she took a long breath and stared at me. Inside I heard the words, *'You are Rhory? I am Ariane. You are the last of us, aren't you?'*

Now I started shaking, but whether from the cold in the park or in this strange stone room I couldn't tell. My mouth had become quite dry. I concentrated.

"*N'est-ce pas?*" she said out loud.

I concentrated as my legs quivered. Outside, a flock of birds swirled past the window. Distant rooftops glowed in the evening sunlight. We were high up, in some sort of tower. I looked back at the girl and connected with her brown eyes. She waited.

'Yes, the last I think. There are six before me.' I formed the thoughts as clearly as I could.

She smiled as she held up a crystal scarab beetle, the one that had belonged to the Egyptian priestess.

'She is the first. Susan.'

'Shoshan,' I said out loud. "Yes, she is Shoshan."

'The Lotus!'

'The Lotus,' I agreed within, for that is what the young

priestess's name meant. She'd been the first person from another time to make contact with me. I'd seen her offered as a sacrifice to a vicious wild boar only a month or two earlier.

I smiled and nodded.

Ariane held up the bag of polished stones that I knew so well. In fact this bag, looking somewhat older, even now rested in my wardrobe, tucked inside an engraved silver sphere.

I nodded and smiled and we both shared the thought-word *'Dimitris'*.

Ariane smiled back. She held up her hand, and on the right index finger a silver thimble sparkled in the sunlight. She pointed to herself as she placed the thimble in front of her on the table.

The scarab, the bag of ten stones and the thimble each rested in a circle of inlaid wood on the tabletop. Just as I'd seen in the temple deep below the bandstand, six circles surrounded a central seventh. Ariane moved something from her lap and held it on her palm so it glistened in the light. I recognised the silver pommel of the sword that I'd found with the other objects, hidden inside the time sphere. With a flourish of her hand Ariane placed the silver pommel in the central circle.

Immediately, the whole chamber darkened and became freezing cold. The walls of the room faded away and Ariane vanished. Instead of the light from the setting sun, a bright moon illumined everything. Where the Hammerford council offices ought to be, a hill blocked out much of the light of the stars. At the top, bare rock glimmered in the cold blue light. Seen from below it had the shape of a kneeling man, a huge kneeling man.

Tiny ice crystals formed on the sleeves of my parka. My breath floated in front of my face, a little cloud of warmth rapidly defeated by the bitter cold. I tried to stamp my feet as my toes were losing all sensation. I stood about six inches deep in crusty snow. Forming a wide circle all around me, jagged stones of granite stood like some giant's silvery teeth.

I'd no idea what land I was in and what time I was in. Worse than that I didn't have the vaguest notion about how to get back to Hammerford Park. My shivering had taken on epic proportions. I quivered from head to foot and couldn't feel my fingertips. I rubbed my hands together and blew on them.

'Move to the door.'

The voice inside me had to be Ariane's.

As I'd walked straight into the bandstand I judged that the entrance lay directly behind me. I turned through one hundred and eighty degrees. My shadow spread as a pale smudge on the snow in front of me. Looking around the stone circle, the unblemished surface of the crisp white snow revealed no other footprints. I stepped in the direction of the bandstand opening. Five crunchy paces later I stopped. I could hear something. I looked to my left. Somewhere in the distance a tiny light shone, reflected back from snow-heavy trees and what might be a hedge.

A voice spoke. The circle had no one in it but I could hear something breathing. Whatever it was, wheezed to my right. The voice again, from the other direction. I twisted round. Just beyond one of the stones in the circle, a figure stood motionless, picked out by moonlight. His padded coat, white with embroidery at its edge, looked much warmer than my winter coat. A tall furry hat on his head shaded his face from the moonlight. His breath floated around his head. I couldn't make sense of what he was doing as he raised his right arm level to his shoulder and extended his left straight towards me. The moonlight glinted on a rod or thin pole in his left gloved hand.

Effing heck, he's going to shoot at me with a bow and arrow.

A squeal and a huff sounded to my right.

I lunged forward, ducking as I did so. The snowy landscape vanished as the moon disconnected. The steps leading from the bandstand were at my feet and I stumbled down them. All around me the air felt as warm and balmy as a summer evening on holiday. The snow on my shoes melted. I eased my way back up the first three steps and reached for my satchel.

A voice floated by, saying something like, *'hearken, hearken'*. I spun around, to see who had spoken. The park remained empty. Not even dog walkers were out and about. Above me the clouds sucked the last of the light from the sky and the damp breeze became cold once again.

Sensation didn't return to either my numb toes or my fingertips until I had reached home. Mum commented on my ruddy complexion and asked if I'd run all the way. I mumbled something, fixed myself a hot cup of tea and beat a retreat to the safety of my bedroom.

I sat on the bed and tickled Jester's ears. He purred, and then for reasons of his own, scratched my hand and jumped off the bed. I stared at the closed door to my wardrobe. Behind it I could visualise where the silver sphere, with its ancient objects, lay in a box hidden under an old pullover. I sighed. I now knew for sure that defeating the fat old priestess back in ancient Egypt hadn't been the end of things. Maybe, only the beginning.

I cradled the hot tea in my hands and grimaced.

Judge Circle

Sweden – about 1520

The arrow thrummed through the air and smacked into the hay bale. The girl watched for a while, standing with her feet planted asunder, as white feathers drifted past. She pulled up another arrow from where it was stuck in the snow next to her boots, drew the string back steadily, keeping her left arm straight and still, and a moment later the second arrow quivered right next to the first. A white chicken feather settled on her hair and another touched her cheek. She brushed it away and turned.

"See, Inge, I'm getting really good."

The young woman sitting on folded sacking on the steps leading down from the kitchen, smiled.

"You are, Eira, you are. Mind you don't get too cold now."

Inge's breath floated in the air. She rubbed her fingers together to keep the blood circulating. Plucking a chicken couldn't be done wearing mittens, just as shooting an arrow couldn't. Her fingerless gloves helped, but the cold seeped up from the frozen stones below her. She stood up, clutching the half-plucked chicken to her pinafore and stamped her feet, before sitting down once more. Feathers floated off in all directions and settled in the rutted snow of the large courtyard.

Charcoal, the children's black cat, had emerged from the warmth near the kitchen range and nuzzled her. She shoved it away and it skittered down the steps before walking, tail erect, towards the nine-year-old archer.

Eira landed another arrow close to the first two and walked over to retrieve her shafts. The sound of hoof beats caused her to stop and stare across towards the archway at the far end of the yard. The wooden doors to the courtyard stood open. A man rode in, ducking slightly under the archway. His dappled grey horse whinnied and skittered sideways a pace or two.

"Stable-boy, ho," he shouted, turning the horse to ride out towards the front of the house.

Inge stood-up when the gentleman arrived, for Kaleb Pettersson was an important man, the biggest landowner in these parts and someone known for his abrupt manner and short temper. The chicken bounced off her knees and landed on the thin snow and frozen mud of the courtyard.

Ralf came out from the stables at the far side of the yard, with a pitchfork in his hand. "Did someone call?" He addressed Eira, who just shrugged and nodded towards Inge.

The young woman retrieved the chicken, brushed it down and pointed to the gate.

"Get on with you, Ralf, Mr Pettersson won't brook no waiting now," said Eira.

Ralf looked stricken and, dropping the pitchfork, loped across the yard and disappeared under the archway. Inge grimaced slightly and yanked more feathers out of the increasingly denuded bird.

"The sooner you're in the pot the better for us all," she said to the lifeless head that bobbed around on her knees, as a freezing gust of wind lifted the feathers up towards the leaden sky. Inge surveyed the dull heaviness of the clouds and concluded more snow was possible before the day was through. A thaw had come three weeks back, and then a further freeze. "Will this winter never end?" she grumbled to the chicken.

The boy hung the two rabbits from a low branch of a twisted old tree and made his way across the snow towards the dark-grey stones, standing like huge sentinels in private conversation, each topped with a slight crusting of snow, like so many moody old men. The Judge Circle of tall stones had stood forever. Possibly built by the frost giants, according to his mother, although she smiled when she said so. No one really knew how the standing stones, arranged in a rough circle, had come to be at the base of Torsberg, the hill rising at the far end of the clearing. The jagged rocks of the hilltop could, in a certain light, look like a vast hammer smashed into the crest or, some said, a kneeling giant.

Both their farmhouse, the bridge over the river and the small town two miles beyond could be seen from its peak. Down by the Circle, Håkan's view was circumscribed by the forest of birch trees that crept towards the stones but never reached them, held back by some troll magic, he didn't doubt.

The snow had been disturbed around the stones. Someone had ridden a horse there not long ago, for the tracks were fresh, as was the dung that hadn't yet frozen solid. Whoever had trespassed had ridden completely around the Circle without entering it. The snow encircled by the stones themselves was unblemished and glowed a dull white, reflective of the ash grey sky above.

Håkan pulled his gloves tight and carefully gripped one of the tallest of the stones, much taller than the height of a tall man, but one that he could climb. His felt boots were not designed for rock-climbing and he eased them against the fissures to ensure a good grip. He didn't fancy falling. Gaining the top he stood, flexing his knees and swaying slightly. The air, so still until a few moments earlier, now had a slight breeze. His breath drifted away in front of him; the highest branches of the birches waved to each other slowly; a clump of snow tumbled from a branch nearby. Otherwise the silence held.

This was where the boy had appeared, if boy he was. He'd appeared and just as quickly, disappeared.

Håkan had been standing very still, watching a boar who'd emerged from the trees on the far side of the clearing. It snorted around but didn't detect him, as the wind carried the pig's boarish stink across to where Håkan clutched his bow, arrow notched and half drawn. The boar did see the strange boy as he walked within the stone circle. It snorted and lowered its head.

The boy, dressed in the oddest clothes Håkan had ever seen, looked at the boar and then towards him. He took another step and promptly vanished. But not entirely, for his tracks remained in the snow. When Håkan looked again the boar had also gone but he could still be heard crashing through the undergrowth.

Håkan surveyed the area carefully. No troll boy today, just the tracks from the horse and rider. He could now see where some man had dismounted for a while and relieved himself in the snow. Håkan shook his head to clear both mysteries, and surveyed the other ten stones. Each one would take a small army to lift. He doubted their wagon would be sturdy enough to carry the weight of the smallest, even if it could be pulled out of the frozen ground. In fact, the stone he stood on would be longer than the wagon, and that was only the bit he could see above the ground.

He checked the snow behind him. His bow and arrows leant against the next rock, well out of the way. He didn't wish to land on those. He took a breath, feeling the chill burn across his teeth. He positioned his feet and extended his arms, as he had been taught. Turning his face towards the clouds, that seemed but a hand's breadth above Torsberg, he bent his knees, fell backwards slowly and then jumped sharply. Keeping his body extended he made a graceful arc, turning completely in the air and landing on his feet, facing the tall stone on which he'd stood moments before. His feet punched into the crisp snow. He wiggled his boots to free them. Heart racing and grinning to himself, he collected his bow and arrows and set off to pick up the rabbits. In half an hour it would be dark and he wanted to be home well before then.

Inge had just completed pulling out the final feathers when the door to the kitchen burst open. She heard the cook say something and a man's voice raised in anger. Pettersson swept out through the back door, ignoring Inge, and shouted for his horse. It took

Ralf a few moments before he led out the dappled grey.

"Bring it here, boy, and look sharp about it, I don't have all day."

Pettersson stood on the small landing that extended from the kitchen door, the stairs descending to one side.

"'s Blood, mind, girl," he said, forcing Inge to take a couple of steps down, while he swung his leg onto his waiting mount. He turned the horse without a word of thanks to Ralf, and trotted towards the archway. As he passed through, an arrow embedded itself in the wooden doorpost. If he heard he made no sign.

"That was very, very naughty," said Inge to Eira, as the girl strolled over to retrieve the arrow.

"No, he was very, very rude," said Eira, "and I'm a good shot. He was in no danger."

Kaleb Pettersson

The thick broth made from chicken and potatoes filled the room with welcome aromas. Håkan's mother, Signy, led them in a prayer of thanksgiving. She sat next to his father's empty chair; his place was laid as was the place of his older brother.

"They could return any time," his mother often said. And he hoped the words carried as much truth as the assurance with which she said them. A letter received three weeks back had spoken of a skirmish, but neither man had been injured.

"They are doing the Lord's work and He will protect them," Signy had said, but she had also brushed away a tear.

Candlelight and the substantial fire bathed their faces with rippling light. Above the fireplace, the huge broadsword from Håkan's great-grandfather's time acted as a reminder that the Ekland family were not just gentlemen farmers. A pitcher of small beer and a plate of salted herring accompanied the bread and the soup.

Inge, with her ample bosom and close-set eyes, hovered near the door. Her blonde hair more or less managed to stay within her bonnet. She'd been with them now for two years and helped out in the kitchens. Fifteen, and quite pretty, she'd be married soon, and word amongst the servants suggested the apothecary's son in the village had his eye on her. Signy had been happy to give work to one of her crofter's daughters; a large household needed plenty of willing hands. Håkan didn't like her much. She'd twisted his ear more than once and he frequently spotted a scowl on her face if caught unawares.

"You may tell the cook the broth is excellent, Inge," said Signy. "There should be enough for all of you too. The hen seemed hefty to me when Gregor caught her."

"Yes, Mistress," said Inge, bobbing slightly but still managing to look petulant.

"Off you go then. We'll call you if we need you."

When the door had closed, Signy sighed and pushed the platter of bread towards the two children.

"Eat well. This winter seems set to last right into summer. I'm glad your traps worked fine, Håkan. The two coneys will make a welcome change once they've hung a bit. The leg of lamb in the outhouse is all but finished now, and smells ripe even to me. It may be time to let the dogs take it." Håkan's mother took a cloth from her lap and wiped the grease from her lips, before cutting a thick trencher of bread.

"Our neighbour called today and it wasn't pretty."

Håkan looked up sharply.

"Pettersson?"

"Yes, Kaleb Pettersson himself, dressed in all his velvet glory, and full of all his papist certainties."

"What did he want, Mother?" asked Eira.

"He wanted what he'll not get," said Signy, laying down her knife and putting her hands flat on either side of her bowl. "Your father's land has been in his family for generations and it's special. Our hill and our Circle, they are sacred and for safe keeping."

"But he can't just take the land can he, Mother?" Håkan's younger sister pushed her chin out and her eyes blazed.

"No, Eira, he cannot, for the land is ours, even if worked by our crofter, Bengt. Mr Pettersson claims he has papers showing the land is in dispute. Papers from generations back. He says he will go to the Bishop and also will petition the King. He offered me a significant sum in gold if I would accept his papers as legitimate."

"But what does he want that land for?" asked Håkan, his stomach tightening. "It's no good for crops and Bengt and his son can barely scrape a living from the birches and brooms."

Signy nodded, the candlelight being kind to the wrinkles around her eyes and mouth. Outside the wind had picked up and moaned its way around the farmhouse. A log settled in the fireplace releasing a cloud of sparks.

"He won't say, of course, but it's the Circle and Torsberg Hill he wants. It's as well not to enquire too closely why, in my opinion. Certainly not to do the Lord's work." Signy looked at her children in turn. She banged her fist softly on the table several times.

"Well he won't get it, not while I have breath in my body," she said.

"We cannot do anything till Father returns, can we, Mother?" said Håkan.

Signy sighed and checked that the door remained closed. In a softer voice she said, "Pettersson's uncle is close to the Danish king and I think he plans to use that connection now our family has shown clearly where it owes allegiance."

"I thought Father said that, as Swedes, we owe allegiance only to God and Sweden," said Håkan.

"That's true, and your father and I are one in this as you know. But it is sedition to speak against the King, and we must all have a care." She looked again to where the thick wooden door remained closed. "Power lies with people like Pettersson who are more Danish than the Danes themselves."

"But if Lennart and Father succeed—"

"Hush, child," said Signy to Håkan, "as far as anyone is concerned they are away trading. We know different but it's not wise to speak of this where we may be overheard. Now, young lady, it's time for bed. The sandman will be looking for you."

"But—"

"No buts, Eira, you've finished your food and beer and it's dark now. Take a candle to light your way. And remember that what we have spoken of here is only for us. These are far from easy times."

After a little more pouting and prevarication, Eira left for her bed.

Håkan and his mother sat in silence for some moments. A fresh log on the fire hissed and sputtered and the wind rattled the shutters. The cat landed at the end of the table making them both start.

"Down, Charcoal," said Håkan to the black cat, who took no notice and explored a particularly insistent bit of fur on its hind leg. A blast of wind sent smoke into the room for a moment.

"Chimney needs cleaning," said Håkan's mother.

Håkan stared at the flames as they danced and fluttered. For a moment he thought he'd almost seen an animal stare back at him. He rubbed his eyes.

"The Circle must never be in the hands of such as Pettersson," said Signy. "The Circle and Torsberg have been in the Ekland family for as long as we have records. Your father does not say much about it, but his mother, God rest her soul, told me that both are a sacred trust and important in ways today's churchmen don't appreciate."

Håkan swirled the remains of the small beer around in his beaker.

"Mother ..." he started, and then paused.

Signy looked at her son and said nothing. Håkan took a deep breath.

"Mother, I've seen things. Heard things."

Still Signy did not speak.

"I'm not sure what. Whether it be troll or devil or winter madness." Håkan looked at his mother, who nodded, unsmiling, her pale-grey eyes deep and unreadable.

Håkan described seeing the boar and the boy, and how this strangely dressed lad had appeared and disappeared within the Circle.

"The second time I just found tracks, Mother. Tracks that started of a sudden within the pure snow of the Circle and ended a few paces later. I cannot see how anything human could have made those."

"Why didn't you tell me of this earlier?"

"I wasn't sure if it was a trick of the devil or my imagining."

"Did you tell the priest at confession?"

Håkan looked at his mother and shrugged.

"I'd nothing to confess. I doubt the priest would have understood. He told me once our circle of stones was built by evil people long since fled this Christian country."

Signy studied her son's face for a bit and then the play of flames in the fireplace. She compressed her lips and nodded.

"You wait here, child," said his mother. "I'll be back in a moment. There is something that now I must share with you."

The Drum Prophesy

The wind had completely dropped and the house held its breath. Even the flames in the fireplace glowed and wavered with less urgency than before. Outside an owl hooted, seeking prey that scuttled around the barns and outhouses. A creak sounded from the stairs and moments later Signy returned with a lamp in one hand and a wooden box in the other. When seated once more, she took a small key from around her neck and opened the box.

She withdrew a piece of parchment, yellow and slightly cracked, and unfolded it. Around its edges were little figures depicting men and women, with a moon's face at the top and a spiky sun at the bottom. Arising from the sun a snake or road worked its way up towards some text and a stylised hill with three trees. Near the bottom, two boys or small men confronted a bear.

"Your uncle painted this drum after a vision he had."

"My uncle? Stefan?"

"No, not Stefan or Goran. They are your father's brothers. No, my brother."

Håkan shuddered as though an angel had walked over his grave. He shook his head.

"Your brother? But you were – sorry, are – an only child, Mother. Aren't you? Grandfather always said how you made up for lack of sons."

"Yes, he did. He loved me and never let me feel unwanted. For he truly loved my mother, your nana, Livli. He went against many conventions to marry her."

"I know. Which is why we all have Sami blood. But she only had one child didn't she? Which is why grandfather said—"

"No. She had a son from her first marriage. He's called Garral. His father was killed in a whaling accident. Your grandmother had to face the world alone and pregnant at fifteen. Think about that. That's Inge's age, just two years older than you."

"So what happened?" asked Håkan, spearing a bit of pickled herring on his knife tip.

"My father lived in a settlement near Livli's village. He traded with Livli's people. Livli struggled to raise Garral without a husband. But she had two great gifts, one obvious and one less so. Your grandmother's first great gift was her beauty. We all get our pale-blue eyes from her and skin that goes hazel in the sunshine, when we finally get some." Signy smiled and sipped some beer, dabbing her mouth again with a cloth.

Håkan nodded. He, Lennart and Eira all had grey-blue eyes that could even appear dusty green in certain lights. A contrast to their father's brown eyes.

"What was her other gift?"

"It's the one I share and the one I think you may have too. It's a certain way of seeing things. Seeing more than is right there, more than can be touched. My mother would say she could see the music of the gods behind the beauties of nature."

"The gods? Surely, a Christian—"

"Yes. Your grandmother raised me Christian as I've raised you. And rightly so. But in the lands of the night lights, where the sky fills with wondrous colour, the old gods have never been completely forgotten, and the ancient pathways have never been completely blotted out. I, and she, can see the hidden power in plants. That's how I can use them to heal, just as she taught me."

Håkan nodded. He loved the barn where Signy dried her herbs and prepared her salves from berries and roots. People came from all over to receive her healing. And Brother Niels, who took care of the health of the Cistercians in the monastery outside the village, was a frequent visitor and family friend. They would talk for hours about the properties of certain leaves and the healing value of poisons when used in tiny amounts.

"And I think you can see, too," added his mother.

"What do you mean?"

"It is not by chance you spend so much time at the Circle. And it is not by chance that you've seen an apparition there."

"I go there to practice my tumbling. You know that Mother. The deep grass breaks my fall if I make an error and the snow does the same in winter, unless it's frozen solid."

"Yes. Your tumbling," said Signy, with a faraway look in her eyes. "I'm not sure whether to be grateful that we gave shelter for so long to those travelling players and vagabonds—"

"They weren't vagabonds!"

"I tease you, my dear. No, they were not. Many an interesting talk I had with the leader of their band, and many an interesting tale he told Matts and me. And I loved their skill with balance and falling, juggling and singing. I'm more than happy they awoke in you a love for the pipes. And the leader had the healing gift as well and much valuable knowledge. But throwing yourself off rocks has never brought me calm."

"But what of this parchment, Mother?" said Håkan, pointing with his knife.

"Your uncle, my half-brother Garral, has the far sight as well. In him it has a different quality. He won't speak of it. He says to do so is to squander its power. He cannot command it. Even among his kinfolk some considered him mad. Some said he would become a great holy man. All he wanted was to hunt whales like his father. But the visions would fall on him at times and he's known as a great drum creator."

"Drum creator?"

"Yes. The visions of our northern kin are written on drum skins. When these drums are played the power of the story is reawakened or so they say. That is why this parchment is circular. See. Here is where the stitching went." Signy pointed to tiny holes perforating the edge of the parchment.

"And the writing?"

"Father taught both Garral and me to write. He loved the sound of our Sami language and its power to convey the hidden mysteries of stories. He'd quickly learned our language in his trading and knew the value of being able to record the written word. He taught Garral before moving south with your nana."

"Why didn't Garral come as well?"

"He was a man by then, having seen sixteen summers. He stayed with his father's family. They needed his strength and skills."

Signy spread out the parchment, moving Håkan's beer mug. She tapped the writing at the centre of the drum skin.

"These are the words that came to him in a sweat-lodge trance. He made the drum and played it into power. After a time he sent it to me here. It arrived the day of your birth. He told the bearer it was for my second boy. I'd not seen him then or heard from him for nearly fifteen years. But he knew somehow I was pregnant and with a boy. That's the sort of power he had or has, assuming he's still alive."

"But what does it say?"

"Look closely, Håkan. See the central writing is surrounded by eleven figures. And to one side a small mountain is drawn."

Håkan felt fire jab its way through his limbs. The room came and went around him. He took a deep breath and leant forward on the sturdy wood of the table.

"It's Torsberg and our Circle."

Party Time

England – about now

"How come you were invited to this party?"

Juliette was fixing her make up in the bathroom, as I applied copious gel to my hair.

"Sorry, sis, if you think I'll be an embarrassment. I won't cramp your style."

I took hold of her bra strap and pulled it a little so it snapped against her back.

"Don't DO that!" said Juliette. "Ooh, you're so irritating."

Juliette drew a line under her eye. I ran a comb through my hair, achieving the casual but neat look. I squinted at a white head that had appeared near the tip of my nose.

"Blast."

"I can put a dab of make-up on that if you want."

"No, I'll just squeeze it," I said, and used a flannel and water as hot as I could bear. The method worked. Juliette pulled a face.

"So," she said, "how come, little brother? Who asked you?"

"The guy holding the party, Sebstian … Sebatane—"

"Sebastian!"

"Yep, Seb. He sort of invited me. Not that I know him, but he's still at the school that Bishop came … Charles Bishop came from. The Hospital School or something."

"Christ's Hospital," said Juliette. She applied glistening lipstick, made a kiss mark on a tissue and then added, "I nearly took a scholarship there."

"I thought it was a boy's school," I said, noting the way Juliette had managed to remind me of her academic precocity.

"It was. A long time ago. But they let in girls, naturally, to improve their results."

"So why didn't you go?"

"Oh, I didn't want to dress up in medieval garb with all those buttons down the front, and that funny white thing hanging like a limp tongue at your neck."

"Oh, they come from that school, do they, the people we see in Hammerford Carfax sometimes? The boys in blue skirts?"

"Not skirts, gowns."

"I don't blame you, Jules. Hammerford High is much more your thing. No uniform at all for years twelve and up." I used my comb to spike my hair.

"But Jolyon is throwing the party isn't he?"

"I think both brothers are. Seb is a good mate of Charles's. Will your … will Lucian be going?"

Juliette looked up at me from her perch on the bathroom stool and nodded. I'd the impression she just might not need to use the blusher, whatever that is. She cleared her throat.

"Jolyon and Lucian were also at school together before Lucian went to Scrivener's. They were in the same fencing team."

I nodded. Something about Lucian weirded me out but I couldn't have said what. He'd been nice as pie to me the few times we'd spoken.

"When do you want me to pick you up, kids?" asked my dad, as he drove past the Town Hall.

"It's okay, Daddy," said Juliette, "we'll walk back."

"All right then, but no calls in the wee small hours, please. Mum made a particular point that you must be back before one in the morning."

Given that the party was not even starting until nine o'clock that seemed a bit draconian.

However, neither of us had said yes. I'd a suspicion that Juliette would be coming home with Lucian; I'd be wandering the cold, wet streets of Hammerford on my own.

We crunched over the gravel in front of the imposing house.

Jolyon, a tall boy with longish dark hair and a self-satisfied smile, greeted us at the door. He ushered us in, paying particular attention to Juliette, and showed us where we could leave our coats. The large front room had a scattering of people, most of whom I didn't know, and pulsed with some rapper doing his thing. We placed the cake Mum had made on a table already chock-a-block with salads, bowls of nuts and crisps and lots of tiny pork pies. Mum had created the cake with its layers of cream and raspberries topped with meringue – my favourite.

Jolyon murmured something in Juliette's ear, smiled to himself and glided off. We approached the kitchen via a passageway full of pictures of horses held by grooms.

The kitchen bubbled with a hubbub of chatter. My mega-sized bottles of coke and fizzy orange joined the forest of wine bottles and the tub of ice and beer. Juliette helped herself to a half beaker of wine and I took a plastic cup of coke, having snaffled a piece of ice from the beer tub. We squeezed our way out of the kitchen and into the relative calm of the passageway. Down the hall, the rapper stopped rapping. Juliette took a sip of her drink while I investigated the painting of a man in a bottle-green coat standing by a tall, dark-brown horse. He had an angled top hat on his head. Cool dude.

"I'll be back in a jiffy." Juliette, a tad furtive, headed towards the hallway and the stairs.

I wandered past more horse paintings into the front room. Techno music thumped out of a couple of humongous speakers. Small candles and a lava-light struggled to defeat the darkness.

In the murk I wasn't sure if I knew anyone. Splayed on the settee were a few boys from Scrivener's but they weren't in my class. One of them gave me a slight nod but not enough of a welcome for me to join them. I found a chair and plonked myself down. A group of girls by the fireplace responded to a story with fierce giggles. I practised various lines in my head I might use if I went over to them.

"Hello, I'm Rhory, who are..."

"Hi. You're cute. Fancy a dance..."

"Hey gorgeous, Look who just walked into your..."

I sipped my coke, took a breath and remained seated.

Two boys and three girls were dancing rather half-heartedly, not quite with each other. I could've joined them. I liked dancing. But I remained on my chair, lit by the lava-light.

Official announcement: I'd joined the wall-flower club. I was a lemon. I leaned back in the chair, let the music swirl about me and closed my eyes.

The experience in the park had unnerved me. I'd thought a lot about Ariane, the girl in the dark-green gown. She'd known my real name and the names of Shoshan and Dimitris, my companions in time travel. When she'd moved the object on the table in front of her – the sword pommel – I'd found myself leaving the warmth of her tower for a bone-chilling snowy waste.

Is she in charge of everything? Am I part of a game of three-dimensional chess across time? I've seen her before, I'm sure of it.

"Are you sleeping, mate?"

I looked up to find Charles Bishop looking down on me with an amused smile on his face. His puffy right eye showed where Calvin had thumped him.

"Not really, Charles, just thinking. But how are you after your ... after the..."

He pulled a quizzical face and said, "After the prizefight? I'll certainly watch myself around Calvin in the future. He's not here, is he?"

"No. I don't think he knows Sebastian."

Someone came up behind Charles carrying two drinks. She had her wavy brown hair gathered back with a hairband. She looked exactly like Ariane, the girl in the tower.

Caroline

"Are you all right for a drink, Rhory?" said the Ariane look-alike.

I nodded, like one of those silly toy animals people keep in the back window of their car.

"You okay? Looks like you've seen a ghost. It's only my sister, you know," said Charles.

"I know, I know. Really nice to see you. It was just for a moment—"

"That you thought I was someone else," said the girl.

She didn't say it as a question, rather she was making a statement. Charles went off in search of drinks.

She stood there rocking sideways from foot to foot, a half smile on her face. I struggled to remember her name.

She began to turn away as I blurted out, "Caroline!" I'd finally remembered.

"Yes?"

"Er ... um, is Natasha coming, do you know? You said you were a friend of hers."

She nodded, her eyebrows arching slightly. "I think she's off with her mother, clearing out some old lady's house."

I did more of my nodding-dog act.

"Oh my goodness, you mean Aunt Bridget."

Caroline frowned a little. "I don't think Natasha told me her name."

I stood up, nearly spilling my coke. I'd just realised that I had to speak to my cousin.

"I'm going to have to make a call. I don't know if I can get a signal here. I must speak to Natasha." I started to walk between the groups of kids holding drinks and chatting.

"I dreamt about you the other night, you know." I only just caught the meaning of her words through the blather of the music.

I stopped. Caroline was staring at the carpet with her hands clasped in front of her. She frowned even more.

"Oh. That must have been pretty boring."

My innards contracted. This conversation wasn't going well.

Caroline looked at me, raising her eyes rather than her face. She shrugged.

"Actually, it was a really clear dream. I've dreamt about the room before, and a really unusual table, but I've never seen anyone in the room – 'til this time."

I didn't say anything. Panic crawled around inside me. I didn't know what to say that wouldn't get me into all sorts of difficulties. Anyway, the noise level meant we could hardly hear each other, and I didn't want to shout.

Caroline continued, "In other dreams, I've even been able to walk over and look out the windows. The tower is near a harbour. Strange ships with huge sails come in and out or are rowed by loads of sailors."

I knew the room she meant. She'd dreamt herself into the same room I found myself in, when I entered the bandstand.

She looked me straight in my eyes. "I saw you in that room. We talked about something but I can't quite remember. Then I saw you standing in some snow with a wild boar right behind you."

"I've got you a drink," said Charles, who had taken all this time to get to the kitchen and back.

I still didn't know what to say. Caroline had just added an extra tangle in the threads of my life. Up to now I'd only had to deal with people from the past; now I had found someone else dreaming of the past, only this time it was my past as well.

I took a deep breath and moved closer to Caroline. I caught a whiff of her perfume. Something tangy and sweet. "I have dreams, but sometimes those dreams—"

"Do you think we ought to help ourselves to some food?" said Charles. "I think it might get busy quite soon, there are still people pouring into the house."

We looked over to where a queue had formed by the table. We decided to join them, preventing me exploring the visions Caroline and I shared.

Half a sausage roll later, I remembered that I must speak with Natasha. I left my food in the protection of the Bishop brother and sister and found a good signal from my mobile just outside. I couldn't get Natasha to pick up, and left a longish voicemail message, reminding her to look for the key and to search for the old journal that had been hidden in the commode. I reminded my resourceful cousin that the commode had been changed into a drinks cabinet, and had a locked drawer that would be easy to miss if you didn't know it was there.

When I came back in, I could hear two drum rhythms. The first came from the front room where Lady Gaga or someone similar belted out a disco beat. Higher up in the house I thought I could pick out a simple rhythm from a drum set. I had to go and look.

The wide stairs curved up to the first floor. The wall had framed photographs all the way up. Every picture showed a woman standing near a famous landmark. The women changed but the landmarks were entirely recognisable, like the Eiffel Tower, the Leaning Tower of Pisa or the Colosseum. I guessed that Jolyon and Sebastian's mother or father fancied themselves as a photographer. On the first landing I clocked that the percussion sounds came from higher up in the house. I found a narrower staircase and made my way up.

In a small room at the top of the house a fantastic full drum set clustered in the corner. I'd once done a drumming course when we went on a family break to Center Parcs. Out of the ten or so kids who followed that course I'd been far and away the best. Even though I was only eleven at the time, Tom the instructor had said I ought to be in a group.

Someone was tickling away in a half-hearted manner on one of the kettledrums. I asked if I could have a go.

"Yeah, why not," said a boy with red hair, a squarish face and freckles.

"You sure?" I said.

"Yep. Sure. They're mine. I'm Seb. Who're you?"

"I'm Rhory."

He frowned slightly before responding. "Juliette's brother?"

I nodded.

"I better be nice to you then. My brother Jolyon fancies her to bits."

I didn't know what to say to that. She seemed to have this thing for Lucian. Where was my sister anyway? I hadn't seen her for ages.

I sat down and surveyed the kit. Nice one. Sparkly purple sides and silvery adjustments. I could tell no one had played it much.

The kettledrum at the side didn't match the rest and had the rich tone I'd heard all the way to the bottom of the house. I eased my foot onto the bass drum pedal and started to work up a beat: boom, boom ba-boom. The toms had been tightened to give a sharp staccato and the ride cymbal produced a satisfying swish of sound. I twiddled a stick around in my right hand, and tried out the floor tom-tom.

Seb and the boy who had been fiddling around with the kit stood nodding in time to the beat that was now flowing nicely. I closed my eyes and let myself feel my way into the rhythm. The thump, crash and patter of sound filled the room. When I next opened my eyes I could see several other people had come in. I hardly registered them as I built to a thundering climax, ending with a blast of sound from the crash cymbal. Yeah. Boom boom, yeah. Crash.

I looked up. The door had filled with faces. Lucian stood there, his blond hair a corona of golden glow from the hall light behind him. Juliette nestled in beside him.

"Rhory," said Lucian, "that's really, really good. I didn't know you could play so well."

"You can see why Mum refuses to let him get a set though," said my sister, smiling. I could see I'd managed to impress even her. She'd never bothered to come and hear me play when we had stayed at Center Parcs, so she didn't really know what I could do.

As I made my way back down the stairs, Lucian called after me that I might be needed later. I nodded but my mind had filled with the plate of uneaten food downstairs, including a large slice of my mum's pudding, and also the problem of how to talk with Caroline. I looked at my watch. Gee, I must have left Charles and her for ages.

The Blonde Lady

The front room had become a sea of bobbing bodies in a murk of low lighting. A well-known anthem filled the room and everyone sang along as they twisted and writhed. Groups of boys danced with boys and girls with girls, but some couples appeared stuck by glue and unable to separate no matter how much they wriggled. I made my way over to the chair where I'd left my food with Charles. My food peeked out from under the seat. Someone else sat on the seat, a girl of about fifteen perched on his knee. She wobbled up and down in time to the music. My mum's pudding had vanished.

I made my way to the food table. All the plates had gone. So had most of the food. A smashed raspberry smeared on our cooking dish showed where the pudding had once been. I found a slightly dried-up cheese sandwich on white bread and a few crisps and balanced them on a paper napkin.

Three girls stood near the doorway into the hall. I could just make out Caroline. Her face caught the light every now and then when one of her friends moved. Her spooky likeness to the Ariane girl in my bandstand vision was – well – spooky. I'd no explanation. One of her friends poked her and pointed in my direction. Caroline shrugged and walked out of the room. She didn't look my way. The other two girls hunched their shoulders and whispered. They both looked over at me. I could feel a red glow creeping up my face and felt mildly sick.

"Hey, Rhory. Brucie. Come on, mate, come and dance."

Some of my classmates had arrived and were in a gaggle gyrating away at the street end of the room. I joined them for a bit, and we all grinned at one another, wiggled around, became serious, tried to look cool, failed and grinned again. When J. Lo or Jessie J or some other diva finished, I mumbled something about a drink and headed for the kitchen.

The floor gripped at my feet as I moved over its stickiness. I wove through the chatting groups in search of Caroline and a replenishment of coke. The table, once neat, now had puddles of sticky liquids, many half-full and empty bottles, and plates of nearly finished food dumped everywhere. One had a large slice of Mum's pudding in the centre, surrounded by pristine china. The only problem – a cigarette had crash landed in the meringue layer. I found a more-or-less clean beaker and topped up with nearly fizzy coke. Caroline wasn't in the room.

As I made my way out, a couple of people said, "Great drumming." I smiled but felt all lopsided. I hadn't meant to just dump Caroline, who'd clearly wanted to talk. Maybe she'd gone home. Not often a pretty girl wanted to talk to me and I'd gone off to produce a riff on some drums.

I worked my way up the stairs once more, past the cityscapes with their languid ladies in glorious black and white. One room had the door wide open and I could see people sitting inside. I hovered by the entrance, sipping my coke and scanning the room for Bishops. I didn't spot Charles, but glimpsed Caroline talking with Sebastian and another boy I didn't recognise. Near the fireplace, complete with roaring log fire, sat a woman. Her long legs were tucked to one side of her armchair and she wore a black dress with silver markings on the shoulder. Her hair, blonde, had been beaten and burnished into brilliance and cascaded in curls down to her shoulders. She extended a slim white arm towards Lucian. He leant over and said something to her, revealing Juliette standing beside him.

I wondered if I had the nerve to go over to Caroline. I didn't really know Seb and thought I might get a chilly reception. I took a breath and entered.

"Rhory!"

Juliette beckoned from near the fireplace.

"Rhory, you should meet Victoria. She's Seb and Jolyon's

auntie. She's the policewoman here tonight."

The blonde lady extended her hand to me now. A black ring, set in silver, flashed. I took her hand and she smiled, looking deep into my eyes.

"I'm pleased to meet you, Rhory. I should point out I'm no policewoman. More of a friendly adult just here to be on hand if needed. I thought I'd be watching TV quietly but I've had great fun talking to your sister. I can see why Lucian is besotted."

Lucian struck a pose of refined coolness, his lips slightly pursed. His hand moved to Juliette's waist.

"I think that Lucian just wants help with his English essays, actually," said Juliette, arching her eyebrows and pulling away from Mr Boy-Band.

"Come on, Jules, we need to set up next door. It's just the right sort of night to explore the other side," said Lucian. I'd no idea what he meant. Juliette half-winked at me as she went past.

At the door, Lucian turned, and said, "We may need you in a bit, Rhory."

I was no wiser as to what they were up to or why I might be needed. I really wanted to have a quiet chat with Caroline. Seb had left the room with Lucian, and Caroline now sat in an armchair on her own, flipping through the pages of a magazine.

I crossed over and said, "Hi!"

She looked up from her magazine but didn't say anything.

"I got waylaid earlier," I said. "Do you know they have a full drum set upstairs?"

Caroline shook her head.

"I just had to have a go. I've not had my hands on a proper set of drums for about two years. Mum just wouldn't let me have all that kit in the bedroom. They've even got a kettle drum up there."

"I didn't know you played the drums."

"I've only got bongo drums at home. They're a great way of releasing tension after a tough day at school."

Caroline nodded, and smiled slightly. I took this as a sign of peace and sat down cross-legged at the side of her chair.

"You saw me as well, didn't you?"

"No." I looked up at her. "I searched for you downstairs and in the kitchen. I didn't realise you'd come upstairs."

Caroline poked me in the shoulder. She leaned forward. "In the tower room. I saw you in my dream, but I think you saw me too."

I shook my head slightly. I didn't know how to respond. I really didn't know anything about Caroline.

"I think it's real. I mean the tower. I think it's real, and I think I know where it is. I'm just not sure about when. I mean when I've been there, always in a kind of dream, I've never thought to ask what year it was. It's more like I'm part of someone else's life that they're living, and I can see what they're doing as though I'm them."

Caroline looked at me and her eyes seemed to be watching from far, far away. I felt that Ariane held me in her gaze in the upstairs lounge of the big house. A log shifted in the fireplace and a spray of sparks danced above the fireguard. The blonde lady with the black earrings stared at us. I felt an icicle drop inside my stomach.

Caroline poked my shoulder once more. "You've been there, haven't you?"

I nodded. "I don't know how I got there. One moment I was crossing the park and the next I found myself in that tower room. You ... well not you, but a girl who looked very like you, who looks very like you, sat at that strange table."

Caroline smiled. "At least I'm not going crazy. Or if I am, I'm not on my own." She closed the magazine and leant over to put it on a pile of other glossy journals on the table next to her.

"I hear her voice sometimes. Ariane's voice." She turned back to me and touched my shoulder. "Believe it or not, Rhory, she spoke to me when I first saw you, and my dad gave you a lift. But

I knew before that. I knew when Natasha told me about you."

Everything in the room felt less and less real. Out of the corner of my eye I thought I saw a cat moving. I looked around and caught the gaze of the blonde lady by the fire.

"Rhory, they're going to want you to do something. It'll put you in danger. It'll put all of us in danger."

I looked back at Caroline and again sensed it was Ariane who spoke.

"Can I borrow this handsome fellow for a moment?" Lucian stood just behind me with his most winning smile directed at Caroline. "Juliette asked me to fetch you. We need your special skills."

Lucian extended his hand down and helped me to my feet. "I'll only take him for a few minutes, then you can have him back."

Caroline leaned back in the armchair. Her eyes were fixed on Lucian, her mouth a tight line. She shook her head, but Lucian had me by the arm and chatted coaxingly in my ear.

Ouija Board

The bed in the room next door rested flush against the far wall, allowing a low oval table of polished wood to dominate the centre of the room. Arranged near it were various cushions. Candles dotted around the room provided the only illumination and the shadows of the young people gathered there danced on the wallpaper. Above the unlit fireplace a panther grasped the branch of a bleached-white wood tree, and surveyed the room through yellow eyes. Not a picture I would choose to have in my bedroom.

On the table, letters from a Scrabble lay in two neat half-circles, in alphabetical order. In the gaps between the plastic letters two pieces of paper stated 'Yes' and 'No'.

"You could sit here if you want, Rhory," said Lucian, indicating a cushion on the far side of the table.

"That makes sense," said Jolyon. "He can be next to me."

"I'll just sit here then," said Juliette. She took up a place at the narrower end of the oval table. Lucian sat down next and a girl I had not seen before took the final cushion.

"So how do we do this then?" said Lucian. "What's the form, Magda?"

The girl sitting opposite to Juliette looked around at each of us. Her thick dark hair did not obey the usual rules and extended from her head in odd directions. She had a short black skirt covering thick stretch pants, also black. Her feet were bare, and in the candlelight her toenails also looked like small black talons. She had a silver ring round one of the big toes. A pendant hung from a silver chain at her neck, and a stone was clasped by four tiny silver hands. The candlelight caused the stone to flicker and glow with a dull purplish light.

"It's simple really. One of us asks a question, and then we wait. If we are lucky a spirit will guide our fingers, and the answer will be spelt out," said Magda.

She reached under the table and placed a crystal tumbler upside-down in the middle, between all the letters. "Now," she said, "we all put our right fingertip onto the base of the glass."

We did this and shifted our position on the cushions until we felt comfortable.

"All right," said Magda. "I will ask the first few questions and we'll see what happens."

She turned to another girl, with long brown hair, sitting nearby on the edge of the bed, and instructed her to write down the letters that the glass moved to.

"None of you are to push the glass. Understand? If you push the glass towards a particular letter we will all feel it. We will know someone is cheating. It's best just to keep your finger very light and let the spirit do the moving."

I'd no idea what she was talking about and felt quite nervous. Juliette grinned, her eyes on Lucian. She didn't look across at me.

"First question. Are you there?" Magda paused. "Do you wish to speak to us?"

The tumbler started moving. I knew I wasn't pushing it. I even eased the pressure of my finger almost off the glass. The glass still moved. It drifted around within the plastic letters and then, turbo-charged, it shot across towards one of the bits of paper.

"YES!" several people said at once.

"Great," said Magda. "Good evening, and thank you for talking to us."

I wondered if everyone was having a joke at my expense. Had Juliette and Lucian set this all up?

Someone behind me said, "Why don't we ask which horse is going to win the Derby?"

"No, they don't answer questions like that. We have to ask questions that are important to us. Then we will get proper answers," said Lucian.

"Okay," said Seb. "Who was it who really killed President Kennedy?"

Magda looked at him, her face betraying nothing. The glass started to move slowly at first, and then zigzagged between letters so quickly it was hard for the girl writing down each one not to make a mistake.

The boy, interested in winning at a betting shop, leaned over the table and said each letter in turn. "T–H–A–D–I–S–B–E–Y–O–N…"

It happened so fast, I couldn't work out if it made sense or was just gibberish. The glass stopped moving.

"Cool," said the girl on the bed. "Seriously cool." She tapped her pencil on the pad where she had scribbled down the letters. "Look, it says 'Thad is beyond'."

"Thad? Who is Thad?" said a voice behind me.

"I think," said Magda, "that you wrote down D instead of T. They sound really similar."

The glass started to move again spelling out more letters Y–O–U–R–P–A…

When it came to a standstill, the girl with the notebook sat for a few moments, her hair hiding her face. She looked up.

"Now it says, 'That is beyond your pay grade'! That's kind of creepy isn't it?"

The betting boy said, "Come on, do you expect us to believe that? One of you is pushing the glass around."

"No! No one is pushing the glass around," said Juliette, looking quite indignant.

"We are just resting the tip of our fingers so lightly on the top of the glass, no one could be pushing it," said Julian.

Magda raised her left hand and looked around at the people standing near us. Her eyes were cold and she frowned slightly. "Come on, guys, this is serious. If you don't believe it that's fine. But don't hang around here spoiling the atmosphere. We've made a great connection and I don't wish to lose it. If you want to stay watching that's fine. Just keep quiet. All right?"

Somebody left the room, but those who stayed just nodded. Magda was one of those people you didn't contradict. I shifted my position on my cushion, to deal with my aching knees.

Magda then asked a question that sent a jolt of fear into my stomach. "What is meant by pathways of time?"

The tumbler started to move rapidly, and Juliette spelt out the letters the glass touched. I felt as though the edges of my body were being rubbed out by some giant eraser. I no longer belonged completely in the bedroom. I was slowly dissolving. The table, the letters and the glass moving around became somewhere far and distant. I stood before a small hill with trees off to my right and rough pastureland on my left. My finger kept moving on the top of the glass and I could hear Juliette's voice from a great distance. But I could no longer remember what that was all about. I needed to climb to the top of the low hill. Above my head clouds raced over the night sky, revealing and obscuring the moon.

The Three Women

My feet scraped on gravel. I followed the track towards the hill. Something snorted. Behind me the field I'd been standing in gave way to scrub and low trees, but I could make out nothing in the darkness. Again, a huff of breath from further back on the track. I crouched down. The moon came out from behind a cloud and a metallic glint revealed something approaching. I sensed, rather than saw, a figure on a dark horse. The man, his face partially hidden by a dark hood, rode up to me with his sword drawn. Blond hair shone in the moonlight. A face I knew half-smiled at me.

"Julian," I said. "What are you doing here?"

The moonlight had shown enough of his face, and I was looking at a person who appeared the exact double of the Julian who was back in Hammerford. The man threw back his hood. His hair, longer than Julian's, moved in the breeze. On the right side of his head he had a long thin plait dropping over his cheek. He didn't speak, but pointed with his sword towards the top of the hill. The other, younger, Julian said something indistinct and far away and I couldn't make out the words.

I had feelings, but I couldn't tell what they were. My body floated rather than walked to the top of the hill. The horse snorted again and whinnied. A little way down the hill, the track I stood on led to a crossroads. Three figures stood where the two roads met, staring up at me.

I could feel something in my stomach being dragged towards them. They each carried a lantern which cast a flickering light on them, and on the ground around them. As I drew closer, they began a strange dance, with their backs towards each other, forming a small circle facing outwards.

Icy, paralysing fear worked a jagged path through me when I recognised Magda, and also the blonde woman I'd seen earlier that evening. All three women were dressed in long flowing pale robes that swayed in the moonlight. The third woman, bigger than the other two, had her back to me, but as they moved, her face, crowned with thick, dark-red hair, came into view. The last time I'd seen her I'd been in ancient Egypt, and she'd been trying to destroy me. If her eyes could speak they would have said 'Gotcha'. Her mouth formed a tight line of triumph. I felt the damp heat of the horse's breath as it drifted past me.

Some distance from the women, a leafless tree scarred by an ancient lightning strike stood out in the moonlight and watched over the women, a brooding presence of sepulchral white. A silvery feline shape I'd come across before flowed along one of the skeleton-like branches of the dead tree. The eyes of this mercurial cat held the same cruel joy that I could see in the faces of the three dancing women. The cat stretched and let out a mewling cry that sucked all the strength out of me. I knew if I reached the crossroads I was lost. Part of me would never truly return to that room somewhere in another universe, where I sat with my sister and her friends.

The three women stopped dancing and beckoned to me. Their eyes, hidden from the moonlight, were sockets of deep gloom. I fell slowly towards them.

"She's collapsed."

A great distance from me, my fingertip rested on cold glass. People shouting squeezed into my awareness and then melted away.

The three women frowned and the cat, as big as a small leopard, jumped down from the tree. The man on the horse trotted forward and I felt something hard jab me under my right shoulder blade.

"She's just lying on the floor. She fell over and is twitching."

Three women gestured more urgently and the fat lady looked as though she might explode with fury.

"Just turn and walk away."

I knew that voice. A girl I liked.

"Walk back up the hill, ignore everything else."

Warmth and a little feeling flowed back into my limbs, and I turned to face the horse. Julian, if it was Julian, no longer looked solid. His sword had become a pale vapour glowing slightly in the moonlight. The horse resolved itself into shadows and nothingness. I walked right through the spot where he had been sitting so proudly only moments before. The cries of the women behind me clutched once more at my stomach and curled snakelike around my throat.

"Keep walking," said Caroline.

Now I recognised the voice. Charles's sister, who'd not wanted me to go with Julian.

I strode up the hill and the sounds of the women behind me became faint and plaintive.

I'd never seen Juliette look so frightened. She stood, holding the glass clutched tight in her hands, staring at Magda. Julian looked at me, a slight smile on his face and his eyebrows raised with an unspoken question.

Magda lurched to her feet, jarring the table and knocking the plastic Scrabble letters all over the place.

"You're not serious." She said this pointing at Juliette, while her eyes swept the room, ending up resting on me like search-lights in a prison yard.

"What's happened?" said the longhaired girl on the bed.

Someone silhouetted in the doorway responded, "A girl has collapsed. She's lying on the floor next door. She's twitching and shaking."

Feet thundered up the stairs. A voice I recognised shouted, "Caroline!"

Charles sounded frantic. I moved from the table and followed the voice. In the room next door, Charles was pulling people away from where someone lay on the carpet.

"Give her room to breathe, move away. Somebody get a glass of water." Charles eased his sister into the rescue position.

Far away, on a bleak hillside, three women wailed. Something went pop in my ears, and I knew I'd come fully back to Hammerford. I left the lounge, descended the stairs three at a time, pushed my way – all grit and purpose – into the kitchen. I rinsed out a glass and filled it with fresh, cold water. Once back upstairs I gave the glass to Charles. Caroline was now sitting up, leaning against an armchair. Charles held the tumbler to Caroline's lips and she sipped some water. She murmured something to her brother that I couldn't quite catch.

"Don't worry about a cat," said Charles. "There are no cats here, Carrie."

"We've got to go," said Juliette. She held my elbow in a grip that threatened to dislocate my bones.

"We're going home," I said to Charles.

Caroline had moved herself onto her knees. She sipped more water, the glass shaking slightly in her hand. She looked up at me,

"You're okay, Rhory?"

"I'm fine," I said. "But what about you?"

"It happens once in a while. I have epilepsy. I'm used to it. It's more scary for other people. Especially Charlie. I'm pleased you got away, Rhory."

"From the Ouija board you mean?"

Caroline shook her head slightly and shrugged. The claw biting into my elbow became more insistent.

"From the man with the horse." Caroline smiled. "And his friends."

"We have to go," said my sister.

I felt Caroline's eyes follow me out of the room.

Pirates

"So how was the party, mate?"

Nick grinned at me. We stood in the inner playground waiting for break to end and experiencing global cooling first hand.

"No, it was all right really," I said. "I mean it was cool. Seb and Joly have this amazing drum set. I got to do a few—

"Seb and Joly ... wooo," said Nick, with a see-who's-joined-the-upper-classes look on his face. Nick and I pretty much hang out together. Best mates and all that. I'd take teasing from him.

"Actually they were sort of okay. Amazing house. Lots of booze and lots of girls."

"Oh yeah?" The sideways twist in Nick's mouth suggested that the numerous girls wouldn't have come anywhere near me.

"Yeah. Actually." I said. "I even went home with one!"

"Really?"

"Yes, really."

Nick nodded and shrugged slightly.

"Unfortunately she was called Juliette."

I received a jab in my ribs for my effort at humour.

"Hey, Rhory."

Charles came and joined us.

"I got a note for you. From Caroline. She wanted to, you know, write." He gave me a pink envelope with a tiny picture of a pixie in the upper right hand corner, and my name written carefully exactly in the centre.

"Ha!" said Nick.

"It's complex," I said, feeling suddenly defensive.

"Always is, mate," said Nick, as the school bell told us it was time to go to the French hut. I pushed the letter into my inside pocket.

After French we went straight to the gym. Someone said as they were leaving, "It's set up for Pirates."

Fantastic. I beamed inside. I'm not amazing at gym, but I run fast, jump high and can out-swerve most. I've even been known to win. But usually it was Bizet who survived longest. He, after all, had been in the England junior team for gymnastics. Steve Bizet ("pronounced Bizzett mate, I'm not some French woofter") was okay. He didn't flaunt his success and even got to miss class on occasion. His picture graced our little hall of fame in the school foyer. His nickname was Carmen. Not sure why.

We rushed into the gym and saw the mats spread out like green islands on a brown sea, with the ropes dangling from the ceiling at various strategic points. Some of the mats were connected by narrow benches; a sort of bridge over shark infested sprung-wood flooring.

"Okay, boys," said Mr Palmerstone to our assembled class, in our regulation blue shorts and white T-shirts, "you know the drill. I select the two pirates. The rest of you are escapees. You're safe on the mats, benches and the wall-bars. If your feet touch the gym floor you've drowned – whether you are pirates or escape artists – and sit over here."

He pointed to a row of benches at the far end of the gym. We nodded. Nick and Calvin became the pirates. Anyone they touched would join the eye-patch and parrot brigade. They took up positions on the mat furthest away from the rest of us. The loud chirrup on the whistle started proceedings. Feet thundered around the mats, with boys leaping and shouting, and banging over the benches from mat to mat.

Carmen immediately climbed the wall-bars and hovered near the ceiling. I pulled a rope close, to be able to swing to a distant mat if necessary. I never get caught early on, being able to outrun even Nick, for all his rugby prowess. Calvin lunged for me, I dodged and he stumbled onto the gym floor. The trill of the whistle confined him to Davy Jones's benches. I was quietly crowing inside when someone whom Nick had nabbed made a lunge for me. I swung on a rope, didn't make it across and had to start to climb; normally a good strategy, for a time, as only the strongest would bother to climb up to catch you. But in the end they always do.

I tried to get the rope swinging once more, to make it back to a mat, but the end was seized by a passing pirate and I lost my grip. I joined Calvin and several others on the benches.

Two boys decided to corner Carmen on the wall-bars. He let them get close and then scuttled sideways and slightly down to where he could launch himself to a safe mat. The two irate pirates chased him, but he gracefully cartwheeled along the bench from one mat to another. This so shook one of his pursuers that he lost his balance. "Splash!" we all shouted from the sidelines.

Carmen remained safe for a bit whilst other less nimble boys were dragooned into piracy or drowned in the attempt. Four pirates started to corner him.

"Go on, Steve!" someone shouted.

He stood on his mat, near a wall, his hand nonchalantly holding the end of a rope. I couldn't see a winning strategy from this position and awaited the inevitable. Barry Chasemore, an elephantine lad, all puppy fat and rosy cheeks, banged across the bench, his arms outstretched, with his tongue peeking out of his mouth as a result of concentrating so hard. He made it to the mat. Carmen had no way of escape.

"Hey, Bizet, you're done for!" shouted Calvin.

Just when Barry should have presented Carmen with his final black spot, starting a new game, our gymnast flicked the heavy rope away from him, so it started to swing. He loped swiftly towards the wall and ran two complete steps up the white brickwork, narrowly missing the red fire alarm box and twisting sideways. Momentarily horizontal to the mat below, he launched towards the rope, catching it on its return. Turning with his head down and his legs in the air, he swung far out over the 'water'. Barry extended his arms wide, awaiting the return swing, which never came.

The empty rope headed back towards the hapless pirate, but Carmen had dropped into a handstand on the floor, and walked on his hands into deeper water.

"Ha, you're drowned," said Calvin.

We all looked towards Palmerstone.

"It says, in the rules, sir," Steve Bizet said from his aft over telescope posture, "you drown if your feet touch the water. You will notice my feet are dry." Palmerstone grinned and we all hollered.

"Nice one, boy. So you get to be the pirate now. Okay, lads, to your mats."

I don't know if Steve Bizet had watched the film *Singing in the Rain*, but that evening proved a little spooky. When I returned from school, Juliette had her iPad on and she and Dad were hooting about something. I came over.

"Look at this guy, Bro," said Juliette. "He's amazing."

"He is actually," said Dad. "When I saw a remake at the National Theatre they didn't find an actor who could do this. Rewind it, Jules. Let Rhory see."

The scene showed two dudes on a stage set. One sang and danced and generally made a monkey's backside of himself, wearing a funny hat. The song, if it could be called that, was *Make 'Em Laugh*. Dad laughed like a drain and Juliette giggled. I thought it straight forwardly old-fashioned and boring.

"Wait, wait, Rhory. Just wait," said Juliette.

"Yeah, it's Donald O'Connor's most amazing dance."

Well, the man in the funny hat started courting a headless dummy. Now that struck me as quite neat. After the dummy and he flew in all sorts of directions, he finished by running straight up a wall, and doing a back flip. Twice. I went hot and cold all over. Just like Carmen at school, sort of. For a crack between two seconds, I sensed seeing this deep underground with nasty people intent on sacrificing me or worse.

"You all right, Rhory? You don't seem to have much of a sense of humour these days," said Juliette.

I mumbled something and left the room. I had to pack anyway. In two days' time I was scheduled to fly to Egypt with Natasha and my aunt and uncle. I negotiated the hallway, avoiding the ski equipment that reminded me of the choice I'd made. My stomach lurched. Serious people were out to do me harm. I might be much safer on a snowy piste than staring at blooming pyramids.

Back in my bedroom I remembered Caroline's letter. I fished out the pink envelope from my jacket pocket and turned it over. In neat letters on the back, just where the flap had been closed were five letters: S.W.A.L.K.

What on earth did that mean? Should I open it? Maybe the answer was inside.

It wasn't. Just a letter, with the current date and writing so neat, only girls can achieve it. At the top of the pink paper another pixie waved a wand distributing fairy dust. I felt I needed that at that moment.

Dear Rhory,

How are you? I am well. Charles probably explained I have epilepsy. I fall down and froth at the mouth and all. I've had it now for five years; ever since I came across the tower.

At the party I worried about you. I sensed something. Or the girl in the tower sensed something, which is sort of the same. Like a web being woven around you, sticky and dangerous. I know it doesn't make sense but I did not want you to do that squeejee thing or whatever it is. Stress doesn't usually bring on a fit, but it did on the night of the party.

I saw you – in a sort of vision thing. More than a dream anyway. And I saw the man on horseback. I shouted really loud and he heard me. The picture then broke, like smashed glass in one of those films when an actor is thrown through a window. The vision broke and so did the web.

But the girl in the tower, she said something. I heard her voice. She said, "Bring back the tumbler."

I don't know what that means. Do you? It is a message for you.

Yours sincerely,
Carrie.

Ceramic Tanks

The blonde lady with the Armani cream suit flicked open her compact and checked her lipstick. She augmented the pale pink gloss, adjusted some errant strands of hair, straightened her jet-black necklace and looked steadily at the middle-aged security man by the massive front door. He dropped his eyes.

"Follow me out after three minutes, Graham, and then head back to the office."

The young man behind her, standing to the side on the black and white checked floor, nodded. He put down the heavy holdall and flexed his fingers.

"Okay," Onyx said to the security man, and he opened the door to Number Ten.

The cameras were lined up outside and the policeman on the steps appeared taller than on TV. The Prime Minister would be making a statement shortly about the situation in the Middle East. Onyx didn't look over at the journalists waiting by the barrier or the microphones that would catch the PM's words later. She knew most journalists had no idea who she was and would assume she worked as a political lobbyist. Only the most unobservant would think she was a secretary. Perhaps only one had rightly guessed she wielded more power than most of the British ministers who met regularly in the Cabinet Room at Number Ten. *Just how I like it,* she thought, as her heels tapped out a tattoo and she speed-dialled her mobile.

"Coming out," she murmured, walking up towards the high iron security gate and Whitehall beyond.

Ten minutes later she settled back into the soft leather of the Mercedes S65 as it softly purred past the House of Commons. Big Ben sounded the hour with its customary flourish, a sound that briefly stirred something patriotic inside her. She pushed the irrelevant feeling aside and pondered how the morning had gone.

The multi-national company, of which she was the youngest Vice President, didn't have an immediately recognisable name, and its logo – a female human body with a lioness's head – put fear in the heart of only the most knowledgeable. Bastet, the ancient Egyptian deity that slaughtered all who got in her way, provided a suitable symbol for the ADR Corp.

The Prime Minister's aide had introduced her as the Vice-President of the Advanced Defence and Response Corporation, in charge of NLW, or New Level Weaponry.

The PM had shaken her hand with a firm grip, smiled a slightly smarmy smile that men often offered her, assuming her very good looks couldn't possibly be combined with ruthlessly focused intelligence.

Onyx had introduced Graham Cavendish, her assistant. He had a cluster of degrees from both England and the USA, as well as his experience from a brief and secret attachment to the Navy. Graham understood how the weapon they were to demonstrate actually worked. Onyx understood politics, power and high finance. She understood the way to use fear of the unknown.

"I thought we were to have a briefing," said the PM as Graham began unloading the tripod and assembling the various shiny black and grey parts of the weapon. He looked unsmiling towards Onyx.

"A demonstration – a simple illustration of the powers of the Disintegrator – will be worth a thousand Power Points, Prime Minister. Most people have no idea that scalar technology exists, and very few at all are aware how it has been miniaturised. ADR have led the field, and we have been careful with our patents and our security. Even our closest competitors cannot imagine what we have now developed."

A secretary knocked at the door and the grey-haired aide went across to collect the tray of coffee and freshly baked biscuits, a favourite of the Prime Minister. Graham worked steadily and the weapon appeared bit by bit at one end of the table. When he was done with his clicks and twists, an 'H' shaped device, somewhat like the hull of a catamaran, sat on the top of the neat, dark tripod. He flicked a switch and a red oval of light appeared towards the far side of the shiny mahogany surface.

"This won't damage the table, will it, Victoria? It's nearly three hundred years old and is irreplaceable. Lord Wellington wrote most of his major speeches seated here."

"No, there will not be a scratch, Prime Minister, I can assure you. The beam has no effect on wood. Graham can focus the beam to within a millimetre..." She smiled, all perfect teeth and blue-grey eyes. "I'm not exaggerating. A millimetre, right, Graham?"

The young man gave a slightly nervous smile, nodded and said, "Yep. That's how it is." He took a small silvery control from his pocket.

Onyx crossed to the bag and extracted a white ceramic shallow bowl a bit wider than a dinner plate.

"Are we making soup?" asked the aide, raising his eyebrows as though he had said something very funny.

"Sort of," responded Onyx. "Did you bring the expendable object in metal as I requested?"

"No, I did that," said the PM. "Lead is metal and I brought along some lead soldiers from my collection. Seemed appropriate somehow."

"Are you sure, Prime Minister?" asked Onyx.

"Yes. Absolutely. They are surplus to requirements."

Onyx took the three little figures, each pointing rifles. They were much heavier in her palm than she expected and slightly cool. She arranged them in a tight formation at the centre of the bowl. They stood bravely, in their red coats, facing outwards.

"Sort of Custer's Last Stand," said the aide.

"Please be so kind as to put on these goggles." Onyx gave out the protective glasses. She shepherded the group behind the beam projector.

"With the glasses on you can watch the figures. Without them on your eyesight might be damaged, so please do not remove them until the demonstration is over. When you are ready, Graham."

Turning two of the three serrated circular controls, Graham adjusted the laser light until the three figures glowed with an even brighter red colour. He stood back and undid one button on his dark-blue suit. He toyed nervously with the knot of his tie. The beam projector hummed almost imperceptibly. Outside the room a phone rang. Otherwise they stood in silence.

Onyx touched the Prime Minister's hand. The aide frowned. "You can say 'when', Prime Minister."

The PM looked at her, smiled and then turned towards Graham. "Go on, young man, do your worst."

Graham nodded and tapped a button on the remote control. For a moment nothing happened. Then the plate vibrated slightly and the three figures radiated dazzling white light. A sound like steam escaping from a pressure cooker ended with a soft whistle. The figures had entirely disappeared. The bowl had a slight smudging of grey ash.

"Here, touch this," said Onyx, carrying over the bowl.

"Goodness. Goodness gracious," said the PM. He took off his goggles. "Blow me down. It's not even hot." He had gone pale.

Onyx marvelled at how strong men blanched when they saw technology they neither understood nor quite believed.

The PM cleared his throat. "So what happens if you point this at a tank?"

"The tank disappears, the people inside do not, unless they have metal inserts in their joints or something. Mind you, they would be completely blind."

"Ah," said the Prime Minister, pouring himself a glass of sparkling water. "Would you...?" he said to Onyx, offering to pour her a glass.

"No thank you, Prime Minister. You're a busy man and we have to let you get on with running the nation." In fact Onyx had a meeting she considered equally important as this one, in another part of London.

The Prime Minister sat down near the ceramic dish, and watched Graham disassemble the beam projector. He tapped his fingers on the table as though playing chopsticks at a piano. He looked up at Onyx.

"So we will have to build our tanks out of ceramics."

Onyx nodded slowly. "Something like that, Prime Minister. But you may find hemp is a more viable way forward. Henry Ford used hemp on early prototypes of his car. It's immune to this beam technology."

Onyx checked her red nails for blemishes as the Mercedes purred its way past Buckingham Palace. Her driver, one of the stalwarts of CEC, or Cavendish Executive Cars, knew not to engage her in idle chitchat. Drivers only made that mistake once. He wore the company shade of blue-grey suit. His hat rested on the front seat.

"After you've dropped me at The Athenaeum that will be it for the day, Peter."

"Thank you, miss," came the reply. "Will you be needing me tomorrow?"

"Not sure," she responded. "I'll call your office if I do."

"Right-oh," said Peter.

The meeting with the PM had gone as planned. Actually it had worked out better than planned. She knew even now phones would be ringing off the hook, if they still had hooks these days, in the offices of the Ministry of Defence and the Treasury. The technology developed by ADR could – and probably would – change the balance of power in the world. And the British PM knew the company would sell to the highest bidder, or at least to the bidder who offered their company the most advantages.

Onyx popped a small peppermint into her mouth. They were

passing the Ritz and the railings of Green Park. In a few moments she would see Sardius. And she hadn't seen him since that dreadful boy from Hammerford had wrecked their plans and played havoc with work on a time scale so vast few people could begin to comprehend it. She straightened her skirt in anticipation of alighting at the hotel.

And to think I nearly destroyed him last week. That would have been so, so sweet, she thought to herself. But the girl in the next room had had a fit and that had literally and comprehensively broken the spell. So much time and thought had gone into planning to get Rhory to that party, along with Magda and the useful but slightly vapid Lucian. Her self-absorbed nephews had come in useful. Stroke of total luck they lived in a big house in Hammerford's famous Causeway. But it all came to naught and now the boy was warned. Onyx was now sure the Hammerford Brat, as she had named him, had helpers too although she doubted he knew entirely who they were.

"Game on," she murmured.

"Sorry, Miss? We're here, Miss." The car came to a gentle halt outside one of London's most exclusive hotels.

The Athenaeum

Sardius, impeccably dressed as always, adjusted the knife-sharp creases of his grey flannel trousers, and crossed his legs. The gold buttons on his dark-blue blazer gleamed softly in the muted light of the hotel lounge. He smiled slightly at Onyx and sipped his filter coffee, which he took without milk.

"So what exactly happened?" he asked, setting down his cup with precision on the saucer. "I thought you had the boy by the short and curlies?"

"So did I," said Onyx. "So did I. One of those odd coincidences that sometimes occurs, occurred that night. As you know we had set up the party entirely to entice the Bruce boy into a psychic space where he could be neutralised. Both Magda and Emerald worked with me. And, my friend, we had him." Onyx crossed her legs and leaned closer to her silver-haired friend.

"When I danced on the inner plane, I could see him approaching. We had set up what we call the Vortex of Hecate. Once he'd entered that we would have had a lock-down on his mind. It would be more effective than one of those military implants. It utilises ancient Egyptian science – what the uninformed would miscall 'magic'. We could have tracked him across time should he ever venture forth again."

She took a sip of the sparkling water the waiter had set in front of her. When he left she leaned across once more.

"More importantly, we could have cut his psychic strings at any point that suited us, turning him into a bumbling moron. At least for some hours. He would have just found himself feeling very confused."

"So what went wrong?" asked Sardius, looking down his nose.

"We were interrupted. A girl had a fit in the next room and everyone's attention became diverted."

"So you failed."

This wasn't a question. As Sardius made his statement Onyx sensed the ice behind his normally charming eyes. She took her time with her glass of sparkling water, depressing the wedge of lemon with a teaspoon. Her hand held entirely steady. Good.

"Hmm ... not completely." She put down her glass, faced the steel in Sardius's glance and slowly smiled. "You might say we marked him. Although we cannot disrupt his mind as intended, a skilled psychic like Magda will, if the conditions are right, be able to work out where he is. And if he bends TS then we will know."

"TS?"

"Time-Space or, more specifically, the time-space continuum. He is one of those who can – in effect – move bodily through time, at least for short periods. He is actually there ... or possibly there – " she made 'air-quotes' with her hands – "constitutes itself around him. You know this stuff is complicated, Norman." She corrected herself. "Sardius."

He nodded slowly, without smiling.

"You didn't anticipate this unfortunate occurrence? I thought Magda could move forward in time, at least see forward in time, to find probable outcomes. The Irish girl..." He moved his hands in a slow circular motion.

"Kelly Prendergast," said Onyx.

"Yes her. Shelley Prendergast."

"You're right. Shelley. My God, she caused us headaches."

"Yes she did," said Sardius. "But before she turned traitor, she provided amazing information. Her early work has borne remarkable fruit."

Onyx felt something shift inside her. She sensed Sardius knew something that he was choosing not to share. She waited.

Her companion stood up with graceful agility, impressive for a man probably the wrong side of seventy.

"I must go to the little boys' room, excuse me. Too much

coffee."

Onyx sighed and relaxed back into the plush opulence of the armchair. The slim, silver-haired man disappeared in the direction of the foyer.

When her private taxi had driven off from dropping her, she'd entered The Athenaeum Hotel to find three geishas standing in the reception area, in full kimonos, with their hair held beautifully in place with what could have been lacquer ware chopsticks. It had taken Onyx several seconds to realise they were mannequins, and she might not have guessed except for their preternatural stillness. Two held fans to just cover their mouths. One clasped both her hands just in front of her heart.

Onyx moved closer to admire the real silk kimonos. They appeared hand-painted, as far as she could tell. She knew kimonos like this could be worth thousands. The banner behind the three static women announced the Japan-London Festival.

"Impressive, aren't they?"

Sardius had greeted her. He kissed her hand. Something only an old rascal like him could get away with. He now sported a little grey goatee beard. She didn't remember that from the past. Surely he couldn't have grown that in the six or so weeks since they last met?

"Let's sit in the lounge. I know we could have taken a conference room, but the best ones are full of Japanese produce apparently and the lounge is quiet at the moment, and free."

They'd made small talk while they awaited the arrival of the drinks they'd ordered. Sardius made some disparaging remark about the British Prime Minister. Onyx didn't let on that she'd just been meeting with him at Number Ten. Information like that she kept from Sardius and the other 'Stones'. This was one of the main reasons they used these pseudonyms. They cooperated on their really important work to do with controlling the direction of time. Their other interests were only shared to the extent they were relevant to their desire to gather greater and greater power and influence into their hands.

"You've seen Emerald?" asked Sardius on his return.

"No. No, I haven't. I have spoken to her on the phone several times. And we used her particular abilities when we were trying to ensnare the Bruce brat. But I understand she's been on extended sick-leave after … after what occurred."

A waiter arrived and placed a silver tray on the table between them. Onyx paused while he opened a second small bottle of sparkling water. She noted the hotel biscuits were inferior to those served to the Prime Minister.

Emerald had been very ill in the aftermath of the great debacle, when the Bruce boy and two others from different corners of history had turned up in Ancient Egypt, completely disrupting a crucial ritual. If successful, the outcome would have cemented the direction of time for millennia, to the great and lasting advantage of the Society of Secrets. As it was it had ended in disaster, possibly leaving their leader, Diamond, trapped back in the dim and distant past.

"She's staying in her house in Devon. She told me a car comes down daily from London bringing papers and things, so she's kept up to speed."

"Yes, I heard the same," said Sardius. "She remains a key player at MI5 despite her set-back."

"Well, her set-back nearly killed her. Her consciousness could have been left halfway between Ancient Egypt and now. She would've been a complete vegetable."

Sardius gave a slight shrug as though suggesting stuff happens.

"We've seen it in the past and it's not a pretty sight."

"Yes. Indeed we have," said Sardius. "One of the reasons I keep my consciousness firmly anchored in the here and now." He pointed with deliberation at the floor in front of him. He leaned forward and poured himself some more coffee from the second glass flask that the waiter had just delivered.

"You need to go and see her, Victoria. Rhory Bruce is a threat to all our plans. But we know he cannot just be taken out. The Irish girl totally established that we may, just may, need him. We cannot take the risk of destroying such a potent link with the crucial past eras, the ones where time is bent and focused. He seems to be able to reach at least some of those nodal points. That's what Prendergast's research showed."

"Yes. And Magda agrees. One positive outcome of the party was her glimpse into his personal future. Or rather his personal past. He's going to find himself in Alexandria."

"Really. Really?" Sardius looked intensely at her. Onyx felt his gaze like that of a deadly reptile, something out of Jurassic Park. "Now that is interesting. Perhaps we can use that to put things back on track."

"How do you mean?"

Sardius leaned back into his settee. He moved his copy of The Telegraph over to the far arm, and reached into his pocket. He drew out a long coloured object and, with a flourish, revealed a highly decorated fan. The missing fan from the third geisha?

"I borrowed this from the lady by the door. She won't miss it," said Sardius. "It illustrates what has happened rather well."

He propped the fan against the back of the settee. It displayed the motif of various birds sitting on the branches of a cherry blossom tree in full bloom. He pointed at the base of the fan from which all its various folds emerged.

"We had found this nodal point. The Egyptian girl, the one with time-penetrating gifts, was to be sacrificed here." He tapped the little metal ring at the bottom of the fan. "That act so early in our aeon, that blow, would have controlled the flow of time in the direction advantageous to us now. Of itself it would have been sufficient. But it went awry."

"Because of the Hammerford brat."

"Exactly. And I think we now find ourselves on a different part of the fan, a different path in time."

Onyx frowned and waved her finger at Sardius. "What do you mean?"

"Time shifted, within narrow parameters, but it shifted, and not in a good way for us."

"How?" Onyx knew a lot about the military experiments with time. There were many, many more than the public realised, but that they had shifted onto a different time-line? Surely not.

"I don't know how," said Sardius. "And as you understand, such a shift changes everything – personal memories, records, even archaeology. Ironically, the one person who will definitely spot the shift is young master Bruce. He was elsewhere when it happened. His consciousness will be on the old time line. He may find anomalies that we wouldn't notice because now they are no longer anomalies."

"When we did that ritual in the Wiltshire house, when Kelly … sorry Shelley, turned on us, we would have been a little outside of time ourselves."

"Yes, we would."

'That explains your sudden goatee that I don't remember.' Onyx didn't voice her thoughts. She experienced a chilly grip of tension in her legs. Things were getting out of control. Being out of control was something she hated.

She agreed to go down and see Emerald, as soon as possible, to decide how to proceed.

Knuckle Bones

Alexandria – about 380 CE

The sheep bones pattered onto the top of the cask.

"Ha, only one," said Devorah.

Resting on the back of Nysa's hand lay the single polished bone; the other four had bounced off.

"Best of three then. I've not played for a long time."

Nysa gathered up the bones, enjoying their smoothness against the palm of her hand. Cradling them with her curled fingers, she leant close and blew. With a flick of her wrist she tossed the five knuckles in the air and flipped her hand over, moving it in an arc.

"There. Four. I think Hephaestus was with me that time." She dropped the bones back onto the barrel beside her.

Devorah stuck out her tongue, and then laughed. She scooped the sheep's knuckles from the cask and adjusted her position on the pile of sacks where she sat. She shook the bones between her hands. Behind her, dust swirled and sparkled in the beam of sunlight from a high window near the eaves of the storage building; sacks were piled up far higher than the height of the girls, amidst row upon row of heavy clay jars. The bones soared in the air, one flashing as it passed into the sunlight. Devorah swept her hand around, her eyes gleaming with excitement.

"Best I could manage was three!" Devorah dropped the bones back on the top of the cask and pointed towards the harbour. "Look, Nysa, the men have dropped one of the jars."

The girls stood up from the sacks of wool and moved to the edge of the shade near the entrance of the huge storage hall and surveyed the spreading pool of oil on the quay, near the gangplank of one of the boats.

Nysa glanced to her left, to where her father sat outside at a table under an awning, his papyrus ledgers in front of him. His face remained impassive but she knew he would be seething underneath. She'd no idea what an amphora of olive oil was worth, but it had been brought all the way across the sea from Crete and now the handsome profit drained into the sticky harbour dust. The two slaves that had been carrying the large flask, strapped between two wooden poles, hovered, unsure what to do. The foreman raised his flail.

"No!" shouted Nysa's father, standing up and moving into the bright sunshine. His reddish-brown robe kept the winter chill at bay but he had to shade his eyes from the sunlight. He walked over to where the foreman tapped his switch against the palm of his brawny hand. The merchant inspected the twine holding the amphora to the staves and said something to the foreman who promptly shouted to the slaves, who'd all stopped working, to get on with unloading.

The girls drifted over to the table, with its pens and inkpots. Devorah joined her father who stood near the wall of the storage hall, squinting at the quayside. Nysa's father walked back and rested his hands on the table, watching the gangs of men continue with the unloading. He sighed, sat down, picked up one of his pens and dipped it in a small jar of ink.

"Will you whip them, Father?"

"No, Nysa, I won't. I only use the whip when a slave deliberately does something wrong. They didn't tie the amphora to the poles. That was done on board ship and those sailors are not my men. What I will do is reduce the captain's commission by the price of all that oil and he will ensure better work in the future. See, he's already shouting orders to his men."

"A wise decision," said the other man. He had a long, straight grey beard and a small black skullcap clipped to the silvery hair that fell as far as his shoulders. His woollen robes had vertical stripes of grey, black and off-white. He remained in the shade standing by the table. Although Nysa had been to Devorah's house several times now, she'd only seen her Jewish friend's father from a distance as he moved from his library to his work room. His face had many tiny creases and wrinkles, whereas her father's face remained smooth.

"Ah, that is what I've been waiting to see," said Maimonides, turning to his daughter. He crouched down slightly and pointed to a ship entering the harbour and approaching its great lighthouse. The front sail with vertical red and white stripes strained in the wind. The second, larger sail had already been furled and the rows of oars, like the legs of a mighty centipede, beat rhythmically into the water. The large eye, painted on the prow, stared unblinking at the Palace of Cleopatra passing by on the left of the craft.

"More wool from the north?" asked Nysa's father.

"In part, my friend, in part. But the most valuable cargo is slaves from the Rome market." He narrowed his eyes. "Including someone exceptional, someone important."

Maimonides leaned back on his heels and clasped his hands together close to his belt. He rocked back and forth for a few moments. "Yes. Someone I've waited for, for a long time."

Nysa hoped he would say more. She loved mysteries and important slaves would certainly be mysterious. She dared not ask him a question and Devorah was entirely absorbed watching the men, soaked in sweat, begin to carry casks into the storage hall where they'd just been playing knucklebones.

On the far side of the harbour, on the Isle of Pharos, white-robed figures moved near the Temple of Isis. A single horseman waved to the priestesses and passed through the gate onto the causeway, his blue cloak billowing out behind him. Halfway across he halted and looked into the harbour, where the slave ship had slowed, perhaps awaiting a place to dock safely. The clack of the horse's hooves carried for a moment on the wind as the great black horse trotted the rest of the distance across to the western harbour. Devorah leaned at the door of the hall, watching the men pile up the casks. Maimonides and Nysa's father studied one of the ledgers together. The rider had stopped his horse near the quayside and looked directly at Nysa. Now he had approached she knew she'd seen him before, when she'd returned from Devorah's house with Myrna and they had also seen the enormous man. She remembered the giant had spoken with this horseman, with his dark hair and – even at this distance – arresting eyes. For a moment, a moment that extended on and on, Nysa and the horseman held each other's gaze. Something seemed to open in the centre of her chest. Vistas filled her mind, of deserts and temples half buried in the sand. An Ibis flew past and turned inland towards the Great Library.

"Do you want to play another round?" said Devorah, rattling the knucklebones in her hands once more.

The Ibis glided overhead.

"Sorry? What did you say?"

"Do you want to play again or are you too chicken?"

The quayside was deserted. Not true. The quayside had files of men carrying sacks towards the great storage hall, but the rider had vanished. Nysa looked along the city walls towards the Caesarium with its huge granite needles and then the other way, to the fort that dominated this part of the harbour. No rider. No black horse.

"Are you listening, Nysa?"

"All right. Let's play another round," said Nysa, with both confusion and excitement swirling inside her.

"That won't be possible," said Maimonides. "Our ship has docked and I have important cargo to check."

The long ship had anchored some stadia out from the quay. Smaller craft were rowing towards it. Light flashed where spears and buckles of the armed men on the ship caught the sunlight. Water dripped down from the oars, raised with precision all at once from the sea, and partially withdrawn into the ship.

Nysa knew, she didn't know how, but she knew that the

person Maimonides awaited hadn't yet arrived. He remained far away. But not for long.

That evening Myrna sat in her sanctuary room at the northeast corner of the Maimonides household. She had prepared her writing tablets earlier, smoothing the wax held within the wooden surrounds, so that she could write with her pointed stylus. A neat pile of tablets rested on a low table by her knee, as she sat cross-legged on a large cushion. Two oil lamps, suspended from the ceiling and hanging just behind her, provided a quiet, warm light that combined with the candle on the table, enabled her to write.

She'd learned to write at her mother's knee and could form words in both Greek and Latin. Being mute, people often thought she must be both deaf and stupid as well, but Myrna understood many of the tongues spoken in Alexandria, even the Egyptian language, although that she couldn't write. Maimonides had asked her once if she could read minds.

"No," she wrote, "I cannot just enter another's mind and look around. But if they form their ideas clearly with precision, and do not seek to hide their intentions, I can hear the meaning behind their words when they speak, even if I don't understand each separate word."

The Jewish scholar waited patiently while she wrote and took the tablet from her, tracing her letters with his fingers.

He looked at her for a while, his eyes wandering over her face. He took a breath and sighed.

"So you couldn't read my thoughts just then?"

Myrna shook her head and picked up a fresh tablet to write.

"No. I have to wish to do so. It takes an effort and is tiring."

Maimonides read her words and nodded.

"That is good ... that is good. I trust you, Myrna, but I also need my privacy. I prefer to choose what you share of my mind. But on occasion a silent communication between us may be advantageous. I think we will both know when."

This had been how they'd communicated since, with Maimonides speaking and waiting patiently as Myrna wrote her answers. Myrna knew her master could not Hear, not in the way she and her mother could Hear. But she had found he could share his thoughts in clear word pictures when the situation demanded it. He'd done this on returning from the harbour as he stopped near her on his way to evening prayers.

'Where is the boy? The boy we seek? Is he on the ship that docked today?'

All this had arisen in her mind as they stood in the colonnade looking at the fountain sparkling in the evening light, as other slaves bustled by.

Now, in the privacy of the room where she had permission to do her work, the work other slaves must not know about and the work never to be mentioned to other Jewish scholars, she looked for the boy they both knew would arrive soon. She took a few deep breaths and allowed her eyes to wander, softly, over the diagram drawn with such care on the papyrus in front of her cushion. Made of multiple overlapping circles of equal size, the patterns, still at first, gradually began their dance. Maimonides had told her this image contained all wisdom in terms of number. "In it, Life itself flowers and Wisdom has her abode." Myrna had not known quite what he meant but knew that the circles could form patterns that her master suggested explained the whole of creation and the very key to Time itself. But you had to learn to see it aright.

Flight to Egypt

Over Europe – about now

The painted mannequin had stood in the centre of the aisle. She'd taught us how to put on a life jacket and how to breathe if the plane ran out of oxygen. We were now cruising at 33,000 feet somewhere over Germany. A steady breeze shushed down from the little air vent above my head. Natasha offered me a wine gum from a clear plastic bag. I chose my favourite, one of the black ones.

"What's he watching?" I asked.

"Who?"

"The tall git sitting next to you."

"Don't know," Natasha stage-whispered into my ear. "Looks like some historical thing. All swords and horses and distressed maidens."

Natasha didn't really have to whisper as the guy had large cans on his ears and looked engrossed in his movie. We'd hoped we would have the three seats to ourselves. We'd agreed I would get the window seat on the way out and Nat would have it on the way back. Just before the door closed the man got on, complaining to the stewardess about the fact he'd booked a seat with bigger leg room. The bloke's legs were squeezed in to our particular part of the sardine can. His white hair suggested he was Granddad's sort of age. We were sharing his wine gums.

"It's amazing. We got right through this term and hardly saw each other," said Natasha, "what with my football commitments and all. Who sealed the well in the park, do you think?"

"I don't know. I couldn't believe it. You know Jules is totally sceptical about what's happened to me. Well I told her some of it. Not the going back to Ancient Egypt bit, but the fact that the well existed and the bandstand had a temple under it and all. So she says I must show her. And when I do the blooming well's been sealed, hasn't it, and they've put new flooring down on the store room in the bandstand."

"You must've been gutted. Who did it d'ya think?"

"Don't know. I just don't know. But I did see this guy … in the park. I mean I think he was the same guy that shot at me—"

"Shot at you?"

"Yea, I told you. At Aunt Bridget's house, when I'd climbed the tree."

Natasha scrunched up her face.

"What on earth were you doing up a tree, you noodle?"

"I just wanted one last climb. You know. I sensed Aunt Bridget would die and all and I wanted, well you know…"

Natasha nodded. We each took another wine gum and gave the bag back to the man at the end of our row of seats. A powerful lime taste filled my mouth and I savoured it for a moment with my eyes closed. Natasha poked me in the side.

"Why are they after you?"

"I really don't know. But I'm glad I gave you the Time Sphere objects, 'cos I think my bedroom was searched."

"You're kidding me, right?"

"No. I sort of sensed that I was being followed. Or I became paranoid or whatever. Anyway, once I had dropped it off and you'd hidden it in your bedroom I did that James Bond thing."

"What James Bond thing? Jumping out of a plane without a parachute sort of thing?"

"No. With a hair. In the bedroom."

"What do you do with a hare in the bedroom? What, like a rabbit?"

I stared at Natasha. I couldn't tell if her dead pan face was designed to wind me up. Then I understood.

"No. Not a hare. A hair. You know, from your head."

"What on earth has that got to do with James Bond?"

"It's in *From Russia with Love,* I think. He sticks a hair from his head with a bit of spit across a wardrobe door, to see if anyone searches his room. He also uses talcum powder. I didn't go that far. But one day when the house had been completely empty I found the hair had fallen off."

"Well, it probably dried out."

"Could be, but I don't think so. You see I'd put a paperclip in the bit where the lid of Auntie's box closed. You know, so when someone opened it, it would fall out. Well ... it had."

"You're saying someone broke into your house and actually searched your bedroom?"

"Yes, I am. I think it was the guy who shot at me."

At that point the stewardess came round and offered us lunch.

The pasta with nondescript meat had been okay, but I preferred the wedge of soft cheese and the single biscuit. I hoped we would get a proper meal once we arrived in Alexandria.

"You think Lucian's involved in all this in some way?" said Natasha.

"I don't know. It's weirded me out really, but I don't remember him at school even though he's been at Scrivener's all year. He seemed to just appear after Christmas."

"And you saw him in this vision thing?"

"Along with that creepy girl Magda and the Ice Queen, Victoria. She really gave me the creeps. But worst of all was seeing the fat priestess again, the woman with the red hair."

"The one you'd seen in Ancient Egypt?" said Natasha

"Yes. And in London that time."

"Maybe—"

I slapped my forehead, upsetting the dregs of a plastic beaker of coke.

"I forgot. The journal. The journal in the commode. Did you get it?"

"I texted you."

"Did you?"

"Yes. The weekend you were at the party we went to help clear Bridget's house. I found the key, just like you said, hidden in a tiny round tin, beneath the statue of the boy in the garden." Natasha used her paper napkin to wipe drops of coke from her jeans.

"And…?"

"As I wrote, I looked in the commode. In the hidden drawer – well, not so hidden, just unexpected."

"And…?"

"And nothing. The journal had gone."

I brooded while the plane hummed and passed high above endless expanses of cotton wool. I'd thought the journal would both help me understand what I'd experienced and be proof I could show others. Like Jules. Now we'd lost it. Probably to the burglar, though I couldn't fathom how.

Natasha nudged me.

"Do you have your phone?"

"Yes," I said.

"Can I have it?"

"Why?"

"Just let me have it, Rho, I've an idea."

I passed it to her and continued staring at the clouds. Another plane, like a tiny toy, flew way below ours. I checked my watch and guessed we must now be flying over Greece.

"Ouch!" Natasha had jabbed me in the ribs. "What—"

"Look! Look what's on your phone."

I did. At first the picture didn't make sense. People dressed in fancy dress were rioting on stone steps somewhere. I swallowed and my head spun and became as light as a soap bubble.

"OMG," we both said in unison.

"You've got it. You've got proof," said Natasha.

"Wow. Yes. I remember. I used the phone to distract and fool the mad priests who were attacking us."

I looked more closely at the picture. My Greek friend Dimitris struggled with a priestess with garish make-up, who held his arm. Her mouth made a perfect 'O' and her eyes were red, not because she was a fiend, but because I hadn't done red-eye correction. Further below, a dark-haired priest stared towards the camera.

"See. You do have proof. Something to show Juliette at least. Now she'll have to believe you. Now you can demonstrate you travelled back in time. And – " Natasha bit her lip and narrowed her eyes – "this being the oldest photograph ever, will be worth millions."

The Lighthouse

Alexandria – about now

I dumped my sausage-bag on the floor of the bedroom and opened an inner door. *My own bathroom. Mega cool.* My limbs ached from having been awake so long, and the endless journey. It had taken ages for our bags to clear at Cairo, and then the drive to Alexandria had lasted, like, forever. I'd tried to sleep in the car but car horns and trucks thundering past had made that impossible. Natasha had fallen asleep with her head on my shoulder so I'd got a crick in my neck by not moving. I rubbed it and circled my shoulder.

The double bed had a green silky cover, with greeny-yellow fringes. It had a bunch of small cushions, which I tossed into a corner. A large rectangular picture hung above the bed with a faded black and white photograph of a religious procession, with priests dressed in, well, dresses – or ceremonial robes of some fancy kind. Judging from the clothing of the onlookers, which included men in funny upside down plant-pot hats with tassels, I reckoned it dated from early last century.

Sitting in an armchair in the corner of the room, I eased off my trainers and sniffed my socks. They wouldn't do another day and joined the cushions on the floor. A tap sounded at my door.

"Hey, you got the big room." Natasha grinned as she hovered in the doorway.

"Yup. Boy's prerogative. This is a man's world, well at least here in Egypt."

"Yeah, well, I've got a balcony. Mind you, it's bleeding chilly outside at the moment and raining. I thought Egypt was a desert. People come here for winter breaks, don't they?"

"Auntie said the weather should improve tomorrow." I lowered my voice. "Her parents seem nice, don't they?"

Natasha nodded. "Tomorrow we go exploring. That driver, Mohammed, is going to be our personal chauffeur, apparently."

"We're going on our own?"

"No, silly. Auntie Aida is coming with us. In fact she and I are visiting one of her female friends. They're quite strict Muslims, so you'll have to wait outside." Natasha's face lit up with a wide grin.

"What, with the driver who speaks no English? Oh great."

Natasha winked and skipped off down the dark passageway. "Breakfast's at eight," was her parting shot.

I crossed to the other side of the room and heaved back the heavy curtains. The multiple layers of material snagged on the runners. It took me several moments to suss out how to work the sliding glass doors, but I failed to get them to move. In the bedroom, the one bar, electric fire crackled in the corner, making minor inroads into the chill. Everything seemed bigger and smaller all at the same time. I yawned. 'Dead beat' didn't begin to describe how tired I felt, but I wanted to see if I had a balcony too.

Finally, I found a wobbly tab and with that pushed up the large glass door could be eased open. I don't know what view Natasha had, but my balcony looked straight out over the harbour. I yawned again, rubbed my eyes and eased my shoulders and neck. Being this tired gave me a floaty feeling and I knew I would sleep the sleep of the dead when I hit the sack in a few minutes.

Alexandria hid in dark patches illumined by faint moving lights. The moon shone somewhere behind Auntie's apartment block and I could see the temples near the harbour picked out in ghostly white. I'd no idea that Alexandria had such well-preserved monuments. Tomorrow might be interesting after all. I moved to the front of the balcony to get an unobscured view. At the far side of the harbour, a tall building rose against the blackness of the sea, its windows flickering with faint warm light. Unlike most high buildings this one had no neon sign advertising a bank or similar. At the top, a room shone with brilliant light. *This must be the famous Alexandria lighthouse. We would visit it tomorrow for sure.*

I covered my ears against the distant drumbeat: "Zulu warriors," someone said. The thumping went on. And on.

"Rhory!"

I woke up to find Natasha standing fully dressed by my bed.

"Are you totally deaf? It's five past eight. The driver comes at eight thirty. Everyone's waiting to start breakfast. Jeez! I thumped on your door but you just snored on. I could hear you. Now hurry up."

My cousin flounced out of the room and I pulled on my jeans and decided the fragrant socks could manage another day as I'd not opened my sausage-bag yet, except to pull out my pyjamas. I wasn't even sure I'd packed other pairs of socks.

"No, you can sit in the front today," said Aida. "We girls get the comfort of the back seat."

I'd only had time to eat pale yellow cornflake look-a-likes with weird-tasting milk, and cram a sweet roll, covered with tooth-tingling ultra-sugary jam, before the door buzzer announced that Mohammed had arrived with the car.

I sank into the front seat, and rested my hands on the slightly cracked leather. "This is an amazing car, Auntie. What is it?"

"A Daimler," said my aunt from the back, as the driver eased his way into the honking traffic edging past the apartment block. "My father used to own a car dealership before things became difficult. He's managed to keep this car running. It's his pride and joy. Mind you, it drinks petrol like a rugby player drinks beer."

I squinted up at the fifth floor, as we pulled away. I thought I could see my balcony. Leaning forward I looked at the other side of the road. Apartment blocks pushed up towards the leaden sky.

They were six or seven stories high, topped with spiky metal aerials and satellite dishes. *So how had I seen the harbour last night?*

"Will we see the temples today Auntie?"

Mohammed the driver looked across at me, frowning slightly.

"What's that?" said my aunt.

"We were wondering what we would see today," Natasha said.

"Well we have to go and visit my friends first. I was at school with her, and her daughter is soon to be married. They are pretty strict Muslims, Rhory, and it's best you do not come up. We won't be long."

"Oh, okay," I said. We were caught behind a cart being pulled by a large donkey. Our driver had turned off the main road down a narrow side street, and it hadn't proved to be a short cut. People stared at the car and a couple of boys with white skullcaps and wispy beards ran up and pointed at me in the front seat. Mohammed accelerated past the cart at a point where the road widened. A man in a white turban sitting at the front, waved and grinned a toothless smile.

Something someone had said to me yesterday floated back into my mind. "Will we see Cleopatra's Palace today?"

"How good's your swimming?" said my aunt. "And how long can you hold your breath?"

Natasha snorted.

"But it's by the harbour isn't it?" Someone had told me that. It was the grand building overlooking the harbour. Perhaps I'd spotted it last night from the balcony.

"It is by the harbour, Rhory," said Aida, "but it's metres under the water."

Natasha made a strange choking, snuffling sound. Even our driver was smiling slightly, his cheeks with white bristles moving like he was chewing something.

"Oh!" I managed, my arms tingling with embarrassment.

"Yes," Aida continued, "we now believe it was destroyed by a massive earthquake that consigned it to the sea bed. It's one of the reasons I'm here. One of my archaeology friends wanted me to do a little exploratory work for her."

"You're going diving?" asked Natasha.

"No. That won't be allowed, I'm afraid. Mind you, I'm not so keen on snorkelling, let alone aqualungs. No, I'm going to be helping her with, shall we say, locating certain things. Remember I told you about what I did when you visited me before Christmas."

"The reason you lost your job?" said Natasha.

"Yes. Pretty much. The officials here don't much like unorthodox methods. They can't control the outcome. But my friend thinks that some of the things stored at that palace may have been hidden elsewhere in Egypt. Important things."

"How would they know that?" I asked, turning around to squint at my aunt.

"Oh, you know," she said, smiling at me and raising her eyebrows.

I didn't. And then I did. Aunt Aida must be in contact with someone who could do what I seemed to be able to do. Someone who could end up sliding into the past and then back again.

A statement I'd heard recently sounded in my mind. *'The treasures of the past and the future are stored there but soon they must be moved. Times are changing and not for the better …'* I heard the voice of the woman quite clearly. I'd heard her say that to me yesterday, or the day before. Then I remembered that the day before I had been in Hammerford. I could nearly remember what the woman looked like and how she dressed.

I caught the driver looking at me: the wrinkles around his eyes had become a little bit more wrinkly. He cleared his throat and looked back at the traffic. Mohammed wore a white turban and had a deeply tanned face, a bit like the man on the cart except Mohammed appeared to have most of his teeth. I couldn't easily judge his age.

We pulled out into a wide road.

"Here is the Serapeum," he said in perfect English, with hardly an accent.

The sky had cleared a bit and sunlight gave the wide-open space a warmer hue than the high-rise apartments that surrounded the monument which remained in shadow. The archaeological remains lay lower than the road, in an area the size of a couple of football pitches. Three coaches were drawn up by the side of the road, and groups of Chinese tourists were about to follow a woman with a headscarf holding a stick with a red triangular flag. High above the coaches, many of the balconies had damp clothing hanging on short lines, no doubt to welcome the sun back to Alex.

"We'll visit here properly in a day or two," said my aunt. "It was a temple once, until the early Christians destroyed it, dedicated to a strange god called Serapis. Hence it's known as the Serapeum."

We drove slowly along the road bordering the site. One tall column still stood and sitting sphinx-like near its foot was – well – a sphinx. Made of black stone, it stared at the world with all the mystery of a feline Mona Lisa.

Aida said something to Mohammed in what I assumed was Arabic.

"We just have time to take a dekko at the harbour," said Aida, "before we need to meet my friends. Really the harbour is the best view in Alex."

"I love the little palms," said Natasha, as we drove past a row of small, squat palm trees.

I did too, but found them less fascinating than the billboards that sat on posts the height of a bus stop, advertising something or other, but with no pictures.

"There're fewer billboards here than in Hammerford," I said.

"That's true, Rhory," said my aunt. "Remember, we're in a Muslim country and generally we don't show pictures of people or animals – it's forbidden. Certainly no girls in bikinis selling motorbikes."

A Giant Intervention

We pulled out onto the broad two-lane road following the long curve of the harbour. Trees and lights adorned the middle of this dual carriageway, and hotels lined the road with stunning views out over the sea.

"What sea is this, Auntie?" I asked.

"It's the Mediterranean," said Natasha.

"I thought that was the sea off France and Spain and Italy," I said. "I know I have heard people talk about the Libyan Sea with all those immigrant boats. I thought this might be the Egyptian Sea."

"I wish," said Aida.

"So where are the palaces and temples?" I swivelled around, but could see nothing like the building I had spotted from the balcony the previous night.

"Hardly anything is left," said Aida. "The streets still follow the pattern that Alexander the Great mapped out, but we have lost nearly all the buildings. Fires, earthquakes and mobs have done about equal damage."

"But ..." I took a breath and stopped myself from making a bigger twit of myself than I had managed already. Obviously I'd had one of my things last night. I hadn't needed the bandstand to slip back through time. Just being tired had been enough. I'd seen Alexandria as it was then and not as it was now. A shiver went right through me.

We drove the full length of the harbour. Grey waves complete with white horses rolled towards the beach until they petered out on the cold, dark sand. I hadn't brought my swimming trunks. Now, that didn't appear to be a mistake. Mohammed turned the car into the city once more.

He parked in a wide street with trees sprouting from convenient gaps in the pavement. At ground level, shops and cafes spilled out onto the pavement. Aunt Aida and Natasha disappeared into a doorway between a men's clothing shop and one that specialised in old fridges.

"Do you wish to sit in the car, young man," said Mohammed, turning to me, "or do you wish to stand on the pavement?"

"Um ..." I wasn't sure how to respond to that.

"I'm going across the road to that tobacconist. I will have a smoke and a black coffee. I will be no longer than eight minutes. But if I leave the car I must lock it, you understand?"

I did. The car door swished closed behind me and Mohammed came round and locked my door after his. Apparently the Daimler pre-dated central locking.

"There's a bookshop behind you," said the driver. "By all means go in. I will find you there."

"Thanks," I said. The idea of browsing books in Arabic didn't appeal. I fished out my phone and my earbuds. I would pass the time losing my mind in techno whilst leaning on the car.

A bus on the other side of the road delayed Mohammed. He could have been military, the way he stood upright, with his broad shoulders and powerful arms. He had a jacket on over his ankle length robe. His hands on the steering wheel had looked almost too big for that job and the hairs on his hands, unlike those on his face, had been black. He disappeared into the shop opposite, with its one small table and chair outside already occupied by a man with a white skullcap, reading a paper.

People walking past generally ignored me. Mostly it was men striding purposefully. A couple of women, with only their eyes showing, and shapeless, dull cotton robes covering themselves, went by with their eyes averted. I drifted over to the bookshop.

The books had sat in the window since Alexander the Great left for India. The covers had faded and only the blue tones remained. The window had a crack low down on the right-hand side. A wooden screen, peppered with regular small holes, prevented me seeing into the shop. Wire hooks on the screen displayed several books more prominently.

The Mystery of the Sphinx, said one. It had a black and white picture of the Sphinx with the pyramids in the background. A man wearing a pith helmet stood in front of the stone monument. *Hypatia, the Last of the Mysteriarchs,* said another. A woman with large eyes looked out from the cover. My knowledge of archaeology and ancient history was pretty much zilch, but she looked Roman rather than Greek, I thought. Roman and infinitely wise.

A man of enormous size swayed his way towards me. The two women looked like pygmies as they passed him by. He'd the sort of physique that makes enormous wrestlers with rippling muscles, blanch. In fact he looked like he might eat a couple of wrestlers for breakfast. Although he was about 50 metres away, I wondered if I should cross to where Mohammed was. Something about this man spooked me.

The techno music rose to a shrieking crescendo and then resolved into a squeal of brakes. A car had screeched to a halt just in front of the Daimler. It had darkened windows. Both doors on my side swung open and two men sprang out, followed by a third. All had shades on, even though the sun had long since given up the struggle with the clouds. All had dark suits. All were staring at me. One spoke into a mobile and then said something to the others. They moved across towards me.

I moved as quick as my pounding heart would allow and reached the bookshop door. I pushed on the handle but it jammed. I tried again. Not jammed – locked. One of the men grabbed my phone. A second grabbed my arms from behind.

"With us. Now. Or we hurt you. Very bad. Very bad."

I kicked the man who had my phone and, flexing my knees, cracked my head against the chin of the man behind me. I had the satisfaction of hearing him howl and seeing the other man wince before a vicious slap nearly separated my jaw from my face.

One of the men jabbered something in their own language and

the man sitting at the wheel of the car shouted.

The man behind me let go. I think he hit the car without his feet touching the ground. The man who'd just slapped me was held, by his neck, by the giant who had arrived at my side.

"Mistake," said the giant to the man, who struggled to breathe and to reach into his jacket. He also thumped into the car, and with a movement of ballet-like suppleness, my saviour-giant scooped up the gun that had fallen onto the pavement. He dropped onto one knee and pointed it at the driver, who wouldn't have won a quick-draw competition, and decided to speed off once his passengers had flung themselves onto the back seat.

The man with my phone was legging it in the other direction. My phone. The one with the only proof on it that I had been to ancient Egypt.

"Fricking heck. Come back!" I shouted.

The huge guy looked at me from an expressionless face. It dawned on me, rather late, that if he wished to take me captive there was nothing whatsoever I could do. His deep brown eyes searched into mine, and he grunted, as though confirming something to himself.

"Cross road," he said. "Stay with Mohammed." He nodded, and checked his wristwatch that had a band with the circumference of a side plate. "Then safe. Safe until we meet again."

Georgina Rillington

England – about now

Hanging Copse, Bog Copse, Windgate Copse … where did they get these names from? Onyx took a sip from her water bottle, kept cool in the armrest of her car. Woodland surrounded her on both sides of the road. The heavy rain had completely cleared and clouds piled up in massive confections of pale candyfloss, impressively white against the blue of the spring sky. An image of a headlight on her dashboard reminded her that her lights were still on. She switched them off. Checking her watch she muttered a swear word and pushed down the accelerator. Her tyres swished through a deep puddle, sending a great spray of water into the bushes beyond.

About an hour earlier, the storm clouds had made it so gloomy she'd needed headlights to see a few metres into the wall of rain that had greeted her as she drove through Dorset. The roads had been awash, and several times she'd had to drive slowly through floods.

The satnav showed the route in bright blue with arrows pointing the way. A female voice with a reassuring British accent guided Onyx through the maze of country lanes. Just as well as the journey had now become complex. Typical that Georgina Rillington, the most important female spook in the country, had her home in the heart of a labyrinth. Onyx had been to her London flat once for a semi-official government party, but she'd never visited her country residence.

Georgina Rillington lived at the edge of an obscure village in Devon. Georgina Rillington gave her the willies. Not many people could do that to Onyx, but 'Emerald' wielded a lot of power, both literal and metaphysical. The spymaster connected in some weird way with a priestess far back in time. Maybe more than one. Emerald didn't talk about things like that and Onyx hadn't seen fit to ask.

She braked to cope with the lorry carrying manure, crawling along in front of her. Her window glided up too slowly and allowed in the rich countryside aroma. She wrinkled her nose, tried not to breathe and switched on the air-con. That only made the smell worse. The narrow road curved this way and that, and she didn't quite dare to overtake the ancient lorry and risk meeting a combine harvester or something equally rustic coming the other way. Her Maserati had amazing acceleration, but could still skid off into a field from a road that had – minutes before – been converted into a river. She banged her hand on the steering wheel in frustration. At this rate it would be nearly an hour before she reached Emerald's country hideaway. Or at least that's what the satnav calculated.

She'd left Hampstead while darkness still hid the large houses of the very well-heeled who lived there. She cleared the outskirts of London before the milk floats hummed their way through the suburbs. She wanted to complete her meeting and return to London all in one day. She absolutely did not want to spend the night with the person she needed to visit. At first she'd headed towards Oxford. Twice, when the roads were quiet, she had gone right round a roundabout before taking her exit. Once she'd done a quick U-turn in the middle of the road. When she was quite sure no one was following her she changed route and headed south-west. Before setting out she'd used a scanner to check no one had planted a tracking device on her sleek sports car. This meeting today was above Top Secret. Only Sardius knew about it.

The smelly lorry slowed even more. The blinker on the right of the vehicle had a broken glass and only one brake light worked. The driver had his hand stuck out of the window and Onyx breathed a sigh of relief as he turned right into a field, taking his pungent aromas with him. She zoomed past, only to jam on her brakes once more to prevent driving into a horse's rump. Ahead, a woman on horseback held out a red flag. She trotted at the back of a file of horses, each with riders wearing bright yellow reflective bands and mustard-coloured jackets saying 'Treetops Riding School'. Onyx could see nothing coming and, ignoring the red flag, pressed her horn and accelerator at the same time, speeding past the seven or so schoolgirl riders and receiving a shout from the corpulent young woman on the leading black horse. Glancing in her mirror she could see one of the girls' horses had skittered to the wrong side of the road. "Blast them," she said to the lady on the satnav who calmly told her to continue straight for the next three miles.

"You have arrived at your destination," announced the softly spoken voice from within the dashboard. A checked flag waved triumphantly on the screen. To the left a hedgerow bordered a large field that sloped away towards woodland. Near its centre a few cows gathered by a couple of nondescript trees. Ahead a church tower suggested the heart of the village wasn't more than half a mile away. To her right a high wall of ancient pale grey stone had tiny flowers and green plants clinging to the crevices and glistening with raindrops. An impressive entranceway announced Featherstone Cottage. Onyx pressed the button on the entry-phone, conveniently placed at driver height. The large wrought iron gates swung open. In front of her a substantial two-storey thatched cottage dominated the large front garden. A statue, invisible from the road, showed three women dancing, facing outwards, their arms linked. "Hecate," Onyx breathed. "Immortal Hecate, we honour Thee." A frisson passed up her arms and neck.

"Come in, come in," said the imposing woman, "you're later than I expected. I have held off my mid-morning coffee." Emerald led the way down the dimly lit hall, with its dark beams, burnished horse brasses and impressive displays of flowers. Her tweed skirt had twisted slightly off centre and her solid calves were swathed in thick blue stockings. She wore what Onyx's mother would have called 'sensible flat shoes'.

"Emerald—"

"Georgina," said the older woman as she balanced her walking stick against the side of an imposing floral-print armchair. "Here, it must be Georgina! We don't want to frighten the horses ... Victoria." Emerald smiled, but only with her mouth. Her eyes watched Onyx with the attention a female praying mantis gives to her spouse before eating him.

The front garden, with an impressive sweep of gravel, had a profusion of tall country flowers, none of which Onyx could name. The back garden, laid to lawn with military-precision stripes left by the lawnmower, had roses of all hues thriving on the right-hand side. There, a grey-haired man with a sloppy blue-grey knitted pullover, brown trousers and green wellies, pushed a wheelbarrow. Trees of magnificent size graced the edges of the property. Onyx had noted approvingly that the house could not be observed from anywhere outside.

"My husband," said Emerald, nodding towards the gardener. "You'll see him at lunch. You are staying for lunch I take it?" She didn't wait for an answer and went straight on. "There's no denying it's a mess. Plans made and followed over the centuries have been thrown awry. You and I and Magda have to set things straight."

Over coffee they discussed how the trap set in Hammerford had been sprung and the Hammerford Boy had avoided their snare.

"We know a lot about his heritage," said the stout spymaster. "It's not by chance he's a Bruce. Bloodlines are far, far more important than most scientists realise." She tapped a little dark wood side-table with her silver coffee spoon. "And if they do realise it, we prevent them publishing!" Emerald's ice-queen smile chilled the room once more. Onyx glanced at Emerald's ankle and noted the slight bulge of a bandage.

"War wounds," said Emerald, demonstrating her uncanny knack for noticing what others were noticing. "The upset caused by those three interfering time-hoppers had some irritating physical side effects for me. I went blind, you know, for nearly a week. Thought I'd been consigned to darkness. But my vision came back all of a sudden."

The woman paused, took a sip of coffee, and fixed Onyx with a stare.

"Inner and outer vision. Inner and outer."

Onyx nodded, not quite sure what Emerald meant, but guessing her psychic skills, already phenomenal, had been enhanced in some way. Or maybe that's what Emerald wanted her to think.

Both women paused as a voice could be heard in the hallway outside. The door to the lounge opened and a largish young woman came in wearing a mustard windcheater top with a badge stating 'Treetops Riding School'. She had the same dumpy features as her mother, and the same thick, somewhat unruly hair showed beneath her riding helmet. She held out her hand with all the enthusiasm of one of her schoolgirl riders. Onyx stood up and introduced herself.

"That your Maserati gleaming in our drive?" she asked.

"It gleamed when I set out but I think it's got half of Devon's mud on its sides now," said Onyx. If the girl recognised Onyx as the one who had frightened her horses earlier in the day, she didn't let on. Her eyes had none of her mother's steel in them, but had a similar lack of affection. *The feeling's mutual,* thought Onyx.

"Lovely car," said the young woman. "I'll leave you to it. I need a hot bath now, to ease the tired old muscles. Ebony's Dreams needed quite a work out today Mother. Toodle-oo."

With the door to the lounge safely closed once more, and Mr Emerald snipping away at his rose bushes in the garden, Onyx raised the question she desperately needed answering. She framed it as neutrally as she could.

"So what happened to Diamond?"

Emerald looked up. Her lips tightened.

A prolonged beep sounded.

"Our other visitor, I think," said Emerald. "Excuse me while I release the front gate." She eased herself out of the armchair and using her stick for support, left the room.

The Crypt in the Garden

Lunch completed, the three women returned to the lounge. Emerald sat near the unlit fireplace. Onyx sank into the soft leather armchair opposite. Magda, wearing neatly pressed jeans, suede boots with some kind of glitter, and a dark and light-grey pullover that slunk off her shoulders, eased herself into the luxury of a smart wingback chair. Outside, Mr Rillington had returned to his roses, this time with a spade.

"The situation is getting out of control," announced the dark-haired young woman, crossing her legs and jiggling one suede leather boot.

"I agree," said Emerald, "and we'll sort things today. I have everything prepared."

Onyx had no idea what she was referring to but kept her counsel. At lunch, conversation had ranged from horse breeding to dressage, the Grand National and the Derby. Onyx quite enjoyed all things horsey, as she had partial ownership of a rather fine racehorse related not too distantly to the famous Red Rum. She'd even passed close by the Queen at Ascot on more than one occasion. Emerald announced over the tiramisu served for dessert, that they were not to be disturbed and would be using the outhouses.

"Now that the three of us are gathered once more, there's something I want to share with you," said Emerald. She reached down for her small brown-leather handbag and removed a mobile phone. Switching it on, she fiddled with the buttons for a few moments, and said "there," as she held it out towards Onyx.

The photo on display on the screen of the phone looked like a still from a film. Taken high up on some steps it showed men and women in costume, holding flaming torches. An imposing man with dark hair stood in the distance near what looked like the gate to some sort of stone enclosure, swathed in darkness, except for a blur of white that might be someone huddled inside. Using her fingers, Onyx zoomed in on the man.

"But …" she hesitated.

A half smile played on Emerald's face.

Onyx passed the phone to Magda, who studied it with care. She shook her thick black hair away from her face and, like Onyx, zoomed in on a face.

"So," said Magda, "we have a picture of Diamond."

"We do indeed," said Emerald, "and this is the first photo of its kind ever. The Bruce boy appears to have the capacity to carry objects across the time pathways. In a way he has irrefutable proof of time travel, not something HMG would like widely broadcast, to say the least."

"No, Her Majesty's Government needs secrets like that kept secret," said Onyx. "In fact, most of Her Majesty's Government have no idea time penetration is possible. 'Far Viewing' is on the far side of science fiction for them. Actual movement through time … well, you would be laughed out of the London clubs they so enjoy."

Magda shook the phone, holding it between her thumb and fingers. "You got this how?"

"In a way, by chance," said Emerald, "if any of us still believe in chance these days. We had planned to pop Rhory Bruce in a bag once he'd reached Alexandria. The snatch team were tracking him and found an ideal opportunity."

Emerald paused and straightened her tweed skirt, pulling the hem down closer to her dumpy knees.

"And?" Magda stood and returned the phone to Emerald.

"Well, it went wrong. Someone intervened. We're not quite sure who, but the team said they stood no chance. It appears this Bother Boy has powerful assistance. But we did get the phone, and that in itself is a great boon. The picture it contains is worth more than all the tea in China. In effect it is priceless for our purposes. Seems the gods were on our side for once."

Emerald glanced up at the large clock on the mantelpiece.

"We shouldn't waste any more time. Three o'clock is perfect for what we need to do." She explained to the other women what they would accomplish mid-afternoon.

Half an hour later, the women left the house by the back door from the well-appointed kitchen and emerged into the back garden. Onyx hunched her shoulders as a chill breeze caught her. The leaves on the trees danced and rustled as the wind twirled them, now this way and then that. Of Emerald's husband there was no sign. *He obviously took his marching orders seriously,* thought Onyx. Some distance from the back of the house they passed through an arch in a high yew-tree hedge and reached a double barn that dominated this part of the garden. Built of slatted wood painted with the darkest varnish, it had a thatched roof, just like the house. The two parts of the barn were connected by a small clock tower above double gates that completely sealed off the outside world. The first barn proved to be warm and to have spacious cubicles, allowing each woman to change with privacy. Onyx slipped out of her outer garments and put on the deep blue robe, tied with a silver cord. From her handbag she took the silver moon-shaped pendant that she always kept with her. Re-forged from silver dating back to pre-Roman times, it had, she believed, special powers of protection and projection.

At five to three the women, all robed, left the first barn and, protected from prying eyes by the large yew hedge, entered the door of the second barn. A landing with a balustrade had just enough room for all three of them. Emerald closed the door and locked it with a great bolt. At the end of the landing, stairs descended to a lower floor several metres below the level of the garden. One tall wrought-iron lamp, standing in a corner of this lower room, augmented the illumination from the two small windows on the garden side below the thatched roof.

Emerald led the way. Onyx studied the faint lettering on the vast slabs of stone that made up the floor at this lower level: writing that had been almost smudged out by hundreds of years of footfall. The few legible words were in Latin. They were walking over someone's tomb. Curved stones protruded from the side of the structure closest to the road outside. Onyx stroked the cool, slightly rough surface of what must be part of a stone column.

"A church?"

"Well, a crypt," replied Emerald. "The chapel above received the unwelcome attention of Thomas Cromwell and his reformation. We believe it was burned to the ground. But the crypt and its ante-room remained. That's where we are."

Magda, wearing a long robe of maroon over a grey underrobe, spun slowly in the centre of the room. Her clothing swirled around her. She stopped and held her hands up towards the roof.

"Powerful. Powerful energies. Dark and light spinning together. A plait of power."

"The Abbey stood on a dragon line. This is a nexus point," said Emerald.

Her deep-green robe, reaching right to the floor, allowed her to appear almost slim. "It's the reason we bought this house. What is achieved here is like some of the vortex points in the City of London. It affects everything else. If we are going to reconnect with Diamond it will be here."

Opening a large oak door she led the way into the next room. Only candlelight illumined the space and pale shadows danced over the plastered walls. On their left some of the ancient stone wall still remained. In the centre of the room a massive wooden table had been almost completely covered with a dark-red cloth. On this cloth, to the right, lay an unsheathed sword glittering in the candlelight. At the other end of the table stood a chalice, made out of the top half of a skull. A shudder passed through Onyx: a shudder of distant fears and ancient pleasures. This underground room already stood between two worlds. She made her way to the large wooden chair set at the narrow end of the altar. Magda sat opposite her. Emerald took the chair to the West. In front of the Eastern chair stood a blow-up of the picture so handily taken by Rhory on his visit to Ancient Egypt.

"There is our gateway," murmured Emerald. "Through similitude we will pass."

Visions of Ancient Times

Darkness clawed at the car. A light drizzle necessitated windscreen wipers, but did not provide enough moisture to prevent them squeaking every now and again. Trees, surprised in the bright headlights of the Maserati, lurched and shivered in the gusting wind, pushing the car towards the ditch at the side of the road. Onyx put the radio on, but found the reception to be poor and switched it off again. She braked sharply to avoid a large branch that had fallen into the lane and eased her way around it.

In retrospect, they'd wasted too much time over lunch, with Emerald's dreadful daughter going on and on about everything horsey and Papa Rillington holding forth about bees, of all things. Who gave a flying chamberpot about bees for goodness' sake? Onyx flexed the fingers of each hand and braked once more as something badger-like scooted across the road in front of her.

"Blooming countryside."

The ceremony had started out all right. Emerald had given them each little leather-bound, hand-written notebooks. The paper, heavy and yellowing and cut to a shape longer and narrower than that found in Ryman's Stationers, surely dated from the 19th century. All were hand-written in a clear copper-plate, with a skill long lost.

"We are doing the Third Rituale," Emerald announced. "It's about halfway through. *Rituale Permeo.*" As there were only three of them and the ceremony required a minimum of six, she explained how they would double up the parts. Each of them had long passages to read, with occasional Latin phrases that Onyx had to squint at to ensure she read them in a way a Roman might actually recognise. About halfway through Emerald stood and, with the picture kindly provided by the Hammerford lout behind her, read something in a language that sounded nothing like English or Latin. She held a translucent piece of paper in her hands and when the reading was complete, she set it alight, dropping it smouldering into the skull goblet.

"Now we wait," said Emerald. "Best to close your eyes."

Onyx knew all three women were adept at loosening their subtle bodies to do far viewing. She didn't expect the feeling that her limbs were slowly melting and that the room itself would vanish like mist in bright sunshine. Except she hadn't found herself in bright sunshine.

"Turn right and then turn left." The satnav brought her back to the problem of negotiating her way out of Devon. She'd thought it would be easy to make her way back to London and had confidently not switched on her dashboard companion. Result? She ended up facing what could only be the entrance to some farm or other with a horse staring at her over a barbed-wire fence.

When the ceremonial had come to an end Onyx had greater respect for Emerald. Without that woman's psychic brio she wondered if she would've been lost in some ancient snowscape for ever. But she'd seen Rhory blooming Bruce, though all three women had struggled to make sense of this vision.

Back in the kitchen the horse girl, Emerald's daughter, received a summary command to go elsewhere – no doubt to whisper to equine ears in a far-off stable. The three women sat in silence for some time, nursing cups of tea and trying to make sense of what had occurred.

"Well, we didn't see anything of Diamond. At least I didn't," said Magda, her silver rings flashing as they caught the light of the setting sun.

"We all didn't," stated Emerald, banging the point of her middle finger on the kitchen table. "His whereabouts remain a mystery."

She muttered an oath under her breath. "It's developing into a right mugger's muddle!" Only she didn't say mugger.

"What are we dealing with here?" asked Magda. "It's as though the boy drags us around in his slipstream. We should have been back deep in the first times of Ancient Egypt with the photo and phone giving us coordinates, and instead we end up in a Greek city somewhere, with crazy Christians and Roman soldiers straight off the film set of Cleopatra."

"Yes," said Emerald, "you're right, Magda. Quite right. Of course. We were back in ancient Alexandria, which is in Egypt, actually." She continued to attempt to poke holes in the tabletop with her finger. "He must be back in Alexandria at some nexus point of the past."

"Good," said Magda. "Let's hope he stays there and gets crucified by some Roman senator just for being a snotty brat."

"No, it's not good," said Emerald. "Whether he finds his way back or not, he has power he doesn't understand, to play with the winds of time. It's as though his actions change the settings, the vectors. He may unravel everything. He must be stopped."

"We need to study what we experienced and see if it gives clues as to how to stop him," said Onyx. "We know we're not alone in this and the visions were for a reason. Mine was bizarre and definitely not Egypt."

Onyx set her mobile phone to record as the women described their experiences in turn.

Onyx found herself riding a horse. Even in the altered state of consciousness a part of her smiled at the irony of that. Her leggings were leather, with slightly itchy undergarments to keep the biting chill from entirely freezing her… She realized her consciousness now piggy-backed on that of some man. *That's a first.* Her boots, made of thick felt or suede, had hefty socks that did little to keep her toes warm – *or, strictly, his toes*. Her riding gloves reached halfway to her elbow and something heavy pulled down on her shoulders. *Not just a cloak, chainmail as well. Saturday night fever, I'm bouncing along in the mind of a soldier!*

The sky above pressed down with a uniformly chilly, gloomy grey. If any sun shone above the clouds, clearly pregnant with yet more snow, it gave the barest minimum of light to allow the description of day. The track along which the soldier rode had been trodden by many hooves, but had frozen ruts and icy fissures, and the rider picked his way with care. The wind bit at his face, and the scarf pulled over his mouth scraped its frozen cloth on his chapped lips. Every once in a while he stopped and listened, scanning the thinly-forested hillside to his left, where it rose steadily towards a ridge half a mile away. On his right, the ground continued to fall away, blanketed with pristine snow with only the tracks of some small animal to show anything had passed by.

Onyx felt his pulse quicken as he saw human tracks high up on his left. At precisely that moment a horn sounded somewhere ahead. He spurred his horse forward. Rounding the next bend he saw a clutch of people on the road. He loosened his sword. Pleasure rose from his loins as he contemplated what he would do to these people in just a few minutes. He didn't rush, as he could see his soldiers fanning out on either side of the road; being higher than his prey, he could spot that the soldiers and the people he hunted hadn't yet noticed him. One of the boys shouted something and the other spun around and then pulled at the woman's sleeve. They'd seen him and the soldiers. Now they knew they were trapped.

He drew his sword and cantered up. The woman, a matron in her forties by the look of her, had both boys gathered to her. One looked just like her, with his blond hair peeking from under his cap. The other, with darker hair and a paler face… *Rhory Bruce, Rhory Bruce!* thought Onyx, preparing to see blood spatter over the snow. Onyx felt the elation surging through the man's limbs. He knew in some otherworldly way that these boys must die, and die now. He didn't care about the woman. The boys must be destroyed. But he would do it slowly. That would work best. Some force or intelligence seeped into his mind – Onyx could feel it – it instructed him. He'd seen the darker-haired boy before, in a vision, a vision with Hecate. He crossed himself, drew his sword and raised it. The boy held out his ski sticks, as though these would protect him, and clattered his long skis around. The shorter boy also moved, but glanced to his right. The soldier decided where he would skewer the taller boy first, just enough to bleed like a pig but not enough to die.

The vision had ended there with the soldier about to strike and the boys hollering, as though that would make a difference. Onyx had felt sick as she struggled to open her eyes in the crypt. The other two women jerked back into awareness of their surroundings in Devon at the same time. Emerald muttered to Onyx, "We nearly lost you," but said nothing more. They'd left and disrobed in silence before repairing to the kitchen to compare notes.

Onyx finally reached an A road and saw London signposted. She left the satnav talking to her as a great weariness settled in. A sign told her a Little Chef would appear in five miles. She contemplated another cup of tea accompanied by egg and beans. Not the wine bar meal she'd planned for this evening, but hours had somehow been lost. It often happened when you played footsie with time. Instead she reached over to her phone on the passenger seat and switched on the playback. Emerald had spoken first.

Simoneas

The phone produced a high-pitched whistle, the sound of a kettle nearly boiling coming through the tiny speaker. A chair scraped on the floor and Emerald's disembodied voice spoke.

"No tea for me, thanks, Magda."

A clink of cups followed by another chair moving.

"At first I saw a series of still panoramas. I think I was tuning in to someone's memories, something they looked at a lot. A barren hillside, with a few rather sad looking palms, the long wooden cantilever that the Egyptians use to draw water from a well. A camel. A hut made of mud and palm fronds. A large wooden cross by a pile of stones."

Emerald cleared her throat.

"I could sense rather than know that the woman whose consciousness had entangled mine was rejecting something behind her. She only stared at this view with its makeshift altar.

"After some moments that picture faded and I could see the sea from the edge of a city. What shook the woman – I could feel her loathing – was the huge structure built on an island across a stretch of harbour water. She stared at it and irritation pulsed through her. It took me a moment to recognise as it was illumined by daylight. The building that irritated her so much had to be one of the Seven Wonders of the World, the Lighthouse in ancient Alexandria. But she used this building to steer by. Once she knew for sure what she could see, she set off walking. People were all around her. I could feel their fear of her. No, not so much fear, as awe. She carried a cross made of two gnarled bits of wood bound together with twine."

A clock in the dining room struck the hour and Emerald paused.

"She walked for ages along the quayside. Boats were drawn up. She'd no interest in them and only gave them sidelong glances. I on the other hand would have dearly loved to study them, but only saw what she chose to look at. She stole glances at the people around her, watching

her. I could feel the little jets of pleasure that people were staring and pointing. Some smiled and waved. Some even cheered. Children ran ahead. I think they'd guessed where she'd chosen to go.

"The harbour extended a long way and her limbs ached, but she had an iron will and kept walking, with the sun hot on her neck.

"Ahead she focused on the spit of land that extended across the harbour, providing a narrow causeway to the island that held the lighthouse. Something there she hated even more than the lighthouse.

"On our left were storage buildings for goods unloaded at the port. People sat there working or shifted barrels. Lots of activity, but everyone was aware of this strange woman."

A dull thud reminded Onyx that Emerald had thumped the table making the phone bounce.

"Then I saw him. The snivelling little nuisance, our own Luke Time-Walker, the Bruce boy. He stared at me. Well, not me, the old woman who had snagged my consciousness. But he stared, as though he knew. And she stared back, even stopped walking for a moment. A girl whispered something to the brat and he looked away."

A car overtook Onyx and the male driver threw a glance her way. She braked and let the other car pull ahead.

"So his presence pulled you to Alexandria? Is that what you're saying?" Magda's voice asked tinnily from the phone.

"Yes. I think it must be that. His presence back there completely overrode the intent in our Rituale to contact Diamond. But I'm sure we can turn this to our advantage. We'll discuss that in a minute. My story's not complete yet."

"Sorry," said Magda.

"Leaving the Bruce brat behind, she continued along the harbour and turned onto the causeway. People now sensed where she was headed. Children ran in front. Some people looked manic. Really gleeful. Others pale and shocked. It took forever for her to walk over this bridge. The sea pounded on our left and I could feel the spume in the air. She looked neither to left nor right. Her shadow slid over the cobbles on the roadway in front of her, cut with two deep grooves made by chariot wheels and

carts, I would assume. She banged her cross on the stones at her feet, using it as a walking stick and making some sort of point. She didn't look up.

"Eventually we reached the far side. Then she stopped and took a long look at the building she'd come to visit. It was a temple. Women stood on the steps, priestesses who served there. A woman descended, perhaps their leader. An old woman, quite bent.

"I could hear people chanting. It took time to realise they were chanting a name. 'Elizabeth, Elizabeth.' This had to be the name of the woman whose mind I inhabited. She raised her cross and slowly turned round in a great circle, looking at the crowd. On the far side of the water I could see Alexandria with its pillared buildings. In front of the temple soldiers stood guarding the bottom steps and the priestesses. The men looked unhappy. They clearly feared this woman. The elderly priestess did not. She walked down holding a golden ankh in her hand. I felt her power. As a priestess, she could see deeply. I even think she sensed me. Moments later I returned in consciousness to our room."

Onyx hit the pause button. Both Emerald and she had been drawn to where the Hammerford boy had been. These times must link in some way; some resonance must hold them together. She desperately wanted a cigarette. There were none in the car and anyway she'd successfully given up some time ago. But the urge was there. A red and white sign glowed in the darkness ahead, and yellow lights lit a rain-swept courtyard with a few parked cars. The Little Chef. She would have a cup of tea and egg and chips and work out what all this might mean.

Muzak inconsequentially reminded everyone in the café of the theme from the film *Titanic*. Onyx pushed her smeared plate with its cold chips to one side, and fitted an earpiece into the phone. She fiddled with the controls until she found where Magda started her story. The young woman's voice, smooth and dark, flowed into Onyx's ear.

"My vision also started with still images. Amazing really. Three-dimensional and frozen. In the first picture I, or the person I became,

studied a papyrus scroll. The lettering looked Greek. I couldn't read it but felt the meaning. It had to be old, very old, even then. But I – or Simoneas – which is who I was, knew it to be relevant to now. And to me – or rather to him. It gets confusing doesn't it!"

"Next he's at the docks of a busy port. Perhaps Alexandria. I could only see what was captured in this panoramic still image. Faces of children, lots of children. All of them frightened. Tears and snot, that sort of thing. Older people, not well dressed, stand with their heads bowed. I hear again and again in this guy's consciousness. 'Where is he? He must be here. I MUST find him.' But he doesn't. I think the children and young adults must all be slaves.

"Then I'm with two other men. Tall black men with fine clothes and tightly curled oiled hair with beads. The men are as black as night. And identical. Twins I guess. I sense their cruelty and power. We're all looking at a cage or prison of some sort. It's before dawn, a smudge of pale green in the sky and flickering torches."

"Come on, Magda," the voice of Emerald butted in. *"I like the scene setting but we have work to do. Did you also see the Bruce boy?"*

A pause while Magda took a slow sip of tea. A clink as she set down her cup.

"My Simoneas is one of us. He can see more than most. It's a girl, or young woman who catches his attention first. I register she's not part of his prophecy, or whatever it is written in Greek on the papyrus scroll. But he senses she's unusual. He thinks he may have seen her before but cannot remember where. Then he sees his quarry. The one he seeks. And yes, Emerald, it is Rhory, as clear as the day is long. Our schoolboy is caged in with other children and dressed like a Greek. Of course my visionary doesn't know he's looking at an English boy from far in the future. He's no way of conceptualising that. He thinks the boy is from some different realm. Some far-off magical land. But he knows the boy is the key to power, immense power. And he wants him. He wants him really badly. To steal his power if he can."

"Does he get him?" asked Emerald.

"I don't know. The vision more or less ended there."

"More or less?" Onyx heard her own voice ask a question.

"I saw one more image. Still again. A huge man, tall, wide, immensely strong. He's staring at me. Well, not me, you understand. Simoneas. At that point the vision ended."

Onyx removed the earpiece and leant back in the plastic settee. How to make sense of all this? Emerald had suggested they'd dipped into a possible past. A past that might lie on an adjacent trajectory to their actual past. She couldn't see how the boy from Hammerford could have returned to the actual past with the portal in Hammerford Park closed down.

Onyx had a different theory. Young master Bruce had found another way of moving back through time and would have a real and possibly permanent impact on their plans unless he could be stopped.

For a moment the buzz and kerfuffle of the restaurant faded and Onyx found herself linked with Emerald and Magda in their dance as Hecate. The man on horseback, with flowing blond hair moving slowly in the dark wind, pointed his glowing sword at the three of them. Then she knew.

Back with a bump to the strains of a dreadful theme tune from a film she couldn't remember, surrounded by overweight truck drivers and thin salesmen finishing their suppers, it was the three of them who'd opened the portal. In trying to capture Rhory Bruce on the inner planes, they'd opened the doorways of time to him. And he'd passed through. Now they had to turn it to their advantage. Their vision had shown them how. The boy from Hammerford was their key back to the nexus point in time in old Alexandria. Now they must use him to move things the way they wanted. After all, he had no idea what was happening. How could he have? He was just a pawn, and she was queen of this particular chessboard.

She paid the spotty youth at the till, and went back to her car with a smile on her lips and a wobble of her hips for the truck drivers who were all watching. She had a plan.

In Limbo

"Hey, look, Rhory, we've got seats right by the stage," said Natasha.

Mohammed walked ahead with Aida and pulled a chair back for her. The stage area, sitting in the middle of an enormous tent, had rows of tables all around. Ours had a prime view.

Jugglers, and people on tall stilts, wandered round by the tables, giving everything a festive air. Although this Tent Extravaganza, as our programme announced, was clearly aimed at the tourists, there seemed to be plenty of locals. Egyptians enjoy a good circus act, apparently. Natasha looked pretty hot with her eye make-up on and a miniskirt over leggings. Her hair, now more or less grown back since her brush with cancer, shone ultra-blonde where it caught the stage lights. Music, from a frenetic band over to one side, crashed with Eastern promise into our ears. We could hardly hear each other. Our table had olives, dates and dips. Some bread arrived shortly after we sat down. We swatted away the occasional fly but the mosquitoes left us alone, as Auntie had drenched us in anti-mozzie spray when we reached the Desert City.

We'd left Alex by the main Cairo road and hummed along in the Daimler. Mohammed drove quite fast and I clocked him checking the mirror once in a while. He spoke to Aida in Arabic for a bit, and I could hear concern in her voice as she responded, but Natasha pointed out a colourful truck we were overtaking and I didn't tune in to what they might be saying. Shortly after, we took a side road and spotted sand dunes picked out by weak street lighting. We parked the Daimler on a flat, gritty car park, directed by a man dressed in white, wearing a turban and a red sash at his waist. Aida pointed out the night sky as we crossed to the large central tent.

"Later in the evening they'll put out most of the lights so we can see the stars, but you can get a fair idea even here. Luckily there's no cloud tonight."

"It's pretty chilly though, Auntie," said Natasha, hugging around her shoulders a shawl she'd been lent

"They light a bonfire too, and set off fireworks."

"That should be fun," I said, being a sucker for fireworks.

Natasha and I ordered cokes and Auntie had a small, very black coffee. Mohammed didn't join us at the table, but sat some distance away with some men he seemed to know.

"Mohammed told me you were mugged, Rhory. You should have said." My aunt took off the glasses she'd been using to read the programme.

My mouth went dry and I searched for the right words. This conversation could quickly get out of hand.

"Someone stole your phone, is that right?" asked Aida.

"Yes, Auntie," I said.

"Can you survive without it or do we need to buy you another one?"

"No, I'll be fine."

"He can use mine," said Natasha, "if he needs to."

"Well, use the landline if you want to talk to your mum and dad. Or Skype. I guess that's cheaper."

"I'm not sure how, Auntie," I said, "they're skiing in Switzerland, remember?"

"Oh yes. Silly me. Of course, they're skiing." Aida glanced over to where Mohammed sat with his burly mates. "Well you're safe enough here."

It hadn't occurred to me until that moment that I might not be safe. I looked around to see if any of the men who'd tried to grab me might have joined us in the tent, but the lights all went out. The musicians played twangy Middle Eastern type music and a spotlight illumined a belly dancer. The entertainment had started.

The needs of nature being what they were, I went in search of the loos. Directed to some tents a distance away from the Extravaganza tent, I'd done what I needed to do, holding my breath most of the time. On my return, I checked out my knowledge of the stars. The inky-black sky sparkled with individual pinpricks of light. One, much brighter than the rest, surely had to be Venus. And above me I could recognise the Big Dipper. Or was it the Great Bear? The stars shone with a far greater brightness than when we'd arrived.

I had on the neat leather jacket Mum had given me for Christmas, but the wind proved icy cold. The sand under my feet gave way and my mind nearly did as well. The Tent City had vanished. The stars sparkled with total clarity because all the lights had also disappeared. I stood ankle-deep in snow and the wind carried sub-zero temperatures straight to my bones. I stumbled on a few paces, towards great chunks of stone and a forest of trees whispering in the icy wind.

The music of Abdul and his Three Brothers came back as suddenly as a sound system being switched on, and the cool Egyptian night felt positively tropical.

"Are you all right?"

I swung round to find Mohammed a few feet away, a cigar in his hand. Some distance behind him the man mountain I'd seen by the Alexandria bookshop stood lighting a cigarette.

"You know, Rhory," said Mohammed, "some people think there is a temple complex beneath these sands. They sense it you know. Your aunt sent me to find you, the limbo dancing is starting."

"How you feeling?" asked Natasha.

"Totally grim," I said.

"We all had the same food in the tent though and Auntie and I are fine. So's Mohammed."

I turned on my side, a wave of nausea sweeping through me,

chilly and sharp. It passed and I eased myself up onto the pillows of my bed.

"You're sweating," said Natasha.

"I feel really cold," I said, but my forehead proved moist as I wiped my hand over it.

I'd been fine on the way back to Alexandria. Confused about my vision of the snow and the great stones, but otherwise fine. This morning I'd woken up to find I'd a major dose of the runs. I'd degenerated as the morning went on, unable to face food, and water passed straight through me. Aida's dad had given me a small brown pill he said would help. It had a bit. I hadn't thrown up since I'd taken it. But I was cutting a groove between my bed and the bathroom with the frequency of my visits.

"You were great doing the limbo last night," Natasha smiled.

The downside of being so close to the stage meant we'd been chosen to come and follow the professional limbo-dancers. I'd hit the bar with my chin at some unimpressive height. Natasha, fit from her football, and much more supple than me, had been truly impressive.

"I had those chicken wings, remember?"

"Oh. Right. I avoided those," said Natasha. "Must have been them. You said they were too spicy."

"Sorry, Nat," I said, dashing to the toilet, unsure which end to aim at the loo first.

The Danish Captain

Sweden – about 1520

The sled bumped and ground its way along the frozen ruts of the forest lane. Gregor's breath formed clouds that combined with the hazy fog arising from the flanks of the two horses. He cracked his whip above their ears.

"They don't like the icy road," he said to Håkan. "Their shoes slide."

"They've a fair old weight to pull."

"True enough," responded Gregor.

Håkan glanced over his shoulder at the piles of neatly chopped firewood and the bundles of broom. Sitting at the back of the sled on a stack of broom-wood, his legs dangling over the end, was Bengt. His thick winter cloak pulled close, he had swaddled his head in a wool cap and old scarves to keep out the bitter wind.

"Why didn't you go with my father, Gregor?" asked Håkan.

"I dearly wanted to, son, but someone had to stay and help your mother keep the farm working as it should. We were raised together, Matts and me, and our friendship was firm as children. It's remained so, so it has. It's my honour to serve your family as it was my father's before me, may he rest in the Lord's peace."

Håkan glanced behind once more at the back of Bengt and the snow-dusted trees surrounding the lane they'd travelled on this last half hour. Gregor leaned close.

"It's all right, Håkan. He cannot hear what we say. Old Bengt is really deaf you know. I have to shout now to get him to hear."

Gregor pulled his fur-lined jacket closer, as the wind provided an impromptu snow flurry from the trees above. His weather-beaten face didn't have the lines and crevices of Old

Bengt, but his cheeks sagged slightly and grey hair peaked out from under his woollen hat. His dark eyebrows bushed above his keen blue eyes. He jerked at the reins to avoid a fallen branch at the edge of the lane.

"So why have Lennart and Father gone? Mother won't really tell me. I know they're not trading. Or at least that's not all they are doing."

Gregor tugged at the curls in his grey beard. He dropped his voice and leant closer to Håkan.

"These are very dangerous times. Sweden knows its destiny has to be grabbed. The King won't give us our country back because we smile nicely." He spat to the side of the lane.

"But the King is ordained by God. At least that's what Father Joseph says at the church."

"It suits the Catholic Church to say that of a Catholic king, right enough," said Gregor quietly. "But there are those who doubt the sanctity and true holiness of the king who rules in Rome. There are those who think the whole edifice of Christendom has become corrupt. There are those who would sweep out the spiders who grow fat at the expense of ordinary working folk. We need to take brooms like those Bengt makes and purify this rotting Church. So we do."

Håkan felt a grin lurking within his face. He'd never heard anyone be so rude about the Catholic Church. The forest on either side remained empty of listening ears, as far as he could tell, although the thick underbrush could hide an army.

"Ho there. Pull over. Pull over, I say!"

Håkan jumped, his heart racing. The voice, thick with a Danish accent and imperious as a Roman Caesar, came from behind.

"Whoa, whoa there," Gregor shouted to the horses as he pulled back on the reins.

Håkan pivoted round. Right behind the sled was a troop of horse, led by a young man with ash-blond hair, gathered in part in a thin plait flapping on his face. He'd been blessed with the sort of good looks saints are given in the statues in the church. How neither Gregor nor he had heard them he couldn't fathom, as the men were jeering and the metal fittings on their horses were jangling. They carried the Danish King's pennant.

"Pull over, you slovenly idiots," hissed the young man. "We are about the King's business and will brook no delay. I'll have your ears if you hold us up further."

Gregor kept his eyes down and urged the horses off to the frozen edge of the road. Cold leaves slapped against Håkan's face and the runner of the sled dropped into a deep rut. The stop came so suddenly, Håkan had to grab the wooden backrest behind him to keep from falling.

The troop of horse thundered past, with an explosion of muddy ice crystals from the frozen road and without a word of thanks.

The sled wouldn't budge.

"We're lucky the runners didn't break," said Bengt.

"True enough, old friend," said Gregor. "There's nowt for it. We'll have to unpack a bit to get the sled movin' once again."

Unpacking all the broom and some of the logs proved tiring work but brought a sweat to Håkan's face. Half an hour later they were under way once more. Gregor glanced at the leaden sky and sighed.

"We may make the monastery before Vespers, I guess," he said.

"Vespers? That's evening. It's only been light two hours hasn't it?" said Håkan.

Gregor grinned revealing a mouth of crooked teeth with a couple of gaps.

"Here," he said. He reached into his leather satchel and drew out a dark-green bottle. "You've done men's work – have a man's drink. Warm you up, young master."

Håkan removed the stopper and sipped. The cold, thick water

met his tongue, ignited, ran like liquid fire down his throat and cascaded a thin stream of warmth that spread miraculously throughout his body. Once he had stopped coughing and Gregor had stopped thumping his back he grinned.

"Aqua Vitae!" said Gregor, as though that would explain everything.

"Better than the warm piddle that passes for beer at the ale house, any day," said Bengt, when he had taken a draught.

"They are killing people that oppose their Danish king," resumed Gregor, after a while. "They're the Pope's mailed fist."

Håkan felt a cold space open up in his stomach. The Danish soldiers had been well armed.

"So Father and Lennart are in real danger?"

Gregor sniffed and grimaced.

"They are doing what I would do if your father had not ordered me to remain and protect the family. Sweden will always be under the Danish spurred boot if no one tells them otherwise."

He flicked the left flank of the left horse.

"Turn, Odin," he said to the horse, as a narrower lane opened on their left, cutting through the oaks and lime trees that the monks had planted over the years.

"Best we leave our converse there, young master," said Gregor as they drew near to the walls of the monastery. "I have something to deliver to one of the brothers, and then we will proceed to town."

No trees grew close to the monastery, and the posts and nets of the vegetable and fruit gardens could be seen under their thin blanket of snow. Somewhere distant a cow lowed and the pungent aroma of dung reminded Håkan that the monks produced tasty cheeses from their smelly cows.

The gate to the monastery courtyard opened and a monk came out. He had a blanket clasped around his shoulders and a woollen hat on his tonsured head, but otherwise he wore the usual brown cassock of his order, topped with a white surplice.

His bare feet, a rosy pink colour, had only thin sandals to protect them from the snow and ice.

"Good morning to you, dear Gregor. You are a welcome sight. As are you, young Master Håkan. And the venerable Bengt, if I'm not mistaken. I would ask you in but we're about to meet with the Abbot."

"And we have to get to the town, Brother Niels. Bengt has been working hard, as you can see."

"Ora et labora," said Brother Niels. "Prayer and work, Håkan, prayer and work. It's our motto, and a right blessed one at that."

Håkan nodded, feeling none the wiser. But he knew Brother Niels worked hard at his healing and visited his mother once in a while to discuss berries and roots, using words like emetics and diuretics.

"It's all right, my dear Brother," said Gregor, "what you want I have right here."

He drew a small parcel wrapped in cloth and tied with twine.

"Ah bless you, and bless Mistress Signy," said the brother. "Her treatment for chilblains and cold-sores is sent from the Good Lord Himself." He smiled as he crossed himself, and Håkan found himself smiling too, both at the way Brother Niel's face lit up and in pride at his mother's skill.

"Have you met the big German?"

Gregor frowned and shook his head.

"He was here last night. I told him of Mistress Signy but he appeared to know of her already. Mysterious man, with a prodigious love of ale. But he has a wondrous materia medica. Maybe you'll see him in town. You cannot miss him, his voice carries a full seven leagues."

Brother Niels threw his head back and laughed, a full-throated celebration of life that had Håkan grinning back.

"We'll keep our eyes duly peeled," said Gregor, smiling and clasping Brother Niels's outstretched hand. "But we should be under way before some ice-maiden comes and takes you to her crystal cave, Brother."

The Apothecary's Boy

The chill wind kept most people wisely indoors within the town. Håkan made his way up the main street, glad of his thick gloves and the warm muffler over his mouth. They had left Bengt at the covered market near to the church. Brave souls would be out shopping today and had need for his brooms to sweep both dust and snow. Gregor had taken up his usual position at the far end of the square, and would sell his firewood by weight to those who needed to keep their stoves hot and their houses warm. A friend and neighbour at the market had a charcoal fire going to keep them warm. When all the chopped wood had gone, Gregor would return to the farm.

"Go to Gunnar the blacksmith, Håkan, and collect the runner for the sled. Bring it back here if you choose, or walk back if you're not minded to wait about here all day," Gregor had said.

"I'll walk back, then," said Håkan. "Weather looks okay. We might even get some sun."

A pallid disk hinted at where the sun couldn't quite break through the clouds, although to the west, where their farm lay, a patch of blue sky looked like a snowbound lake. Håkan picked his way with care between icy ruts and frozen puddles.

The blacksmith's smithy lay a short walk from this street, up a lane too narrow and steep for Gregor's sled coming from the market end of town. At the corner stood the apothecary's shop. Valde Löfgren, the apothecary, had made it clear in the past that he disapproved of Signy and her work with herbs. Håkan's heart sank as he saw Klas, Valde's son, standing with a few friends outside their shop. Klas might be interested in Inge, but that hadn't made him any friendlier towards Håkan.

Håkan walked into the road to avoid passing too close to the youths. He slipped on a piece of ice and only just kept his balance.

"Hey!" said one of the boys.

Håkan looked across at Klas and his two friends.

"Where you going?" said Klas

"Good day to you, Klas Löfgren," said Håkan, nodding at the others whose names he didn't remember. "I have business with Gunnar."

"Ooh," said the taller of the two other boys, "business with Gunnar. What are you now, a blacksmith's errand boy?"

Håkan ignored this and muttered, "Good day," once more in the hope that would conclude the chit-chat. He would return by a different way.

"Horrible Håkan a heathen heretic," said Klas in a voice that carried clearly up the hill.

Håkan turned, a tremor of anger sweeping through his body. He made a sign with his gloved hand that had only one interpretation.

One of the boys was about to chase after him up the hill, but Klas stopped him by grasping his arm. He leant close and whispered something.

"Ha ha, heretic boy," came the shout from one of Klas's friends.

Håkan, furious and uneasy all at the same time, ducked into the glowing warmth of the smithy. Gunnar, bare-armed and incredibly muscular, with the furnace white-hot behind him, raised his arm and brought a heavy hammer down on the glowing tip of a piece of iron. With each clang sparks flew and the metal dulled slightly. He plunged the glimmering metal into a tank of water, producing a hiss worthy of some giant python.

"Hey, Håkan! How are you? No Gregor?" Gunnar grinned as he laid down the iron pole, waved at one of his apprentices to keep the bellows going, and wiped his forehead.

"Gregor's in the market—"

"Of course he is," said Gunnar, "of course. You've come for the runner brace, I expect."

"Yes, I have," said Håkan, unsure what he should call a man his father's age whom everyone called Gunnar.

The big blacksmith reached for something hanging on a hook on the wall at the back of the smithy. He carefully unwrapped the curved metal, with simple but pretty workings.

"I've kept the design. It'll match in with the other three, don't worry. I expect Gregor knows how to fix it to the sled. He's done it enough times."

Håkan nodded. He'd no idea if Gregor knew what to do with the curved metal or not. Gunnar tapped the brace with a smaller hammer. It produced a clean ting-sound, not as deep as a bell, but suggesting there were no cracks anymore.

"This'll stop you ending up A over T in the snow. It's a wonder the old one held together at all."

He wrapped the metal up in sacking and bound it at both ends.

Having thanked the blacksmith, and confirming that Gregor would settle the account the next market day, Håkan returned by the longer upper road that wound round the edge of town and, crucially, avoided the apothecary. The long icicles extended down from the eaves of the wooden houses like luminous and sharpened giant's teeth. They glinted with dull luminosity in the dreary winter light; although they did not drip, Håkan avoided walking under them. He'd once seen a dog speared by a long dagger of ice and didn't fancy the experience first-hand.

The Witch's Brat

Once back on the road towards the family farmstead he breathed more easily. Klas Löfgren had a reputation as a bully. Since the trouble between his mother and Klas's father, Håkan had kept away from him. Valde Löfgren had even used the word 'witch' to refer to Håkan's mother, Signy. He didn't get a very sympathetic hearing, even in Catholic Church circles, as most town dwellers had benefited from her skill with herbs at some point in their lives, and the Cistercian Monastery used many of her medicaments. But since his father and older brother had gone on their travels, hostility amongst some in the town had grown. He had overheard Signy and Gregor in discussion about how to deal with Löfgren and their bully of a neighbour, Kaleb Pettersson, on more than one occasion.

"I can always go north," his mother had said mysteriously, one time, but had not explained how that would help.

The snow and ice crunched under his boots and the metal runner for the sleigh grew heavier to carry with each step. He moved it from his right to his left arm and counted 100 paces before moving it back again. As he passed the turning to the monastery some crows took off from the trees ahead of him, cawing as they flew. He hoped the cause was not a wild boar, or even worse, some wolves. Apart from the crows, nothing stirred and the snowbound woodland held its breath. Except he could hear breathing. Håkan stopped and held his own breath. Nothing. The snow-spattered trees kept their counsel. There it was again. A snigger suppressed.

"Hey! Who's there?"

His shout disappeared amongst the trees. He shifted the metal runner so it would make a more effective weapon. He'd the strongest sensation of being watched, but peer as he might into the irregular ranks of tree trunks, and the dimly lit bushes that grew in tangled profusion amongst them, he could discern nobody.

He swallowed, took a deep breath to calm his nerves and concluded he was spooking himself unnecessarily. He walked on. The tracks left by the troop of horse that had nearly caused them to lose the sled's runner, were to his right. Håkan wondered if the soldiers would be staying in town or moving straight on through. He would happily never see them again, especially their leader with his cruel eyes.

"Haw, haw, haw, Håkan!" A voice sounded behind him. He turned to see two boys a couple of years older than him emerging from the trees. A cold, hard clump of snow exploded off the back of his head. Staggering and turning again, Håkan ducked as another ball, more ice than snow, whistled past. Klas Löfgren and another boy from the apothecary stood a few paces in front of him, cutting off any escape route. His only hope would be to run into the forest, but the bushes and frozen shrubs would impede him and anyway the boys would likely catch him.

"Well, snivel-face, what have we here? Something stolen from the smithy no doubt. We should take that back, should we not?" Klas addressed the two boys behind Håkan who cut off his route to the town or monastery. Håkan had no doubt he could outrun any of them, but to do that he would have to get by them, and the stick held in Klas's hand and the knife stuck in the boot of a boy behind him made that a hazardous enterprise. He backed to the edge of the road and held the metal runner to one side so he could swing it if he had to.

"The witch's brat wants to fight," said Klas. "And there we were being friendly and passing the time of day. But then, snot-features, if you are asking for a fight, we won't disappoint you, will we?"

He moved down the lane towards Håkan, but kept an eye on the metal in Håkan's hand. Another snowball smashed into his left shoulder, as the boys nearest the town closed in on him also.

Håkan ignored it and, feeling almost outside of his own body, flexed his knees and measured where to place his feet when he sliced the metal runner at Klas's neck. He would get in one good blow and he wanted to make it count.

"You know –" a voice with a strong German accent sounded from the trees behind him – "I really … really do not like bullies."

A horse's head appeared between Håkan and the boys on the town side. The steed snorted as it moved sideways towards the boys. Their horrified faces stared up at the rider, whose massive shoulders would have put a woodsman to shame. They turned and fled towards the town.

"Now then," said the man, "that makes it a bit more even. Do you want me to umpire? I might even dismount and then it would be two on two. That's a man's fight. Are you up to it?"

This final question, the man directed at Klas.

"Sir. I don't know who you are. We were only having a joke. We know Håkan, you see. Just a joke. And not really the business of a stranger."

"I will decide what is my business and what is not," said the man, drawing his sword and urging his horse on.

Klas stepped backwards, slipped and just caught his balance.

"Sir, please, sir," he said, his voice rising a full octave.

The man raised his sword and swept it through the branches above his head. Clumps of snow rained down on Klas and his friend. Klas screamed, lunged sideways and ended up entangled in a roadside bush, with snow all over him. His friend charged into the forest on the other side of the road, and a further horde of crows took flight, filling the air with their gritty cries.

The man winked at Håkan and beckoned him to walk past Klas.

"Just a joke, as you say," said the man. "See, I'm laughing." He sheathed his sword and did indeed grin at Håkan. "Now, begone with you for I will indeed thrash you if I come across you in similar circumstances again."

Klas struggled up, his dignity, like his clothing, all askew. He had lost his hat but ran off down the lane towards the town.

"Give me a moment, young sir, and then we will make acquaintance of each other," the man said, his Swedish coming out as though he'd sat on it first. He rode off into the forest, ducking between trees, and emerged a few minutes later leading two smaller packhorses, laden with panniers.

"I was collecting berries," the German said, as though that explained his sudden arrival on a small Swedish lane. "Maybe you can render me an assistance?"

Håkan nodded, not at all sure what might come next.

"I am looking for Signy Ottosdatter, married to Matts Ekland."

Håkan bit his lower lip. The big man's florid face had widely spaced eyes, and under his leather hat, curly light brown hair peeked out above a forehead much creased by frowning. His mouth, with full lips, remained half-open as he fixed Håkan with his gaze. His breath hovered about him in the cold air.

Something in Håkan settled. The man's eyes, although watchful, had no guile. And he'd just saved Håkan from a beating or worse.

"That's my mother, sir. I'll take you to her."

"That's good," said the man, "very good. My name is Bombast. At least that's how your joking friends will learn of me. But to you and your esteemed mother, I am simply Paracelsus." He threw his head back and laughed, the sound rolling through the trees.

Paracelsus

"I'd expected two of you, you know," said Paracelsus to Håkan as they all sat down to dinner that evening.

"My brother, you mean?"

"No. No, I've met your brother, and your father, the estimable Matts Ekland. Indeed, it's because of them I am here."

Everyone spoke at once. Signy held up her hands to her children. "Quiet, quiet." She turned to her guest, who'd been given pride of place at the head of the table, and sat there beaming at them all. "You met Matts and Lennart? How are they? Are they well? Have they been wounded?"

A look of horror swept across Håkan's mother's face. "They are not—"

"No. They are both alive and they had all their limbs when I last counted. But –" his face became serious, his cheeks glowing red in the lamplight – "but Matts had been wounded. That's why I met him."

"Wounded?" said Eira. "Father is—"

"Your father is lucky to be alive and lucky – or blessed by the good Lord – that I was there. Without my medical skills I doubt he would have recovered. But recover he did. You see, battles are great for doctors. Gruesome but informative. I've learned much from the battlefields of Europe. It's one reason I travel so much. That and annoying local so-called doctors so much, it's wise for me to move on."

The big man chuckled and drank some beer. He wiped his mouth with the back of his hand.

"He took a thrust from a lance."

Signy's hand shot to her mouth. Håkan felt cold steel move through his innards.

"It was a clean wound and missed all vital organs. Your husband killed his assailant before the lance could be twisted—"

"Oh!" said Eira, putting both hands up to her bonnet.

At that point Ralf opened the door and Inge entered, carrying a large plate of steaming mashed potato with blood sausage. She set it down, looked at Paracelsus and went to stand in the gloom by the wall.

"Thank you, Inge," said Signy, with scarcely a tremor in her voice. "We'll call you when we need you."

Inge flicked her chin up and left the room. The door closed with a notable thump.

"Is he walking?" asked Signy.

"Better than that," said the German, "he's able to ride. A trauma to the body like that requires good cleaning, excellent stitching and skilful rebalancing. I could do all those things. When I first saw your husband, Mistress Signy, he had a high fever. The risk was infection. I dealt with that. He is choleric and needed something to cool the humours."

Paracelsus spoke at length about what medicaments he'd used and why. He thumped the table gently with his fist to emphasise key points and confirmed the value of prayer in a doctor's armoury.

"Healing comes from God, through the hands of Paracelsus! Without God nothing. Without Paracelsus …" He threw back his head and laughed, before drinking a long draught of beer.

"Please fill our guest's beaker, Håkan."

As he did so, the German doctor held his wrist.

"As I said, I expected two of you, and not your brother Lennart. You're not hiding someone away?"

Håkan shook his head, completely bemused at what Paracelsus meant.

"Well. He'll come, I'm sure. And when he does there are things I must show you."

Before Håkan could ask more about what he meant, the German doctor had launched into a discussion about the new medicine and the value of alchemy. He could see his mother was torn between listening to a man with astounding knowledge of healing and wanting to ask more about her husband and son.

Paracelsus rubbed his hands and looked round at the others. He nodded slowly.

"I've come to learn from you, good lady," he said to Signy, "if you will feel able to teach an oaf like me."

"I don't know what I could possibly teach you," said Håkan's mother, shaking her head slightly.

"Your husband was sure you could and so am I. The berries that grow in these northern climes have remarkable properties. I can see that when I look at them. But how to prepare them? That is wisdom learned over years, if not over generations. And that you know, I believe."

"Yes," said Signy, with a suggestion of a smile, "I believe I do. And will do so happily if you will tell me everything, and I mean everything, about Matts and Lennart."

"Gladly," said Paracelsus, "once the good young master has replenished my beer once more. Beating off knuckle-heads has proved thirsty work."

Håkan held his breath, but the doctor didn't explain and Signy didn't ask. He poured more beer. Paracelsus took a long swig.

"And I will share with you what I can of my exceptional knowledge, for fair is fair in this world of ours, is it not, Mistress Signy?"

Most of next day, the German doctor and Signy worked in the outhouse next to the stables and the building where the sled and sleighs were housed. Gregor applied himself to the sled, adding the mended runner in the right position. Håkan took Paracelsus and his mother cheese, bread and beer at midday. They sat at a table in the room that had the pleasant musty fragrance of old herbs. Countless bunches of dried plants hung from the rafters. On the table Signy used a pestle and mortar to grind and crush certain seeds she was discussing with the big man. He made notes in German in a great notebook, with pictures scrawled in black ink in the margins. Later in the day Håkan watched from the platform outside the kitchen as Paracelsus removed packages from his panniers in the stables and replaced them with parcels wrapped by his mother. That night Signy took her meal with the doctor alone. Next morning, before the sun had risen, he'd gone.

"He wanted me to give you this message," said Signy to Håkan. "He'd seen our Judge Circle in a dream. It contains both hope and danger for you. He said the angels of the portals watch over it and over you."

Signy fell silent, her forehead creased in a frown.

"Did he say anything else, Mother?"

"He said much else. Much, much. We should be ready to leave at any time. He's a man much given to visions and the subtle worlds are close to his sight. He has the eye just as my mother did and just…" she stopped.

"What do you mean, leave?"

"Just that. He didn't explain. He's a man much aided by either our good Lord or the devil. He's not good in the way Brother Niels is good, that's for sure. He's too taken with the passion to know. And even he would not pretend he was humble." She smiled. "But he's more than generous with his knowledge and is off to town today to give healing for free to any of the poor who wish for it."

"He will go to the monastery then?"

"No. No. He said he would rather be poked with Satan's pitchforks, even after I told him about Brother Niels. He said I was the one he had come to see." His mother cleared her throat. "He knows what your father and Lennart are about. He supports the same cause. He cares not a jot for Swedish independence from the Danish yoke, but believes the new teachings of Luther are the Word of God for our time. He carries a bible written in German. Imagine! He showed me, but I couldn't read a word, their letters are so thick and chunky."

"Like his Swedish," said Håkan. He and his mother laughed just as Eira ran in shouting.

"Tell me, tell me," she demanded.

Shoshan

The walls glowed with a light of their own. The smooth passageway was made of large separate stones, each of a slightly different size and angle. The high ceiling, coloured blue, glowed like a benevolent sky and the multitude of five-pointed stars added their golden aura. The walls displayed writing etched a deep black against the glow that emanated from the stone. Håkan walked in the centre of the corridor with a feeling of extraordinary calm. For the walls radiated more than light. They bathed him in love, and somewhere deep inside himself – he could not have said where – he recognised this place.

The room at the end of the passage had paintings all around of men and women with extraordinary headgear, and some with animal heads. Near the centre of the room stood a girl of about his age dressed in a long pleated robe of delicate white material. At her neck she wore a pendant, a lustrous stone with a crease down the middle that reminded Håkan of a beetle's back. This too glowed slightly. Her dark hair was bound at the temple with a plaited cord of soft red strands, which in turn held a feather in place.

The girl, taller than Håkan, beckoned him to approach. He took in a breath to speak but she held two fingers to her lips and then pointed them at him. She moved a forefinger to each ear and stared at him with a smile in her eyes.

Silence gathered all around, like a deep ocean of possibility. Håkan could hear nothing, nothing at all, but in that nothing lived all sound, and every sound had beauty. He felt a pressure in his chest, as though something wished to gain admittance. His heart started to thump. Still the girl smiled, a smile of kindness. She reached out with her hand, palm upwards. Håkan extended his own arm and, guided by the deep silence, held his hand palm downwards and touched her fingertips.

The sensation was akin to jumping into the great lake to the north of their town, the lake that extended like a small inland sea towards the north of Sweden. The silence engulfing him swirled and bubbled with texture and meaning, if he could only hear it. And then he did.

'My name is Shoshan.'

Håkan sucked in a deep breath,

"Oh, I can—"

Shoshan frowned and put both hands to her ears as though he had shouted at the top of his voice. She shook her head, smiled and extended her hand once more. When their hands touched, and Håkan could sense the deep connection, he sensed the words, *'We talk within, dear friend, only within.'* Håkan nodded and tried to say inwardly, *'My name is Håkan.'*

The young priestess smiled.

'Yes. Yes. A "high born son". That is certain.'

Håkan wasn't sure what she meant but she had moved deeper into the chamber where a large stone chair stood facing one of the walls.

'Sit. Sit here.' She stood to one side of the chair.

Håkan eased his way onto the cool stone surface of the seat. Only then did he see that he too had on a long skirt of some fine cotton, with a simple shirt of similar material. Confusion swept through him and he tried to get up. Shoshan touched his arm, and then rested her hand on his shoulder.

'You are here in your Ka. Your Ka wisely takes the clothing appropriate to this sacred and timeless hall. No need for fear. You are gifted to travel this way and you have travelled so many times. It's just you have forgotten. This journey you will remember.'

Håkan looked up at the girl and thought for a dreadful moment he, or his Ka – whatever that was – might burst into tears.

'It's good for us to be together. We are never really separate, any of us. But we all forget. Katesch tells me that we are each like a jewel on a

necklace spread through time, divided and united at one and the same moment. Our work is one but the place of the work each of us must do is wherever we find ourselves.'

'Who is Kat Esh?' asked Håkan, inwardly forming his thoughts as clearly as he could.

'Katesh?' said the tall girl. *'She is the leader of our priestesses. She is our teacher. But High Born Son, we have work to do. Soon you will have to return and there is something I must show you.'*

She indicated he should close his eyes. Håkan did so and found, bizarrely, he could still see the wall in front of him. He now realised it had the picture of a man with the head of a dog or wolf. In one hand he held a staff and in the other a cross with a loop at the top. Then in less time than it takes for a thought to cross the mind, Håkan was walking behind a large dog, or perhaps a small wolf, through snow-laden trees.

The path had fresh snow which reflected the moonlight and was crossed with soft shadows in deep blue from the birch trees that bounded it. Håkan could feel the fresh coolness of the snow under his bare feet. The wolf led him on until the point where the path descended towards an opening in the forest. Here it sat and turned its moonlit eyes towards him. Håkan felt an intelligence behind those eyes that went far beyond any of his father's dogs. He knew the wolf wished him to proceed carefully down towards the clearing. He took a few paces on his own and turned back to see if the wolf would follow. It had gone. The snow under the trees and on the pathway had no tracks. None at all. Neither his feet nor the wolf's had left any mark. But looking back in this way he recognised where he was.

'Just watch. Just see. Don't do anything more.' Shoshan's voice sounded clearly inside him as though she stood at his elbow. He walked carefully down the slope towards where the trees thinned out and he could observe the whole of the Judge Circle. He discovered others were by the circle as well.

Three men sat on horseback; one Håkan could easily recognise as he knew the horse. Kaleb Pettersson wore his high plumed hat and had gathered a dark-red cloak about his shoulders. The other two riders faced away from Håkan towards the circle. The smaller of these held a chicken upside down, by its bound feet. Footprints extended all over the inner part of the circle. Someone had used thick cord to tether a goat at the far side of the stones. It started bleating and struggled to get free. The horses startled and the boy with the chicken pulled hard on his reins to bring his steed under control.

Klas, thought Håkan, and his father Valde the apothecary. What on earth are they doing on our land at dead of night?

Torches, held by the two older men, burned with a flickering light that proved hardly necessary given the moon and the clear sky. Pettersson held his torch up high and looked towards where Håkan stood in the shadow of several trees. Håkan pressed himself against the chilly bark of a tall birch tree. The three men stared in his direction.

"It's nothing. Just an owl," said Pettersson. "Let's get on with it. We know tonight is perfect for the sealing. You have your knife, boy?" This last question was directed at Klas.

He grunted. The blade flashed in the moonlight. Klas Löfgren eased his horse into the circle. The chicken struggled. When he had the horse near the centre he raised the knife and the chicken.

"Make the blow clean and then—"

"I know," said the boy, "splash blood on each of the stones."

Håkan closed his eyes. He'd seen many chickens killed and twisted the necks of several himself. All boys raised on farms did that. But this killing nauseated him.

'Open your eyes.'

He did so and looked up at Shoshan.

'Now you see what's happening,' said the young priestess with words that floated into his mind.

He nodded.

'This is a sacred circle and they are desecrating it. It must be purified. There is one close to you who knows how and it must be done tomorrow. Look again.'

He did, and from somewhere high above the circle he could see three figures riding fast towards the bridge back to town. In his nostrils he sensed the smell of rotting flesh.

'But how—'

Shoshan had removed her hand from his shoulder and the words echoed around his own mind. He opened his eyes once more and could see the quivering flame of the small night-light in his own bedroom. He'd been dreaming and already the dream had started to slip from his grasp. He needed to pee and reached out for the pot by the bed.

'Don't forget!'

A voice – a girl's firm voice – sounded in the room. Håkan nearly wet himself. He searched the shadows. Lennart's bed lay flat and empty. No one was in the room except for Charcoal, and he doubted the sleeping cat had spoken to him. Then with puke threatening to erupt from inside him he remembered. Everything.

He got down on his knees and prayed. The devil had clearly been at work. Either here or at the Judge Circle. He would check in the morning and decide what to do.

A Rare Gift

Gregor led out the two horses with embroidered blankets and light saddles.

"Are you sure you don't wish me to accompany you, Mistress Signy? In this snow we could take the sleigh."

"No, thank you, Gregor. Håkan and I will go with our dear friend Paracelsus. He's interested in seeing Torsberg and our Judge Circle."

Gregor dropped his eyes and nodded. He sniffed and then searched the sky. The clouds, a mottled panoply of pale greys, pressed down on them.

"Could turn nasty if the wind gets up as well. Will you be warm enough?"

This last question came Håkan's way.

"This coat keeps out all the cold, thank you, Gregor," Håkan responded. "And we won't be that long."

Gregor nodded again, offered a salute and went back into the stables.

As Signy ducked under the courtyard arch she murmured, "He didn't believe us, but there it is. Gregor is totally trustworthy, a virtue I'm not sure is shared by Inge."

Håkan had seen Inge peeking through a crack made by the partially open kitchen door. He smiled at his mother.

"If she knew the full story I doubt she would stay for a minute longer. It is beyond belief, truly, and strange indeed that Paracelsus is with us at this time."

That morning, after they had broken their fast, Håkan said he must talk with his mother. She had insisted they did so in the dispensary, where the herbs were prepared. She had work she must complete. When Håkan arrived he found the big German sitting there, well wrapped against the cold.

"I want our friend to hear what you have to say, Håkan."

"But—"

"He will be able to help," said his mother, in a tone of finality.

After a few stumbling starts, Håkan described his dream from the night before. He started with following the wolf to the circle, but when questioned further he admitted the vision of the strange young priestess and the stone chair. The two adults listened in complete silence, punctuated with some short questions. They made no comment until Håkan had finished.

Signy stood up, walked the length of the room and then back again. She looked at their guest.

"It's as I thought. The time has come, though quite what we're to do I am not sure."

Paracelsus pointed his finger at Håkan.

"You have a rare gift, boy. The power to see as you see is vanishing. I have the gift in my own way as does your mother, but to travel as you have..." He stuck out his lower lip and sighed. "To travel like that..."

"Well, that is your Sami blood, I think, Håkan," said his mother, finishing Paracelsus's sentence. "And it ties in with the drum picture I received at your birth. I showed that to our friend last night. And now you tell us our beautiful Circle is spoiled and must be put right."

They'd decided they should leave as soon as they were able. Paracelsus had to ride to town and said he would meet them at the bridge two hours beyond noon. Normally the town's church bells carried as far as the farmstead, but with the wind from the west they had estimated the time and hoped the German would not have been waiting too long.

He waved when they came in sight. As they drew close Håkan noticed Paracelsus wore his sword once more. He had saddlebags just like Signy. Both contained substances to purify the Circle, Håkan assumed. A sled was attached to his horse by two strong cords; it had a stack of neatly chopped firewood bound to it, sprinkled with a light frosting of snow.

"You ride well, boy," said the German, drawing alongside Håkan.

"I've ridden since I was a sprat," said Håkan. "Just wait a moment. Wait here, please."

He cantered ahead for some distance along the path and then turned his horse. He knew his pride had taken hold but he went ahead anyway. Keeping it at a steady trot, he eased his feet out of his stirrups, and taking a firm hold of the front edge of the leather saddle, tipped his head and torso forward at the same time as he raised his legs. Moments later he rode past his mother and Paracelsus doing a handstand on the top of the horse.

Håkan jumped down, never letting go of the saddle and jumped back again, riding up to his audience and struggling not to grin.

"A tumbler? That's quite a trick, lad. There's many a Cossack on the Russian plains who would be happy to be able to do that!"

"Håkan's been impossible since we had a group of travelling entertainers come and stay. They also had arcane knowledge of healing and I made them welcome. They rewarded me by turning my son into a village square juggler."

Paracelsus raised both arms above his head.

"Bravo. Bravo. It takes courage to do what you have done, boy, and you've been given an angel's gift, I think, when it comes to the juggler's art. Your mother says you play the pipes as well."

"I do," said Håkan.

"Well I hope you have brought them with you. Music through a wind instrument has a powerful effect on the bogles and sprites we'll be up against."

"We are lucky you were here, Paracelsus."

"Luck is never part of it when the wicked practitioners of the dark and forbidden arts are abroad. Too many folk doubt the reality of what they do and think a few bells and holy water will do the trick. But they're dangerously naïve. They think they know it all with their psalters and shaved pates. But they know nothing of those who dwell invisibly and balefully. I do. And we will open once more this sacred gate, or my visit has been in vain."

They took a longer route than normal towards the stone circle, to prevent the sled with its cargo of chopped timber from becoming snagged. Signy led the way and Håkan came last, taking care to avoid his dark-brown horse putting one of its white-socked forelegs on the wood. Paracelsus held up his arm and called, "Mistress Signy." Håkan's mother stopped and turned. The German beckoned to Håkan, who came up alongside.

"Do you feel that?" he asked.

A Gateway to Hell

Håkan could feel the cold and the slight chill of the breeze on his cheeks. His ears, encased by the woollen flaps of his hat, picked up nothing out of the ordinary. Paracelsus kept looking at him. Håkan looked through the trees in the direction of the Judge Circle. A dank, dark void pressed in on his chest. Fear, unbidden, rippled through his limbs. The surrounding trees and the other two riders were close by and far away all at the same time. Despair, doubt and great tiredness crept over him.

"Yes," said Paracelsus, "that is it. Now you must banish this foul river of devil's bile. For we must draw closer but not become submerged into what's been invited here."

He leant over and grasped Håkan's shoulder with his gloved hand.

"Always remember you have your own angel wherever you go. That angel and all it rules is your certain protection at times like this. It is a flame of the Fire of God and an Eternal Benediction of the living Christ. Call on it within and it will choose to be with you. You cannot command your angel but when freely invited it will choose to guide and protect. Just will it from the purity of your own blessed soul and it will make its presence known. For no prayer goes unanswered. Ever."

Håkan had never heard of his own angel before and looked towards his mother. She sat motionless on her grey mare, her lips moving silently. Håkan spoke in words of silence as best he could to his feathered friend. A wind passed through the branches above their heads and a spattering of snow fell around them. The tight band that had constricted his chest eased and the feeling that he'd gone far away and couldn't breathe gradually dissipated.

"Look." The German doctor pointed upwards. "Can you see?"

Håkan raised his eyes. The bare snow-topped limbs of the

birch trees spread like branching rivers of wood against the dull glow of the sky. The marbled clouds, drab and snow-heavy, formed a motionless canopy high above. But beneath these clouds and within the confines of the spidering twigs of the trees, something danced. When he looked, nothing showed itself. But when he didn't look, Håkan saw, or felt he saw, movement, as though a greater intensity of air formed itself and swirled about them. This intensity had the playfulness of a squirrel combined with the insubstantiality of steam as it vanishes into the air around it.

"The air's alive."

"Yes, boy. That is so. And at one time all knew it, all country folk could see it. But now the doctors in their universities, taking their fat rewards and sitting on their fat … sorry, Mistress Signy. Now the doctors deny the reality of the sylphs of the air. But when we three call on our angels the sylphs dance and sing and cavort, for it is their pleasure also to be wafted by an angel's wings. And today we must invite the sylphs, the flaming spirits of the fire, the glittering denizens of the earth and the flowing undines of the water, to work with us in driving out this abomination invited last night by your Swedish neighbours. And you will be the leader of the sylphs, Håkan, when you encircle thrice the stones and charm them with your pipes."

At that he clicked his tongue and his horse started forward. A few moments later they could see Torsberg rising above the trees. They approached the stone circle from the southern end furthest from the farmstead. Paracelsus said, "Wait" and released the cords holding the sled of wood. He rode slowly forward. Some fifteen paces from the stones, his horse reached where Håkan had seen the three riders in his nighttime vision. Paracelsus unsheathed his sword and held it by the blade, the handle and handle-guard forming a cross. He lifted it high above his head and rode in a slow circle before returning to his companions.

"It is worse than I thought." He hawked and spat. "The one

who wove this spell, who invited the dire and the dreadful into this sacred confine knew what he was about."

At that point his horse passed wind.

Paracelsus grinned. "Exactly, Thomas, exactly. You always doubt the power of evil and so do I. The devil and all his works meets his match when he meets Bombast Theophrastus Paracelsus! Right. We must make a start. Watch without watching, Håkan. You may see or know things that are and are not at the same time. To believe them is to give them power and it is power they will take in less time than it takes to sneeze. But watch sideways and learn. The forces we will banish from here are but delusions who think they are real, conjured from the absolute nothingness of darkness and folly. We're more than a match and we'll start with you. Dismount and take to your pipes, young sirrah! But first we must protect ourselves with the salamanders of fire."

Paracelsus kept talking as they prepared a fire about twenty paces from where the circle started. Having cleared the soft snow with cut branches from a nearby bush and used their gloved hands to scrape the icy remnants from the tufts of grass, they placed logs in a triangle and used the space between for the kindling that Signy produced from one of her saddlebags. When prepared, Paracelsus stood facing the fire and the gaunt hill beyond the circle and opened his tinderbox. As he sought to get a spark it span out of his hands and tumbled into the snow. A twitch of fear travelled across his face. He stooped to pick up the box and gather its contents.

"It's all right, my friend," said Signy, "I also brought a tinderbox." She collected it from the same saddlebag that held the kindling and passed it to the German doctor.

"I'll take off my gloves this time," he said, "and not underestimate the sorcery that's been done here."

Moments later the fire surged up and he added more kindling. In a few minutes flames flickered and roared as the dry wood caught and burned bright. A spot of cold snow settled on Håkan's cheeks.

"We must make speed," said Signy, looking up at the sky. A few wisps of snow drifted downwards like orphans from the clouds above.

Paracelsus directed them to make a second fire ten paces to the right of the first, in order to melt snow in a pot that Signy had brought for the purpose. To this she added small pinches of crushed herbs. Paracelsus walked over to this bubbling brew, but his back masked what he did next. Håkan looked over to the Judge Circle. Dark stains dribbled down the purity of the stones. Blood spots lay like old wounds on the scuffed and trampled snow inside. Something lay at the foot of the stone nearest Torsberg. Håkan struggled to see what it was. Surely not an animal hidden beneath the snow, its head just… Then the dark dreadfulness oppressed his chest once again. A band tightened all around him and he found breath hard to come by. The stones of the circle had become as the teeth of a giant maw. A gateway to hell itself. Light disappeared into this abysmal hole and eyes watched Håkan, unblinking. On the rock closest to him, shimmering malevolently, sat a silvery polecat. Its size kept changing and its form rippled.

From far, far away a thought pushed into the last dry corner of his conscious mind as he sank into the cold, dark waters of a freezing bog. "Watch sideways, High-Born Son, watch sideways."

He gasped a breath. In the darkness swirling within the tooth-like rocks, a deeper darkness formed itself into a massive dog, a hellhound of dread and doom. Its eyes, dull red emanations of chilling fire, sought to find him and freeze him.

A thought settled in his mind like one of the wisps of snow; the thought of his angel. He let it spread through his mind. Great wings unfurled around him. With a howl fit to crack a mountain in two, the growling dog withdrew to the far edge of the circle.

The silvery cat washed itself and winked at him.

Something sputtered nearby.

"There," said the German. "That will help."

Steam rose from the pot, and a fragrance reached Håkan, so pure, so tender, and so sublime it might not be of this world.

"Come. Inhale," said Paracelsus. "This will help and protect."

And so it did. When Håkan next looked at the circle of stones they had lost the appearance of an ancient curse. The blood and severed goat's head still desecrated the space, but the constricting darkness had lifted, at least a bit.

Watch sideways.

Håkan took up his pipes and blew to fill up the cloth bag. The drone sounded its buzzing note and with the pipes Håkan picked out a simple melody of light and laughter. His feet carried him without effort around the stone circle once, then twice, then thrice. Something in the aroma made by his mother and the strange doctor had certainly helped. When he completed the third circuit he glanced towards the top of Torsberg. There, next to the hammerhead rock, sat a wolf silhouetted against the sky. Håkan turned to his mother and Paracelsus.

"Look."

They looked at him.

"No. On the hill top."

But it had gone.

"That was just for you," said his mother, when Håkan told them of the wolf.

Paracelsus collected ash from the fire in a separate pot, and holding it carefully in cupped gloved hands entered the circle. He muttered Latin words that Håkan could not make out clearly. At each quarter of the circle the doctor stopped and traced out a simple device in the snow, by pouring hot ashes. At the northern end he picked up and threw out the head of the poor goat. When he returned to the south he put down the pot as though it held precious and delicate treasure rather than smouldering ashes. He drew his sword and walked three decisive paces towards the centre of the circle. He plunged the sword, using both hands on the hilt, deep into the snow and soil beneath. Then, standing to one side, he unscrewed the pommel of the sword and walked slowly, with head bowed, to the centre of the circle. Once there he shook the pommel three times each, in three directions. A drop of some liquid flashed as it curved towards the snow. For a brief moment sunlight broke through the clouds and the snow-blessed top of Torsberg glittered with light.

Paracelsus left the Judge Circle with his sword and carefully screwed back the pommel.

"It is done."

"It certainly is," said Signy. "Just look."

Snow had started to fall heavily, quickly obliterating the footprints within and around the standing stones. Right in the middle of the circle stood a boy, dressed in a short tunic and wearing light sandals that strapped up his calves. He stared at them and swung round, taking a pace behind him. He stopped, rubbed his eyes, looked up and slowly turned back to face them.

Soup in the Sleeping Room

I couldn't stop shivering. The great chunk of hollowed-out bread, served with a thick, hot stew, had helped but hadn't fully done the trick. In truth, what had happened when I went into the bathroom expecting to be sick had scared me nearly witless. One moment I was about to throw up and the next I was standing in snow, surrounded by dark-grey obelisks of stone with three strangers staring at me from beyond a fire.

I tore off more of the bread, dipped it into the dark-brown soup and fished out a chunk of carrot. It tasted wonderful. Opposite me, in the sleeping room with wooden walls lit only by candles, sat the boy who apparently had been named Horken. He didn't smile much and watched me steadily, with his pale-blue eyes tracking every shaky movement of my hand. Like me, he had a chunky woollen blanket around his shoulders and sat on a bed covered with a fleece from more than one sheep, sewn together, that still retained its sheepish smell. The plank of plane wood on my legs, now thankfully encased in woollen trousers, quivered as my legs continued to move of their own accord.

I think Horken, and his mother Signy and the big German doctor, had been as frightened to see me standing there like a fairy without wings as I'd been to see them. Horken shouted something in a strange language that ceased to be strange when I realised he spoke Swedish, albeit with a really thick accent. Swedish and Norwegian are close enough languages for me to understand any Swedes I meet, and I once spent a long summer holiday in Sweden with friends of my mother. I pick up languages quickly.

"He may be a trowel!" I thought Horken shouted.

"Are you a trail?" said his mother, as the big German lifted up his sword by the blade, so the top formed a cross. As I was neither a trowel nor a trail, nor a vampire, that had little effect beyond confusing me even further.

Then I got the word.

"No." I said in passable Swedish. "I am a boy. An English boy. I'm not a troll. I have just come from…" I stopped. I might do better passing for a troll than someone moving from one epoch to another, switching countries on the way. Mind you, how on earth can anyone explain suddenly turning up in the middle of a mini Stonehenge, wearing what looked like a dress?

Inexplicably, the big German, who introduced himself as Philippus Aureolus Theophrastus Bombastus von Hohenheim, said, "We were expecting you. Welcome!"

He kindly gave me his cloak to wrap myself in. From that point on, a combination of the snow, the sub-zero temperatures, the wind and the general sense of total unreality, led to me shivering so hard I couldn't get words out in gobbets of more than one syllable. The three of them had a hasty consultation, too quiet for me to hear, and invited me to mount a horse. The last time I'd ridden had been on the beach at Bognor. I stared at the stirrup as the horse cast a baleful eye in my direction and snorted its derision. The German's massive arms plucked me out of the snow and, bare legs on either side of the horse's neck, with him behind me, I started the brass-monkey route back to where this odd trio apparently lived.

With much whispering I had to follow Horken up to the bedroom he shared with someone called Lennart without meeting anyone else in the house. His mother Signy brought in the food. Of the German with the ridiculous long name there was no sign.

Horken moved back on his bed to rest against the wooden wall. Dried flowers were tied to each of the bedposts and their pleasant fragrance did something to counter the sheep-dip nature of the room.

"So…" he said.

I took a breath and welcomed the brief interlude between

bouts of shivering. He continued to stare.

"So," he said once more, "how come this time you stayed when the other times you vanished?"

I set the plank of wood that served as a tray to one side on the bed, and also moved back to give myself the support of the wall. Finally warmth had started to return to my limbs.

"I don't know," I said in Swedish.

I wish I did. This is all very confusing. I guess this boy is one of the Seeds of Life, but he doesn't seem friendly – not in the way Shoshan and Dimitris were friendly.

His eyes had grown so large I thought he might be turning into an animé cartoon. He bit his lip.

I wonder if he can hear me?

He nodded slowly.

"Holy Mother of God!" he said. "Jesus and all his saints. Yes, I can hear you."

His hand reached inside his jerkin and he pulled out a small cross that hung by a leather thong around his neck.

"This is devil's work."

"No." I said out loud. "No it isn't. It's just that we've forgotten how to use this skill. I think our ability to hear each other's ideas may actually be really, really important."

Horken stood up, walked over to a small table and poured himself a drink from the jug Signy had put there.

"Do you want some small beer, Rhory?" he asked. For the first time he didn't sound antagonistic. I nodded. In Sweden and Norway small beer means weak beer. Even Dad allowed me small beer when we were in restaurants in Norway.

"I've had very strange dreams," he said, "and seen some pretty strange things. Even here. Right in my sleeping chamber. I also met someone. I met a … a girl. I think a girl or maybe an angel…"

Shoshan.

"Yes." He said out loud. And then inwardly, *'The Blue Lotus girl.'*

"I met her too. Shoshan. It means…" I couldn't think of the word in Norwegian. "It means Lily."

"Lotus," he responded.

"Hm, yes, Lotus. That's right."

"I saw her in some strange hallway, far, far away. With a great big stone chair. And when I sat in that chair I had a vision."

Sipping the beer and then helping ourselves to some more, we recounted our tales. I spoke about the image of the god Anubis appearing in my bedroom at night and meetings with druids and Pythagoras and Dimitris. I described, as best I could, the clash at the evil temple and how I'd got in the way of the redheaded priestess. Horken's mouth dropped open at that.

"We are working against some really bad people," he said. "Mother says the folk she comes from, the Sami, have tales about a war in heaven. She thinks we're fighting on one side in that war."

I nodded. Frankly, it felt like a war on earth that Horken and I were caught up in.

"It's certainly something like that," I said.

"So you have moved backwards, you have come from … from a place that doesn't yet exist?"

I rubbed my chin and made what Juliette calls my 'monkey face'.

"Well, it's complex. Actually this time I've just come from North Africa and I think I'm meant to take you there."

The door opened without ceremony. The big German, apparently called Paracelsus by his friends, stood there with Horken's mother Signy.

"Things are moving faster than expected. We must return to the Judge Circle at first light. A prophecy must be fulfilled for all our sakes. Then you'll head north."

"Why?" said Horken.

"Because," said his mother, "Pettersson plans to have us

arrested for fomenting rebellion. He's the magistrate and will come tomorrow evening when the Danish soldiers have returned."

We Enter the Circle

Håkan beckoned me over to the window. Icy air poured over us as we looked out through a gap in the shutters. Weak moonlight gave some illumination and a lone dog barked a few times. In front of the house a tree-lined pathway meandered towards the lane that led, according to Håkan, to the nearby town. I'd become used to eau-de-sheep-skin, but being this close to Håkan reminded me that people in the Middle Ages didn't wash that regularly.

The previous night I'd found out the date. We were slap bang in the middle of Henry VIII's reign, if we were in England. Here, a cruel Catholic king ruled from Denmark, even though followers of Luther grew stronger in Sweden every day. That was why Lennart and Håkan's father were not at home. People like them were organising in the south of the country. They wanted Swedish independence. Not surprising really. Håkan asked me if Sweden succeeded. He couldn't understand when I said I'd no idea, but they must have succeeded some time, as Sweden was 'now' Lutheran.

Håkan could write. He showed me how to spell his name with a tiny 'o' on top of the first 'a'. I wrote my name for him and explained I might be distantly descended from a Scottish king. Not so distant for him, of course. He smiled, more or less, and nodded.

Dark, bulky shapes glided in front of the house. A figure on a horse led other horses and two silent carts, which floated over the snow.

"We have two sleighs. Gregor is getting ready."

"For what?" We were both whispering.

Håkan looked at me.

"I'll explain later. Too dangerous just now. We don't trust the housemaid. She has ears like a cat."

"Oh," I said, trying to picture their feline maid, until I understood. "Oh right."

A few minutes after Håkan's mother, Signy, knocked at the door and let herself in. She had a pile of clothes. Moments later she returned with a tray with beer and pickled fish, some cheese and tough white bread. Breakfast Swedish-style, circa the 16th century.

"You'll need to dress warm, Rhory," she whispered, and slipped out again. The door squeaked closed.

Håkan grimaced and said, "Eat well. We may not get another meal for a bit."

After washing down pickled fish and cheese with weak beer, I studied the clothes. I'd never seen anything like them. Håkan showed me how I would have to put on the leggings first. They had buttons front and back.

"In this cold you don't want too much exposure." Håkan grinned.

Over these went pantaloon thingies of thick corded material, held by a broad leather belt. I had two pairs of socks to put on and a leather jerkin to go over the top of several shirts and a woollen sleeveless pullover. The hat, with patterns woven in, fitted my head and snuggled over my ears. I thought that I might finally get to feel warm. Lennart's boots became quite snug with an extra pair of socks. By the time I'd dressed I realised Mother Nature required I take swift action. Once in the freezing cold privy – too disgusting to describe in detail – I gave thanks for the back flap on my long underwear. The icicles on the door of the loo indicated it had no heating beyond my breath that hung around for ages.

The stable boy had two horses ready when we slipped out of the front door. Paracelsus sat on one and Håkan and I climbed on the other.

"Thank you, Ralf. See you tonight," said Håkan in a loud voice.

I looked around in alarm. Up to that point everything had been whispers. At the top of the house something pale caught the moonlight. A face looking down on us from a window.

Once well beyond earshot of the house, Håkan explained that Ralf could be trusted but lying wasn't something he did well. Håkan's words had been for the benefit of other ears.

"Cat woman?" I asked.

"What?"

"The maid."

"Yes her. Inge," said Håkan. "We'll not go back to the house again now, not for…" He trailed off, and shrugged.

"I see," I said, not seeing anything much. I didn't even know where we were riding.

We picked our way along a narrow track between tall trees with pale bark. The horses' hooves crackled on the ice. A little more snow had fallen as we slept. The slight pallor of dawn showed the trees with icing sugar on their branches.

At one point Paracelsus stopped us and dismounted to pick a few blood-red berries and slipped them into a little sack at his waist.

"Never eat those," he said to the forest in general and us in particular.

Moments later the crag of a low hill showed above the trees and we came out onto a field of pristine snow. The stone circle appeared innocent and pure.

"We will keep the horses here. The energy is only right at dawn for a venture like this. The horses could disrupt it. You will have to enter on your own, but together. You, the two of you, will be the key."

His German accent did not help. But he made about as much sense as a rap song that you can't quite hear. I'd no idea what he was burbling on about.

"Dismount," Paracelsus said, "and stand here."

He looked up at where a quarter moon hung pale and interesting just above the trees. A few brave stars still managed to shine as the sky turned from charcoal to grey. No clouds meant the frost had already given the snow a slight crust on the surface. Thankfully, no breeze sucked the little remaining heat from my extremities.

"The moment is just right. Look, the morning star." He pointed to the side of the hill with its brooding rocks. A single bright star shone to the right of the crag. Paracelsus pulled a piece of parchment from inside his bulky coat. He read something out loud. I didn't understand a word but guessed it might be Latin. I remembered too late to listen within and only caught the meaning "time is eternity flowing."

"I have a teacher," said the German. "He actually knows things worth learning. Not like the quacks at the universities. He is a true alchemist. Valentine. He foresaw this moment and told me I should come here. I've had confirmation from, well from…" He spread his hands around as though the woodlands that surrounded us were full of teachers. As he did so I'd a sense of a small face watching on the far side of the stone circle. Shivers went up my spine, this time not from cold.

"You must enter the circle together. You must take a gem of value to heart and spirit. That is the key to your return. Look. Learn. Much depends on you both. All the signs suggest that. All."

We nodded. I didn't like the idea that anything too much depended on me. But if all we had to do involved going between a few stones and coping with fairy folk peeking at us, then let's go for it.

Paracelsus shook something out of a small leather pouch onto his gloved hand. He handed me a small brooch, set with a green stone. Håkan received a ring.

"This is my mother's."

"Yes, they both are. She treasures them as heirlooms. It is that treasuring that'll bring you back safely."

My heart started to thump. Where were we going? Only into a set of old stones. Why the big deal?

"Now," said Paracelsus. "You need this now." He'd undone the pommel from his sword. The pommel I recognised. The pommel from the Time Sphere that should be with Natasha. He removed his glove and shook a bright drop of liquid onto his thumb tip. It glowed in the morning light, catching moonbeams or something.

"Aqua Vitae. The alchemist's greatest treasure."

He muttered more Latin as he pressed his thumb tip on my forehead. The liquid should have felt icy in the sub-zero temperature, but it spread a warmth all across the front of my head. The trees glowed with a vibrant flickering luminosity. The stones had increased in weight, as though they held the knowledge of the whole world in their crystal depths. Håkan and I moved forward together. Within the circle the snow glistened, a pool of purity stained with dark shadows. As we passed between two of the biggest stones, everything reversed. The glowing white turned to darkness, the stones glowed and flared, and the trees vanished. A silent whispering crowded in on me. The ground fell away into an inky nothingness.

The Tower of Time

Håkan's story

Håkan stumbled. The light had been sucked away and his eyes hadn't adjusted. He didn't feel snow beneath his fur-lined boots but something hard. He closed his eyes, so they could adjust to the gloom. He took a few deep breaths to calm his racing heart.

To his left a huge curving wall extended as far as he could see. It had no top. It had no beginning, just extending downwards into a perpetual gloom. He closed his eyes and opened them again. The sticky liquid Paracelsus had put on his brow tickled and prickled. It sparkled. To his right the English boy clung to a railing that ran as far as the eye could see, just preventing them both from toppling into the yawning abyss at their feet.

Of the Judge Stones nothing remained. Håkan now stood on a walkway that extended in a huge circle: a curving path that would take at least an hour to complete. The walkway would allow two people to move abreast. It appeared to be made of silver and glowed slightly, catching its light from within the glassy wall that rose above their heads and fell endlessly beneath their feet. He closed his eyes again and caught his breath. His left hand hurt, it gripped the railing so hard. Once more he looked and made out filaments of illumination, with their roots far below him, extending unbroken up parts of the wall like vines. Nearby, rivulets of deeper darkness ascended in contrast like creepers. These were thicker and stronger than the strands of brightness but never completely overpowered them.

Leaving Rhory, Håkan moved to the left. Movement within the wall drew his attention. The glassy surface proved partially transparent in places. He could see as though looking through clear ice on a lake, only here the icy walls were vertical. He touched the surface, causing ripples to radiate slowly in the wall.

Where his glove contacted the transparency increased.

Beyond, or within this fluid wall, a woman sat alone on a horse. At first she remained static, like an illuminated picture of a saint, pausing on the lane that connected their farmstead to the town. He took a breath and rested both hands on the wall. Light and form crystallised into his mother, riding; she reined in her horse and looked in his direction, a puzzled expression crossing her face. On either side of the horse were two panniers. She shook her head as though to clear it of something and crossed herself. Twitching the reins she rode on faster and did not look across again.

Sadness swept through Håkan, and he grasped her ring tighter in his right hand and murmured a quick prayer. He turned back and could see no sign of Rhory.

Walking swiftly he found where they'd entered this strange realm. He peered into the faint glow at the shapes beyond the wall. Several black stones stood as sentinels and he could just make out the two horses beyond the icy wall. He nearly pushed through, knowing that if he did so he would be back with Paracelsus but unable to return to this space, whatever it was.

He continued to his right and searched for where the English boy had gone. A sound pulled his attention upwards. Walkways extended in circles high above his head, as far as his eyes could see. The vast chimney in which he stood did not ascend vertically, but gradually curved so he couldn't see to the very top. He couldn't make out Rhory, but he thought he heard a sound. He tried to shout, but his voice immediately vanished. He pressed ahead and came to a narrow stairway going up. To its left the walkway continued so one person could progress. The stair had a high gate in front of it, and unclimbable silvery railings. The gate, ornate and solid, had a large lock and he couldn't get it to budge. It looked like Rhory couldn't have gone by this route.

A little way beyond the stairway he found a ladder that he could climb down. He had to place his feet with care on the rungs. The next circle down also reached the full circumference of the vast chimney with its liquid walls. Everywhere he stopped he could see activity within the glassy depths. People getting on with their lives; armies marching; families going to church. He recognised one place as Gamla Stan in Stockholm, where the royal palace stood. A bishop led a procession with a flower-festooned statue of Mary, surrounded by priests and choirboys swinging censers.

He walked on more quickly. Images flickered past. Ships at sea; great cities thronged with people; battles raging with men on horseback and soldiers with long pikes. Something pulled him forward. He wanted to get to the beginning. Where did this place start? Stairways and ladders appeared with greater frequency and he descended fast. In fact he hardly had to move his legs, just to think clearly about going down and he would be much deeper and further away from where he could re-enter the stone circle.

Håkan stopped. Someone had spoken. A voice loud within him and silent without. A woman's voice, full of resonance and kindness.

'Look now,' said the voice.

He did. He was standing by a filament of bright glass that had its origin far below him and stretched in a branching shape high above. He could see a bustling city lit by a brighter sun than Sweden ever managed. Tall thin trees of amazing height lined wide boulevards. Huge houses or palaces with columns and red-tiled roofs sat alongside squares bathed in sharp sunlight. Soldiers moved in squads, wearing helms that caught the sun and shone like gold, slashed with bright red plumes. Beyond the thriving buzz of the city the sea glittered with sunlight flashing from countless wavelets. Ships with brightly coloured striped sails moved into the several harbours. Some craft, with oars moving like the legs of a vast insect, pulled away from the city.

On an isle close to the harbour wall stood an impressive palace, its roof dazzling red in the sunlight. As Håkan studied the building he drew closer. He didn't move from the walkway, but his interest pulled the building closer to his vision. A woman stood at the gate to this palace. She wore long flowing light robes that moved gently in the breeze. He'd never seen clothes like this, so light and graceful. The woman carried something in her hand. A tube of wood, bound with a ribbon. She opened the tube and drew out a scroll which she unrolled a little way and read. Now Håkan approached so close he could see her face. Her hair, held by combs and pins of tortoiseshell, was a lustrous brown; her eyes looked towards him and she had such dignity and grace Håkan felt tears forcing their way to his eyes. He knew her in some way he couldn't explain.

'We will be reunited soon,' she said. *'In Alexandria.'*

If he pressed through he'd be standing with her on the steps. But she turned away abruptly, and in a flicker of an eyelash he could see the whole city once more. The palace, set on an isle in the harbour, became barely discernible.

'Come,' said a different woman's voice. *'Descend a little more and we can meet. There is something you must see.'*

The Mirror

Rhory's story

The tall grey stones faded and expanded. Of the trees I could see nothing. We were standing on a kind of platform within a huge tube of glassy rock of enormous proportions. I reached out to grab the railing in front of me, to avoid toppling right over, and promptly released the brooch into the void. For a moment it caught some light, flashing before it vanished. Sheer panic swept through me. My only way to get back to the real world had fallen into some bottomless pit. I wanted to puke. I tried to speak to Håkan but words wouldn't form. He stood with his eyes closed. I had to descend and at least try to get hold of the precious stone that would allow me out of this place, whatever it was.

I stumbled off to my right, leaving Håkan standing stock-still. I kept the awful void on my left as far away as I could. My right hand, thickly gloved, slid along the glassy smoothness of the wall. An arc of light ran just in front of me; where I touched the wall a glowing ripple ran ahead. I stopped and studied the surface of the glassy barrier that surrounded me. I could pick out blurred shapes on the far side. At first I could make no sense of what I could see; it looked like a photo badly out of focus, studied through distorting glass. But as I watched, the shapes resolved and sharpened.

A road, snow-covered and tree-lined, gradually appeared. Still at first and then with movement, a troop of soldiers emerged. They carried a red pennant with a white cross. The man leading them held up his hand. He cocked his head to one side as though listening. He drew closer, moving without actually moving, and I could make out his face. He wore a helm that reflected the dull light. His horse, a dappled grey colour, tossed its head and he leant forward and whispered something to it. A soldier riding slightly behind him spoke but he shook his head and made a dismissive gesture with his hand. If I didn't know that Lucian remained in Hammerford in some other fork in time and history, I'd have sworn he led a troop of horse on this snow-swept road, somewhere nearby. But I'd seen this blond-haired officer before; he'd confronted me in the dark vision brought on by the Ouija board.

His eyes searched for mine once again. I pulled away and the scene faded into greyness as the glassy wall became opaque.

I pressed on and found a stairway going up. That wouldn't work. Some metres further on a stairway descended. I went down two steps at a time. Panic threatened to overwhelm me every moment that I glanced down into the void. I stopped when I reached the bottom of the stairs, dizzy and nauseous.

I'd no idea what realm I'd entered by coming into this stone circle. By descending I moved in time in some way. Had the brooch dropped down to the beginning of time? Would I find Eve puzzling over it in some overgrown but rather lovely garden? I didn't feel the least like giggling but I could see the ridiculousness of walking back to the beginning of time. I needed some guidance. I turned my attention inside and listened. I needed assistance. *'Help me.'* The words clarified inside me. *'I think I'm lost.'*

'Not really,' said a voice distant and yet clear inside my mind at the same time. Not my voice. The voice of a woman. I half recognised it.

'Nothing in the tree of time occurs by chance. Look carefully around you. Follow your heart. Be cautious. We'll meet soon if we can.'

A deep silence welled up inside me, comforting and lonely. I knew I wouldn't hear the voice again, not until I'd looked as she suggested. The wall at the base of the stairs I'd descended glowed red, the warm colour of a setting sun. I pressed my hands against the wall. At first I could only sense the reddish glow. Gradually, the walls of a wide room appeared, extending out towards a balcony. A woman sat at the far end, her back towards me. She wore a white gown embroidered with pale gold fleur-de-lys. The setting sun gave her dark hair a reddish hue. Beyond her, the turquoise of the sea echoed the blue-green of the sky at dusk. The woman half-turned her head as though she sensed my presence. She held something on her lap.

I pulled off my thick gloves and stuffed them into the inside of my jacket. Feeling a little bit like the roly-poly Michelin Man, I entered the room. I knew the woman connected in some way to ancient Egypt and I found myself near her without my legs really moving. Her hair hid her face and she held something in her right hand, close to her body. Her gold-coloured slippers peeked out beneath the folds of her gown.

At last, her voice sounded inside me. *'You are close.'*

Still she didn't raise her eyes.

'I've waited ages for this moment.'

I longed for her to look up. I remembered the love in the eyes of Shoshan's Egyptian teacher, the priestess Katesch. Something magnetic drew me closer. Now I felt—

'Here, boy, look!'

She held up the object in her right hand, still averting her face. It flashed in the sunlight, a bright slash of coppery light. She moved her hand so that I'd be able to see into its polished surface. A copper mirror. *What was it about a copper mirror? What had someone said?*

I looked, but the mirror shifted as she stood up. Even in that fraction of a moment, I sensed a shard of icy coldness, enough to freeze the hearts of all who loved me.

Aunt Bridget had told me not to look in the copper mirror. She'd said this in the hospital. I slashed my fist at the woman's wrist as she tried to grab at me with her left hand. Her face turned towards me as I struck the hand holding the mirror. The flashing copper span away into space, tumbling from the balcony. Her eyes, glinting daggers of pure hatred, were framed with red hair. *Emerald.* I recognised her at once. The bad priestess; the fat woman from the theatre in London.

But already she'd drifted far away. I stood back within the relative safety of the glassy walls.

Next to me stood a woman I could trust.

'Welcome once again, Red King.'

The Heart of Time

A huge sense of relief flooded through me. *'Ha–si–na'*. I recognised the graceful and very tall woman who'd once been my guide across the Plain of Time. I'd only been able to actually see her when we were near to the early days of Ancient Egypt. I assumed that must be so now.

'Yes, Red King. You are right. We stand once more near the beginning of things, even as you, our sacred brother, stand near the end. Come, there is something you should now see.'

I followed her as we walked by the wall that gently glowed with a soothing light. I caught blurred shapes as we passed, of great courtyards of stone and a mighty river flanked by palm trees. She stopped and indicated to me an archway made of hieroglyphs that moved slightly as though the glassy wall here was alive. Within the boundary of the arch, the wall thinned to something as slight as one of Mum's silk scarves. The tall priestess held out her hand and together we passed through. The passageway we entered also shimmered and glistened like vibrant water. The floor, dark and soft, revealed nothing. Above my head glowed hundreds of five-pointed stars.

'We move in the sacred realm of the Goddess here, Red King. You've earned the right. For within time, whatever passes, however dire, however blessed, is embraced by the healing perfection of She who Watches All. It is truly said, All Will Be Well. But how that outcome will be reached and over how many aeons, that is the mystery of time.'

I loved the sound of her voice bubbling up through the ideas within my mind. She walked ahead of me, leading me with her hand. I wasn't at all sure what she meant. Sounded cool though.

We came out into a large circular space. Above us a dome extended, higher than the one in St Paul's in London, decorated with a painting of a woman who seemed to be dressed in stars and doing a handstand at the same time, except her feet were on the ground. Her body made a great hoop in the painted sky above us.

'We're in the Sanctuary of the Mother.' Hasina smiled at me.

I nodded, as I didn't know how to respond to that piece of info.

'The Mother is the Heart of Time.'

Hasina let go of my hand and I folded my arms. I hoped I wouldn't be tested on all she beamed into my mind, as I couldn't quite get the relevance. The priestess smiled.

'No, Red King. No examinations. Your big exam is your life. That is true for all of us.'

I'd forgotten my inner thoughts would be broadcast as though I shouted into a loud-speaker.

'Look around you.'

The chamber, with many archways, was made of the same glassy material as the huge tube we'd just left. It pulsed with soft light but I could make out no forms within or behind the semi-transparent walls. We'd entered through an archway that had different coloured columns on either side; or rather one column had been hewn from a dull black stone and the other from one that remained pure and pearly white. Each doorway into the chamber differed. One, red on both sides, seemed to flow like red wax as it melts down the side of a candle. It gave me the creeps, like the entrance to a particularly foul ghost train at the fun fair. Only with real ghosts. Far away from this arch stood another, where light played in the softest of hues. I couldn't even name the colours they were of such delicacy and beauty.

'Look up, Red King.'

I did as asked and found that the painted goddess who moments before had watched over us, and indeed the whole dome, had faded. We stood on a platform suspended between great Time Trees. They flowed with light, now dark, now bright, sometimes bruised with dull colours and sometimes radiant with joyful hues. Yet they weren't trees. They would join and then separate again above our heads, weaving around one another like a great plait. Some thick trunks would split and split again, only to come back close to one another and then re-join.

To one side with the arch of great beauty, the tree of light grew straight and unfolded into a blaze of coloured aromatic flowers. To the other, a misshapen ugly shape ended as though blasted by lightning. Yet from both, branches extended towards each other, joined and continued skywards.

In less than an eye-blink, the great twisting trunks vanished and the dome, with its long-legged goddess fresco, had returned.

The priestess looked over at me.

'No two people ever see the same, Red King. For time is a mystery and the way it unfolds is not for us mere mortals to fully comprehend.'

I gathered my thoughts as best I could.

'So what did I see then?'

'You saw how what is merely possible becomes actual.'

She pointed to the black and white archway through which we had passed.

'Here you see how the great act of betrayal, the murder of our most blessed Pharaoh and his wife by the priests of Set, has made a black stain that flows ever onwards towards the time of the Great Decision. Your time, Red King.'

I swallowed. I'd enough trouble deciding what game to buy to play on the family Xbox. A Great Decision sounded rather too difficult.

'The way time will flow is determined moment by moment by all our decisions. Yours, Shoshan's, Dimitris's, Håkan's and all of the Life Seeds. Time responds. Courage matters, and facing the Chaos released by the Servants of Set is something the Mother of us all requires.'

'Oh, so that's why it's okay for people to shoot at me when I climb trees?'

The priestess frowned slightly and then nodded a little.

'Come, my young friend, the hours pass even within the Chambers and Passageways of Time. There is something you must see before you

return.'

Once more, she took my hand, and we went through the archway with the black and white columns. The soft darkness embraced us. A familiarity returned. My time and my history is what it felt like.

'Younger brother, if I may call you that, this is where we must once more part. I cannot follow you where you now go. For this is a moment where your decision will be paramount and you must decide alone.'

I nodded. I felt a bit like those times at Scrivener's when we had exams in the hall, with all the desks set in rows, but I hadn't done any preparation.

She held out her hand. There, in her palm, lay the brooch given me by Håkan's mother. So I would be able to get back after all.

'Don't lose this. You may not be so lucky twice. Hold it, Red King, and ask to see the point of the Great Decision. After that you'll be able to return as though you'd taken no time at all.'

I took the brooch and clasped it tightly in my hand. She watched me, her eyes soft and deep and getting farther and farther away. I closed my eyes for a moment, wondering how to wish correctly. I wanted to get the words right. When I opened them Hasina had entirely vanished. I stood at the bottom of a tall ravine. Jagged rocks rose above my head up towards a cleft of blue sky. Trees clung to the rocks, but only just. The floor of the ravine, where I stood, had partly filled with rocks that had crashed down the steep sides. No way could I climb.

Ahead of me the ravine split into two. Each side had a pathway, rock-strewn and matted with spiky shrubs. Rocks, with smooth sides, stood at each entranceway. On one a huge white comma had been painted with a black dot in the centre. On the other a black comma held a white dot.

Time to decide. Apparently.

Return Home

I chose the white comma with the black dot – I think. It may have been the other way around because it all happened so fast. I went towards one, then switched to the other. I thought I would walk a few metres in and see what it looked like. "You take the high road and I'll take the low road..." as my dad likes to sing. One gets to Scotland quicker, the song said.

Anyway, I'd entered a few metres and looked behind me only to find solid rock. The gully now extended back the length of a football pitch. Carved stone steps mounted towards a blank cliff-face of rock. No point going back that way. I went forwards. As I did so darkness descended so suddenly I blundered about for a few moments while my eyes adjusted.

Streetlights cast a mournful glow on the grubby pavement. The low cloud cover, a murky grey, flared a jaundiced yellow as it caught the headlights of a distant car. A police vehicle or ambulance wailed its two-tone cry.

I recognised where I stood: I'd stumbled into North Street in Hammerford. Outside of several closed shops, black rubbish sacks lay like huge, sedentary slugs. Maybe the dustbin people were on strike? Most of the shops had metal shutters down, displaying crude graffiti. I couldn't remember any shops needing protection like this on our high street.

Two policemen walked steadily my way. They were chatting quietly to each other and headed straight at me. I pressed myself against a shop window, one that had no shutters. The officers passed by without a glance in my direction. One had a half-smoked cigarette in one hand. The other hadn't shaved for two days. Both carried machine guns. It was like being in France.

I looked up at the shop sign. It said Targett's. Inside the display area lay a selection of dusty bric-a-brac. I didn't remember an antique shop here. Across the other side, Howell's the Bakers stood where it should, though the woodwork looked in desperate need of paint. Next to Howell's should have been the newsagents where I picked up Dad's newspaper. Instead an illuminated sign, with garish red letters, said, 'Adults Only'. The shop window had curling magazines and strange candles.

A Monopoly set, caught in the yellow glow of the street lamp, lay next to old roller-skates in Targett's shop window. The man with the top hat and monocle stared at me. The extra details added to his hat, moustache and cane, had been made by Juliette when she was about ten years old. I also recognised the missing corner to the lid. Why on earth would this flea pit of a shop have our only Monopoly set?

I walked on down towards the Carfax, passing the cinema which, although open, didn't say what films they were offering this week; just three red 'Xs on the display board, the last one having slipped slightly as though it had lost the will to live.

The wailing of the car drew closer and flashing blue lights swept over all the graffiti on the shop fronts. It sped on up towards the station.

I stopped. It had to be early evening as the sky still had some light of its own, even with the dull grey cloud cover. But no one walked on the pavements. And the only car I'd seen belonged to police who fancied themselves as rally drivers. I turned into the Carfax, and headed towards where the Post Office should be. Two bus shelters, with all their glass smashed out, suggested buses mightn't be running. The shops in the inner road of the Carfax were also closed and shuttered. Light sneaked out from the corner of a window of a pub in the distance. Perhaps I could go there and ask what had happened.

I hardly noticed the person sitting on the steps of the closed chemist shop; I thought the crumpled shape was an old coat dumped there. The elderly man's head rested on his chest. He loosely grasped a half-drunk plastic bottle of water. Or I assumed it held water. He looked old enough to have taught my granddad. Some useless beggar.

A woman made her way towards where I stood and the man half-sat and half-lay. She had way too much make-up on and her hair piled up in curly clusters on her head. She tottered on very high heels with a skirt much too short and a coat much too long, but open and showing her tight blouse underneath. She carried a polystyrene box in her hand.

Just like the police, she didn't look my way at all. She stopped by the man and sighed, looking up at the sky as though to check for rain. The light fell full on her face. My heart rose full into my mouth. Tears sprang to my eyes. Juliette. Not Juliette as she is or was or whatever the frickin', twinkin', blinkin' hell was happening. But Juliette as she might look in ten years' time if life had been really, really cruel.

"Here, Dad," she said. "It's the best I could do tonight."

The old man looked up. One of his eyes had turned milky white but the gleam in the other showed my father hadn't lost all his spirit, even though he appeared to have aged half a century.

"I know. I know. No one gave much today. One person stopped and asked me to play *Danny Boy*. I did my best, but the mouth organ is not what it used to be and they apologised for having no change. They gave me their water bottle though, so I suppose we should be grateful."

My hand hurt horribly. I squeezed the brooch so hard it bit into my palm. I moved to where Juliette would see me clearly, but she looked through me.

"Dad," she said.

He looked up from his job of dividing the noodles with the plastic fork that came inside the box.

"Dad, I had the strangest sensation." She stared right at where I stood. She sniffed, wiped her nose with the back of her hand and let out a sigh. "Doesn't matter though. I'm probably just hungry."

"No. No. No. No!" I shouted, pushing the hard metal of the

brooch further into my hand. "No. Take me back, I'll choose again. I want to go back."

Tears blinded my vision. I squeezed my eyes shut. A hand touched my shoulder.

"Are you all right?"

The Crystal Boat

Håkan's story

Håkan stood in the narrow gully wondering which way to choose. His mind whirled. Hasina, the tall dark-haired woman dressed in flowing robes, with a feather embroidered on the shoulder, had quickly won his trust. Something about her calm assurance and the warmth of her presence made her easy to follow. He'd never seen a woman so effortlessly graceful. She'd led him into a large circular room. She didn't speak outwardly, but inwardly he heard her words tumbling around his mind.

'The Gods created time that mankind could be free,' she said. *'Free to choose as their minds decided. At any point in time much is possible, good and bad, and if you have a place to stand and see, like this place, the results of all those possible choices flow forward like massive strands.'*

The woman went on: *'Few indeed are permitted to see the future. Those are the world's great prophets, and hard is the path they must walk. But you, a Seed of Life, may see the Great Choice that is to be made. If you so wish.'*

Håkan nodded, not really knowing what she meant, and moments later here he stood, faced with two smooth rocks marking two different ways forward, and painted with signs he didn't understand. He shrugged and took the pathway marked by the white tadpole with its black eye, if that's what it was. He liked frogs.

At first the gully narrowed. He had to squeeze between two thorn bushes and his sleeve caught. He couldn't free it and the leather tore, leaving a tuft of his sleeve quivering in the slight breeze. He emerged onto a ledge, somewhere high enough that clouds swirled below him. He had a choice, to go back or to descend these impossibly narrow steps cut into the rock face.

Looking back, the thorn bushes appeared to have grown and to block his return completely. He trusted his head for heights and, carefully keeping his balance, he started to descend. The cloud swirled close and he could only see a few feet in front of him. The steps went on downwards for a long way. Had he met someone coming up, he doubted they could have wriggled past each other without one of them falling. He came to a slight hollow in the cliff-face where he could catch his breath. His heart raced and even though the foggy cloud made his hair damp, he could feel sweat trickling down his back. The steps now turned in the other direction, descending still further. He grimaced and set off once more. A gust of wind caught his jacket and for a moment that lasted more like forever, he thought he would tumble. His gloved hand found an indentation in the rock, just enough to save his balance. He clung there for an endless moment, not daring to look down to where the cloud had begun to clear. His knees weakened and for several breaths could hardly bear his weight.

Below him he could see a landscape stretching out towards the horizon. Sun sparkled on a river that meandered through a forest of great trees, their deep green leaves shifting in colour as the wind moved them in the bright sunlight. Scattered across the forest were clearings, each with a cluster of buildings unlike any he had ever seen before. Between these buildings he could see the occasional flash of reflected light, suggesting small rivers feeding into the great river that flowed off to his right, where farmland provided a checkering of browns, yellows and turquoise.

With the sunlight now providing a better view of the steps ahead, and the width of the steps increasing, Håkan made quicker progress. After a couple more turns a handrail appeared and Håkan descended two steps at a time.

When he finally reached the bottom, the sun had moved significantly lower in the sky. Above him the cliff face rose sheer, with an occasional tree just about clinging to a crag. He couldn't see the top of the cliff, nor where he had started from, as clouds still tumbled and flowed, blocking his vision.

The purity of the air and its freshness suggested he remained quite high up, or that he was in a land like Sweden where even sunny days cannot quite drive away the glorious freshness of a summer's day.

Some way ahead, a boat, tethered to a post, bobbed on a narrow river. He'd never seen a remotely similar craft, for the whole of it might have been cut from crystal, and it flashed and glittered in the sunlight. He looked for oars but could see none. The stream, if stream it was, ran more or less parallel to the rock face. Too wide to jump, he didn't fancy walking for miles to find a bridge, and anyway he couldn't see one in either direction. The banks of the stream were full of flowering plants, and dragonflies darted around, their red and deep blue-green bodies, flashing in the sunlight like sparks from the blacksmith's forge. Above, a hawk or maybe an eagle slowly circled, high up by the clouds.

He stepped into the boat to see if he could use his hands to paddle across to the far side of the stream. As he untied the line that tethered the boat, it moved. A sound, somewhat between a woman's humming and cat's purring, filled the boat and it vibrated slightly. Håkan nearly lost his balance as the craft, now with a mind of its own, took the centre of the gently flowing stream and moved steadily, its prow parting the water in two distinct waves. Håkan crouched and started praying. He remembered many childhood stories of enchanted boats and expected any minute to sweep into an inlet in the cliff face and find himself presented as lunch for the local trolls. At the moment he decided to jump out of the boat and swim to the far shore, it slowed, keeled over to one side and turned, entering a wider waterway heading for the distant trees. This river had sides too straight to be natural and felt deeper than the stream, with the banks considerably further away. In the clear water occasional shapes appeared and darted by, suggesting fish bigger than any he'd ever seen before. So instead of being a troll's lunch, he might end up on a fish's smörgåsbord. He decided to sit it out and see where the boat took him. His exhaustion from descending the rock face and the rocking motion of the enchanted boat lulled him into a doze.

"Come!" said a voice, in Swedish. "This is no time to sleep. You will have a sore neck for days if you lie like that much longer."

Torsberg

A boy, somewhat older than Håkan, led the way. He wore a jerkin of soft wool, and wide pantaloons of a material Håkan didn't recognise. Their deep-green colour changed slightly as they moved and caught the light. His feet were bare. The grassy path up from the river had a softness unlike the tracks Håkan knew in the forest. The trees here stood taller than those around Signy's farm, and their great limbs were thicker. At one point two children, sitting high up in the branches, waved to him. He didn't wave back as he assumed they were fairies, or worse.

Birdsong surrounded them everywhere. Occasionally other paths gave off from this one, also softly grass-covered. They reached a bridge, and a craft, like the crystal boat that had carried him here, bobbed at the bottom of a few steps. Flowers tumbled down the banks of these waterways, and tiny birds with long sharp beaks flashed between bulrushes.

Over the bridge, the track rose up towards a hilltop. As they reached the crest Håkan studied the rocks that broke through from the rougher grass. They were familiar. Very familiar.

"This is—"

"Yes," said the boy. "This is Thor's Hammer as we call it. It is famous for who lived near here once and what took place here once."

The boy pointed down the hill towards the familiar shape of the stones of the Judge Circle. Nearly all the birch trees had vanished, to be replaced by this huge forest. Within clearings, buildings made of similar crystalline material as the boat glinted in the sunlight. Closer to Håkan and below him, buildings emerged from the hillside with curving walls as clear as spring water and roofing covered with grasses and flowers. Inside these strange homes, made he knew not how, wooden floors caught the warm light of the afternoon sun.

The boy moved in front of Håkan. He placed his hands on the younger boy's shoulders. His eyes were moist.

"I'm allowed to show you this. I'm not allowed to tell you much though. That's been made very clear." He smiled, and went on, "If I did so you wouldn't be able to live your life in the way you choose and that would be wrong."

"But everything has changed."

"Yes. Yes it has, hasn't it. And the part you are to play in that is not a small one. You have seen why the Great Decision, so long ago for us of course, why it was – and is…" He cleared his throat and looked out across the forest. "Why it's so important."

The older boy moved away and started to descend the hill towards the Judge Circle. Håkan looked back to where the distant cliff face should be but could see nothing of it. The landscape, though altered in appearance by the size and colour of the trees, remained similar to what he knew of home.

Running down the hillside, as he often had in the past, the wind caught his hair, and the unfamiliar fragrance of many herbs wafted around him. Try as he might he couldn't overtake his new friend. Once at the bottom he started to remove his jacket as he caught his breath.

"No," said the boy. "No. Keep that on. You'll need it." He looked up to where the sun approached the tops of the trees. "We must hurry. There are things you need to do and you cannot do them here."

The taller boy walked to the edge of the Judge Circle. He stood right by the stone Håkan sometimes used to jump off when he practiced his somersaults. That at least looked unchanged.

"Do you have the jewel?" asked the boy.

Håkan had no idea what he meant.

Once more the older boy looked towards the sun which brought out red glints in his hair.

"The jewel you were given when you entered this circle."

"Oh," said Håkan, feeling a bit silly. It rested against his palm, even as they spoke, safely tucked in his glove. "Yes, Yes, I do."

The boy pointed back up the hill. At the crest, by the austere rocks at once so familiar and yet now so strange, many children stood. In their hands they carried flowers. They appeared around the edge of the hillside, talking to one another and pointing down towards where he stood. Music drifted by on the breeze. Håkan listened, holding his breath. He knew that music. The pipes. Someone playing the Swedish pipes. He heard the children laugh and in a rippling wave of colour they shook their flowers in the air above their heads, allowing petals to fall like rainbow snow.

The boy moved behind him. Within the circle, the light dimmed and a freezing cold blast of air hit Håkan in the face; just at that moment a hand pushed him between two of the standing stones. He stumbled in. His feet crunched on crisp snow, as flakes swirled around his face. He looked back but the boy had gone and Torsberg stood empty, grey and bleak. Someone sobbed, someone else in the circle. The English boy stood there with his eyes closed, fists pushed against them and snow settling onto his leather hat. His cheeks glistened with tears. Håkan, glad for the first time to see his companion, walked over and touched his shoulder.

"Are you all right?"

Paracelsus's Gift

Sweden – about 1520

We'd ridden most of the morning, and my legs screamed out for mercy, or would have done if they had a voice. We'd left the Circle quickly after Håkan had jostled me back into the here and now; well his here and now, even if not mine. As we followed twisting paths through the forest the unreality of it all gradually ebbed away, aided by the piercing cold air and thin flurries of snow. I still couldn't shake out of my mind the image of Dad begging in the Carfax and Juliette looking so miserable and at a loss. I had to do whatever it took to prevent that from ever happening to those I loved most. Håkan had had a very different experience in the time-tubes or whatever we'd clambered about in. He chuckled and burbled on in Swedish as we shared his horse, but I didn't listen. Håkan's saddle found every sore spot on my nether regions.

Paracelsus led the way, even though Håkan gave directions. He kept a hand on his sword and looked about frequently. We neither saw nor heard anyone. We'd not followed the route away from the standing stones that we'd taken earlier that morning. Håkan said we would be less likely to meet anyone if we went across the land of Bengt, the woodcutter. So we followed the narrow paths and forded streams flowing swiftly with icy water, till we finally came to the edge of fields covered in pristine snow. Håkan pointed at his house in the distance, but said nothing, and we kept within the trees until the farm had been left well behind us.

At one point, Paracelsus spoke to us quietly, over his shoulder.

"We can't afford to stop long today. Your mother is well in advance of us and we must meet with her before night closes in, and that's just a few hours off."

The German doctor had remembered what I'd forgotten, that during Swedish winters days are very short and nights are very long. He'd not asked us about our experience. Once we had crossed the monastery land without being seen and circled the town, he relaxed a bit.

"You know, visions of the Other Worlds take their own price. When you boys crossed over, the sky darkened as though going backwards into night. The fire sucked down into itself, and I had to keep adding kindling or it would have gone out entirely. I can tell you, my young friends, I said many prayers, some I've not said since I matched your years. But I always place my faith in The Lord, and He's always blessed me." He sniffed, hawked and spat.

"Woodland sprites gathered too, you know. I could sense their delicate presence all around, but they went just before you returned. It's good, this work you did. It's good."

When we stopped for a quick lunch of chilly bread and tangy cheese, Paracelsus fiddled deep in one of his saddlebags. He stood for a while, his hand inside the leather container, and listened.

"It's time," he said, apparently satisfied that no one stood in earshot. "I couldn't be sure until today, but now I am. You are the boys my teacher told me of and it is right I hand this burden on to you."

Håkan and I glanced at each other. He shrugged, and I shifted around as my legs ached so much from riding. Paracelsus held a soft leather package, bound with a thin silvery cord. We stood near a tree stump that provided a rough and ready table for our lunch. He squatted down and gently unfolded the packet and spread it out. There, displayed under the silent canopy of the trees, were several of the items that I'd discovered in the Time Sphere, once I'd learned its secrets: Shoshan's scarab necklace, the small bag of ten stones that Dimitris had received from

Pythagoras, the thick Greek coin, and the silver thimble.

"You must guard these well," said the doctor, his eyes glistening. "We all depend on their safe-keeping over the rolling years."

He straightened up and fiddled with the top of his sword that he had kept close while we ate. He took off his glove and placed the pommel of his sword on the palm of his hand.

"Here, Håkan. Add this. What it contains you and Rhory will need once more if you are to succeed in the far north. And once more again ..." he looked up at the sky, his eyes narrowing, "...to the east. What it contains is prepared by an alchemist far greater than I will ever be. And I'm certainly the greatest doctor currently alive."

He beamed at us, his rosy cheeks making him look almost like a boy once more.

"And now, now we must go. Snel. Vite. Fast."

Håkan carefully wrapped the package, and glanced at me with what looked like anger – but could have been fear – in his eyes. He slipped the package with great care into his jacket and buttoned it up once more. We remounted the horse, which snorted and decided at that point to relieve its bladder. Surrounded by a cloud of steam, my legs complaining of medieval torture, we set off.

"The Witch's Lair"

For some time we'd been descending. The snow still speckled down, but with less belief in itself. The sky no longer loomed just above the treetops and pale blue patches hinted at brighter weather to come. My legs had given up, going beyond aches, through pain, past torture and had arrived at a complaining numbness.

After our quick lunch and the revelation of the time-travelling objects, we'd ridden for a while, each deep in our own thoughts. I didn't know what Håkan made of Paracelsus suddenly revealing he had objects from times and lands Håkan had hardly heard about. I couldn't make head nor tail about how he'd ended up as their custodian, like my great aunt. Did this mean Paracelsus also had to be an ancestor of mine? That idea seemed preposterous, and clearly he wasn't an ancestor of Håkan's.

Paracelsus interrupted my thoughts. "They're searching for you, you know. They even know one of you is English."

"How do you know," I asked.

"I stopped yesterday in the tavern. It's dark inside there. The rush lamps give scant light and the fire less heat."

He turned on his horse, to look across at us.

"The booths and tables are separate and soldiers talk loud. They were speaking Danish but I understand it quite well. It's not so different from low German and Swedish. They said they'd be coming to the witch's lair today, once their captain returned."

"The witch's lair?" said Håkan.

"It was a phrase a soldier used. I guessed they might mean your farmhouse. Then that neighbour of yours, Pettersson, raised his voice. He explained that the Danish officer would come to the house to question you all about your father. Local people stared into their beer. They fear this man, but I know also they like your mother. As the soldiers became drunk on Pettersson's money, I slipped out and rode back last night to warn Frau Ekland."

"She's gone ahead, by this same route," said Håkan. "And Gregor led the way early this morning with the sleighs."

"The sleighs?" I said.

"Of course, the sleighs," Håkan snapped, though leaving me none the wiser.

Now, with the dusk approaching and my legs belonging to someone else, I'd ceased to care. The trees began to thin and we came onto a wider road. Paracelsus held up his hand, keeping us within the cover of the trees. He listened. The silence hovered around us telling nothing of its secrets.

The sky had cleared to a washed out blue-green. In front of us lay the biggest skating rink I'd ever seen. The spattering of snow had stopped. Little flurries blew and tumbled in the wind over the black, flat surface of the ice that stretched as far as my eyes could see. The sea, or lake, or whatever it was, extended both ways on the far side of the road. Our horses panted, as they waited for us to decide which way to ride. Beyond the road, the steep bank fell towards a jetty, its wooden poles and slats glistening with ice crystals. I couldn't make out the far side of what had to be a lake.

Håkan gave out a low whistle. An answering call, like some marsh bird, came from a little way to our left. We crept forward. I could feel the tension as Håkan looked for the hidden whistler.

"Here," said a voice.

The old guy who looked after the stables and horses and who had left so early in the morning, stepped out from a copse of trees. Dressed in a long white jacket and pale leather hat, he'd blended in with the tree trunks in the dim light. Behind him a pile of furs moved and Håkan's mother appeared. Another movement and Håkan's little sister Eira rose from a cocoon of fur, with her bow in her hand.

"Thank the Lord," Signy murmured. "We must hurry. A lone soldier passed this way only minutes ago. He saw nothing but we'll be caught like fish in a bucket if they come back this way."

Håkan dismounted, and compressing his lips gestured for me to get down. My legs wouldn't obey. I started to lean to one side and rub my thighs to get feeling back, when the old man, Gregor, moved over.

"Come, young sir," he said, "I don't think you live in the saddle, do you?"

I shook my head, feeling tears might not be that far away from disgracing me.

"Just tumble my way, I'll get you."

I came down in an undignified heap, his strong arms supporting me all the way. For a few minutes I walked around as though my legs were acting out the shape of the letter A. Håkan moved closer to the water's edge. The doctor, Gregor and Signy talked together, their heads almost touching.

"You'd best go quickly, doctor. Your religion and your nationality are not in your favour, you know," said Signy.

Paracelsus held Signy's hand for a few long moments.

"You will be safe, you know," he said. She nodded, but without much conviction.

"The lamps are lit," said Håkan.

"Then we go," said Signy.

Paracelsus remounted and held both his arms above his head in a salute, first to Håkan and then to me. He leaned forward in his saddle offering us a bow and eased his horse round to go back up the track we'd just come down. Gregor mounted Håkan's horse in one easy, graceful movement. He touched his hat to Signy, nodded to Håkan, blew a kiss to Eira, and smiled at me. I sniffed, wiped away tears from each eye and felt Signy's hand on my arm. The two men had already disappeared into the forest.

"Come," she said. "We cannot tarry."

We followed a small path down towards the jetty and some steps that in summer must lead to the water's edge. Tucked under the landward end of the jetty stood two sleighs. Håkan arranged the furs on the big one. The smaller one had room for two people at a squeeze. Both the sleighs had a single lantern lit, with fresh horses munching from sacks looped around their heads.

Håkan went round each of the horses removing sacking tied to their hooves. Their horseshoes glinted with tiny spikes.

"Crampons," I murmured in English to no one in particular.

"Stops them slipping and sliding all over the place," said Eira. "Great on ice. Rubbish on land."

"Ah," I said.

"Shhh..." said Håkan.

Signy pointed to the stars beginning to emerge. She spoke to her son, her voice urgent and her gloved hand moving this way and that, angled towards the sky.

"When they rise, both of them, put out your lamp and steer right."

Eira tugged my sleeve.

"Come on, Rhory." She grinned at me. "I've got my bow, you're quite safe."

Her bright eyes, so earnest, caught the light from the lamp in the larger sleigh.

"We're going in this one," she said. "Get in."

Feeling the world had entered a topsy-turvy stage, I climbed in next to Eira. After arranging thick furs over us like some mother hen, rather than an eight- or nine-year-old girl, she kept her bow in her hand and the quiver of arrows just behind her.

Signy finished her instructions to Håkan and came over to our sleigh. She held up her gloved hand, hissing, "Shhhh!" as Eira began to say something. A jingling sound accompanied by shouts and hoof beats came from the trees.

"Go, go, son," said Signy. "Now."

Sleigh Ride

He flicked the reins on his smaller sleigh, and with the tinkling of many tiny bells he set off. We followed immediately, although our sleigh had no musical accompaniment. We fell in behind Håkan, whose lively horse set up a swift pace. The sleighs shushed their way across the ice, running parallel to the shore. Eira had turned around to watch behind us. She had an arrow notched in her bow. Something whistled overhead. I turned as best I could.

"Be careful!" shouted Signy, no longer showing any caution about noise. "Don't knock anything off, we cannot go back for it."

On the bank a file of blue-coated horsemen descended towards the jetty. One rode out on the planks, the drumming of his hooves carrying across the ice. Two horsemen started riding on the ice, but the horses hesitated. Wrong horseshoes, I guessed.

"They're shooting," said Eira.

"Keep your heads down," said Signy.

I waited for the flash and bang of a gun, but none came.

"There!" said Eira. "They're rubbish."

Something small and black drew a line in the snowy ice to the right of us. In a moment we overtook where it stopped.

"A bolt," she said.

My puzzlement must have shown.

"From a crossbow."

I nodded. Crossbows didn't sound too dangerous. Already the soldiers were becoming grey smudges, as the jetty faded into a blur. The officer shouted something, his hoof beats crashing over the wooden planking once more. The horsemen on the ice rode back up the bank and disappeared into the trees.

For some moments the only sounds were Håkan's Christmas melody of tiny bells coming from in front of us, and the thrumming of the hooves of the two horses on the ice, their clever spiked shoes gripping with ease. The soldiers on the road were charging at full speed. They appeared and disappeared as the trees hid and revealed them. In a few minutes they'd be on the bank above us and well within bolt shot. Signy didn't seem bothered and she and Håkan held the same steady pace. The trees on the lake side of the road disappeared entirely and I could see the officer leading the charge. My stomach contracted into a sick ball of sharp pain as I recognised the Lucian look-alike of my dreams. Even in the final dying moments of dusk, the glow from the snow as he emerged from the trees left no doubt. He reined in, as the road took a sharp turn to the left. The lake had an inlet here and the shore fell away from us. Håkan and Signy must have known the danger from the soldiers would quickly pass.

Eira and I settled back into the furs. The biting cold wind played over my face and I eased my scarf out of my jacket and over my mouth, pulling my hat low on my forehead. Above us more and more stars appeared. We glided over the flat blackness with the deepening dark of the sky twinkling and sparkling. If my legs hadn't been quite so full of aches and my tummy rumbling with the need for a juicy hamburger and fries, and if soldiers led by the army captain from hell weren't hot on our tail, I might have enjoyed the beauty of it all.

Once darkness had completely fallen and we could no longer see the shore, just an increasing gloom around us, Håkan slowly stopped. He walked smartly over to our sleigh, and snuffed out the lantern. Briefly, he held his mother's hands, blew a kiss to his sister, murmured, "Look after them both," to me and returned to his sleigh. The tiny bells tinkled their message once more, a sound, so loud as we sat still that it had to carry to the shore to our left.

Very slowly, Signy eased our horse to the right, with a few twitches of the reins, until we were heading at a considerable angle to the route Håkan had taken. Now Signy kept the horse going slightly slower than before. She looked over at us and smiled a tight smile.

"Maybe it'll fool them. I don't know. It's best they don't know which way we are going, then we may get away from them. It's about three hours before the moon rises. When it does, we'll eat. As long as we show no light we'll be invisible from that shore."

She pointed to our left. In front of us but on the side closer to the shore, we could see Håkan's light. Of his sleigh, we could see nothing.

Someone touched my cheek. I awoke from a shapeless dream. Signy stood beside the sleigh, looking down at me, with her finger to her lips. The horse munched on something in a bag at its mouth. Eira rummaged around in a leather pouch. Above us crystal diamonds shared their cold, twinkling light from millions of years ago. The moon, a yellow half-lozenge, lying on its side at an odd Swedish angle, gave enough glow-power for me to recognise the boiled egg that Eira offered me. That, plus bread of a crustiness that might have come from being part frozen, and a piece of cold meat, made possibly the best meal of my life to date. Something about being in the middle of a frozen lake being chased by time-hopping overgrown schoolboys gave me an appetite. We washed it all down with a beery drink that tasted soapy, but very welcome.

Moments later the horse had been debagged; it had let out one of those horsy noises halfway between an old steam train and an opera singer clearing her throat, and we were off. Once more we kept the slightly slower pace. Signy frequently looked up at the stars and made minor adjustments to our direction. I'd no idea how we would have made this journey if the cloud cover had remained, or worse still, it had snowed.

The stars looked close enough for a tall man on a ladder to snaffle one, with one of those things shopkeepers use to get tins from high shelving. I'd never seen so many. Right across the sky a pale whisper of light lay like a forgotten river of fairy milk. The Milky Way! Not something that I'd ever seen in Hammerford.

The sleigh trundled on, and on and on. Until it stopped.

"Rhory, I need you to take the reins. I'm falling asleep. And Eira, sit with Rhory and pinch him if he snores."

I took the reins, after a quick explanation. I had to keep that group of stars just over the horse's right ear for a while, but also to keep that bright single star always to our left and in front of us. We were to wake Signy when the ear-stars disappeared below the horizon.

The horse seemed to know an amateur was holding the reins, and went more slowly than before, something a little more than a stroll but a lot less than a canter. I turned to look at Signy, but she smiled and nodded and the next time I turned around she'd fallen asleep. Eira hummed and whistled tunelessly through her teeth. She nudged me when the star, the pole star I guessed, had gone too far to our left, and I struggled to find the stars that should be by the horse's ear. There were so many. Then I spotted them, gave a few professional tugs to the reins, and we were heading into the right sector of nowhere once more.

The noise of the runners changed dramatically, producing a juddering and crunching. I wondered if one of the runners had come loose or something. I looked at Eira, but she had her head thrown back studying the stars above us, and I could see no concern in her face. A little while later, the noise vanished and we shushed on smoothly like before.

Signy tapped my back.

"Stop now, Rhory."

I looked ahead. The guiding stars had set. I'd not seen them do so. The bright pole star sat where it should and Signy nodded to herself as she studied the celestial satnav above us.

"This is fine. Fine," she said.

She went around the sleigh and removed the lantern. Standing so her body shielded the direction of the far shore from where we had come, she used a tinderbox to get a light. The lamp soon flared back into life, and she placed it on the right edge of the sleigh so the light shone forwards and to our right, and couldn't be seen from the western shore.

"Now we wait. Håkan will see this light if he passes in front of us."

"And if he passes behind us, Mother?"

"We must hope he does not. But there is a little light showing behind, and light can be seen a great distance in this dark."

"But we will see his light, won't we?"

"No, Rhory," Signy replied, "he will have shut off his light before those stars you followed set, and changed his direction towards us."

Goodness, I thought, but didn't say. *What could possibly go wrong?*

We waited. I had another egg and my tummy rebelled by bloating. I moved around on the ice imagining the murky depths below us full of fish and coldness. I could just make out my footprints. I wrote my name in the snow. Eira copied the shapes. I wasn't sure if she could spell, so wrote her name E-R-A.

She corrected me and paced out E-I-R-A.

"Oh," I said.

"Shhh." Signy held up her hand.

We stared into the curving wall of murky gloom beyond where we stood. The ice lay like a flat dull-grey plain all around us. Ahead, nothing moved. Then we could all see Håkan quite clearly, and quite close. But no bells rang.

He drew up beside us, his horse panting and producing his own cloud system in our lantern light.

"I threw away the bells when the moon rose, and put out the light when you suggested, Mother. They will think we're ahead of them on the western shore. Now we have the advantage as they have no idea where we have actually headed."

"What's that?" said Eira in a tone that made us all jump.

Off to our right, far away, we could see a light move. It appeared and disappeared, making a shaky progress northward.

"Thank you, Lord. Thank you, Jesus and Mary and all the saints," said Signy. "It's the eastern bank. We're close."

Just then a crack, like a rifle shot went off.

"Spread out," said Håkan, "that's the ice cracking."

Myrna

Alexandria – about 380 CE

Myrna smiled as the young girls danced around the fountain. They whirled and twirled so gracefully, so full of life and giggles. Even though a winter chill lingered in the air, the sun shone brightly on the far side of the courtyard, picking out the starry whiteness of the jasmine that climbed part of the inner wall. The girls moved in and out of the sunshine, clapping their hands and spinning on the spot, dipping and rising just as they had been taught by the Lady.

Cat watched them from a patch of sunshine under the jasmine bush. Her yellow eyes switched from one to another, and the silver ring in Cat's ear twinkled in the bright light. She raised a paw and delicately but purposefully washed her nose.

"That's enough," said Anastasia, flicking her long wavy black hair from her eyes and stretching her arms high above her head. "I need to breathe."

Nysa, the slimmest of the three, settled herself on a part of the low stone wall of the fish pond that had not been soaked with spray from the fountain.

Devorah, the young lady of the house, turned and shouted, "Drinks, Myrna, we're completely parched!"

She's imperious, that one, thought Myrna, *but underneath she's kind, and so very clever.*

"Yes please, Myrna," added Nysa, always careful to be polite.

Myrna put her hands on her hips and sighed. The stub of her tongue ached today and she moved it against the sharper part of her back teeth. That gave a little solace. She focused her attention on Nysa. Something had changed. She had danced with a precision that escaped the other girls and her movements had the supple fluidity of a gazelle. Myrna closed her eyes and looked.

Nysa's colours had expanded. A new and deeper blue played delicately around her neck. Myrna nodded to herself. *As I thought. This one can Hear. Now I understand what the Lady meant. 'She is the bridge'.*

Someone clapped their hands. "Really!" said Devorah, "we're actually dying of thirst here Myrna, and you're in a dream."

Myrna opened her eyes and slowly moved her hands from her hips. Nysa frowned and whispered something to Devorah, who compressed her lips and turned to stare into the fishpond.

Minutes later the girls had drunk their weak beers and bolted down honey cakes. They were licking their fingers and giggling again. Myrna, sitting on a stone bench in the deepest shade in the courtyard, pulled her woollen shawl closer around her shoulders. The sweetness of the honey stuck to her teeth and she sucked at them and loosened a flake of sugary crust with her fingers. Across the deep blue of the sky a cluster of white birds appeared above the roof, nearly cleared the whole distance and then wheeled as one, flying right over where Myrna sat. *A sign?*

Over the past few nights she'd heard her mother's voice quite distinctly. Her mother, dead these twenty years or more. Her mother, who'd taught her to read and write and assured her of the reality of the Old Gods whom Myrna sensed even as a child. *Speak with her,* her mother had said, *it is time she learns the inner voice.* At first Myrna had thought her mother meant Devorah. Certainly she served the young Jewish girl, although she belonged to the girl's father. But now, seeing the play of those delicate colours at the throat of the pagan Nysa, she concluded it was this girl who had awakened the old gift, the gift of hearing. The three young friends now sat on the stone bench across the courtyard from Myrna, their faces turned towards the warmth of the sun, their eyes closed, the gentling effect of the honey having done its work.

Myrna closed her eyes once more and focused again on Nysa. She held the young girl's image, with her brown eyes and pensive mouth, hovering before her. She delicately wove a cord of light between her solar plexus and that of the girl relaxing on the far side of the courtyard. She projected in words that were more than words the thought, *'Listen, Nysa, and do not speak. Stand. Move towards the fountain.'*

She waited three full, slow breaths and then repeated the message. She sensed a responding thought, chaotic, but there. Opening her eyes once more Myrna found Nysa standing just to the right of the fountain. All colour had drained from her face. She looked around the courtyard as though seeking someone and then her eyes came to rest on Myrna, who nodded slowly to her and impelled the words *'You can Hear. It is a gift. Keep it secret. Use it wisely.'*

Nysa sat once more on the edge of the fountain. She looked up at the sky above and down again until her eyes met Myrna's. She bit her lower lip and took a deep breath. Then she let it out in a rush and shook her head as though to clear it. She closed her eyes. The silence deepened around Myrna. A breeze played with the folds of her gown.

'I must go. Will you walk with me?'

Myrna heard her words distinctly. As always the meaning settled first in her mind and then the words clothed the meaning. She nodded. *'So, we who both follow the old Gods, can hear.'* She stood up from the bench. Anastasia and Devorah were sitting oblivious to what happened so close by them, enjoying the sun and the music of the water in the fountain. She crossed to them and tapped Anastasia's knee. When the girl had opened her eyes, Myrna pointed to the sun lowering in the sky and to the great door to the street. She made walking gestures with her fingers.

"Oh, all right!" said Anastasia, standing and smiling. "I suppose I have to go. Leah will be annoyed with me anyway for having stayed away so long. You ready, Nysa? Seems like Myrna wants to march us home. Goodness, it looks like you've seen a shade! Are you all right?"

Nysa nodded. "Just a bit tired," she said.

"We will meet again on Aphrodite's-day?" asked Devorah. "Isn't that when the Lady needs us?"

"Yes," said Anastasia, frowning slightly. "Though Leah says I shouldn't call it that – I should call it Preparation-day."

"Pfft!" Nysa snorted, now having joined them. "We have these wonderful names for the days of the week and your sister wants to call them by numbers. Preparation-day follows what? Fourth-day?"

"No, it follows Fifth-day, the fifth day after the day of Our Lord."

"Oh it's all getting much too complicated," said Devorah. "I know we don't really believe in them, but I like the names of the Gods. Father says if we banish those Gods we banish our heritage. Knowledge is not something to be broken up."

"Not your heritage, though, is it, Devorah?" said Nysa.

"Sort of," her Jewish friend responded. "After all, we have lived in Alexandria since my great grandfather's time. We have the temples all around. My family came here because of all the knowledge you Greeks and Egyptians have tucked away in your libraries."

Myrna clapped her hands and pointed to the door. The girls pouted, giggled and ran to get their cloaks.

The Man on the Horse

For a while Nysa walked in silence beside Myrna, with Devorah's family watchman walking a respectful distance behind them, his heavy cudgel designed to deter anyone who might bother the young slave and her charge. After leaving the Jewish quarter, they had taken Anastasia safely to her home.

Nysa looked up at Myrna.

"So you can, sort of … you know, you are actually able, even though…"

Myrna did not help her out. She had accepted her fate long ago and Nysa needed to toughen her mind. She kept her eyes on the road in front and steered the young dancer safely past shiny horse dung.

"Even though you are mute you can talk," said Nysa, colouring.

Myrna looked across at her but kept her face blank. She wondered if the girl could commune inwardly with her out in the bustle and grime of Alexandria's busy streets. She had absolute certainty that if the Old Gods conferred a rare gift like this, it would be for a purpose. It had been so for her. Would it be so for Nysa?

The girl bit her lip again and her walking slowed a little. Myrna matched her stride and drew silence around them both as best she could with people bustling by them and horses, carts and mules to avoid.

'You can talk even though they took your tongue. So cruel.'

Myrna nearly stepped into a puddle and had to jig to one side to avoid it. Nysa's words had arrived so clearly it had almost blotted out her sight.

She drew the young girl into the lee of a building at the edge of the Jewish Quarter and out of the throng of the street. The watchman stopped several paces behind, his eyes watching but not watching.

'The new powers in Alexandria consider these gifts as witchcraft. Let no one know you have them.'

Myrna held the dark-brown eyes with her own.

'Gather your thoughts with care. If you can Hear you can also Speak inwardly. Beware of letting the wrong people hear your thoughts. These are dangerous times.'

As if to provide emphasis to the thoughts Myrna had just shared, a squad of soldiers marched past, all flapping leather straps and thumping of boots. The men had their hands resting on the hilts of their short swords. A couple of them cast sly glances towards Myrna and her charge. One man stuck out his tongue and wiggled it around. Myrna pulled Nysa further back into the shadow of the wall.

When the backs of the soldiers with their red cloaks were a good distance down the road, Myrna nodded to Nysa and they set off once more. The soldiers had returned to the Macedonian camp on their right and Myrna turned left to put as much distance as possible between them and the leering men.

They walked on in silence for a time, both inward and outward. Over the past two years, since the awful Desert Mother, Elizabeth, had started her wild preaching against all the Old Gods and against the Jews, the streets had become less safe. Myrna glanced over her shoulder to check the watchman was in place. Behind him, just three or four paces to his rear, walked the biggest man Myrna had ever seen, a mountain of flesh on legs. His head, either completely bald or shaved, rose from a neck that would have done justice to one of the oxen pulling carts through the market streets of Alexandria. His arms dropped from vast shoulders like the carcasses of sheep hanging in a butchery. His hands looked like they could crush a coconut without difficulty.

Myrna walked a little faster. Perhaps they should have taken the litter and been carried by four powerful slaves. She had heard rumours in the market place of young pagan girls being snatched and turning up in slave markets far to the south. She hoped they were just that – rumours. Glancing back once more she received a wink from the watchman. Behind him the man mountain had vanished. He must have turned up a side street.

"Are you all right?" said Nysa, her forehead puckered.

Myrna nodded and touched her young charge's arm. She pointed ahead. The blue of the sea could just be made out now, and in a moment or two the full glory of the Royal Harbour would be visible.

"Can we get some of those? I have a little money." Nysa had paused near a table where a street vendor had laid out fresh dates on palm leaves. Myrna also had money and gave the man a few staters, receiving a toothless grin and some dates in return for her coins.

Myrna loved dates, although she had to use her fingers to shift the sweet flesh around her mouth and remove the pit. Having no tongue resulted in more than having no speech. She wiped her sticky fingers on the edge of the green leaf and dropped it in the gutter. Yes, she loved dates, but she loved coconuts more. Maimonides, her owner, had shared some with her occasionally, when they worked on a difficult translation together. His wealth could manage that great luxury, for coconuts came from far away, often in the boats owned by Nysa's father, who had even greater wealth than Maimonides.

The harbour with the huge Pharos lighthouse came into view. The beauty of her home, with the multi-coloured sails of all the boats and the splendour of the old palace of Cleopatra, never ceased to delight her. She lived where the greatest ideas of the world were gathered. Alexandria was the most civilised city on earth. She had seen Rome as a child, from the wrong side of a slave pen. She knew Alexandria surpassed the brute grandeur of the Emperor's city in both its beauty and its learning.

Her breath caught in her throat when she realised that the huge man stood in the public gardens to their left. Next to him a man with military bearing but wearing civilian robes, sat on a jet-black horse of magnificent size. He had the tanned face and build of a soldier and leaned forward talking steadily to the giant, who nodded occasionally. The man on horseback smiled, raised his hand in farewell and rode forward. He looked directly at Myrna and Nysa. Myrna stared back. He changed the direction of his mount to pass more closely to the slave and her young friend. His eyes had a blue-green colour and his dark hair, uncovered, had suggestions of silver at the temples, highlighted by the setting sun. His mouth formed a firm line and he had the prominent chin of one who knew how to command. Myrna felt as though she'd become transparent, that the man had the ability to see within and through her. She sensed the vastness of the desert in the man's gaze and the sweet sanctity of ancient temples. He switched his gaze to Nysa and pulled the horse to a standstill. Nysa still looked out towards the harbour with the sunlight twinkling on the blue of the waters. The man carried a short staff of ivory. He touched it to his temple, nodded at Myrna, kicked his heels into his horse's silky black flank and cantered off, his back as straight as a stone column.

Once more the big man had just melted away. He must have walked amongst the trees in the garden whilst Myrna looked at the strange horseman. She shuddered and took Nysa's hand, walking fast towards where the girl lived beyond the Sun Gate.

Passing the gymnasium they came close to the Temple of Saturn. This building, with its high columns and cool colonnades, always pleased Myrna. While Saturn, or Kronos as the Greeks called him, had little to commend him as a God in terms of kindness – he had after all eaten all his own children until Zeus defeated him – there was a profound stillness and clarity within the temple that Myrna found soothing. Shouts and bellowing caused both the young women to turn.

A group of young men ran down the street shouting abuse about the temple. One bravo picked up horse manure and threw it at the temple steps. "Filth to filth," he hollered, and raced on with his friends, hooting and yelping.

Nysa and Myrna walked on in silence. The older woman sensed the young girl's pain; her gods were being desecrated. The new Christian God was usurping their place. The tolerance of centuries had given way to bigotry and hatred.

When they reached the door of Nysa's family house the girl turned to Myrna.

"I've had dreams. Strange dreams. Dreams of flight to distant places." She paused, searching Myrna's face. "Maybe to distant times."

Myrna nodded and waited. She knew much of such dreams.

"Someone is coming. I sense it. Someone who I know already even though I've not met them. Someone who can..." She stopped talking and took the hand of Myrna in both of her own.

'Someone who can also Hear.'

Neither knew whose thought that was. It arose within and between them. Myrna's eyes filled with tears and she touched Nysa's cheek. Her hand returned involuntarily to the silver chain at her neck, the mark of her slavery. Her master, Maimonides, treated her well and respected her gifts, but now this young girl, true to the old Religion, had proved to be a real kindred spirit. A warmth spread around her heart, and the deep pangs of aloneness that had been with her ever since her mother was struck down before her and her own tongue taken from her mouth, lessened just a little.

'Thank you, Nysa. Your thoughts will always find me. Just hold my image clear.'

She reached into a fold in her clothing and drew out a feather, the sort of feather worn by priestesses long ago. She gave it to the little dancer.

'This will help.'

Cold Comfort

Sweden – about 1520

Fear jabbed cold electricity up my limbs. I moved away from the sled. The cracking continued, changing the black silvery ice at my feet to a mosaic of crystal lines. I moved towards where we'd seen the light. A dark mass rose ahead, resolving into a hillside covered in trees. Someone shouted behind me. I stumbled on, my legs still not fully my own. I heard a shout from the land and stopped. *What if the soldiers were there?*

The ice first sloped and then sank. I went down with it. The buoyancy of my boots and thick trousers slowed my sinking, or maybe it was the plate of thick ice, dislodged below my feet. When the water met my skin it seared with an angry chill, sharp as a knife. I'd never felt anything so cold. I couldn't see or think. But I did spot that my life didn't flash in front of my eyes. *What a disappointment.* I hung onto the ice in front of me, completely alone. I could see no one, as low down the mist hid everything. I tried to kick my boots loose, but they were laced and becoming as heavy as lead as they filled with liquid ice. I could still breathe, but not well enough to call out. What if no one had seen me fall? What if they'd also fallen as the ice broke up beneath us?

Each breath became a battle as water burned against my skin and stole all feeling.

Dad sat next to me, the water nearly reaching his knees.

"You know, Rhory," he said, "ice is amazing. It is actually lighter than water, which is why it floats. If water did not have this unusual quirk there would be no life at all. Water is heaviest at four degrees Centigrade."

I tried to nod. The cold had sent living icicles into my brain and my thoughts now moved slower than schoolboys asked to tidy their bedroom. Perhaps Dad knew how I could get out of this fix. I didn't, and the water – painless now – pulled my numbed body, down into it. *It'll be warmer at the bottom.* Had Dad said that or did I imagine it?

A voice spoke in my ear. Speaking in Swedish. *Stop tickling,* I tried to say. But the words had frozen in my chest and curled up and refused to move. Someone or something far away said, "Now we have you." Maybe the schoolboy from hell? Maybe the fat priestess? Whoever spoke they were welcome to the tiny candle flame that remained of Rhory until it faded.

"Rhory ran the wrong way," Eira's mother shouted as Håkan sprinted to the larger sleigh.

The English boy had headed to where the river came in; there the water was warmer and the ice was thinner. Someone on the bank waved their arms about but the boy didn't see, stumbling on to where the colour of the ice changed.

Even before he sank, after the great cracking sound that sent lightning flashes of white lines across the ice under their feet and beyond, Håkan was tying the rope around her waist. Eira knew why. But he told her anyway.

"You're the lightest."

He took off his belt.

"Hook this under his arms, thread the rope end through, tie it. Tie it well. Go now."

Eira walked with her lightest steps across the ice. Rhory still had his chest out of the water. As long as he could hold on she knew there was a chance. When she came within a few paces she lay down on the ice and edged forward, using her boots to push against the slippery surface, almost like swimming. She had the belt and rope in her hands. Her gloves lay on the ice, well behind her. She knew she could not tie knots with gloves on.

Rhory couldn't see her. He had slipped further and the dark stain of the water crept up his back and lay only a couple of handbreadths below his collar. Eira knew that in water this cold, he would by now be unable to move. She could hear him snorting, every breath a fight. Another loud cracking sound stopped her, but the ice remained firm. She edged forward.

"It's okay, Rhory. It's okay. Don't worry. I'm here."

Getting the belt under his armpits proved to be easier from behind. He didn't see her to grab at her to pull them both under. He didn't sense her presence.

"Tie the rope!" shouted her brother.

Icy water flowed up her jacket sleeves as she pivoted onto her back. She had threaded the rope end through the belt, which she'd already fastened at his back. If he sank now he would pull her in headfirst. A simple knot would do as long as it didn't slip. Her numb fingers wouldn't obey. She started again. A crinkling, scraping noise filled her ears. She expected the dark waters to choke her any moment. She pulled. The knot held.

"Now!" she shouted. "Pull now!"

Already her body moved over the ice. The rope tightened around her chest. She lay staring up at the sky. Nothing moved. Then, as a swish of freezing water passed her, stinging her face, she jerked away from the bank towards the firmer ice by the sleighs.

Did I dream? I don't know. I had memories of being held by a woman. I thought an Ice Queen. I will be king of the dead where the icicles dwell. But the woman hurt me horribly with her warmth. My legs, back and arms screamed for mercy before I slept once again. When I woke the woman had gone. A dog lay to one side of me; I could tell by the smell and the fact it panted in my face and licked me when I turned that way. On my other side a boy, I think it must have been a boy, snuggled up. My teeth rattled a tattoo and my whole body shook.

"He's still so cold."

I woke in the night. Voices spoke quietly somewhere and a fire crackled nearby, sending shadows dancing crazily around the timbered ceiling. *Out of the frying pan into the fire, except it should be out of the freezer into the fire.* I hoped the timbers wouldn't be set alight by fiery shadows.

That night or next, I woke and felt something hard and warm by my knees. I tugged at it. Something heavy unwrapped and I burned my fingertips. At that moment I realised I'd survived. Whoever had done the saving had also put warm stones in the bed, wrapped in cloth.

Someone rubbed my arms and prodded my legs.

"No frost bite. Lucky this one. Very lucky. I thought at least he would lose his toes."

I went back to sleep. This conversation did little for my sense of well-being.

Eira fed me soup. She scowled as she did it but grinned when I managed to swallow something. A woman I'd never seen before, with a flattish, nondescript face, gave me a hot drink. It burned down my throat, sending tiny streams of fire to all my limbs. I sat up.

"Careful now," she said.

As she left the room she spoke to someone outside.

"Feels like my own boy, this one. After all, I more or less suckled him."

This somewhat disturbing news came before a cackling. Three females laughing together, apparently at my expense. Not a sound I enjoy.

"You can leave him here, Mistress Ekland, if you wish. We could do with a handy boy, once he's learned to avoid the springs." She cackled again. I retreated into sleep.

The urgency of my bladder taught me to walk once more. Håkan held my arm and we crossed the snow to the midden. I peed and peed. Well, all the soup I'd eaten had to go somewhere. A smell of animal, straw and manure proved strangely comforting. Better alive in a stink than dead in a pure lake.

"We must go," said Håkan, his eyes a mixture of irritation,

alarm and anger.

"Where?" I said. I'd no idea where we were headed. Why hadn't I asked? Perhaps I had. I found it hard to remember much before I went into the ice. "Is Dad coming?" I asked.

"What? Who? My father?"

"No," I said, confused now where the thought had come from. "Sorry. It doesn't matter."

"A group of hunters are going north. We will travel with them a bit."

"On the sleighs?"

"No. It's too steep on this side of the lake. The road runs on the western side. Here, on the east, the fishing villages connect with smaller tracks and it is much more hilly. We've sold the sleighs. We may buy them back, when..." He trailed off.

"Where are we going then?"

"North. We'll be safe in the far north. The track by the lake is not snow-bound."

"Good." I said. I figured I didn't really have much choice. Someone had said I must go north. No idea why. Alexandria and the heat of Egypt were about as far away as they could be now.

"We'll ride. You will have your own pony, for a bit, until we change to skis. It'll be easier. You can use skis, can't you?"

"Yes," I said. "Yes I can. I can do black runs."

Håkan looked at me as though I'd just spoken in toads and frogs.

"Hard to explain," I added. But skiing would be much easier for me than riding. In fact if I hadn't gone to blooming Alexandria I would be skiing now, with hot chocolate to look forward to at the end of the day, plus a good movie on someone's laptop.

Palanquin Journey

Alexandria – about 380 CE

All three girls trembled and bounced. Anastasia fingered the beads at her neck and leaned forward to get a glimpse out between the blinds. A sudden lurch nearly put her on the floor. The three of them giggled.

"I should have them whipped," she said.

"Who?" said Devorah.

"The porters, silly."

"You would make a cruel mistress," said Nysa. "Anyway Myrna wouldn't let you."

"Then I'd have her whipped too," said Anastasia, winking.

"Yes, you and whose legions?" said Devorah. "I tell you this, I wouldn't cross Myrna for the world. And Father would never let anyone beat her. She's much too useful to him."

"I make a good mistress, actually," said Anastasia, pouting towards Nysa. "My body maid loves me." She wiggled her shoulders back and forth.

"Well, you'd whip her if she didn't," said Devorah.

Anastasia pouted some more and then all three girls dissolved into giggles. The palanquin stopped and Devorah pulled a gap open in the curtains.

"It's another of your Christian processions," she said, pulling her head back in and talking to Anastasia, "taking up the Emperor's roadway."

Sounds of cymbals being clashed and horns blown combined with shouting and laughter.

"Trouble is," said Nysa, "these processions of yours often end up with heads being broken. And the heads are often ours."

"I know," said Anastasia, her face pensive. She played with the beads at her throat. "I hate the violence. The teachings of the

Nazarene do not allow such behaviour. He was a man of peace. A man who would turn the other cheek. A man who cherished all others."

"I wish all his followers would realise that and behave accordingly," said Devorah. "Alexandria is not the safe place it once was."

"You sound just like my older sister," said Anastasia.

"My mother says the same," said Nysa. "She says many Christians have become zealots. We all used to get on well and respect each other's gods. But no more."

The curtains parted a little and Myrna's face appeared. She smiled and raised her eyebrows.

"We're fine," said Devorah. "How much longer?"

Myrna held her finger and thumb a short distance apart.

"You always say it's a short distance," said Anastasia.

Myrna moved her head back and forth and pulled the curtains closed.

"I forget she can't speak sometimes," said Anastasia. "It's almost as though she does."

Nysa felt a strange glow in her chest. *Am I the only one who can hear her?* She didn't want to ask her friends. The way Myrna's words just floated into her mind still confused her. She didn't doubt her experience, though. The words were so clear and Myrna responded to her inner talk, too.

"Why doesn't she ride with us?" asked Anastasia.

"I invited her," said Devorah. "She sometimes does when it is only me and her. I think she walks because the porters' feet might sink into the road with four of us."

They started moving again and soon Nysa could feel that they were descending.

"We're going to the Harbour Palace?" she asked.

"Yes," said Devorah, "the Lady sent word to Father that all three of us should meet her and the others at the east harbour."

"Have you been there before?" asked Nysa.

Devorah glanced towards Anastasia and back at Nysa. She rubbed her nose. "I may have. Father's work takes him all over and he knows the governor quite well."

"They say Cleopatra's shade still walks in the gardens. Someone saw her once," said Anastasia.

"Did she actually live there?" said Nysa. "I thought her palace stood closer to the Serapeum."

"Well, she may have used it for ceremonial occasions, like all the old Ptolemies," said Devorah, looking intensely at Anastasia, "but I'm told it has a smaller library and also a room designed by some old mathematician."

"What? Euclid? Oh, that would explain everything. That's why the Lady wants us there. She positively loves Euclid."

"Even if he's four hundred years old now or more."

"He eats sensibly and always waters his wine," said Anastasia.

The cry of sea gulls and the unmistakable aroma of fish told Nysa that they were close to their destination. A few moments later, the jolting stopped and the palanquin went still. Myrna drew back the curtains and unfastened the heavier cloth that formed a partial door. The girls emerged into the blinding dazzle of the sun.

The bearers stood naked to the waist, glistening with sweat. One drank from the end of the leg of what once walked around as a goat, the thin stream of water or wine arcing into his mouth. Myrna smiled, little beads of perspiration on her upper lip. She pointed towards the palace.

It stood on its own island, not as big as Pharos with its famous lighthouse but large enough for the impressive palace, gardens and a small temple to Artemis. It could only be approached by boat. Nysa studied the gap from the jetty to the large square in front of the palace steps, with their seated lions with raised paws resting on huge stone spheres. *No doubt designed by Euclid to teach about conic sections,* thought Nysa. She remembered someone telling her that the size of the gap was enough to prevent a galloping horseman from jumping over. The walls of the courtyard area rose sheer from the sea. On the side away from the shore, sharp rocks would break the sea's winter fury, but today the deep blue waters gently lapped against them. The only way to the palace involved climbing steps up from another jetty on the palace side. *The walls around the courtyard would provide a useful defence,* thought Nysa, *if any pirate should be so bold as to try.* With the Macedonian barracks just off to the right, she doubted any sea raid would succeed long.

"Come on, Nysa, stop daydreaming," said Devorah. "Can't you see Hypatia's waiting?"

The Lady Hypatia leaned against a wall, by the wide stairs ascending towards the great doors into the palace. A slave stood by her, holding a parasol to shade her face. Various young people gathered close by listening to her, but the distance meant Nysa couldn't be sure if she knew all of them. She did recognise Angelos, taller by a head than Hypatia herself and distinctive with his shock of black hair falling in tight curls to near his shoulders. Although a Christian, like Anastasia, he knew her to be the finest teacher in Alexandria and absorbed her words like one of the sponges sold by the harbour.

Myrna led them down to a small boat, and in a matter of minutes and a few swishes of the big oar at the back, the girls alighted on the steps leading up from the sea to the palace courtyard.

Alexander's Sword

Even this early in the morning, the glare of the white stone flagging made the girls squint and Nysa could feel the warmth of the sun passing straight through her light clothing. When they crossed to where the Lady waited for them most of the other young people had already left and disappeared into the palace grounds.

"This is your first visit I think, Nysa?" said Hypatia.

"Yes," said Nysa. "Thank you."

"No. Thank you. The work you dancers are doing is wonderful and important. I'm not sure you quite understand how important."

Hypatia's robe was drawn in under her bust and fell in graceful folds close to the ground. Her sandals, made of soft leather, peeked out. Her brown hair, arranged slightly differently every time Nysa had met her, had been gathered with beautiful grips and combs, and rose above her long neck. She was by far the most beautiful woman Nysa had ever seen. The girls all adored her, even though she didn't smile easily. Her kindness always shone through and once she started talking she could carry anyone to places so magical, time just stopped.

As they entered the palace grounds Hypatia turned to Nysa. "These gardens are my favourite place on earth, you know. The breezes from the sea, the calmness so close to the city but so separate, the shade from these wonderful trees." She moved her arm gracefully towards the tall palms that cast dappled shadows on the stone seats, ornamental bushes and flower gardens.

"Most of all I can sense the presence of the Divine Euclid." She offered a radiant smile to Nysa, laughter playing around her eyes. "He did his most important work in these grounds, you know."

They climbed the steps at the end of the garden and passed

through a grand portico into the darkness of the large reception room. As Nysa's eyes adjusted, ghostly white shapes hovering off the ground turned into statues set in niches in the walls. The floor had an intricate design in mosaic, showing a muscular man in the central circle, wearing a lion skin and carrying a great club. At the corners of the room, smaller circles showed Herakles, Nysa guessed, fighting Hydras and cleaning stables and doing all his labours. An outer circular band of mosaics carried the symbols for the zodiac, so important to Hypatia's teachings. As they passed through the room their footsteps and voices echoed. Nysa carefully avoided stepping on a face of coloured stone labelled 'Poseidon'. You could never be too careful when close to the ocean.

A door on the left led to a broad colonnade with a view over the sea. The water shimmered in turquoise splendour, partly reflecting the pride of Alexandria, their great lighthouse. Nysa, squinting into the glare, could just about make out her father's storage rooms on the far side of the great harbour. Further into the city the famous Library dominated all the other buildings nearby. Two galleys rested, anchored in the safety of the calm waters. A small skiff carried tiny figures towards the shore.

Hypatia, Myrna and the three girls made their way along the colonnade. Angelos walked behind them. To their right, a beautiful carved double door stood partially open. Out of the corner of her eye Nysa saw Anastasia and Devorah exchange a glance and then look at the floor.

"This is the library," said Hypatia.

"But the Great Li—"

"Yes, Nysa, the Great Library is over there." Hypatia extended her arm towards the curving waterfront of the city. "But this library held a special place in the heart of Ptolemy II. He wanted somewhere he could study and this library is not so widely known at all. In these difficult times that is just as well. But look..." She pointed above the door. There, held by large clasps of thick greenish metal, a sword had been fastened, its sharp leaf-like blade parallel to the ground.

"That is the sword that actually cut the Gordian Knot."

"King Alexander's sword?" said Nysa.

"One of them," responded Hypatia. "And the one he used on that famous occasion. You remember how no one could undo the knot, it had been tied so intricately, and Alexander just sliced through it? Well a prophecy says that as long as that sword is above that door this important library is safe."

The Lady paused and turned to Angelos. "I think these girls should see this library. Tell the curator I have sent them and ask if he can show them round. Once they have seen..." she paused and looked once more up at the sword, "...all they need to see, bring them to the Room of the Mathetai."

Angelos nodded, offering a very slight bow.

"Come, fair maids. This is a privilege not even given to all princes. Remember not to chatter like starlings. People come here to study."

Anastasia pouted. Devorah huffed. Nysa wondered how much oil Angelos put on his hair to keep its tight curls from rioting. They entered the serenity of the Palace Library.

A bald-headed man, with robes like a priest and dark lines of kohl under his eyes, came over to them. Angelos greeted him with deep respect and introduced the girls by their name and their family. *I'd no idea he'd noticed me,* thought Nysa, *let alone knew who I am.* The Curator regarded each of them in turn. He held Nysa's eyes for so long she felt a flush of embarrassment spread through her and looked down. When she caught her friends' eyes they were giving her an odd look.

"Our Library isn't like the main one. Its collection has a quite different purpose. You'll see it's laid out in an unusual way. This is where people read." He indicated benches and tables set between a curving Library wall and the windowed inside walls of the colonnade. "We collect the documents for them. They are never removed from the island. Their words are all sacred. Here rests the history of all mankind. Here are the Revelations of the Gods. Come."

He beckoned to Nysa and her friends but as he turned, indicated to Angelos he should remain by the door with Alexander's sword. In front of them, a fresco painted on smooth curving plaster showed maidens dancing with the God Apollo. *The Muses! The creative spirits behind all writing.*

The Curator led them to the left where the fresco on one side and the curving wall on the other carried recesses holding rolls wrapped in cloth. Under each separate recess a geometric shape, some Greek letters and a number, offered a filing system Nysa couldn't quickly grasp. They moved slowly between the curving rows of papyrus rolls in their little cubbyholes. On their right an opening led into an inner concentric circle with further storage. They walked past that opening and several more. Light filtered through from a raised cupola high in the roof. Just above the head of the Curator, unlit lamps hung on long chains from the ceiling far above. As Nysa's eyes adjusted to the muted daylight, she could read the codes for each document.

Every entranceway to the inner circle had wooden columns with painted hieroglyphs. Nysa had learned some of this antique picture writing and loved its mystery and beauty. But the pictograms had a random appearance to her. They entered the next storage circle, turned right, passed by a couple more entrances, and turned left into a circle even deeper in the library. Nysa had no idea now where she stood in relation to the entrance with the sword.

"Walk down there," said the man.

The three girls followed his directions and soon came to a wall, with a painting of a god with the head of a bird.

"Who's that?" asked Anastasia.

"Thoth," said Nysa, "the god of writing and learning. My father says he is similar to the Greek Hermes."

"We'd best go back," said Devorah.

When they retraced their steps the Curator had gone. The girls stopped.

"Which way should we go?" asked Nysa, sensing the other girls somehow knew more than she did.

"I don't know," said Anastasia.

"Surely this is a labyrinth," said Devorah, "designed to confuse."

"Well, we came this way, didn't we?" said Nysa. She looked at her friends and they nodded. They continued forward, passing openings on both sides.

"I think we turned here." Nysa peered between the columns giving access to the wider circle on their right. "Shall we try?"

Anastasia shrugged. Devorah coughed, and dust swirled about them where they'd brushed against some of the cloths wrapped around the scrolls. Nysa led the way and soon met a transverse wall bearing scrolls and entirely blocking their progress.

"Other way then."

They went back the other way, passing the entrance they'd just come through and continuing on. No opening gave access to the outer circle before they met another block.

"We have to go back," said Anastasia, "don't we?"

They did. Nysa could feel a slow nervousness creeping through her limbs, like footprints left by ants made of ice. She couldn't see how they could be lost. Even if the Library was indeed a maze it had to be fairly simple.

"Knowledge is like that," said the Curator, who now stood behind them. "It is so easy to get lost amid all the opinions and the shouting in the market place. Only the pure in heart can find their way in this Library and only the pure in soul can plumb its depths."

Some of the storage areas must slide. That's how he ended up behind us in a corridor we'd just walked down, thought Nysa.

"Come, I'll show you something."

He walked on purposefully, turning this way and that, sometimes in an outer circle, sometimes in the inner ones. The shelving went high and although Nysa thought she might be able to climb it, the top part rose smoothly, with no handholds.

They reached the centre. Light reflected in a corona above them, high in the domed roof. A bull, with a sun disk between its horns, dominated the centre of the Library. The Curator pointed up.

"Our dome, built with the same wisdom that enabled the beauty of the Pantheon in Rome. We have light for our work, but no rain."

In front of the life-size bull, made entirely of bronze and very detailed, a small offertory table held flowers and a brass cup with a cover full of holes, from which the smoke of a gentle incense rose heavenward.

"The Apis bull protects our labyrinth even as the Minotaur protected the labyrinth of Crete." A thin smile spread along the Curator's mouth. "Don't worry, we're not sacrificing any virgins today."

Nysa shuddered. Devorah let out a snort and coughed some more.

"Come."

The Curator led them down a narrow passageway that carried no scrolls. The plaster walls on either side had Egyptian writing and pictures of many of the Gods. At the far end, on either side of a stone doorway flanked by pylons running up close to the ceiling, were pictures of a goddess with wings outstretched, with a feather in her headband. Above the door a winged sun disk rose above the sinuous curves of two snakes facing outwards in each direction.

"We call this room the Temple of Truth. Only those true to themselves can find their way in and find their way out again. Our bull is as protective as the Minotaur, over the learning hidden here."

Nysa peeked in. The room, lit by four suspended lamps, had carvings in low relief all around. Figures waded through water, their clothing rendered both wet and dry with the mason's chisel, with an artistry that took her breath away. A central round pillar partially blocked the carvings on the far side. Some incised symbols had been highlighted in colour. The room held an extra-ordinary peace, the stillness found at the centre of a spiral.

"Those who find their way here uninvited, never leave. It is our joy and our duty to protect that which the Gods have given. Those who built this Library knew that. We have a sacred trust that must not be broken."

The curator let the girls look into the room for some moments longer. Nysa thought she heard something like a sigh, deep, deep below the stone floor, as though somewhere in the rock nearer sea level a god of the underworld turned in sleep. She tried to open her mind to the words that might live in that sigh.

'BEWARE,' whispered the soundless voice. A voice older than Alexandria. A voice older than Egypt.

"Come on, Nysa, we're leaving," said Devorah. "Unless you want to stay here all day."

The Curator had already started the journey back through the long passageway towards the sun-bearing horns of the bull at the centre.

She followed the other girls out, turning this way and that. A path too complex to easily remember.

"Do you want a fig?" asked Angelos, sitting on the step of the entrance to the library.

Time Dance

Nysa continued down the colonnade with her friends and they entered a further large room some way beyond the library. High above their heads the ceiling carried traditional Egyptian decorations. The floor had been laid with pale rose marble slabs. Light came from rows of highly placed windows, shielded from the bright sun by the roof overhang. The cool clear atmosphere of the room enveloped Nysa and she could feel the resonating peace that a place gathers from being used for years for sacred ceremonial. A buzz of voices greeted them. Boys and girls of Nysa's age and older were chatting and some watched as men erected a structure of poles on the side of the room closest to the sea. Near them, a large irregular object the size of a cow or bull lay swathed in cloth.

"Gather around," said Hypatia.

They did, sitting in a large circle as the Lady gracefully perched on a low stool that one of the older boys had offered to her. Myrna sat on a marble bench on the far side of the room.

"Some of you have been here before and for some it's your first time. You all know that the great sage Pythagoras taught 'all is number'. I've told you this many times. We see it in the coiling of the snail shell, in the placement of the leaves of plants, in the rhythms of the Moon and the Sun and in every aspect of these beautiful bodies gifted to us by the Gods for our time on this celestial sphere on which we dwell."

As she spoke the men continued to build whatever they were constructing with their poles and rope. They worked swiftly and quietly and had obviously done this before. Above them, high up, other men were standing outside one of the windows on a walkway. They were working with something metallic, which flashed golden in the sunlight every now and again.

Hypatia was pointing to the floor.

"See where the craftsmen who made this wonderful room incised our floor with the universal numbers of creation."

She stood up and borrowed a thin, straight stick from the same boy who'd provided her stool. Walking within the circle formed by her young audience, she pointed out the geometric designs on the floor. Fine grooves had been cut and pale-coloured dyes marked their course in curves and straight lines. Hypatia spoke of how a single point becomes a line and a line a triangle or square, and how the square evolves into the pentagram. As she spoke, the point of her cane flicked first to a line and then to a shape picked out on the surface of the marble.

"When we dance in here, we animate the Numbers of Creation, we stir the Currents of Time itself. That is the importance of sacred dance. Some of you have been evoking the movements of the celestial spheres for several years, and some of you are just coming fresh to this." She looked to where Nysa sat with Anastasia and Devorah, and smiled. "This work – for it is indeed work – is of the highest importance. These are dangerous and difficult times when the most holy and delicate of truths are in danger of being lost."

For a few long moments, Hypatia looked around her at the shapes on the floor. *She's seeing into the future.* Nysa frowned and blinked. *How do I know that?*

'Because it is true,' came the thought within. Nysa glanced over to where Myrna sat bathed in the pink reflected light from the floor. The mute slave girl winked.

"Today I'm going to share something new to all of you," said the Alexandrian woman. She gently eased her way down onto the stool and arranged her skirts around her. She placed the cane at her feet.

"Nine years ago, to the day, I had a vision. I'd been fasting and living in our Temple of Isis for almost a month. Each night I reached out to the stars, seeking wisdom from the Gods who animate those great constellations. The spirit of Athena drew close."

She looked over to the boy who assisted her.

"I did not see Her, Angelos, no one can see a God. But I knew She had drawn close. I fell asleep."

The boy nodded. Nysa wondered if this answered a question he'd once asked.

Hypatia spoke of her dream and how it had been as real, if not more real, than her normal everyday life. A deer had approached her and led her into a grove of trees. There, three maidens danced and sang, whilst others played lyres and beat tambours. The spring near to where they danced sparkled with sunlight, and these reflected beams the three dancers caught and wove. At first the light beams glowed and vanished, but gradually, as they danced, a shape appeared, a shape beautiful in its simplicity yet full of life. A shape that the dancers span into a key to life. Gradually the dancers withdrew and the shape moved on its own between the women in their pale gowns. As it slowly revolved, crystalline forms appeared, and flowed, and scintillated within it: pyramidions, cubes, spheres faceted with hexagrams…

Nysa could see Hypatia's grove and the shape. The glowing structure of light pulsed with inner forms. She knew they were the ones spoken of by Euclid and the ancient Greeks; some appeared made of fire and others made of water. They flowed in and out of each other like gentle breaths. Their inner dance made the outer shape, which looped in a folded circle that Nysa couldn't quite understand. For a moment the grove vanished and Nysa floated within and beyond this flowing stream of light as it wound its way throughout space, embracing stars and constellations in its dance.

Gradually it all vanished. The others in the room were talking quietly and the men had completed the structure they were building. Hypatia walked past her and briefly placed her hand on Nysa's shoulder.

'You saw. You know. Hold the Secret close. It is dear to Isis.'

Nysa didn't know if it was the Lady who had spoken or Myrna. The room, still and moving at the same time, no longer felt completely solid, as though, if she tried hard enough, Nysa could see through its walls.

A dazzling shaft of light poured into where they sat, lighting up a wide rose-coloured circle on the floor. The three or four boys and girls caught in the brilliance moved away. Hypatia walked over to the men and carefully removed the cloth covering from the object. Built in metal – Nysa guessed bronze of some sort – the shape, made of a gleaming curved rod, formed an exact replica of the folded line of woven light Nysa had seen with her inner eyes. The men attached thin cables that disappeared up into the gloom near the ceiling. Gradually three other men pulling near the wall caused the metal structure to rise in the air. Hypatia guided it at first and then men standing on the platform of poles moved it so it did not swing wildly. Bit by bit it rose until, with blinding flashes, it caught the sunlight reflected in through the high window.

"See," said Hypatia. "In mathematics this is called a knot. This is the Time Knot."

She pointed with the long stick at the sharp shadow cast in the oval of light on the pink marble floor. As the men moved the shape above them, the shadow produced flowing shapes, as though dark snakes chased each other across the cold stone floor. Nysa caught her breath as the floor came to life. The shadow movement dissolved its solidity. Nysa could see into and through the marble. Pictures, forms, songs unsung, poems not yet dreamed by poets all played just below the surface.

"Watch the shapes, girls, watch. Let them seep into your heart, your stomach, your blood and bones. They are the very shapes of life. They are to enlighten, not mesmerise. You will know their meaning only when you dance them."

At some point – Nysa could not tell minutes or hours, for time had vanished – the boys started playing music on instruments they'd placed earlier at the sides of the room. The acoustics were wonderful. The sounds – drumming, fluting, strumming – flowed like the shadow snakes, while the gleaming bronze Time Knot slowly rotating above them.

Nysa stood and danced. Anastasia and Devorah joined her. The other girls span slowly in a weaving, dipping, rhythmic circle around them. The music led the dance; the dancing led the music; and the Time Knot guided them all with its celestial shapes.

"Fight, You Boys, Fight."

Sweden – about 1520

It took three days riding for us to reach the end of the lake. Another three days and we were in a landscape of fir trees and pure snow. The hunters stopped at a lodge where we slept one night in the warm. They would stay here and trap furry beasties. We would go north. I couldn't believe that I felt sad to say goodbye to my pony. Baldur – for that was the name he answered to – enjoyed being in the lead. He pushed to the front, even though my riding skills were by far the least accomplished in the group. No one seemed to mind. Baldur had a knack of finding the right way to go.

Now we carried small packs on our backs. The skis were very long and narrow: made of wood, they had upturned ends and rather lovely carvings. My boots were strapped in. *No safety catch! Best not to fall over.*

Signy had a map drawn on a piece of cloth that she kept with great care in her jacket. She knew the villages to visit and the ones to avoid. In the summer both she and Brother Niels had travelled in these parts looking for certain rare berries and flowers. In the first few days we often slept where Håkan's mother was known and respected. She'd sewn various small pieces of jewellery into her skirts and used these on occasion to buy provisions for us. Both she and Håkan had some valuable coins. They discussed accounts some evenings, very quietly. I wondered how long we could manage to pay for all our food. On two occasions Signy persuaded a farmer to take us on his sled, when the roads were good enough. My legs, much tougher now, enjoyed the rest. The cold continued to sit inside my bones. I'd never felt really warm since my dip in the lake.

As we headed north the days became shorter once again and,

if possible, colder. I couldn't get either Håkan or Signy to explain why we were going so far north. Something about a drum skin, that didn't make sense to me. We now felt quite safe from the Danish soldiers. That is, until we saw the scarecrow in the tree.

We'd left at dawn from a village where we'd slept near the fire in a large homestead, with dogs and chickens snuffling and clucking around us. I'd ceased to worry about smelling like old football socks days ago. I caught the powerful whiff of the others once in a while, and when dogs stopped barking at us they would sniff everywhere as though we were olfactory entertainment. I don't think anyone washed more than their face and hands in the winter months. Having a … going to do a number two, when you have to break the ice in the privy just to get inside, became an activity best avoided as long as possible. There never was a happy ending, and definitely no puppy-soft loo paper.

The pathway we followed climbed gently with some occasional downhill runs, when the skis swished along and the wind blew the honk of our clothes well behind us. The sun shone brightly and the snow-clad trees looked just right for a picture postcard. We knew we were coming close to another village. We were near the very edge of Signy's map. She'd marked this village with a little dot that meant it looked on Lutherans in a friendly way. Eira, who'd been taking long swishing strides in the lead, came to a stop and pointed. We were climbing the track towards a crossroads, where a great fir tree dominated the view. A shape, man-like and not man-like, hovered below a great branch. In a few strides Signy overtook her daughter.

"We have to pass this way. Don't look children. Such a view never leaves your mind. The poor man is beyond helping now."

Signy's words proved right. I glanced up as we went by and wished I hadn't. In the cold the man looked chilly but normal, apart from the fact he hung from a branch, with his feet a horse's height above the ground – and he had no eyes.

I felt gorge rise in my throat and thought I might be sick. We took the track to the right at the crossroads. Signy had seen that on her map. Anyway we could see smoke curling up quite close by. Minutes later we were in the village. Every door remained closed. This had been where we hoped to find lodging for the night. Sometimes we paid and sometimes we all did some work to cover the cost of our warm hay and salt-fish stew. But to find a place to stay we needed to talk with people and here no one wanted to show their faces to us. We took off our skis and carried them across the rutted frozen mud of the main street. A wooden church stood a little way apart at the edge of the village. The door stood ajar.

"Maybe we can sleep in there, Mother," said Håkan.

Signy went to the door and looked in.

"What do you want?" said a voice behind us.

"Shelter for the night, mistress," said Signy. "That and a little food. We can pay."

The woman looked at her for a long time without saying anything. She stood at the door of a small cottage on the other side of the road to the church. A cat came out and rubbed itself against her legs. She had a white bonnet on her head and a heavy shawl around her shoulders. She could have been any age, but I guessed she was older than my mum.

"I know you," said the woman at last.

Signy waited without saying anything. We three cold youngsters looked back and forth from one to the other.

"You, best come in," said the woman. "I'm Kristina Ralfsdatter."

"Yes," said Signy, introducing herself, and us. "I remember you."

The woman didn't say much after that but bustled around preparing a stew. She even had meat and the smells were beyond mouth-watering. A fire roared in the stove and the room, whilst a bit smoky, had enough warmth so we could take off our outer layers. The cat had found its way to my lap. Outside, the steady clack, clack came from where Håkan chopped wood. He had a real gift for that and an accurate eye.

Once darkness had fallen, lamps had been lit and we were eating, the woman turned to Signy.

"We met once, you know."

"I do," said Signy.

"When things were safer."

"Yes," said Signy.

"Your husband?"

Signy looked up from her trencher of bread, brimming with meat and root vegetables.

"Doing the Lord's work."

The woman nodded. She passed the beer jug around once more before saying, "As is mine. As is mine. May the good Lord keep them safe in their travails."

"Amen," said Signy and Håkan together.

Eira's eyes had grown as big as two king-sized marbles, as she looked from her mother to this lady. She said nothing.

"The man?" said Signy.

"By the crossroads?" said the woman.

"Yes."

Listening to them was like listening to my mum and dad talk sometimes. A code you just cannot quite get because not all the information is divulged at the right time.

The woman leaned back in her chair.

"He unwisely spoke too much."

We waited to see what more she would say. She'd closed her eyes.

"He was our pastor."

Signy leant across and placed her hand on the woman's arm. The woman covered it with her own.

"Soldiers came here looking for a woman on the run with

three children in tow. The pastor spoke for us all when he said none of us had seen any woman on the run. He added, 'What woman in her right mind would run with the snow so thick and the winter still holding everything in its grasp?' The soldier in charge, a cruel man, struck him for those words, with the flat of his sword. But Gustav stood up once more and told the man he wasn't fit to be an officer. If you could have seen him smile then, your blood would have turned to ice."

She clenched her fists and placed them on either side of the trencher of bread in front of her.

"He turned to two of his soldiers and said, 'He is defying an officer of the King. That is treason. Hang him. He is not to be cut down. The birds need to feed. Not much food with all this snow.' And within the hour it'd been done. We were all forced to watch."

She paused for a long time. The wood in the stove crackled and the firelight played on her face.

"Not a man or woman in this village who would not spit on the picture of that papist king now. We're done with Denmark, that's for sure. Before, some were loyal. Said it was our duty to obey. God's will and all that nonsense. Now? Now we are all for Martin Luther." She drank down her beer, her face fierce.

The next day Kristina Ralfsdatter would take no money from us.

"Travel through the woods. Keep going steadily north. Watch the roads. That captain, he's an evil man. Canny. Cunning. Somehow he knew you'd pass this way. Only he got his timing wrong."

She gave Signy a long hug and then held each of us by the shoulders.

"No one here saw you. I didn't see you. Even the cat didn't see you." She smiled at Håkan and me. "Your mother explained something of the task ahead for the two of you. God speed. Those whom the Good Lord looks over..." She stopped, shrugged and turned back into the cottage. Turning once again she pointed at us, using both hands.

"Fight, you boys, fight. We are done with all this evil. Fight."

Lucian's Twin Brother

Signy had been given good directions and we made steady progress. For the second day the sun shone brightly. The snow often tumbled from high branches, falling with a soft humph nearby. Long icicles dripped and sparkled in the light. A buzzard circled slowly, high above us. The food had done us all good and Eira, who skied next to me when she could, whistled her tuneless whistle once more. She'd her bow handy in the hope something small and tasty might come in range.

We'd worked our way on a small track around the edge of a hill. Stones formed a shelter that might have been man-made or might not.

Eira said, "I have to stop here a moment. I'll catch you up."

We nodded, we had all had to make stops like that once in a while.

"There's a wider track down there," said Håkan, "we will wait just inside the trees."

We skied down slowly. In the summer what lay below our feet must be pasture. Some tufts of frozen grass peeked through. Just before we reached the roadway, Håkan pointed off to our left. Something flashed in the sunlight.

"Soldiers," he whispered.

"Have they seen us?" said Signy.

"I don't know. The sun is more in their eyes, but they may have seen movement. The meadow is pretty open."

"We should've stayed by the tree-line over there," said Signy.

"The snow is deep on that side of the hill," said Håkan pointing across the road. "No horse could follow us there."

"Are they on horseback or skis?"

"Danes on skis? Never. No, some are walking, I think, and most are riding."

We heard a shout.

"We'll cross the road and ski down there," said Håkan.

A sound like a thin jet of steam escaping made us all turn. There on the road sat the young officer drawing his sword. His face showed clearly now; he could have been Lucian's twin brother. He could have been Lucian, except his eyes had an almost purple tint and emanated cruelty. The thinnest of thin smiles had crept over his face.

"You might as well come out," he said, in Swedish with a slight accent. "I can see you all and my soldiers are behind you."

I looked back to see our retreat had indeed been cut off. His horse now blocked the route across the road, and his sharp sword, flashing as he turned it this way and that in the sun, didn't look ceremonial. He had a small crossbow hanging from his saddle. Something moved just at the edge of my field of vision. I didn't look towards it because the captain, or whatever he was, had pointed his sword at me.

"Come here, boy. This is a meeting I've been looking forward to for a long time. Now, let me see you properly."

He didn't, because at that point his horse reared and plunged forward along the road, and he nearly lost his balance. An arrow stuck out of the horse's rump.

"Come on," shouted Eira, as she skied straight across the road behind the horse, as it reared once more.

We dug in our ski poles, clattered across the frozen ruts in the road, and gathered speed on the steep slope the other side. The snow-covered meadow had few rocks to avoid and I made a little prayer to the god of green runs that I wouldn't fall on a slope this easy. Eira, leading, leaned this way and that. Håkan did the same. I just kept my head down and thought we would surely already be out of arrow range. One shot cracked out, echoing around the valley. A gun? We were now speeding so fast the wind brought tears to my eyes. The slope continued on and on, deep, virgin, wind-banked snow, impossible for any horse to cross.

Eira still held the lead. She screamed, jumped and sailed for some moments in the air before dropping from view. We were all going too fast to stop. Well, falling off a mountainside might be preferable to drowning in a frozen lake. The snow stopped. I leaned back, losing balance. I sprang. I'm good at simple ski acrobatics, and made an enforced backward somersault, an easy manoeuvre. I saw a flash of dark rock, green frozen water and then snow. Straightening out from a crouch my skis hit the snow on the far side of the gulf, much lower than the hillside I'd just left. I leaned into the slope to bring myself to a gliding halt, in a shower of snow and ice. Eira had made it; so had I. Moments later both Håkan and Signy leapt to safety, although he ended up doing a bum's rush for a bit.

Håkan and I climbed back up the slope to the gully we had just jumped. The gorge fell at least ten metres and we'd crossed about the same distance with our jump. Only the fact that the other side stood much higher than this bank had saved us. The difference in height entirely hid us from the Danish captain and his murderous thugs. The narrow gorge ran as far as the eye could see in each direction. If no bridge existed nearby then we were safe; at least for a while. No horse or even foot soldier could safely descend and ascend those sharp rocks. Signy said we would keep the gorge to our left, and continue to head more or less north.

We skied slowly that afternoon. All of us were exhausted and no one spoke much. We'd hugged Eira for her presence of mind and coolness with the arrow in the captain's horse. Sadly, she'd dropped her bow when she came to the gorge; we hoped it wouldn't be needed again. We trudged rather than skied, as the ground rose steadily once more. Signy hardly answered when we asked if we were going the right way. The horrid death of the pastor, a man we'd never known, had shocked us all. And the near-death experience with the Danish bully hadn't helped.

The path climbed through trees. Sometimes we had to take off our skis to get past a fallen branch or an uprooted tree. This held us up, and the light began to fail. For the first time since crossing the lake, it looked like we might spend the night in the snow. We all knew that with the temperature plunging at night, we mightn't survive that.

The trees thinned and then cleared. Ahead of us lay a valley. The track descended to a little hamlet next to a frozen river, fed by the gorge far to our left. We could see a bridge there. Behind the hamlet the hill rose sharply, with its snow and trees looking impassable. The top of the hill stood shrouded in the mist of a low cloud, even though we were bathed in sunshine.

"It would have helped if Mistress Ralfsdatter had told us of the gorge. She did describe this hamlet. Maybe if we'd followed the road we would've reached here eventually. She thought we would be here by tomorrow night, so I think we took a short cut."

When we entered the small cluster of houses, Signy counted with care. We knocked at the door of the fifth house on the right. A man asked our business.

"We are friends of Mistress Ralfsdatter."

After a pause, bolts were drawn back and we entered the smoky comfort of the cottage. Jurgan, a man in his forties with a pockmarked face, didn't smile much. His room had half-made barrels dotted about. He said he made his living as a cooper. The cottage had walls constructed from huge stones, heavier than two men could lift. I'd never seen anything built like this in Sweden or Norway. Signy told a little of our story and how we'd escaped from a troop of Danish soldiers seeking to capture us. The man nodded but didn't say anything. He put some cheese and bread on the table, with the inevitable pitcher of weak beer. We ate through all he placed before us.

"We leave tomorrow before dawn," Jurgan announced, as he wiped down the table. "I also breed mules. We'll use those. You cannot ski to where we are going." I wondered how he bred mules when they are sterile, but kept my basic biology to myself.

None of us slept well that night. We all shared the thought of fists pounding on the door. Jurgan had courage, certainly. He knew all about the dead pastor. He spat when we told of the Danes.

We gathered by the mules as silently as we could. Nothing stirred in the village. The last dregs of moonlight meant we didn't need torches. Jurgan brought us through his kitchen at the back, past the stench of the privy and midden heap, to the rich aromas of a mule pen. One had already been prepared as a pack animal, carrying our skis. It also had a satchel of food for our journey. The other three beasts carried Jurgan and us, two by two. I again had the joy of sharing a ride with Håkan. I didn't think he liked me very much. He hardly spoke and I think blamed me for holding up the escape so long we were now likely to be caught and … well, who knew, but the eyeless man provided a clue. Signy rode with Eira, who even managed to fall asleep as we climbed a narrow path that started near the cooper's home.

When we were well away from the village Jurgan told us that only locals knew of this route. The proper roadway, difficult to negotiate in winter, would take at least two days even on horseback. He doubted the soldiers would think we would head this way, to his small town.

I wondered about that. The Lucian spooky guy had appeared in my dark Ouija vision. He seemed to be getting intelligence from the nastier places in the universe.

Mule Paces

We rode all morning without stopping, going at mule pace. At one point we nearly emerged from the trees and could see down to the little hamlet, laid out like a toy farm in the distant valley below. A couple of people ran down the main street. Eira pointed. We could all see the file of blue-coated soldiers making their way towards the bridge that led to the village. Håkan muttered something.

"Don't talk filth," said his mother.

"Sorry, Mother," he responded, and then winked at me. *Perhaps he likes me after all.* I grinned back, determined to add the word to my Swedish vocab.

"Don't worry. No one in the village will help them now. They all know you've passed through. They all know where you're going. But they will all say you headed east. We haven't time for the Danes." Jurgan added the same word as Håkan had used. Signy frowned. Eira looked at a spot on her boots. Håkan stared at a mule. I giggled. Then we all laughed, full throated and hearty. The first good laugh since I last took a bath – in the lake.

"Sshhh…" said Signy.

"Don't worry, mistress," said Jurgan, still chortling, "the wind makes so much noise, the soldiers won't be able to hear themselves think. But we best move back into the trees. A sharp-eyed soldier might see what he cannot hear."

We continued climbing. A good hour later we came to a little plateau. Trees grew at the edges, and near some great stones a frozen pond clasped stiff bulrushes in its icy grip. The flat area, close to what might once have been a building, extended for about half the size of Scrivener's cricket pitch. Jurgan led the mules past the pond and through a gap in the overgrown stones. Moments later we were in a substantial cave, and he had a fire going, with melted snow approaching the boil.

"I do this journey frequent," he said. "This is my stopping-off point."

"Was this a building once?" asked Signy pointing outside the cave.

"Indeed, mistress. This was a small but thriving monastery. The monks had taken a vow of silence or some such thing and chose to live isolated like. Our little village down there served them, as did the town up above." He pointed to the roof of the cave. "Where we're headed."

"What happened to them?" asked Signy.

"Before my granddaddy's day, they died out. Perhaps the plague. Perhaps through lack of talk." He spat.

"Don't like monks. Never have. They live off the poor. I've never seen a thin one in my life."

Jurgan added some dried meat from the panniers and a few chopped vegetables. Soon we were dipping in chunks of bread and slurping up hot food.

"Mind you…" Jurgan said as though we'd not all been more or less silent for twenty minutes. "Up there –" and again he pointed to the roof – "I'm as good a Catholic as ever rang a silver bell. When we get there –" he jabbed his finger upwards – "best forget the name of Luther, however much we like him and his reforms."

We nodded. I'd little idea what this Luther guy had done or when he'd done it. He seemed important to Signy though, and I didn't like to ask. Mum and Dad have never been church-type people. But ever since I'd seen a god appear in my bedroom, I'd thought there might be something more to find out. Shame I couldn't use my laptop to look up Luther.

Meal done with, with no washing up except the pot, which he wiped with an old cloth, we returned to the mules. Now Jurgan linked them all by rope, with his mule in the lead, and the pack mule last. I'd a sinking feeling we might be about to do something dangerous. Above the old ruined monastery, which had kindly donated some of its stones to Jurgan's home far below, the rock face rose almost perpendicular, to the height of a sizeable office building. Ice glistened on it, and a few crisply frozen bushes clung to sharp clefts. The pathway allowed the mules just room to go up single file.

"Don't try to steer them," said Jurgan over his shoulder. "They do this route most weeks, up and down. No horse can manage. Not sure-footed enough. I can show you skeletons to prove the point, and not just of horses."

I hoped he was lying, to amuse us. But I suspected my hope was in vain.

"Them soldiers will not be able to follow, even if they guess where you've gone. Not up this bit, any road. And the other way round? Take 'em nigh on two full days. That's why I does this route. That's how I makes my money. Fish up. Furs down. Barrels up. Biscuits down. Beer at both ends." He burped and laughed.

Gradually we climbed. I stared at Håkan's scarf. I stared at the lichens on the rock face. I estimated the length of blue-green icicles (biggest, I reckoned was more than two metres). I studied the sky for signs of snow. I watched a bird sit and stare at us as the mules picked their way along a path no wider in places than a skateboard. Sideways obviously.

I absolutely didn't look down. The path twisted in a hairy hairpin every now and again, climbing ever higher. I don't know how long we rode. A damp foggy cloud settled round us. I could still make out the rock face to one side or the other. I didn't have to worry about looking down. Rock on one side and cloud on the other. Water droplets settled on our sleeves. *Must be above freezing then.* Still we climbed. My estimate of an office block had been way out. *We must be higher above the ruined monastery now than the London Eye.*

"How did you do that?" asked Håkan all of a sudden.

"What?" I said, to the back of his hat.

"On the skis. Over the gully."

"Oh that," I said.

"Yes, that. That looked…" He ran out of words.

"Not so difficult, actually," I lied. I'd crashed on my face and my nether regions many times when practising. But somehow, a back flip came easier to me than any other trick. I could do the same off the springboard at the Hammerford pool in the summer. Race down the board, bounce, and spin backwards, usually entering the water with a huge splash, but feet first. Scared my mum to bits but even Juliette was impressed. Actually doing stunts like that with skis proved easier, with a steep enough slope. Wouldn't want to teach Håkan though, not with the long wooden skis and lashed-on boots.

He half-turned. "Took courage. You were about to fall and you did something grand. I like that. The tumblers who taught me tricks, they could do things like that, turning disaster into something glorious."

Seems like I'd impressed him.

"Tak Håkan," I said.

He shrugged, a friendly sort of shrug.

Lights appeared ahead. In the foggy gloom they spread out like glowing stains surrounded by faint rainbows. The mules developed a sense of urgency and even trotted for a few paces, before deciding that was too undignified. Moments later we reached a big building with a courtyard.

"The tavern," said Jurgan. "You're lucky to be in a good Catholic town. We're all loyalists here," he added quietly. "And you're visiting a relative up north. Right?"

"Right," said Signy, "the Lord's blessed truth in fact."

I wondered what she meant by that but didn't have time to ponder as a door opened and we were met with food smells and a huge clatter of noise.

Daylight Robbery

Our few belongings were stowed in a chamber with straw mattresses, above the main room where we now sat. The warmth of a great fire glowed right through the house. Perhaps having the slow-death-by-mule-ride behind me, perhaps having stewed rabbit inside me, or perhaps drinking what looked like water, but burned all the way down into my stomach, I finally felt warm.

A boy with a pudding-basin haircut, the colour of pale daffodils, banged down beer in front of us.

"Will we pay here with one of your jewels?" asked Eira. "Ouch!" she added. "Don't kick me Håkan."

"You can get a bath here," said Jurgan. "They'll bring hot water to the room for a price."

"Don't think we can afford that," said Signy, rather too loud. "We need to pay you though. We have some Krona."

Jurgan leant across the table. "The herbs you gave me down there –" and this time he pointed to the floor – "they're payment enough. That and the work you're doing. Your family that is," he added quietly.

The pot-boy, or whatever description fitted young master Pudding-Basin's job title, talked with two men at the far side of the room. He leaned into their table. They looked across at where we sat. One had a thin face and darkish hair, the other, who could've been Pudding-Basin's father, had long ash-blond hair that fell to his shoulders. Those shoulders looked like they obtained their size by lifting blocks of stone from the monastery far below.

More clear fiery water arrived and we all drank to Jurgan's good health and fortune.

"Yes, if Mary Mother of God helps me," he said, crossing himself.

We all nodded rather too vigorously. Eira had fallen asleep, her head in her mother's lap. Back in our room, we all fell asleep almost at once, surrounded by noise from below, welcome warmth from the fire and our own particular aromas.

"We must go."

"Right," I said, struggling to awake. "Is it breakfast?"

Håkan jabbed me in the ribs.

"Now," he hissed. I'd fallen back asleep.

Signy had her finger to her lips.

"I paid last night for the meal, the drinks and the room. All we own is here. But we're not in a safe place in this papist stronghold. Did you see the Danish flag as we came in last night?"

I didn't think I knew what the Danish flag looked like, so I just looked expectant. That usually worked. We quickly gathered our stuff and made our way downstairs. The room had a few people sprawled at tables and some curled up by the fire, suggesting that there were two classes of room in this hotel. The sound of snoring drowned out the soft padding of our footsteps. Håkan and I held all the skis, lashed together, and eased our way between the tables to the door. It wasn't locked. We slipped out, letting a great blast of cold air into the room. No one stirred. We were out. We walked through the town until we reached the church. A candle burned inside, accompanied by men's voices softly chanting.

"Matins," said Signy, quietly. She turned right, up a lane flanked by two or three wooden houses.

In the distance a dog barked. Another answered. Then a cock crowed. Our feet crunched on the ice between the ruts of mud. No stars shone in the murky darkness above our heads. The street remained totally dark apart from a lamp flickering some way ahead. A pale glow off to the right suggested dawn might bother to share some more light soon. Our eyes adjusted and we eased our way out of the town.

"Is this the right way, Mother?" asked Håkan in a whisper.

"Yes. Jurgan told me which way to go."

We walked on in silence, hedgerows on either side of us. The lane had been paved in rough ice rather than snow and we stepped carefully, to avoid twisting our ankles. I missed my mule. After about half an hour, with the landscape becoming clearer all the time, we reached some trees. The farmland now lay behind us. To our left, a hill rose steeply with a cluster of tall trees at the top. On our right someone had piled a high cairn of stones.

"The roadway will drop soon. We will go down into another valley. We can ski again. We're getting close."

"Mother," said Eira.

"What?"

"Um, Mother, I need..."

"Be quick," said Signy. "We'll be getting our skis on."

I helped lace up Håkan's skis. The boots had to be firmly fixed so the skis didn't shift around. I took my gloves off to do this and the cold nipped at my hands, dispelling all last night's warmth in a few moments.

"Don't bother," said a deep voice.

In panic we looked around. Standing in the lea of the craggy hill a huge man held Eira by her hair. He walked her forward, pushing her with his knees in her back. She scowled with fury and fear. In his right hand he held a long hunting knife. He moved it in a circular motion.

"Drop your skirts," said another voice, higher pitched.

Emerging from trees to our right came pudding-basin boy, his pale hair sticking out from a multi-coloured bobble hat.

"Now," said a deeper voice from behind us.

Swinging around, I confronted the thin-faced man from last night. Like Pudding-Basin he carried a club.

"Your skirts," said the big man, with the shoulders of an American football player, "quickly."

"Don't be vulgar," said Signy.

"I ain't kidding, you Lutheran cow," said the man. "I'll slit this heretic's throat as quick as picking my nose."

I didn't appreciate his line in metaphors (or was it similes?) and one glance at Signy's face showed she'd run out of strategies.

"Leave my daughter alone, you bully," she said. "What's it you want?"

"Yer jewels, missus," said the blond giant.

"Thems as sewn in yer skirts and then some," said the jerk behind us.

"I can give you money, but you must let us go."

"Yer in no position to bargain," said the giant. "Look, I'll cut this filly's throat, so yer see I'm in earnest, and then…" He had been holding the knife high above his head for effect. His eyes opened wide as the knife span out of his hand and bounced on the icy ground in front of him. He let go of Eira's hair, and clutching his knife hand, he made a sound like a dog listening to Coldplay. An arrow had lodged in his palm, like one of those joke things you get at magic stores, only this one had real blood.

"Drop them," said a voice. "Now, if you want the pleasure of another breath."

We were surrounded by men, with dark skin, dark hair and some with tattoos on their faces. Their jackets all had embroidery. Three or four carried bows, fully drawn and notched with arrows. The rest had vicious-looking spears.

Eira ran to Signy. Pudding-Basin boy burst into tears. He and the thin-faced man dropped their clubs.

One of the weird strangers walked over to Signy. He put his hands to her face.

"Hello, my sister. What kept you so long?"

Night Journey

Alexandria – about 380 CE

Nysa kept to the shadows. A lick of candlelight played on a shutter high above her head; some flute music and the tinkle of small cymbals suggested entertainment at someone's dinner. She could see no one ahead in the narrow street. But just as the shadows hid her they could hide a cut-purse or worse. She came to the broad road that ran to the Sun Gate. Now she would be visible to all, a small vulnerable figure swathed in a cloak slightly too large for her. She took a deep breath, and walked steadily across the large flat paving stones, remembering to avoid the cracks just as her sister had taught her. The soft clopping sound of a horse's hooves on stone carried, as did the cries of a group of young men singing in the far distance.

As she made it into the comforting gloom of the buildings opposite she thought she heard a footfall. She stopped and tightened her grip on the dagger tucked in the folds of her cloak. A band of fear tightened around her chest. The dagger comforted her, but she had no idea how to use it apart from waving it around and screaming, and then running as fast as she could. *Not a very sound strategy.* The wide thoroughfare remained eerily quiet, although a deeper patch of darkness on the far side suggested she might be being watched. She sniffed, walked determinedly in the deep shade provided by the lee of the government buildings, and headed towards the east of the harbour as instructed.

As instructed.

She'd no idea if she'd been truly instructed or not. Ever since the floor in the Geometric Room of the Palace, as she called it, had melted presenting her with the image of a pulsing shape of crystaline light, nothing had been the same. For her at least.

Anastasia and Devorah had also experienced something but all three of them were reluctant to talk about it, as though an experience like this could not really be shared. Anastasia had come closest when she'd said, "Were you frightened when they made us climb down that rope ladder?" Nysa's look of total confusion had caused her friend to shrug and say, "Oh, it doesn't matter." Devorah had been worse if anything. On the way back in the palanquin, she'd blurted out, "No way, no way at all am I going to be a filthy slave." When asked what she meant she'd bitten her lip quite hard and said she must've fallen asleep and dreamed. None of the girls had mentioned the dance in the shadow of the Time Knot since.

One evening at supper, Nysa's mother had announced she'd heard from Maimonides' wife that a large slave market would be held soon, with pliant slaves from the north. "You could have one if you want."

"Good idea," her sister said. "Buy a gelded young man to look after you and protect you from the religious roisterers."

Everyone giggled when Nysa asked, "What does 'gelded' mean?"

Her father had agreed the business could do with a bright young man to help.

Nysa stood with her hands on her hips and said, "What right do we have to steal a young man's life?"

They all laughed at that.

"Nysa, sweet gentle Nysa, their life is forfeit anyway. Usually they've been sold by their family or taken in war, fair and square. With our family they have a safe roof over their heads, food twice a day, freedom to follow the gods they choose and freedom for themselves when I die."

"Don't let's talk of that," said Nysa's mother.

"It comes to us all, dear." He crossed the room at that and ruffled Nysa's hair, saying, "I'll take you with me," and left the room before Nysa could ask where and when. And why.

Later that evening, sitting in her room with her maid asleep on a low settle in the corner, Nysa had felt dizzy. The floor became fluid once more, as it had in the Geometric Room. She lay down before she fell down. The bed span slowly and nausea flooded her body. Struggling to get up to go to the latrine, Nysa found the room completely changed around her and all feeling of nausea or dizziness gone.

She stood up.

'Ah,' said a voice inside her and outside at the same time, *'you are here.'*

A girl sat on an ornate carved wooden chair with a table full of inlay on its surface. *'I've waited for you for a long time. I think this is you, isn't it?'*

She held up a thick coin that glinted in the soft light of the circular room. Nysa should have been terrified but she felt entirely safe, as though meeting a friend long known, who'd been away and had come back. The girl spoke in a tongue Nysa couldn't recognise. The words flowed musically and the girl's arms moved as she spoke. Her pretty face became animated and her thick brown hair broke free just a bit from the golden bands that held it in place. As she spoke, the meaning bubbled up in bursts inside Nysa.

'Yes, you're right. We do know each other. Deeply. Like sisters, only better. Now we have met. Properly. The link is forged, so to say. The chain across time. The Bearers of the Key.'

She smiled at that and Nysa smiled back, even though the words remained pretty close to gobbledygook. Yet she felt a warmth around her heart and nothing but kindness coming from this sister who was more than a sister.

'We don't have long. The flow of the streams of time never ceases and your time and mine are – at the moment – crossing.'

The girl moved her arms in a way that might illustrate time's crossing or might have been an odd way to scratch an itch.

'On the night of your next full moon you must return to where

you've just been, cross the water – the boatman will expect you – and find the library. The special library. A sister to you and me will be your guide. But not her alone. For another and his champion will also watch over you that night. Remember the feather is the key. There, I've said it. Just as you told me to."

The girl's face crinkled up with laughter.

'I don't understand,' thought Nysa. The other girl began to fade.

"Where do I ... why do I...?" Nysa asked, but the vision had gone.

"What, Nysa?"

Nysa opened her eyes to see her maid standing by the bed, a lamp flickering in her hand.

"You were having a dream, I think, child. Now settle down. My, you're not even changed for bed. I've been remiss. I must've dropped off to sleep. Have you washed your face and hands and used the tooth stick?"

That had been four nights ago. Four nights before the full moon; the full moon which bathed the whole harbour in its pale glow and caused the Palace to appear to float above the seawater. Now here she was, about to trust a vision she no longer really believed and hoping the boatman would take her across. She'd a few coins in her purse, assuming the man would be there at this time in the evening. Getting out of the house had been the difficult bit. She'd had to wait until her maid slept. She'd dressed in the dark and slipped out as though visiting the latrine outside. It had a window, too small for most people to climb in but, once unlocked, just big enough for her to slip out.

As she came closer to the sea, a couple passed by in a chariot; Nysa pressed herself back into the harbour wall and they didn't look her way. To her left, near the long causeway built to the orders of the Great Alexander, some soldiers stood in a group, their long cloaks flapping slightly in the sea breeze that tugged at her own clothes.

The paved area leading to the jetty had small kiosks and the little lamps that burned threw their flickering illumination on warm nuts, meat on sticks and sweet things, as well as little trinkets and toys from Rome and Constantinople. She'd come down here with her family in the past. But now it looked alien and potentially dangerous.

Bother that. Nysa crossed the paved area leading to the jetty, walking with a firm step and keeping her face hidden under her shawl. Off to her right a water-seller rang his little bells and held out his copper cups.

Only when she reached the jetty did she see the horseman. He sat motionless, partly hidden by one of the trees that gave shade from the fierce summer sun for those drinking or sitting watching the harbour life. At night it provided a perfect place for a man on a black horse to be inconspicuous. As she had that thought he rode forward. She recognised the man she'd seen weeks earlier who'd looked at her so intently. The same man who'd ridden across the long causeway and promptly vanished.

This night he didn't vanish. He raised the ivory rod he carried in a sort of salute. Then he pointed behind her. Nysa had nearly reached the steps down to the jetty. She looked back. The giant stood fully lit in the strong moonlight, his breastplate gleaming and his legs, like small tree trunks, planted asunder. He'd been watching her all along. She couldn't make out his expression but the man on the horse grinned and, tapping his mount, wheeled round and cantered off in the direction of the Jewish Quarter.

"Come on, miss, I can't wait all night."

This came from the boatman at the end of the jetty. Nysa made her way over and stepped gingerly into the rocking boat. She sat down rather too sharply as it lurched with the bucking motion of a wave. A slap of water gave her face a fine salty spray. The man paddled and they crossed to the palace side. Nysa reached for her purse.

"Don't be silly, duck," said the man, "it's all paid for. And I'm always here, see. You'd be surprised who takes this little trip in the darkness. Your friend is waiting for you, see?"

He pointed up the stairs leading to the Palace. A figure stood at the top of the stairs, his dark wavy hair silvered by the moonlight.

"Look lively, Nysa. You have a library to visit," said Angelos, pointing towards the palace.

The Labyrinth

Angelos opened the library door with a great key in the shape of an ankh. Above his head a soft blush of illumination glowed on the sword of Alexander. Their footsteps echoed as they entered.

"Change in there," said Angelos, pointing to a small door on Nysa's right, one she'd not noticed on her first visit. She closed the door to the oddly shaped chamber, with one curving wall making the room wider as she went forward. She sat for a moment on a stool, catching her breath and bringing her racing heart under control. She trusted Angelos because the Lady trusted Angelos, but she'd never ever been alone with a young Christian man before and here she was on an island, with no one in her family believing she was anywhere except in her own bed. She could be sold into slavery or robbed or... She shuddered.

Two lamps hanging from the ceiling gave a warm, if slightly inconsistent illumination. A little stray moonlight added some cold comfort. Spread out on a table lay a robe of white linen. Next to it sat a smooth leather draw-string bag. On the floor were sandals with silvered leather straps. Nysa quietly secured the clasp on the door to the room, and slipped out of her dark clothes. The soft robe passed easily over her head. Three mother-of-pearl toggles closed the top of the garment and when done up it fitted perfectly. She opened the pale leather bag and drew out a long braided cord of smooth silken threads, with tassels at each end.

A gentle knock sounded on the door.

"Just a moment," she whispered.

She tied the cord around her waist and slipped on the silvery sandals.

Angelos nodded as she stepped out into the library entrance, the quivering light of the lamps enhancing his good looks. He didn't smile but inclined his head slightly.

"I'm honoured to lead you to this labyrinth," he said, his voice a little tight. In the quiet of the night it echoed faintly. "Listen carefully. You must find your way to the source of life, the bull. From there seek once more the Chamber of Initiation."

Nysa frowned. *What's he talking about?*

He held her eyes. His own were fathomless in the gloom.

"Once there," he went on, clearly using words to be spoken as a ritual, "find your way through."

Nysa frowned some more. *Through? Through where? The room didn't go anywhere, did it?*

"If at any point you wish to end your quest, call thrice the name of the Messenger of the Gods, Divine Hermes. We will hear. We will free you. But you will remain a candidate for three more years before you may try again. For some time more you will remain a slave in the twisting coils of time."

Angelos took a breath and raised his chin slightly as though freeing a crick in his Adam's apple.

"Candidate at the entryway to the Maze of Time, do you wish to proceed? Think well. You may tarry here and no one will believe the worse of you."

"No. I'm fine. I'll proceed," Nysa heard herself say, as though from several cubits away.

Angelos nodded, suggesting she'd offered an oracle of great significance.

"It is well. Proceed in peace and may the light of those who have trod Time's Circles and found their true Source be with you."

Angelos crossed to a small table placed by the fresco of Apollo playing music to the Muses. He picked up a pipe with a double shaft and placed it to his lips. The music swirled around her as he backed away leaving her standing at the entrance. His movement – or a breeze from outside – fluttered the flames in the oil lamps and Apollo himself, with light rippling over him, appeared to be playing, and the Muses to be swaying gently.

When the music faded Angelos had gone and the door to the library was sealed fast. Nysa turned back to the entranceway to the labyrinth library. *Which way should I go?* The Librarian had taken them left. She remembered that. But parts of the library could be moved. She was sure. So the path through might well be different tonight. A voice she couldn't quite hear, a voice inside and far away, reminded her to trust her intuition, to look and really see. She turned to the right.

The smell of dust, papyrus, cloth and leather played like a multi-layered tune on her senses. At night the aromas took on a greater power. Ahead of her the passageway of scrolls curved to the left. The glowing lamps hung well out of arm's reach every second cubit or so, giving just enough light to steer by but hardly enough to read comfortably. No matter how gently she placed her feet, her steps resonated. She approached the first opening, bordered by pillars of wood full of Egyptian carvings. *Sandalwood!* The scent arose quite distinctly as she stood close by. Simple hieroglyphs of gods, animals, snakes, eyes, arms, winged suns, all descended incomprehensibly from the lintel high above her, to the point where the pillars swelled as they met the stone floor. Khloe, her older sister, had taught her the meaning of some of these pictures. A shaft with four lines crossing the top had the name 'djed' and represented Osiris's backbone. She stroked the shape with her finger. *I wish I'd paid more attention. Perhaps these are words that say which way to go.*

She moved on. At the next entranceway she stopped. Sandalwood scent refreshed her and something caught her eye. Three or four pictures above the floor, on the right pillar, a lotus plant showed the head of a boy emerging. For under a moment and with less force than a half-remembered dream, she felt a tall girl of about her age standing close by. Instead of freaking her out, the tiny glint of sensation spread through her like a peaceful glow. She passed through the entrance and turned right. Almost at once another opening appeared on her left. Again the sandalwood graced her senses. She closed her eyes and drew a breath. Something gently pressed against her left shoulder; so gently it felt like the memory of a touch. She looked at the figures on her left hand side. Once more she saw the lotus with the emerging head. It caught the light a fraction more than the images above and below. She entered and turned left, followed by the smile of the tall girl. This time she passed three openings on her right and one to her left, feeling nothing special. Then she reached a stone wall. *I've made a mistake.* The utter stillness settled around her.

'Look carefully.'

Nysa couldn't be sure if that was her own voice or a voice from the girl who remained close and yet far away: a tall girl wearing a robe similar to hers, standing in an Egyptian Temple.

'Look. You will know. But look'.

She walked back. At the first opening she felt nothing – just an emptiness. At the second a puff of air made all the hanging flames flutter and the pictures danced. In her imagination something pressed back at her through this entrance. A gloom; cold despair; a chill of loneliness and fear. *How come I didn't feel that before?* Nysa moved on, reaching the third opening. She stood for a long while. Nothing. Silence. The stillness of questions unanswered and impossible puzzles unresolved. She could go on or turn back. *Help me,* she said to her inner friend – the one from so long ago.

'Face your fears,' came the response.

This time the thought arrived with a clear image. The girl stood looking right at her, wearing a pale grey cloak with a feather embroidered near her left shoulder.

Feelings churned through Nysa. Surely she knew this girl. Her face ... *I've been with her in my dreams.* She drew a deep breath, trying unsuccessfully to master her nervousness, and walked unsteadily to the opening that now swirled with eddies of dread. Fear clutched with icy fingers at her stomach. Her legs became weak and her thoughts seemed to flee as a white fuzzy fog took over her mind. She forced herself to look at each pillar. Neither side had a hieroglyph of a lotus. She looked carefully once more. On both sides, at the same height, a single feather had been carved, with other devices below and above. The feather, the sound 'i' according to Khloe, like the feather worn by the girl with the grey cloak. Without thought Nysa stepped through. At once the cold fear departed. Nysa heard a gentle laugh, somewhere beneath her feet, so faint it couldn't be real. The face of her inner friend, tall and beautiful, with long dark hair, smiled at her.

'Now, it's easier.'

It didn't matter which way she turned. The curved passageway, full of scrolls snuggled in their cubbyholes, beckoned her on. Moments later she had gained the centre of the library with Apis, the sun-bull.

Entombed

The passage leading to the stone room pressed in around her. Ahead, the rectangular stone doorway framed the central pillar in the small room, with its carved bands of hieroglyphs emphasised with tiny shadows. Nysa stepped inside the lamp-lit room. A deep stillness embraced her as though all the images around her held their breath even as she held hers. The fine relief carvings on either side, evoked from the smooth stone, were even more lifelike. She could sense the river flowing slowly, pressing against the legs of the men and women wading through it. Above these exquisite stone pictures, a band of symbolic lotus blooms divided the bottom two thirds of the wall from the top. This upper portion to her left contained a familiar scene of a hawk-headed god and a jackal-headed god, weighing a feather on huge scales, against a heart-shaped pot. To one side stood a goddess with a feather rising from the top of her head. To the other, a helmeted god, tightly wrapped in cloth, had a green face and sat in judgement. *The judgement of Osiris.* Khloe had explained a similar picture to her at the Temple of Isis. The heart of the candidate for heaven is weighed against a feather to see if it's been true in life. If the scales remain in balance, the person is safe. If not, some disgusting hippo-type creature eats them. Nysa shuddered. Seeing this picture in a busy temple on market day had been faintly boring; here it accused her of all the things she had done which she shouldn't have.

On the right wall the same picture repeated. *Okay, you've made your point. This is a judgement room.*

Nysa skirted round the pillar and studied the wall in front of her. It had no dominant large images except for a winged sun extending at the top. Below, the walls remained largely bare apart from a row of single glyphs just about level with her eyes and one casting a slight shadow, lower on the left. She moved to explore the hieroglyph that extended into the room by the depth of a fingernail. It contained an etched shape of a strange curved head, with two rectangular ears. *Set,* thought Nysa. And then wished she hadn't. *Not good to evoke the god of chaos here.* She could see no doorway, nothing to slide or push to open a way through. *Except this raised slab.*

She pushed against the stone carving of Set and it slid flush to the wall. Nysa sucked in her breath and bit her lower lip. Nothing happened. Nothing except a grinding noise so faint she thought she must be imagining it. She ran her hands along the other carvings. Nothing else stood out. The stone felt entirely smooth except for the slight incisions made to produce the various pictures.

What on earth am I meant to do now?

Something had changed. The silence, if anything, had just become fuller and deeper. Anubis, the jackal-headed god, stared at her from one intricately drawn eye. The feather in the weighing pan seemed to quiver slightly. She walked back around the pillar and nearly fainted. Where the door had been, stood three figures. The goddess Isis on the left, Osiris her husband on the right and in the centre, Horus, their falcon-headed son. Horus, carved into solid stone at the place where she'd entered the room. Now, no longer a room but potentially a tomb, unless she could find a way out.

There's no door. How do I get out?

Tears pricked against her eyes and Nysa felt a giddy whirlpool of panic opening up inside her. She closed her eyes and leant against the wall. Its coolness calmed her a little.

There has to be a way.

Nysa turned and studied the picture above the fresco. Something didn't fit. She worked her way carefully along all the figures. The gods! Something about the gods. The hawk-headed god, Horus, faced back over his shoulder, looking at Anubis behind him. Nysa circled the pillar to compare with the mirror image opposite. Here, Horus also regarded Anubis, behind him.

Their eyes. What is it about their eyes?

The eyes were detailed and very stylised. On Horus the right eye had been carved, just as it should be. But behind him Anubis had a left eye on the right side of his face. Up above his head three glyphs sat: a tiny, seated goddess with a feather, a thin rectangle with an angled end lying horizontal and then the same shape, vertical.

Maat! They all mean Maat or 'truth'.

Nysa went back to the right-hand wall. Here Horus's turned head again showed the right eye correctly and Anubis with a left eye, this time correctly. Above his head were four glyphs: a feather, a tiny pharaoh's crown, a hawk and a line folding back on itself.

Random, so random.

The wall at the far end of the room had ten little glyphs, nine in a row and then the one of Set, which she had pushed, no doubt closing the stone door to her sarcophagus. All the glyphs she had seen incised above Anubis were there. Surely if she pushed the glyphs meaning Truth, in the right order, she would be released. The stonework had tiny lines around each picture and Nysa felt certain if she pressed them, they would move. She went back and checked. The first glyph showed the tiny version of Maat, seated. She found it and her fingers hovered. The silence closed around her softly, like the desert on a night of total stillness.

Too simple, anyone could guess that. These letters all say Maat. What do the other letters say?

She looked at the letters above Anubis on the right hand side. One of the lamps suspended from the roof guttered, and the figures on the wall quivered. The hieroglyphs spelt no word she recognised. They were nonsense. The pictures stood for 'i', 'n', 'a' and 's'. Khloe had insisted on teaching her the Egyptian alphabet last year. *Inas.* It didn't mean anything.

It has to be Maat in the right order. Surely.

She stared at the row of glyphs on the wall. All the letters were there. But if she got it wrong she would fail. And she so didn't want to fail. She rubbed her hands up and over her face and eyes. Then it came to her.

Wrong eye means wrong way. It has to be the nonsense letters. Inas. Inas. The sound returned to her from around the room.

She giggled. "Nysa! It spells Nysa!" The silent gods at the blocked entrance echoed the words back to her. She thought she also heard a snort as though someone, somewhere, was trying not to laugh.

Probably the Hippo, getting ready for dinner.

Without giving it any more thought she went and pushed the glyphs in the right order – the order that spelt her own name. They shifted in by fingertip depth really easily. The final hawk – the 'a' of her name – was the second glyph on the left. As it slid home, a rumbling started and, at the corner to her right, the floor began to open. A whole slab of stone slid gradually under the wall, revealing an illumined crypt with some stone steps descending. Nysa stood uncertain at the top. She held her breath and the universe did too.

Time Treasures

"Come on, Nysa, we haven't got all night, you know."

Anastasia's face appeared at the bottom peering up at her. Nysa came down to be greeted by Anastasia and then Devorah, who both gave her a big hug. They had huge grins on their faces. Nysa descended into a room a cubit or so bigger than the one above, but with two closed wooden doors.

"You were very quick," said Devorah. "I took much longer before I worked it out."

"We watched you, you know," said Anastasia.

Nysa frowned and shook her head.

"The Hippo. If you look at the Hippo really carefully you'll see its black eye is a space. We watched you through that. Come. We really haven't much time and others are waiting. Are you ready?"

Both of her friends looked like they were halfway between exploding with excitement and about to do something really important. The two girls moved Nysa around until they stood with Anastasia at the front and Devorah at the back. They gave Nysa a small, lit lamp to hold.

"Put your hand on my right shoulder," said Anastasia. Nysa did so, and felt Devorah place her hand on her shoulder in turn. They walked to one of the doors. After knocking, the door that had no handle on their side opened.

Anastasia led her two friends into a room that lay beneath the circular library. Directly below where the Apis bull would be above them stood a granite block bearing flowers in bloom, surrounded by a circle of women, all in long robes. Braziers, on tall stands, cast a warm light all over the chamber. A sweet fragrance filled the air. Each wall held different types of decoration, Egyptian at the far end with Greek figures coming next, at the wall that must face the sea and the lighthouse.

Opposite, a single figure sat cross-legged under a tree, clad in robes of dusty yellow, his eyes closed. A nearby deer bowed its head towards the praying man. Nysa was directed to place her single lamp on a low square block of stone a cubit or so from the taller granite altar. As she did, she noticed it held a finely incised image of a central circle, with six circles gathered around it.

Nysa looked up, straight into the eyes of her sister Khloe, standing on the far side of the flowers, her face lovely in the soft light from the braziers. Khloe nodded. On one side of her stood Hypatia, her calm face unreadable, on the other, the slave girl Myrna. All the women – Nysa reckoned there must be ten or eleven of them – had pale grey cloaks, gathered at their shoulders and covering much of their white linen robes.

"Welcome, Novitiate. Welcome, Nysa. Welcome, Sister," said her sister.

"Welcome, Novitiate. Welcome, Nysa. Welcome, Sister," said Hypatia.

Myrna looked at her, her eyes fiery in the reflected light. The same words just spoken out loud repeated inside her breast.

'You are truly One Who Hears. Say what you have just heard within the sanctum of your mind.'

Nysa repeated the words she'd heard: "You are truly one who hears."

Everyone smiled. Hypatia nodded.

"It is well, Novitiate. You have entered the realm of the dead and found your way through. You are now indeed one of us."

The ceremony proceeded for some more time, with several of the women moving gracefully around the central altar, as Hypatia spoke words of great beauty. Water was sprinkled and fresh incense ignited.

Hypatia came and stood in front of Nysa. Devorah and Anastasia stood at each side of her facing their teacher.

"Look around you Nysa, my Sister. For even as these sacred images convey the essence of the great spiritual movements of our time, so does the teaching of the Holy Ones surround you at all times."

Guided by Anastasia, Nysa looked at each wall in turn. Behind her, with the door set to one side, she recognised Christian imagery, including the Fish of the Nazarene and the Winged Lion.

"All the Great Ways contain Great Truths, Nysa. And in truth they are but One Way."

A woman Nysa did not know came forward carrying a grey cloak.

Silently, Hypatia fixed the cloak around her, pointing out the embroidered feather on the shoulder that matched all the others in the room.

"We are the Ladies of the Feather. Our Founder's words can still be found in the quietest parts of our souls. And our great Teacher on the Ways of Time is one close to you. She has many names. The Lady of the Blue Lotus. The Servant of Neith. But you will know her as we do, simply as Shoshan."

As Hypatia said these words Nysa recalled the presence of a girl about her own age as she made her way through the labyrinth of the Library above them. For just a moment warmth spread through her heart as though she had found once more a long-lost friend.

Anastasia and Devorah left the circle and returned moments later each bearing a box decorated with inlays.

"Here is our token, Sister. Keep it safe. Show it when needed to those who should know. It marks you as one who has mastered the first coil of time."

Hypatia opened the box and removed a large coin. She placed it in Nysa's left palm.

Khloe returned the empty box to Devorah and took the second, slightly larger box from Anastasia.

"My Sister –" Khloe smiled at Nysa, her watering eyes softened and full of love – "these sacred emblems are yours. You are now their Guardian, even as you are a Companion and a Seed of Life. Keep them safe until you find, eventually, one who may secure their passage onwards in time."

Khloe and the three girls emerged into the pale green light of early dawn. Angelos, who'd been sitting in the garden area in front of the palace, stood and bowed slightly towards the group of girls. He sheathed a sword.

"Mother and Father," said Nysa, "they have no idea where I am. They—"

"Are over there," said Khloe.

Nysa looked across the narrow stretch of water to the harbour. Two figures stood by a palanquin.

"They knew all along?"

"We all did," said Devorah. "Hypatia spoke to your parents just as she spoke to mine. Membership of Our Sisterhood is respected by the wise of all faiths here. My father stays here in part because of the teachings guarded by the Sisters of the Feather."

"As do we all, sister, who is now my Sister."

Khloe made a movement with her hands to indicate two different types of sister. "Come. We'll get some breakfast at the harbour. You look like you're about to faint."

"You knew all along, Khloe, and you said nothing?"

"We each have to come to the sisterhood by our own path, Nysa. I joined at about your age. I think the priestesses of Isis and our own dear Hypatia wondered if I might be one of the seeds on the Golden Thread that runs from past to future. But I cannot hear within in the way you do. For me, Myrna has to write things down. Occasionally I pick up thoughts but they are vague and uncertain. We know from ancient records held within our own Labyrinth Library, written by the great Shoshan herself, that all the Companions of Time have inner hearing. It is one of their marks."

"But that only started with me so recently," said Nysa.

"True." Her sister smiled and sat next to Nysa on the bed in her room. "The day you heard Myrna, when you were at Devorah's house dancing, was a day we quietly celebrated. But you still had to find your way through the Labyrinth. That is also a test of your readiness and ability to join the sisterhood."

Khloe placed her hand over her sister's.

"The time is coming soon when the Sisterhood will have to step into the shadows. Our protection within the sanctity of the temples of Isis won't last much longer. We know that. Our greatest seers have predicted this time. They see the coming era as a period of deep night, with only a few stars of brilliance to light the way for those travellers seeking the path. Yet our knowledge will never be lost, for we know the Golden Thread stretches unbroken before us, as long as we all play our part as we should."

"Did you know of these ancient treasures?" asked Nysa, opening the larger of the two boxes: a beautiful work of art in itself, decorated with an exquisite picture of a hawk-headed god. He bore a sun disk above his head and crossed rippling blue water in a narrow boat.

"No. Not until you showed you could Hear. I told Hypatia. She produced this box that she'd been given, as its guardian, from Father's mother."

Khloe stroked the picture on the box with her fingertip. She smiled at Nysa.

"Grandmother died before you were born, but I just about remember her and her remarkable eyes. Hypatia held the box in trust, as she was sure that the Seed would be found within our family." Khloe felt inside the folds of her robe and produced a key. She handed it to her sister. "Neither of our parents is directly connected with the sisterhood. I think Mother attempted the labyrinth as a young woman, but called for the help of Hermes thrice, and never tried again."

Nysa unlocked the box and withdrew two soft leather pouches. One contained a flawless rendition of a scarab beetle in pale jade, hanging on a golden chain. The other held ten small spheres of polished stone.

"I have duties, Nysa. Mother is preparing a special feast today, for tomorrow we must fast, drinking only water. The sisterhood is to do a ritual of utmost importance and you will be needed there."

For a long time Nysa sat very still. Everything still felt somewhat unreal. She'd no idea what it really meant to be a Seed or Companion or any of these things. But the pale jewel lying on the soft wool cover of her bed comforted her. She counted the spheres. *Ten.* She knew about the teachings of the great sage Pythagoras and his Tetractys. Hypatia had shown the sublime meaning of the triangular shape that could be simply made by arranging the points in rows, with one at the top and four at the bottom.

She picked up the scarab jewel. Her hand warmed and a flux of energy spread through her. She closed her eyes. At first she sensed nothing except the comforting weight of the jewel resting in her palm. Meaningless smudges of dark and pale shapes played on her eyelids. Then a face appeared as though a torch had illumined it in a waking dream.

'You are the girl who spoke to me in the Labyrinth,' thought Nysa.

'Yes. We are now truly connected. You have found me in good time, sister and country-mate.'

The girl smiled, her large eyes, emphasised with dark make-up, sparkled.

'On the morrow you must open a crack in the pathways of time. You now have the power. I will be standing just behind you.'

The image faded. The girl's beautiful smile had warmed Nysa through and through. She quietly slipped her treasures back in their bags and stowed the enamelled box, with its Horus motif, deep in her clothes chest.

Reindeer Days

Sweden – about 1520

"They're from the far north," said Håkan to me, as we watched our rescuers trussing up our would-be captors. "Mother's related to these people because her mother was Sami. My grandmother had Garal with her first husband and then was left a widow. Mother says my grandfather fell in love with her for her great beauty."

I nodded. Everything had happened so fast I'd not had time to catch my breath. Of course I knew about the Sami. Nowadays in Sweden and Norway, to call them Laplanders is considered rude or downright racist. I thought they lived beyond the Arctic circle. Surely we couldn't have walked that far. It might feel like we had walked from Land's End to John O'Groats and further, but that far north, in winter, we would be knee-deep in snow geese and polar bears. Here fir trees still dominated the landscape and craggy rocks covered with lichen were not under permafrost.

Signy and the man who called her sister had stared at each other for a long time. She'd wept a little and spoken softly to him. The other hunters had made short work of the three nut-jobs who'd tried to rob us. I was sort of glad they hadn't ended up hanging from a branch, although I'm not at all sure they would have been that kind to us. Now they stood, trussed up with thick cords, their legs hobbled, their gloves firmly bound on, making picking knots even beyond Houdini. Some grey-haired wag with little tattoos on his face had suggested tying them in a circle facing outwards, so when they walked one of them would always be walking backwards.

"Why are you here?" Signy asked her brother. "How did you know to find us? We were almost lost, just walking by the North Star and hoping for the best."

"Look at the trees," said her half-brother, Garral, pointing to the craggy hill rising above our heads. At the top, three incredibly tall fir trees stood, a landmark for miles in each direction. "This hill is called Storsberg, the Queen's Hill. Some think it means a Swedish Queen or a Danish one, but it is sacred to Frig, Queen of Asgard. The drum showed this very hill when Håkan was born, remember?"

Signy shook her head. She'd clearly forgotten or maybe never realised. If we hadn't been accosted by the Danish captain, would we have come this way? I didn't know. It seemed sort of random to me. But here were Signy's tribe ready and waiting, and because of them Pudding-Basin, his dad and their thin friend were going to have to hop, skip and jump for a very long time to get home, if they were to avoid a painful death by freezing.

Large flakes of snow started to descend. The sky, hardly bright with the dawn, had darkened again and looked snow-laden.

Garral studied each of us in turn. He deployed that type of x-ray vision that seems to judge a person from the bones outwards. Taller than the rest, with a deep tan and weathered face, he'd the stance of a man whom even wolves avoid in the forest. His blue hat, round like a large pillbox, had stitching in bright yellow, ear flaps and strange folds on the top. It added substantially to his height. His long, light tan-coloured-jacket had myriad tiny pieces of embroidery forming intricate patterns. A tight belt at waist height caused it to flare into a short skirt, but not in any namby-pamby way. At his throat, a necklace of long teeth added to his warrior street-cred. His thick dark trousers ended in knee-high boots, like all the men.

"Bring them with us," said Garral, who appeared to be the group's leader. The big blond guy started to protest, but fell quiet when a spear ended up tickling distance from his nose. We set off on a side track, down from the hill. For the first time for ages I began to feel we might be safe. The men around us were mainly small, with highly embroidered leather jackets and large hats. Their spears looked well able to tackle polar bears and I'd seen how effective they were, when using a bow and arrow. We reached a copse of trees. Two men emerged, their bows nocked with arrows. They nodded at Garral.

"We'll leave straight away," he said. "The snow will cover our tracks and we'll be like ghosts who come and leave no mark. Hold them for one thousand heartbeats and then let them go. From here it will take most of the day for them to get back where they live. And I wouldn't have them die, though they deserve it."

Something snorted. We moved through the trees to a clearing. There stood a small herd of the biggest reindeer I'd ever seen. Three or four had huge antlers and tossed their heads up and down. They were all attached to sleds by bright leather straps that reached around their chunky middles. None had a red nose that I could make out.

Moments later we were gliding along over the snow, with flakes settling down all around us. Apart from the soft rhythm of the reindeers' hooves, and the swoosh of the sled runners, we were surrounded by grey silence. My Sami – he didn't tell me his name – didn't talk. I leaned back against the front of his chunky jacket after he'd sat down on the sled and given me a rather toothless grin. He held the steering straps for the sled and I squeezed in in front of him. Thick and slightly smelly pelts kept us warm. Even with low visibility we bounded along at a fair pace. Garral knew one snow drift from another, apparently, and occasionally shouted when we changed direction. I wondered about the three men doing the six-legged race back up the steep track and then their long walk home. Well, they deserved it for the way they had treated Eira.

Trees passed by, sometimes close and sometimes blurry in the distance, just visible through a haze of feathery snowflakes. Garral made dramatic changes of direction several times early on. I guessed this was to confuse any possible pursuit. But with the steady snow and the speed of our four-legged transport, we were surely leaving any hunters far behind.

The Perils of Berries

Garral called a halt. The snow had thinned but not quite stopped. Near where the reindeer stood, shuffling and snorting, a great rock rose out of the edge of a hillside. Garral led the other men in gathering green pine fronds. He and Signy placed the first evergreen branches on the snow, starting to make a crescent shape around the rock. At first I could see nothing too special about this grey stone emerging from the snow. But it had drama, almost as though it had a life of its own. The colouring, cracks and shape suggested a language ancient and forgotten. The snow had settled on the top of the rock but didn't cover its lichen smudged face. Håkan and I laid our branches together, near the edge of the crescent, and Eira laid hers next to mine. Signy stood watching as the other men added their branches. When all had become still once more, she nodded, smiled a tight smile at Garral and returned to her sled. No one said anything.

The sky gradually lightened and we stopped once more. My driver, who had definite need of a shave, opened a leather pouch and offered it to me. Inside were berries, chilly but not frozen. They burst into flavour in my mouth, tasting bitter at first and then releasing a faint sweetness. From another bag he took something that looked like old bark. He nodded, offering the stringy bit of wood with his half dozen teeth breaking into a serrated smile.

"It's dry reindeer meat," said Håkan. "Chew it well or you will get a really sore tummy."

I did. Old bootlaces might have been softer. The meat didn't soften quickly, but eventually the strong flavour filled my mouth. Once it had gone from chewy to swallowable, I did just that and down it went. A few more berries, and another bit of tough reindeer and we were off again.

The travelling became hypnotic. The snowscape glided by. It

had stopped snowing entirely and patches of blue sky hinted at the possibility of sun. The air remained incredibly cold, but no wind meant no wind-chill factor. We drew up near a huge tree stump, which, judging by the large number of tree rings, might have been around when the Vikings wore horns on their helmets. Once more we honoured this place with fronds from fir trees.

Garral called Håkan and me over; his blue eyes were cold and flat as a frozen lake. He stared at us both as though searching for whether we'd really done our homework or not. I wouldn't have lied to this man.

"Go," he said.

A feathery coldness of fear spread out from my stomach.

"It's not good to arrive without gifts. Collect berries from within this part of the forest. They are renowned. Collect them in this bag. Be quick. We cannot wait long."

Too late, I tuned into the thoughts within and behind his words. Something he considered but didn't say. His necklace of teeth – or maybe claws – had sharp points that tangled with the thoughts I couldn't quite hear.

Håkan and I moved into the bushes, while his mother and sister, and the Sami, shared more of the delights of dried reindeer. The ground rose sharply for a few metres and we had to scramble with our hands as well as our feet through the snow. I'd no idea what we were looking for but kept my eyes peeled for blackberries, as they were my favourite and hoped we would not find gooseberries, as they definitely weren't. The way the trees and bushes had grown provided a natural path of crisp snow. The only sound came from our breathing and the squeaky crunch of our boots breaking the snow's surface.

We entered a clearing. The sun had finally broken through and shafts of light picked out dazzling white strips on the virgin snow, leaving the nearby shadows a wonderful shade of blue. We were somewhere magical. I started half whistling that Mariah Carey 'All I Want for Christmas' song they play over and over, but Håkan said, "Sshhh," and held up his hand. I couldn't hear anything except the sunlight falling on snow, which remained pretty quiet. Catching the brightness and nestling between two tall trees, a single bush glowed with deep purple berries. We walked over. Each berry had a blush on it of the sort of icing sugar very small fairies might use. They looked absolutely delicious. But they might of course be deadly nightshade, or a Lucrezia Borgia special. I decided not to try one, but it only took us a few minutes to fill the leather pouch.

We turned to go back. We were no longer alone. Dominating the far side of the clearing – blocking our way – stood the biggest bear I've ever met in the woods. Actually the biggest bear, period. His pale brown fur became almost white where the sun lit it from behind, so he also glowed. It reminded me of the pelt I'd been using to keep warm on the sled. I hoped that hadn't been his mother.

Everything felt unreal. His intense brown eyes, too small for his great face, focused entirely on us. *Maybe the berry bush belonged to him?*

"What do we do?" I asked Håkan, out of the corner of my mouth, hoping Swedish boys in the sixteenth century, or wherever we were, knew the answer. My whole body fizzed in that in-the-middle place between craven fear and total excitement. We might be dead in moments, but something about the glowing bear invited wonder as well as terror.

The bear raised its paws, showing claws the size of a Swiss Army knife, and I recognised where Garral had obtained his necklace. The hairy monster rippled with fatty muscle. It dropped down onto all fours, and looked smaller: not cuddly, but not the size of a barn door any more. Who'd said 'never run from a bear'? Well, chance would be a fine thing. The bushes behind ours were thick and tangled and the bear would crash through more easily than two lightly built boys. The bear tossed its head, looked at us both once more while time stood still. Then it turned and trundled off. I finally breathed out. We both waited. The odd crackling sound suggested the bear had veered deeper into the wood. Still we waited.

Håkan had a glassy look in his eyes, staring where the bear had been. The sun had disappeared behind the clouds and the grove in which we stood no longer had the magical fairy-grotto look any more, just a snowy clearing at the edge of an endless forest.

"Come on," I said. "I think it's gone."

He nodded and we started to return. We stepped quietly, looking left and right and ready to leg it seriously, if Bruno showed us his snout once more. He didn't. The path between the trees and the frozen bushes went on much further than I remembered. I looked for our footprints, but we were scrunching through virgin snow. Håkan walked confidently. Just as I thought we'd have to go back, we came to the bank. We half-slid and half-scrambled back down and came out to where everyone waited. Except they weren't there!

"As Seen in the Vision"

We emerged maybe twenty metres from where we'd entered the forest. Over to our right, the sleds stood neatly, with their reindeer staring in our direction. My tooth-challenged Sami stood chewing and staring at us as though we might be wood-sprites or worse. He didn't smile. Faintly, we could hear feet crashing through the forest nearby, and voices calling.

Håkan shouted out. In a few moments, Eira and Signy emerged some way away.

"They're here!" Eira shouted. "It's all right, they're here."

Gradually the men came out of the forest and gathered around the tree stump. They looked towards us but no one grinned or offered a greeting. Led by Garral, once more they arranged green tree fronds, this time in a wide circle around the tree stump.

Garral knelt in the snow for some moments, facing where the mighty tree had once dominated the forest, and then stood up in a lithe single movement. He crossed to his sled and reached into a pack. He walked over to where we both stood. Håkan looked as confused as I felt. Eira had taken off her glove and had her thumb in her mouth. Her eyes had grown in size once more, like two great berries from the bush we'd found.

"Tell me," he said, looking from me to Håkan and back again.

I felt we'd done something naughty but couldn't quite make out what. I held out the bag of berries. He ignored them.

"This is where the leaders of our tribe come. This is the centre of our Yggdrasil, our world tree." He pointed at the vast stump. "It's here we seek for visions when the time is right. So tell me."

"We saw a bear," said Håkan. "A nearly white bear."

A collective sigh washed around us. The men gathered closer.

"What did he do?" asked Signy's brother.

I bit my lower lip and then said, "He stood on his hind paws after creeping up silently, and then looked at us. He kind of glowed, and then dropped down again, and then…"

"He went quietly back into the woods and we could return." Håkan finished my thought with better grammar.

Garral nodded.

"It's done," he said. "As prophesied on the drum. As seen in the vision."

The men around us were humming as though we were inside a swarm of bees.

"You are men now," said Garral. "Come."

In a swift movement he used something to slice down the skin on our foreheads in the direction of our noses. Neither of us moved. A blood drop fell on the snow at my feet, spreading out into a pink blob, only to be joined by another and then a third.

"Here," said the big Sami, and he pressed something hard into my palm. "This is a bear's claw blessed with the blood of your vision-brother." He said the same to Håkan. For the first time I noticed a scar between Garral's eyebrows. Several of the men nearby had the same, but not all. Those men hung back.

"A shared vision happens once every ten generations, or so our wisest say. And for the bear to honour you both is a sign indeed that the spirits are with you and with our tribe. We will make great music as soon as we return."

"And the other part of the prophecy?"

The man who asked the question had been the one who had held the spear to our would-be kidnapper's nose. His hair, slightly fairer than Garral's, stuck out from his large hat in curly tufts. He had a moustache that would make a walrus proud.

"Come," said Garral, "we must go with speed, there are many leagues to cross before we find the comfort of our lavvus."

As I walked over to my sled, Eira ran up and pulled my sleeve. She half-grinned and half-frowned.

"You were gone ages and ages. We'd been looking for you both for so long before you came out. Where were you?"

I didn't have an answer to that question. I lifted her up and gave her a peck on the cheek.

"I don't know," I said, truthfully. "But if I had to have another sister I'd like it to be you." Eira took off her glove and touched her fingers lightly at the centre of my forehead. It stung but I didn't wince. I placed her down again. She ran off to her mother, taking ten-league steps.

I eased my way back into the sled, the legs of my driver on either side, wondering what on earth the other part of the prophecy might be.

That night all the men slept in a large lavvu tent that two of our party had gone ahead and erected. Signy and Eira had a small tepee-shaped lavvu of their own. A fire near the entrance of each structure gave a smoky warmth, helped by the ample pelts. I fell asleep trying to remember what I'd been told about carbon monoxide.

The next day we shoohed through the snow, across a magical landscape of trees, hills and small frozen lakes. The sun glinted and glistened on icy branches and snow-covered rocks. We saw no one else. We did see one wolf in the distance, but he must have smelt Garral because he howled once and then sloped off over the hillcrest. I hoped he'd not gone to contact his twenty closest hungry friends.

We hardly stopped at all, and then only to drink snow-melt water – flat and tasteless – and chew more reindeer meat. The sun lay just above the tree line when we came to a large collection of lavvus in a clearing running down to a frozen lake, much smaller than the one I'd fallen into. At the centre of the lavvus stood a huge unlit bonfire of brushwood and logs. Maybe we would have a BBQ later. My mouth watered at that absurdity. Perhaps dried reindeer left something lacking from my diet.

This time Håkan and I were given a small tent. The pelts inside were soft and would have made a celebrity look great as she walked up the red carpet annoying the anti-fur brigade. Which included me, I remembered, but that was before I would have frozen to death without real fur. We lay down and filled the small space with our ripe odours. I'd become itchy in all sorts of places and hoped the raw bits wouldn't get infected.

"Take off all your clothes"

Signy poked her head through our tent flap, letting in a final shaft of sunlight.

"Can I come in?"

We said yes, and she joined us. I'd so many questions but I let Håkan lead the way.

"Will the soldiers follow us here?"

"Garral doesn't think so. They don't really control this part of the country and so small a force might just disappear into one of the lakes, never to be seen again. So for now, I believe we can enjoy our freedom once more. There is no love lost by the Sami for either the Catholics or the Danes." Signy pursed her lips. "And my people have learned over the years to just head north, if they come up against problems. We can live in the snow and most others cannot."

She smiled at us both, her eyes losing the worry that had been in them ever since the stone circle had been spoiled with hen's blood.

"Show me the berries," she said. I'd entirely forgotten about those and reached into my backpack. The leather pouch protected the dark-purple fruit and none had bruised. Signy took off her glove and held a few on her palm. Her hand shook slightly.

"This fruit is very rare. It has great healing properties, cleansing the blood and giving strength to the mind as well as the arm. But the fruit bushes grow far south of here and are in season in autumn."

She carefully replaced the three fruits in the bag.

"Keep these safe," she said to me. "You will need them tomorrow, when you meet—"

At that point a woman we hadn't seen before put her head through the flap at the lavvu door.

"Bring them now. All is prepared, Mistress Signy." She grinned at Håkan's mother, showing a mouth with slightly more teeth than my driver had.

We left the tent and crossed the compound, led by this woman whose shape approached the spherical, with her rounded body and thick jackets.

"She's my cousin," said Signy, "and so, Håkan, you should call her Aunt."

Håkan nodded and his almost-aunt indicated we should enter a tent slightly larger than the one we were to sleep in.

As we went in, she said, "Take off all your clothes and throw them over here. They may need to be burned."

We heard her chortling outside with Signy as we stripped in the chilly gloom inside the lavvu. I struggled to get my big boots off and the whiff that came when I did, nearly made me gag. The boots went out as well.

Voices and giggling greeted the clothes as we ejected them through the flap. Håkan, naked as a rugby player in the after-the-match-bath, put his head out and asked his mother for fresh clothes. Laughter and general hilarity greeted that request. A drum started beating and a sound like ten Chihuahuas howling became more and more insistent. Hands clapped in rhythm. Håkan retreated into the lavvu, his hands giving him slight modesty. I peered out. I could see the drummers thumping away on decorated drums and the tiny naked dog sounds came from four men playing pipes.

Sami of all shapes and sizes stood in two lines on either side of our entrance, making a leather-clad, laughing and smirking roadway, curving all the way to another much bigger lavvu with smoke rising from its central peak. The people having huge fun at our expense included a lot of women. Signy and Eira were crying. But not with sadness. Eira stamped her feet when she saw me and beckoned me to come out. I snapped my head back in and held the chilly leather closed. The cold air gave me goose bumps all over. I shrank at the prospect of going outside, as did every part of my body.

"It won't get easier," boomed a voice, "it'll only get hotter."

I had no idea what Garral meant, because I recognised his voice.

"Do you want me to send some mothers in to bring you out, boys?"

The general merriment that followed this suggestion indicated that many of the mothers and maybe quite a few of the daughters thought this would be great sport, to be undertaken as quickly as possible. I led the way and Håkan followed.

The snow burned against the soles of my feet. Glancing down I could see they were black with grime and sweat. Everyone clapped now and waved their hands. We ran between the smiling faces towards the bigger tent. I'd started to shiver again as I reached the doorway. We stepped into a tiny outer space made by huge flaps of leather. A hot blast of air blew against my body, giving my front heat while my bottom and back parts were still at refrigerator temperature. Håkan must've had experience of this because he drew open the inner flap and stepped inside. The heat was immense and hot air seared up my nostrils. All the air had a fragrance.

Around the edges of the lavvu, thick upright logs connected with slatted wood set into slots in their tops, provided places to sit that would not leave scald marks on the nether regions. In the centre of the space – a much bigger space than I'd guessed from outside – coals glowed with a fierce red light. Every few moments something outside sighed and the coals glowed once more. A small man, also as naked as we were, used a wooden ladle to slosh water on the coals; as he did so, steam spurted with the sound of a dragon clearing its throat. Already sweat had broken out all over my body. Another man, without so much as a fig leaf to provide cover, showed where we should wash. We dipped wooden pitchers into a leather and wood water butt filled with warm water. We both swooshed and swooshed streams of cleansing warmth over us, and rubbed off the worst of the grime with cloths. I luxuriated in warmth and cleanliness, letting water slowly trickle over my head, eyes and mouth, until it ran in a stream off my chin, into a gully at my feet and out of a hole at the edge of the lavvu. Once in a while a cold blast fought a losing battle with the heat from the steam. Voices outside grew quieter.

"Sit," said the man by the fire, pointing to benches furthest from the heat. My eyes had begun to get used to the gloom and, with something akin to horror, I clocked that as we'd been washing, the rest of the tribe had been filing in. All of them. Men and women, boys and girls – all starkers. I think even a blind man facing the other way would've seen me blush. I turned around to Håkan. He sat, with his eyes closed, naked as nature intended – as the saying goes – with sweat breaking out all over him. I guessed he'd done something like this before – or that he'd not yet realised.

"Come," said the monosyllabic man. He beckoned for both of us to get up. As we walked the twenty-mile long walk to the door, I stared straight ahead. Even my peripheral vision showed no one was looking. Our Sami friends chatted quietly or just sat glowing in the heat.

We exited into the stunning cold.

"Roll," said the man, pointing to virgin snow to the side of the lavvu, where no one had walked since the last snow fall. Håkan, showing an understanding of Swedish life I'd never encountered, plunged into the snow. He rolled around.

The man came over and gave us both some light birch branches.

"Hit."

We did. Gently. Our skin glowed pink in the lamplight from torches that fluttered and wavered near the big sauna tent. At first I'd the uncanny experience of being somewhere really cold and feeling really hot. I'd never ever felt so clean.

Gradually others came out and took a snow dip and a thrashing. Some really did hit themselves hard. As everyone hadn't a stitch of clothing on I lost my shyness, at least a tiny bit. When I started shivering Håkan said we should go back inside. The heat was truly wonderful wrapping itself all around me and encouraging the sweat of fear to pour out.

In and out we went a few more times. Fear left. A great, warm peace took its place. Our chatty friend led us back to our tent and said "dress!" We did. Soft leather over some strange but effective undergarments. Socks that caressed the legs and boots that were snug. Even round hats with embroidery. I didn't have a mirror but knew that after that long in snow and sun even I would pass for a young Sami.

The Three Women

Once more voices sounded outside and the drums became insistent. I stepped out into paradise. The sun had long since set and no moon had risen. Right above stars shone and nearer the horizon, a light both mysterious and wonderful danced in the sky, illuminating the whole encampment. Waving and shimmering, luminous sheets reached up into the heavens, glowing with a green of unsurpassed beauty. I'd never seen anything so glorious before. I forgot where I was. I almost forgot who I was. Sheer joy swept through me. I knew I wasn't seeing the outer edges of heaven, but I might as well have been. I'd always thought of heaven as being coloured green – a silly fancy from before going to primary school. What did they call this: Aurora Borax? Aura Bra-less? No, that couldn't be right. I grinned a private grin to myself. Someone took my hand. I still had so much heat from the sauna, I'd bare hands. Eira smiled up at me, her face dancing with firelight and her eyes green with star-fire. *Yes. I'd adopt her as a sister.*

Later, with the celestial fire filling the heavens above the trees, we ate warm stew and sopped it up with flat bread charred on fire embers and called something like Gahkko. Fish of a loveliness I'd never experienced before came served on more of the delicious flat bread. We drank a fiery liquid that sent warmth to all the final redoubts of the empire of cold that had been within me for what felt like weeks.

The musicians answered the angelic light show with music to match. Then Curly Hair, the man with the big moustache, stood up and danced and the great fire was lit, bursting into flame and sending sparks high into the sky above us, challenging the stars overhead.

Curly danced towards us, and took a drum from one of the players. He beat it with the palm of his hand. The rhythms he made were subtle and tumbled over themselves, defying any music teacher's question 'how many beats in the bar'.

Using the drum for emphasis he started telling a story. Maybe he used Swedish. Maybe he spoke in their own tongue. I saw his story with the inner hearing of the ideas he expressed as they whirled around his mind. Although his words rhymed, I could tell this was not a repeated song but a story told for us now, however many times it had been told before.

The heat of the fire gave us warmth and the words of the story carried us on its own journey into the past.

The Story of the Three Women

Aggu, son of Lavrass, son of Issat
Travelled to the far North
To the far North travelled Aggu.
Wanted to see horned fish, said some,
Wanted to see the fish maids, said some,
Wanted to find the night sun, said some,
Wanted to catch his own whale, said some,
To feed his wife, Maddji, a woman of rare beauty.

The drummer drummed, laughed and winked. The green light slowly rippled its silent music in the sky. The fire sent its sparks higher and higher in a vain attempt to kiss the stars twinkling above. The Chihuahua pipe-band blew and whistled for all they were worth, accompanied by images of a man dressed in dark leather, embroidered in pure silver who rode an elk of amazing size further and further north.

Back home, Maddji made bread, milked the reindeer, produced cheese and dreamed of her one true love, Aggu.

Milked the reindeer? Really? I didn't know reindeer could be milked and wondered if that was what floated in the meat stew we were all now eating? It had a white, creamy texture and tasted sort of … white and creamy.

A woman's face hovered in the space between my mind and the singer, her eyes blue-grey, her pale hair long and partly braided, and her jacket silvery with dark-red embroidery. The woman being drummed into my mind had small, pretty features and was short.

While Aggu, son of Lavrass, son of Issat,
Hunted seal and hunted bear and hunted whale,
Maddji, loved by Aggu, grew.

Too much cheese, I concluded. Not enough exercise.

The pretty woman, with her blue-grey eyes, waited, but Aggu didn't return. The pretty woman, with her pale blue-grey eyes, worked, but Aggu didn't return. The pretty woman, called Maddji, grew. And grew some more.

Judging by the images popping into my mind this woman, quite diminutive, began to become quite spherical, or possibly very pregnant. As this thought arose, the drummer went into a particularly impressive riff, and stopped singing. The drum rhythms rose and fell, elided and folded sounds that chased each other, like paws pattering over flattened snow.

Behind the drummer, between where we sat – Eira on one side and Håkan with his mother on the other – with the distant lavvus dancing their own melody in the firelight, a pack of wolves crossed the snow. I froze and spilled my stew, spoiling my clean trousers. Still the wolves padded past. Still the Chihuahua pipe-band played and the drummer drummed. One wolf stopped and stared right where Håkan and I sat, its eyes flashing firelight. The drummer reached a crescendo and the wolves padded into the dusk where the fire's reach ended and the night darkness began. The drummer's fingers pattered wolf cub sounds. I looked at Håkan. He stared, and held his mother's hand, his wooden platter ignored by his side. Eira had fallen asleep half resting against me and half on the pelts where we sat. The heat of the fire warmed our backs. The singer started again.

Aggu did not return from his adventures. Maddji retired to her lavvu to give birth. Women hurried here and there. Silence fell. A meteor crossed the sky, falling slowly and burning cold fire. A baby cried. And then another, and then a third.

Three girls, small as rag dolls,
Bore the woman, bore Maddji.
One had one eye, one had another eye, one had no eyes,
Bad luck, said the tribe wives, bad luck said the birth wives,
Bring us bad luck, said the jealous men,
Jealous of Maddji and her Aggu, with his courage.

The three tiny bundles were carried out by a birth woman and taken into the forest. Snow fell and a wind blew harshly while wolves prowled and howled deeper in the forest. The woman laid the three tiny children naked in the snow, to perish quickly and save the tribe from bad luck. Another meteor fell slowly across the sky, burning with cold fire. The night lasted for so long the babes would be frozen before frail rays of sun could find their way into that part of the forest. A final meteor crossed the sky.

The pipers played sad, wandering notes to the drummer's slow heartbeat.

Maddji wants her children and as the dawn comes, giving weak light for a few hours, she searches. She searches by the lake and she searches where the reindeer wait and she searches in the forest. But her three babes, one with one eye, one with another eye and one with no eyes, are nowhere to be found. Every day she searches, but in vain. And the tribal women tut and sniff and shake their heads. It's for the best, they say, and nod. Bad luck, they say, and nod. Would have done no good, they say, and nod.

The drummer danced and leapt, as he wove patterns of sound,

his moustache reddish in the glow of the roaring fire behind us.

Aggu returns, returns with silver,
Aggu returns, returns with beaver,
Aggu returns, returns with walrus tusks,
Tusks marked with pictures,
Tusks full of power, and three falling stars.

Near to home, he enters a cave to keep out the winter chill. Tired beyond imagining, he falls asleep and dreams of a great wolf. The wolf licks his face. He awakens to see a wolf who turns and pads out of the cave. Aggu grabs his spear and stands but hears behind him a sound, a very human cry. He is terrified that he has walked into some spirit's lair. But the cry calls to his heart. He makes a fire and by its light sees three little faces looking at him. One has a blue eye and the other hazel. One has a hazel eye and the other blue. One has hair of pure white and eyes of pink. They gurgle and laugh at him. They are fat and healthy, nested in leaves and tree bark. They walk over on all fours and nuzzle him.

Aggu returns, returns with silver,
Aggu returns, returns with beaver,
Aggu returns, returns with walrus tusks
and his three daughters. Returns to Maddji.

The drummer laughed. Everyone laughed. Nearby, a mournful howl stopped even the chief Chihuahua in his piping. A wolf, a real one this time. Silence fell as we all held our breath.

A tall young woman, one I hadn't seen before, walked into the distant glow from the fire. She didn't rush but everyone stopped talking. She wore no hat, even though the air was crackling with frosty cold. Her hair fell straight, and glowed with golden firelight as she came closer to us. She approached Garral, and taking his hand, touched her forehead to it. She turned, her eyes glistening, and came straight up to Signy, who stood slowly at her approach. They looked at each other for a long time. A tiny whisper of a smile appeared on the girl's face.

"You have come," she said. "At last. I have long dreamed it."

Then she came over to us.

This girl had the grit and bearing of Pocahontas and the inbuilt sense of superiority of my sister Juliette. She didn't smile, but looked long and hard, first at Håkan and then at me.

"They will see you tomorrow. The three sisters. They say tomorrow night the stars will dance for you. That is their message."

Portals of Time

Alexandria – about 380 CE

"A large shipment of slaves arrived today," said Devorah. "They've been taken to the plataea by the Temple of Serapis."

Nysa nodded, her mind elsewhere. The girls stood looking out over the harbour from the shade of the colonnade just outside the Labyrinth Library. Soon they were to join Hypatia and many others for an important dance. Myrna came and rested against the balustrade by Nysa and Devorah.

'This dance is of the greatest importance. A prophecy is to be fulfilled. The stars are aligned in a way most propitious.'

Nysa nodded and repeated what Myrna had said to Devorah.

Devorah smiled. "I caught some of it. I think I'm getting better at listening."

Nysa turned at the sound of hand clapping.

"Come inside," said Anastasia. "The room is prepared."

Once more the Time Knot had been suspended, its curving metal shape casting shadow patterns on the geometric lines of the pink floor. The girls took their places as the boys and young men started the rhythmic pulses of the music. Moments later, led by Angelos playing the flute, the senior Sisters of the Order entered. They formed a circle around the dancers. The Time Knot slowly span and the girls whirled and twirled within the shifting, geometric shapes.

As they danced the floor – smooth and cool – became transparent. Nysa's feet carried her on this glassy surface far away from all the others. Behind her a stench arose, a constricting and throat-squeezing pressure; three grey figures also span slowly, weaving trails of cobweb cloud that choked and obscured all it touched. But in front, three short women walked towards her.

Their faces bore tattoos like some of the women of Egypt, but they didn't look at all Egyptian. Their hair, drawn tight and gathered at the back of their heads, fell almost to their waists. One had hair of pure white. Their eyes flashed fire. Each of them beat a drum and as they drummed, the surface behind Nysa shattered like marble struck with a heavy hammer. The spinning cobweb women behind were furious. Their anger lashed at Nysa's ankles and pulled with cold venom at her heartstrings. But the three small drumming ladies dressed in embroidered leather marched closer and closer. Nysa turned to face her oppressors. Wild eyes and screaming mouths shouting cold silence; they tried to jump the gulf that had opened, but failed. Dust and darkness took the cobweb women. A hound wailed a truly dreadful cry.

Turning back towards the drumming, Nysa found a vast herd of massive deer, bearing great antlers, rumbling past. As cold fresh dust arose – like the Olympic snow in the stories – one beast broke free. Huge, with antlers greater than outstretched arms, it drew close, tossed its head and looked straight at her. Scraping one front hoof, it ducked its head low, snorted and thundered off to join the vanishing herd.

Going on a Visit

Sweden – about 1520

Both Håkan and I slept the sleep of the dead that night. Perhaps the drumming had soothed us or the firewater we'd shared had worked its magic. When we woke the sun had risen nearly overhead and the lavvus had a deep stillness about them. We had a breakfast of sour milk and flat bread, and spent the sunny hours chatting. Håkan now accepted me. At least he looked like he did. We spoke about the objects Paracelsus had passed on to him and I filled him in with my adventures. It took a bit of explaining to show how I had come to Sweden from Alexandria, some hundreds of years in the future. But whatever he'd experienced when we went into the time zone of the Judge Circle allowed him some understanding. Håkan had no real grasp of the forces we were up against and listened in silence when I spoke of the tussle with the evil priests and priestesses in Ancient Egypt who had tried to sacrifice Shoshan.

"Are we done now, do you think, now we have escaped the Danish captain?" Håkan asked.

"I hope so," I said, but a niggly worm inside whispered otherwise.

I explained to him about my vision or dream, where I had seen the Lucian look-a-like on horseback supported by three women aspiring to be witches. He crinkled his eyes, took a breath and let it out again without saying anything.

We chewed over the significance, if any, of my arrival from North Africa. He had very little idea about Egypt or Alexander the Great, and did not believe such a man had actually existed. I began to wonder how I would get home to England, or modern Alexandria, or wherever I should actually be now. Time-hopping teenagers could not just look up the next flight. Somehow I didn't fancy spending the rest of my days drinking sour milk and eating dry reindeer meat, even if some of the tattoos the men wore were cool.

Eira came to our tent and told us we were wanted. We had to bring the things the German doctor had given Håkan, and Håkan's pipes, as well as the berries.

"You have your bagpipes?"

"Of course, I played them at the Judge Circle, remember?"

I'd forgotten. I'd no idea the pipes had been in his back pack all along. I collected the berries, which were still entirely fresh looking; neither of us had actually tasted one. At the tent where Eira and Signy slept, Garral's tall daughter waited. She glanced up at the sky when we arrived. Signy and Eira came out at the sound of our voices.

"I will need to take them soon," said the girl.

"Can I come?" asked Eira, sounding and looking her age for once.

"No," said Signy. "The sisters didn't ask for you."

"Why? I was the one who shot the horse wasn't I?"

Signy gave a slight smile and said, "Yes, that's true. But the sisters only asked for Håkan and the English prince."

English prince! Did they know something I didn't know?

Signy held Håkan by the shoulders and looked at him without smiling.

"You're a good boy. I'm proud of you."

She turned to me and said, "Keep safe. We owe you much I think, now and in the future."

Confusion clouded my thoughts and I'm not sure I said anything in response. I thought we were only going to another lavvu and would be back a few minutes later.

"I'm Hilká" said Garral's daughter as she took the lead. We soon left the circle of tents and followed a narrow well-trodden path through the forest. Hilká walked fast and we almost had to trot to keep up with her. The dusk deepened between the tall trees, and more than once I nearly whiplashed my face with a low branch. We climbed a little, and crossed a frozen stream, stepping on a couple of greenish stones to make the far bank. Something snuffled and crashed away through the undergrowth but I didn't see what. Still Hilká walked like she'd entered the Ladies' Marathon.

The path swung to the right and we came into a clearing. Two reindeer stood tethered to a tree with a low wooden trough nearby. Central and towards the end of the clearing stood a lavvu, almost white in colour, made from pale leather, I guessed. A fire crackled nearby. All the men of the tribe stood to one side, talking quietly with each other. They didn't catch our eyes as Hilká led us to the lavvu. She held up her hand to get us to stop, and went in on her own.

The men now looked our way, unsmiling and some with deep frowns. My heart started to speed up and a pool of coldness settled in my stomach.

"Come," said Hilká, beckoning us into the lavvu.

The Woman with Pink Eyes

Inside, the space – bigger than I'd anticipated – appeared empty at first. From the centre, radiating struts of wood ran down to the upright circular wall made of soft leather. Hanging from the struts were many bunches of dried flowers and herbs reminding me of the room Signy used at her farm. The ground, covered with thick pelts, had padded cushions, all embroidered and looking luxurious in the soft light of several oil lamps. The flames flickered and something on the far side of the lavvu glistened. Eyes! Three women stared at us. Three women sitting close together, also dressed in soft leather so light in colour, they nearly merged with the wall behind them. All three were tiny. I mean, they really were very small. Not midgets, but none of them would have quite made the five-foot mark needed to go on certain Disneyland rides. Two had coiled silver hair and one had hair whiter than cotton wool and as fine as silk. Her eyes were entirely pink.

Hilká cleared her throat noisily behind us. I turned and she pointed with her chin at the pouch I held in my hand. I started to move to give it to her and she shook her head. Then I got it. Finally. I approached the tiny sisters. I half-bowed and bobbed and felt a flush rising to my cheeks as I offered the berries in the bag to the pink-eyed sister. Her hands had large veins and papery skin; she opened the pouch. She poured some of the berries into her hands and her sisters examined them. All three smiled in unison and nodded.

Pink-eyes waved to where we could sit. We eased ourselves down onto the comfort of a raised multi-coloured pelt. The sisters in front of us had faces so crinkly no amount of face cream would have made any difference, even if they were worth it. Their features, apart from the peculiarity of their eyes, were virtually identical. I thought they could easily be over 100 years old. But then I thought that of some of my teachers at Scrivener's. Maybe I wasn't a good judge.

Pink-eyes nodded once more. A cold swish of wind suggested that Hilká had left. Silence settled around us as the three crones studied us in their own time. From a great distance I sensed a rushing, as though a huge herd of wild horses charged through grasslands and we could just make out the sound. The tiny woman with snow-white hair raised her eyebrows a fraction, as if to say, "Did you hear that?"

Once more a distant sound arose at the very edge of my mind. A pounding of waves on the shore. The sound gathered and came closer.

"You are welcome here, prince," said the inner voice as the waves turned into words. Pink-eyes looked at me and her eyebrows rose another sliver.

I nodded. I formed the words *'I am not a prince. Just a schoolboy from—'*

Inside my mind and behind the three sisters at the same time, the bear we'd seen south of here, barked and showed its teeth. Håkan sucked in his breath and leaned back. He'd seen it too.

'You. Boy.' The pink-eyed woman pointed at me. *'You are of a chain that must not be broken. The rivers of the destiny of tribes flow this way and that, but they flow true. It is to our ancestors we must be faithful. Those who forget their ancestors are destined to wander alone and friendless till they learn who they truly are.'*

'And you. Blood of our blood,' said the sister on the left to Håkan, *'you will weave the north and the south together, with sweet sound, even as you weave time past and time future with harmony. So the prophecy said. So we saw. So the drums have spoken.'*

And, although the lips of the sisters remained still whilst this odd conversation flowed from them, the men outside struck up on their drums.

The third sister nodded. Her voice rang like a melody half remembered, gentle notes but ones that lingered on and on.

'Those of us who dwell on the edges of this world also dwell on the edges of time. We three see time past, time now and time yet to come. Like the sisters in tales told of old, the threads of many destinies weave their way through our lavvu. We watch. We measure. We see where destiny's sword cuts. Men and women seldom learn the part they play in the whole but you two will know, and will come to know much more. The dark and the light shades have already played out in your vision. We see. We see.'

'All is done and all is still to be done.'

'Conquer the small and the great shall be achieved.'

'Bury the stories deep and the tree of light will illumine all.'

'Fear not the tempest. All will appear lost but all will be saved.'

'Buildings fall into the sea, and cities sink beneath lakes, but the wisdom of the tribe remains with the tribe.'

'The first wisdom is the last wisdom.'

'The known becomes unknown to be known truly.'

For timeless moments the drumbeats encircled us as the sisters' words flooded into our minds. I knew – I couldn't say how – that Håkan heard even as I did. I couldn't tell which sister's words were which. The ideas danced around the lavvu, gradually filling it with light. The sisters seemed to grow, and become younger, their faces radiant. Just beyond them, outside the lavvu wall but in our full vision, the bear – a female bear I now realised – stood on her hind paws.

The pink-eyed sister rose and in a high-pitched, crackling voice said, "Come now, boys, it is time. The stars have awoken."

Hilká, who had returned without my noticing, crossed the lavvu and offered her arm to the tiny woman. They led the way, as the other two moved slowly behind us.

We came out into the fullness of night. So many stars, layer upon layer of them, sparkled in the inky darkness, hanging close but always out of reach. Someone led me to a drum, a drum with paintings. I sat on a cushion on a tree stump and played first with my gloved hands and then with my bare bands. Håkan's bagpipes warmed up, like a few tomcats greeting each other. Then a lilting tune span and wove its way around my rhythms and those of all the other drummers. Pipe music of the small dog variety, created melodies rising far above our own. I drummed and drummed and Hilká touched my arm.

"Look."

The stars simply danced. Constellations gathered, intensified, glittered still more brightly and then faded as others took their place. The names of these star families fell into my mind and I found I knew them already. Above our heads the sky slowly moved, stars chasing each other and forming new groupings. The drumming eased itself into the distance. I stood, maybe aided by Hilká. Håkan also stood, playing his pipes.

The trees withdrew and the snow at our feet hardened and turned dark. Hilká's touch vanished. Walls closed in and geometric shapes clarified in the hard pink ground at our feet. A wave of great warmth gathered close to us, driving out in an instant weeks and weeks of cold.

Twang of Puke

Alexandria – about 380 CE

I looked around. Nobody. We stood in an entirely empty room. The dark chamber, swathed in warmth, had nothing in it except tall lamps with flames guttering and an odd structure made of wooden poles. Håkan's bagpipes wheezed out their last few notes, like someone had just sat on several asthmatic cats. Håkan staggered backwards.

"What's happened? Where are we? Where have the musicians gone? My mother? Oh, Mother of God and Holy Saviour, am I dead?"

"I don't think so, Håkan," I said. "I think we have slipped through—"

"I want to go back." He spun round wildly. "How do we get back?"

That question hadn't really occurred to me. The other times I'd flitted around through time I eventually just returned to the here and now, in Hammerford. It'd never occurred to me I might get stuck in one of Time's coils.

Håkan dropped on his knees. The cool, pink flagstones carried all sorts of lines and curves, some containing colour. Moonlight shone in through high windows. As my eyes adjusted to the gloom I thought I could discern a smudge of lighter darkness across the room.

"I think—"

Håkan threw up. All over the floor in front of him. Splat. Retch. The acrid smell set off something in me and I thought I might be sick too. *What should we do?*

Håkan looked up, wiping the back of his hand across his mouth.

"We must get out of here. The strange smell."

He'd just puked, hadn't he? Did he expect it to smell like a high-class air freshener?

"Like a Catholic Church."

I registered what he meant. The room had a memory of incense. I moved away from Håkan and breathed in. Definitely someone had burned incense, like in one of the Indian shops in the Lanes in Brighton. For just a moment I heard – without really hearing – music. Outside a bell sounded, and in the distance, a drumbeat. This time the sound had a reality. I moved over to the smudge of less dark darkness, where the door might be. It eased open.

I stepped out onto a broad colonnade with a low wall. Beyond this wall, lights from a tall structure reflected on the water. At the top of the building, etched in steps against the sky, a bright beam flared out.

A lighthouse. Not a lighthouse, The Lighthouse. Pharos. One of the Seven Wonders of the World.

It looked just as it had in my vision – or whatever – when I arrived in Alexandria. Sometime in the future. Now here it stood, for real. To the left of the Lighthouse, points of light marked a causeway crossing the harbour and further to my left, a long wharf had little pools of lamplight and people moving about, some carrying lanterns on poles or in their hands.

A ship moved in the distance, oars rising and falling to the beat of a drum.

What time are we in? What on earth do we do now?

Håkan came out into the colonnade and stared about him.

"How come it's so warm?"

We were both still dressed in Sami finery, leather hats and all. His face had a glistening of sweat, but then he'd just vomited.

The colonnade ended in a blank wall on our right. We headed left, keeping in the shadows, and crept slowly and quietly towards the harbour. We passed a double door with what looked like a sword fixed by copper clips above it. Maybe an armoury of some sort? I hoped the soldiers wouldn't emerge as we eased our way past. At the far end of the walkway had another wall blocking our progress, but a door on our left opened onto a further room. I peeked in.

Once more, tired braziers cast feeble light, but here the white floor reflected some of the moonlight and we could make out more detail. We looked all around but could see no one. Apart from the distant sounds from the harbour, silence hovered around us. We went in, walking very gently over stony mosaic pictures. Two larger doors across the room stood wide-open, showing palm trees lit by moonlight in some sort of garden. Between us and those doors a table had been placed. On it two lamps cast a brighter glow, revealing tunics and sandals. Two sets. Looked like we were expected, or if not, this was truly convenient.

"Come on," I whispered, "we need to change."

Håkan followed me as though sleep walking. His eyes had a faraway look and I wondered if he might faint. The faint twang of puke still clung about him.

We both pulled off our leather gear and dropped the embroidered clothes in a boys' bedroom-type heap, on a picture of the head of a man wearing a lion-skin hat. The tunics fitted perfectly, and some cotton undies protected our modesty in case of high winds. They felt like gym shorts but without the elastic or logos. Each of us had a short cape, which tied somehow over our shoulders. I helped Håkan, who didn't understand the concept of a reef knot. His vacant eyes moved around, settling here and there. He sniffed.

We wavered at the door. Swathed in shadow we couldn't be seen, but the equally dense shadows under the trees and bushes could hide a small army. Something hooted or piped. I assumed an Egyptian owl, if there is such a thing.

Moving down the steps, like two reluctant visitors going to a fancy dress party, we crossed the garden and came to a gate leading to the harbour. We'd made it. Or at least I thought we had until I got that we were on a small island. The sea sloshed around at the bottom of some steps, lit by bright moonlight.

"Shoosh," I said, in English.

"What?" said Håkan. "Oh. Shit!"

Hmm, that's what I'd avoided saying, but it sounded okay in Swedish.

Someone cleared their throat behind us. We turned. Standing between us and the museum or whatever it was, stood a man with the dimensions of a small mountain. I heard someone cry out. And realised it was me.

The man raised his fingers to his lips. Fingers belonging to hands the size of a large wicket keeper, wearing protective cricket gloves. That was bad enough but his appearance had my legs turning to jelly. I'd seen this man before. In Alexandria. But not the Alexandria of Greek tunics, rather Modern Alexandria. This man could be the twin of the guy who rescued me from being car-napped whom I'd last seen in Tent City. Only on his head he wore a Roman-type helmet with a short plume.

Putting his thick fingers to his mouth he produced the owl noise once more and beckoned us. Moments after a boat appeared, coming from a jetty twenty or so metres away. Three or four minutes later, we stood on the harbour in Ancient Alexandria watching a small troop of Roman soldiers march. A military man on a black horse rode over towards us, the hooves of his horse clopping on the cobblestones. Now I came in for my second big surprise in as many minutes. The man dismounted and took off his plumed helm. His craggy face entirely matched that of Mohammed, our driver in Alexandria, the one who had picked us up at Cairo airport. Apart from his short military-style haircut, he might have been identical.

He said something in a melodious language. I couldn't understand a word. Perhaps he's talking hieroglyphic? He pointed at me and spoke again, this time more slowly. His voice, a rich baritone with an intonation that suggested he found the world obeyed when he spoke, flowed round us. As it did I 'heard' the meaning of his words inside me.

'You must go with Magnus. Trust him. You know now that you can.' He smiled at me as though I would get his joke. *'For a time you will be in a cage. Don't worry, Magnus will be close by all the time and another friend will be with you. From now on you must pretend to be mute. As though your tongue had been cut out. Understand?'*

My heart thumped blood into my ears so the sounds of his words barely registered, but the meaning did. I nodded, wondering what on earth this all meant.

'You will understand what is spoken, even as you understand me. But you must never speak, unless you can master Greek very rapidly.' A pale reflection of a smile crossed his face.

What happened next happened fast. The horse-rider, or 'the General' as I'd nicknamed him, glanced over towards the far side of the harbour where three figures strode towards us. That was the last thing I saw, as Magnus put a sack or something over my head. But I'd seen enough of the three figures to register that two were tall black men.

'Fear not, my friend. All will be plain shortly and your service is much valued.'

Magnus, the man mountain, half-lifted and half-walked me deeper into the harbour.

An Old Friend

Magnus didn't speak and even when I tried to listen to his thoughts, all I picked up sounded like the scuffling of shoes on cobbles. After an eternity of walking and stumbling through narrow streets that climbed and echoed with our footsteps, the noise level around us picked up. Even through my musty cloth fashion-accessory, I could tell we were in a large square, with people talking in groups and a lot of torches flickering away. I smelt roast meat and my mouth, dry as a bone until a few moments before, gushed with saliva. *I could eat a horse.* I decided that might not be a good wish in these circumstances. Other hands, less kind than Magnus's banana bunches, took my arms and I was pushed at the same time as the hood came off. I staggered into a cage sited at the edge of a large torch-lit square.

The cage floor had straw strewn over it. At one corner my clever nose told me the pottery pot was a privy: a public one and very smelly. At the opposite corner, where a bunch of girls packed in together, stood another larger pot that might have water. I hoped so. My thirst proved worse than my hunger. A girl, larger than the rest, sat right by the ribbed jar, holding a ladle. I sensed she could and would use it as a weapon if any of the boys at my end approached in the wrong way. She was hunched over with her copious dark hair covering her face; one eye glinted between thick tresses, staring right at me.

At my end, near the farmyard smells, about ten boys sat doing disconsolate impressions. One cried. I guessed they were near my age, except for a boy of maybe eight or nine with ash-blond hair and rosy cheeks. He stared into the vast square, where people congregated in groups or walked on whatever business would bring them there at night. Immediately outside the wooden struts of my new home, stood men wearing swords. One carried what looked decidedly like a whip. I would have swallowed except all the saliva had fled my mouth once more. My status had just become clear – Slave-boy. That seemed a rather steep price to pay for being able to slip through the cracks in time. I felt less of a Seed and Companion and more like a sacrifice.

I looked around for Håkan. Panic rose through me. He wasn't there. I tried to remember if I'd heard his footsteps along with those of the kindly giant who'd just brought me here. Standing amongst the boys in the smelly enclosure a deep, fearful loneliness rose over me like cold lake water.

In the middle of my self-pity, words surfaced in my mind.

'Don't look at me. Just listen. Nod if you understand.'

I stared towards the square and nodded towards an impressive statue of a bearded young man standing alone on a plinth in the middle, guarded by four stone lions.

'This is just a trick. You are being watched. It must look like you truly are a slave. A mute slave. Nod if you understand.'

I nodded slowly once more as three men walked towards the wooden pen. A combination of my knees giving way and real exhaustion brought me down to a sitting position.

'Lie down, Rhory. Keep your head turned our way and put your arm over your face.'

I adjusted myself a bit like a cat settling on a duvet, touched some boy's leg and got a kick. I could sense the men had reached the outside of the cage. I couldn't understand their language. It sounded coarser than the horseman at the harbour. But the ideas behind the gravelly words bumped and jostled into my mind.

'Do you think he's here?'

'The prophecy says so. On the fifth full moon, it says, the Key-Bearer will come, a King disguised as a slave.'

Someone hawked and spat.

'But is he here? This is not the only slave pen in—'

'He's here.' A smoother voice spoke for the first time, with words that slithered into the cage like thin snakes. *'We just have to*

work out which one.'

'I still don't know how we lost the way here. After all, the giant's not hard to follow.'

'Well we did, and his trick with the flour sack didn't help.'

'What about the other boy?'

'What other boy?'

'There were two. And a horseman.'

'Are you crazy, I saw the boat. There was one boy and the colossus.'

'And the boatman.'

'Of course the boatman. You say you saw a second boy.'

'And a horseman—'

The sound of a slap was followed by a muted yelp.

'I'll pickle your nuts, you curly-haired cretin! There wasn't any horseman.'

The voices dropped and the ideas became confused, involving birds' eggs and pickled fish as well as whipping and branding. I decided not to follow the logic of all that. Then words reached me loud and clear, along with their instant Google translation:

'I'll buy all the boys and torture them till I know which one is this so-called king. The price we'll get for him will more than compensate. They need him by the next New Moon.'

After that I heard nothing. Something scuttled past my nose on the straw. I jerked my head back. The girl by the water jar raised her face, allowing her hair to part and torchlight to play on her face. I knew her. I absolutely knew her. She smiled.

I'd seen her twice before, once on a tube train in London, and once in the Coliseum Theatre in London, when we'd gone to see the ballet, *The Nutcracker*. Obviously, it couldn't be her. Shelley. Could it? Unless she could also travel through time and was now—

'No, my brave friend. I cannot slip through the byways of time. That is your gift. Mine is different. I can hear thoughts quite clearly, perhaps more even than you. Thoughts at a distance. Thoughts being thought

leagues away and even, if I have … it's best you don't stare at me like a startled hound.'

I turned my head and looked at the other boys. Most were asleep except for the blond-haired boy who looked straight at me. I smiled and received a toothy grin in return. I got up, trying hard to keep my legs from shaking. I walked over to Shelley's look-alike. The girl, or woman more precisely, had dropped her head once more but as I approached she raised the ladle and threatened me with it, whilst making strange groaning noises. The blond boy said something. I turned.

'Don't speak back to the boy. You are mute, remember. You must never speak. Your life depends on it.'

I looked at the lad quizzically, giving a shrug and raising my eyebrows. He spoke again. This time the ideas registered.

'She's a vixen and controls the water. She gave one boy a black eye when he tried to take the ladle off her. She's mute though. No tongue. Just as well. She'll be sold cheap to some cat-house.'

I didn't realise catteries needed slaves or even existed in ancient Alexandria. That's one for the history books then.

'You must approach on your knees,' said the boy.

I did so, and when my body knelt between the ladle-bearer and the boy, she winked at me, and took a deep scoop from the jar.

'Don't worry, Rhory. The water is fresh and comes from our own well. You won't need to use the turd pot every few moments.'

I drank the sweet water. My sense of almost total panic had begun to subside. She refilled the ladle and I passed it to my new friend. As he drank she pulled a biscuit from the folds of her clothes.

'Hide this. Eat it when you can. You need your strength. Don't trust Cupid there. He knows too much for a boy of his age but doesn't know how to hide his thoughts.'

I took the ladle back from Cupid, and returned to the boys' side of the pen. I pretended to sleep but the drumming of my heart wouldn't let me do more than doze. Cupid slumped down where he could watch all the other boys, but sleep did overtake him eventually. As the sky began to turn a sickly pale green, I managed to eat the biscuit. Nothing had ever tasted so good. Not even dried reindeer.

Sold to the Highest Bidder

The shout brought me wide-awake. A man with oiled legs and a whip stood nearby, offering kicks to any boys still sleeping. I made it to my feet before his boot reached me. He had a deep scar on one side of his face. An old gladiator perhaps? The thought that I might end up in some sandy pen with lions and crocodiles as my last companions threatened to return the biscuit to the straw at my feet. Sunlight streamed into our cage. It didn't improve the smell of the privy and I nearly gagged.

They grabbed the boy just behind me and led him outside. A noisy throng of thirty or so people stared up at a low stage, where the boy stood shaking and hugging himself. A fat man sat at a table, his head with all the hairy elegance of an egg. His smile would have put a toad to shame. In his right hand he had a short stick made of something white, perhaps ivory. He spoke, toad-like, to the audience. I concentrated. Numbers came in with other ideas like *'not enough'* and *'rich fool, I'll make a good profit on him.'* We were being auctioned. At the edge of the crowd stood two tall black men flanking a shorter man with dark wavy hair held in place by some sort of grips. He wore make-up. He had a scroll in his hand and kept referring to it. He spoke rapidly to one of his black companions.

"Not this one, I think. Too cowardly."

A glistening on the boy's leg showed he'd wet himself. Probably didn't fancy the awful stench of the privy. I didn't blame him and wondered if I could avoid being sold by—

'Rhory! Watch your thoughts. You're not the only Hearer here.'

Worse than school. Even my thoughts were being monitored.

'Remember, whatever happens, don't talk or open your mouth. You are meant to have no tongue.'

For a while only girls were paraded. One, a particularly pretty girl, had to drop her dress. I dropped my eyes. I wanted to kick the man at the table. Drooling toad. I'd seen her back. It had a red welt across it.

Scar-face grabbed my arm and pulled me forward. Faces looked at me expectantly. The last time that had happened before an audience I'd been playing a cow in the school play of Noah. No after-play party this time. One of the black men came forward. I looked back and forth between him and the other black guy. Blooming heck, they were twins. He turned and nodded to his brother. Their smaller white friend raised his scroll a fraction and the bidding started.

Someone shouted out a question. Scar-face grabbed my hair and yanked my face back. His hands, not as gentle as the dentist from hell, squeezed my cheeks and a finger went into my mouth. I tasted a mixture of orange and sweat.

He laughed. Cuffed me as though I was a naughty nephew. His words came out separately and very clear, clear enough for me to get exactly what he said.

"He's mute. No tongue. Good as a secretary if he can write or a bed-chamber servant."

Neither of those appealed. Someone hooted with laughter. Couldn't I just go home?

What just happened? I mean, like, the guy's just lied. He's on my side.

The black twins and their boss were in a huddle talking rapidly. Someone made a bid. The bald-headed man looked across in surprise. One of the black guys tried to see who was bidding.

"That's a month's wages."

"Must be him then."

"Or a trick."

"Sold."

Scar-face dragged me over to a man with a trim beard and a robe that went partly over his head, sort of *Life of Brian* style, Juliette's favourite Monty Python film. My new master spoke rapidly to Scar-face. Scar-face mounted the platform and whispered in Egg-head's ear. He looked up, turned his head and spat. He pointed his ivory cane towards the girl with dark hair, near the water butt.

"Lot 24 withdrawn from sale," announced Egg-head, his toad-like mouth turning down. "A tenth of her book value will be charged anyway."

When the woman who'd protected me arrived, she looked at me and smiled a tiny smile.

'Keep your head down. It's best you're forgotten.'

Four men who looked like they might be out-of-work wrestlers, arrived with a strange box held by two long poles supported by their shoulders. The bearded man hustled me inside with sharp incomprehensible words. Once he was seated, the swaying contraption moved and soon we left the chatter of the square far behind.

Then we stopped. This time the man spoke much more distinctly, through a gap in the curtains, asking if we were being followed. Apparently we were not.

"I'm Maimonides," he said. He leaned over and touched my shoulder. He nodded and smiled. "This is indeed a blessed, most blessed day. Long prophesied."

I offered him a quivery smile.

"Our friend has to walk outside. We're watched and must remain careful. Her name is Myrna. She is from the Hyperborean Lands and carries their great gifts, the gifts of Abaris and Hu and Hesus."

As I tried to make sense of what that might mean the box on poles bumped down. Maimonides, exited quite nimbly for a man of his age. He helped me down. We stood in a courtyard flooded with sunlight. A fountain splashed and sparkled in the middle. Three girls sat perched on the edge of a stone seat looking at me in the way teenage girls look at Boy Bands. I expected them to scream any moment. Next to them sat Håkan. His legs were stretched out in front of him and he held out a plate to me.

"Come on, Rhory," he said in Swedish, "have a fig. Only don't speak, as you have no tongue." His face cracked into a smile. Myrna smiled and squeezed my arm. The girls came over and looked at me as though I was about to explain the secrets of eternal youth and good looks. I think that was the point at which I fainted.

A Vision in the Snow

The mysterious boy now slept in the room shared with Håkan. Myrna had used some herbs to revive him and said he'd simply become exhausted and not to worry, he hadn't caught any pestilence. A long sleep would renew him, she'd added.

Nysa allowed the sunlight to warm her and she enjoyed the play of light through her closed eyelids while sitting in Maimonides' garden. Cat rubbed against her legs.

Much had happened since she'd traversed the Labyrinth and joined the Sisterhood. Last night she'd met up with all of Hypatia's dancers and musicians and processed to the Geometric Room. As the Time Knot revolved slowly she'd danced, allowing the flowing shadows and pulsing sunlight to be her guide. The dancing reached a crescendo after about half an hour, when her legs began to ache. For her at least, the room started to fade. Moving and swaying, she could see a land far below her feet. Great white plains were broken up by huge groves of tall, dark-green trees unlike anything she had ever seen before. Nysa knew the area was colder than even the worst winter day in Alexandria. Two years ago, snow had fallen, settling like flour on all the great temples. Only the oldest people could remember it happening before. She'd collected it into sling shots and thrown some at Khloe. But the country she could see now had to be far, far colder.

Below her, a fire burned and dark tents caught some of the light. Two figures emerged from the bigger tent, followed by three tiny women. One of these women, with snow-white hair, looked up and Nysa felt her presence. The figures started playing music, one drumming and one blowing a strange set of pipes. Boys. Only boys. But they drew closer, or Nysa descended towards them.

A crash of a tambour and Nysa had returned to the room with its rippling shadows.

"I saw him. He's nearly here, except there are two of them." Nysa waved her hands about. "They are dressed so strangely."

"They approach," said Anastasia. "I saw them too and a great beast with dark fur and huge claws."

"Come," said Hypatia. "Angelos, please guide all our musicians back to the shore. Leave the clothing, two lots of clothing, as instructed. Girls, we must gather in the Library."

Nysa knew that meant a meeting of the Sisterhood would take place.

They went swiftly through the door into the Labyrinth Library and were soon in the ceremonial room beneath. With cloaks on and gathered in a simple circle, Hypatia led them in a beautiful chant, and then they sat, keeping the portals of time ajar, as Hypatia put it. Not much time passed, thought Nysa, before Angelos came in and said the two boys had arrived safely, and a certain Magnus had them in his care.

"Come," said Hypatia, "it's all going as it should. Myrna is already where she needs to be, poor thing, and you girls…" she nodded towards where Nysa stood with Devorah and Anastasia, "…need to make haste to go to Devorah's home."

Somehow, Nysa and her friends reached Devorah's house before the boy from the snowy northlands. Hypatia explained he would have no common language with them and they must show him kindness. He arrived, riding with the stranger Nysa had seen before, the one on the black horse; the one who managed to disappear when he wanted to. This time the man entered the courtyard, and dismounted, before helping the boy to descend from the dark stallion. The boy seemed perfectly at ease, for someone who has just crossed from one aeon to another.

"His name is Håkan. HOR-KAN." He emphasised how it should be pronounced. "He will speak through his friend when they're reunited. For now it's well to keep him within this compound."

Maimonides emerged and spoke quietly with the stranger.

"Make our guest some food," the Jew instructed Devorah's mother, who hovered nearby. "I must away to the Temple of Serapis. There are one or two slaves there of great interest. Not least my own helpmate." The mysterious rider and Devorah's father left together.

They'd all taken a very early breakfast – or late dinner – and the boy with pale hair had eaten for two, if not three. He now appeared wide-awake, and once the sun came up decided to amuse them by walking around the courtyard on his hands and managing to do a complete back somersault from a standing position. Devorah had just rewarded him with more figs when Myrna arrived with the boy from the far west, who promptly fainted.

"We'll be slaves."

The next two days passed in a kind of dream. Two of the three girls left, leaving the smallest of them, Devorah, to look after us. I tried to communicate with her using my thoughts but she couldn't catch anything. I could follow her thoughts, though, and with sign language we managed fine. Of Myrna, the Shelley look-alike, I saw little. She left the compound early both days and when she returned, joined the elderly owner of the house, Maimonides, in his room.

"Why do you think we're here?" asked Håkan when we finished our breakfast, a rather bizarre mixture of fish with honey cakes.

"I don't know. We must have a special link with one of the girls. I thought it must be Myrna, but now I'm not sure. It would help if we could find out what year it is."

"Year?"

"You know. If it's before or after the Common Era."

"The what?"

"The Common ... the year Jesus was born."

"Are we in Israel? Will we see him?" Håkan's eyes took on the same intensity as when he played his wailing bagpipes.

"No. We're in Egypt, I think. Well, I know. In the city built by Alexander the Great."

"The general who cut the Gordian Knot?"

"Yes. That one. But I think we're not in his time but later. In fact we must be because Devorah spoke yesterday about the Christians leading riots."

Håkan nodded. He could follow her thoughts as well, although I think he missed more than I did. We were sitting on one of the stone benches in the courtyard, talking softly as we might be overheard even with the high walls surrounding us. Mind you, not many people in ancient Egypt spoke fluent

Swedish, so we were probably safe. A cat sprang onto my lap, making me jump.

"Hello, Cat," I said, and received a nudge from a cold wet nose for my pains.

The gate opened and Myrna came in accompanied by two girls, the same two girls I'd keeled over in front of. Not a great way to impress the opposite sex.

Myrna smiled across at the two of us.

'There's much to plan. We have to act fast. Nysa will explain to you.'

She came over and looked from me to Håkan and back again. Her eyes smiled. Myrna shrugged slightly and sighed.

'Listen well. Much depends on how you all do.' Myrna turned and beckoned to the two girls. They came and stood by the bench where we sat.

"I'm Nysa," said the girl with shortish curly brown hair, "and this is Anastasia." She pointed to her taller friend, who had dark hair falling halfway down her back. Nysa's wide-set brown eyes flitted between Håkan and me. She bit her lip. Anastasia said something far too fast for me to follow her thoughts as she spoke. Nysa leant back and folded her arms. Anastasia said something more, and I caught the word 'Devorah'. She laughed and passed into the shade of the colonnade before entering the house.

Nysa perched herself at the end of our bench and half-turned to face us. Her arms were still folded. She had a woollen dress in dark blue, with geometric shapes embroidered near the bottom. Her pale leather boots were spotted with dry mud.

'We have to go on a journey. It's to save the important teachings. You will need to meet The Lady. We'll be slaves. It's dangerous. But it's okay. I think.'

Håkan, sitting closer to Nysa, glanced at me. His puzzled expression matched my own feelings, though I expected I had picked up more of Nysa's ideas than he had.

Nysa laced her fingers and stretched her arms.

'I saw you both in a vision.'

"Oh, right," I responded in Swedish. I stood up to face them both, talking slowly so both she and Håkan could follow. "What did you see?"

'You were playing the drums. And you were playing something dreadful on a sheep's skin or something.' She grinned at Håkan, who frowned and then laughed. *'You were near a great group of horned beasts, where tall dark trees grow. And watching you stood a massive monster with dark hair and great claws.'*

"Yes. That was us," I said, "just before we came here. And the monster was a bear."

I put my hands on my hips and then, realising I looked like a nerd, put them down again. "How old are you?"

'I've just entered my fourteenth year.'

"Me too, more or less. And also Håkan."

"What journey? Where are we going?" asked Håkan.

'I'm not sure. The Lady – sorry Hypatia – she will explain. It involves the secret library. Last night the sword was stolen. That's a sign. The fanatics want to destroy everything. We must pretend we are slaves, and smuggle the teachings. There's a prophecy. Hypatia will explain.'

Just as well, I thought, and then realised my thoughts were like speaking out aloud to Nysa.

A wave of sadness crossed her face.

'I don't really understand either – I just know it's important. It has to be us young ones. We are the only ones who can find the Hall. I'm sorry I can't explain it better. I don't really understand it, except we must do it. For the Ladies of the Feather. Well for everyone, actually. It has to be soon – maybe tonight.'

Myrna and the other two girls emerged from the house. Maimonides followed them.

"Come," he said in his own language.

We followed him into a room that ran the length of one side of the courtyard and extended two stories high. At the far end, a mezzanine floor with a balustrade, like a wide minstrel's gallery, protruded several metres into the room. On a table lay Håkan's bagpipes that he'd brought with him from Sweden, and also the Sami drum that I must have carried across the great stretches of time. I'd no memory of holding it when we arrived in the harbour, but then it had been a weird evening all round. Our Sami clothes were neatly folded nearby. Sun streamed in from a window above the mezzanine through an open space in the wall that, from its rough edges, appeared to have been recently knocked through. A large irregular structure, swathed in cloth, stood on this upper floor.

Maimonides spoke slowly. Anastasia and Devorah sat on stools on one side of the room, and Håkan and I perched on the table edge. Myrna, still wearing her outdoor cloak, stood to one side.

'There was a prophecy, many years ago. Received in the last years of Ptolemy I. A wise woman's words, the words of a true soothsayer, a sibyl.'

Håkan looked over at me. I didn't understand all I heard, but images suggested something between a good witch and a priestess had been given a vision that she'd written down, in some Greek guy's reign here in Alexandria. I gave him a quick synopsis in Swedish.

"The prophecy has been kept hidden. Our Great Library is well known to all. We take a copy of every book that reaches this port and buy copies of those that do not. Scholars know our pockets are deep for books of great knowledge or wisdom. But few know we have another library, smaller, but infinitely more important."

The Jewish guy cleared his throat and clasped his hands in front of him.

"Well, there has been a sign. The prophecy stated that that library, the Labyrinth Library, would be safe as long as Alexander's sword hung above the door. Last night it was stolen.

A mob commandeered the boat and beat up the few guards. The strength of the door prevented them entering. That and the curse that will fall on any who wrongfully enter.

An image arose in my mind, of a sticky whirlwind sweeping all before it into a deep gully of sharp rocks. Not a curse I wanted to test. Not with the creepy beast that lived in the gully to contend with.

"There is a secret group here, dedicated to the ancient and universal wisdom. This group has representatives of the Nazarene, the Hellenic and Roman mysteries, the Jews and others from farther East. We all venerate what has been gathered here over more than half a millennium. But now we know it must be hidden to keep it safe for the distant future."

Maimonides looked across at me, his eyes twinkling as they narrowed slightly. The grey-haired man nodded as he glanced at each of the young people in turn.

"And even as the prophecy says, it falls to the young to save the wisdom of the old."

He reached into a fold of his cloak and drew out a tube. Carefully removing the cap, he extracted a small scroll. He came over to the table and spread it out. The writing might have been Chinese for all I knew, it didn't have any letters I recognised. He read to us:

"When the crone who eschews the Great Nile and wears the skin of the goat enters the city between the waters, and insults the Mother of the Hawk-eyed God, then the Secrets of the Ages are in peril. When the man on the pale horse leads a river of flame, then that flame will enrage Jove and His two Brothers. Calamity will follow."

Maimonides looked at us all. His face held a serenity, as well as a cold fury.

"An age of darkness comes. An age when all we treasure will be treated as though it never was, as of no importance. It is written and it has to be. We have been warned. We have been warned so we can act when the time is right. Our Hypatia has asked that she should explain what must happen and has a request for you. No one can rightly force another to do a deed involving great jeopardy. We are all free and free to choose."

He stared over our heads for a moment, looking like some Old Testament prophet about to call a plague down on an errant pharaoh.

"I have ordered two palanquins. You are to travel in secret to the harbour. Hypatia will meet you there."

We Meet Hypatia

Travelling in a palanquin was mega. *Beats taxi rides any day.* The cushions were deep and the rocking motion, if there hadn't been so much noise, would have soon lulled me to sleep. Håkan and I shared the palanquin with Nysa. Anastasia, Devorah and Myrna travelled in a second, slightly smaller contraption. Eight men, who could have just left the set of *Pirates of the Caribbean*, carried us. Cool.

We were told to keep our curtains drawn so, of course, we all took turns in peeking. The streets looked like Hammerford when the local team is about to play an important fixture, only much more so. People swirled everywhere and we often had to stop until a way ahead cleared. Some young men carried torches, their pale flames incongruous in the bright sunlight. At one point a passer-by banged on the side of our conveyance, making us all jump. The fact our bearers were armed probably kept us safe. We were descending quite a narrow street.

'We're getting close to the harbour. We've just gone past the Great Library.' Nysa looked at us both. *'We should come out quite close to my father's storage sheds.'*

I was sorry to have missed the Great Library, which I knew was pretty famous, and was going to suggest we went round the block and had another look, when the curtains to our little travelling room were torn back. The sweaty face of a young man with wavy dark hair thrust itself inside. On his forehead a large cross had been drawn in black ash. Nysa screamed. I think I yelped. Håkan jabbed him in the eye with his finger. The man's head vanished accompanied by a howl. In moments we were joggling along much faster. We could hear shouting behind us. I felt we'd entered a personal nightmare designed for three, with goodness knows what chasing us down the street. The men carrying us were shouting. I tuned into their thoughts as best I could.

'Danger.'

'Run or we're dead.'

'I've got cramp.'

'Who was that giant?'

This last came with its own image. Magnus. My personal colossus. I felt a teeny, weeny bit calmer, which meant just shy of total panic on my Richter scale of fear. The palanquins stopped. We were now safe or about to die. A man about my dad's age looked in.

"You're safe now. We have guards here and you weren't followed." He nodded at Håkan and me, but didn't smile. "The time has come, Nysa. The time to serve our Gods as best we're able."

'Yes, Father.'

We stepped out into the semi-gloom of a huge warehouse, filled with sacks and large clay jars. Just outside, beyond an area shaded with a bright yellow awning, the wharf and harbour teemed with people. Some were working, but most were watching as though a bus with the winning cricket team was imminent, or, when I saw their faces, a tumbril with some luckless French aristocrat about to be relieved of his headache.

"We don't have much time."

A woman sat on a stool in the dimness to one side of us. Her eyes had that quality of soft kindness found in the best of nurses, but also had the ability to see right inside you, given to clever headmistresses. She'd a face of such quiet beauty it reminded me of Shoshan's teacher Katesch. Various combs and clips held her dark-brown hair in place and added to her majesty. Her dress, woven with greens and blues that changed hue as she moved, reached close to her feet.

"Gather round. You do understand me?" This last comment she directed to Håkan and me. We nodded.

"This is Hypatia," Nysa whispered to us, her eyes sparkling.

We sat down on sacks arranged in a small semicircle.

"First, greetings to our newest friends." She smiled at the two of us. "Others will join us soon but they are aware of what is going on. You can see from the streets that we are facing a difficult time in Alexandria. The politicians and the newly appointed bishops are using the blind faith of the masses to gather themselves more power. The latest edicts of the Emperor offer us little comfort, and those who are not followers of the new state religion, Christianity, are being put at risk."

She described how the Governor of Alexandria, a personal friend, protected her and her father Theon, but he too experienced pressure from the zealots who would destroy everything not to their taste.

"They have no respect for the Hellenic Religion, nor the venerable Gods of Rome or Egypt. If the hotheads get their way they will destroy our Great Library and close all our temples, some of which have traditions going back to the time of the most ancient pharaohs." A shadow crossed over her face as someone came in from the harbour.

"Ah, here is Angelos."

A tall young man approached us. He looked about 18 or 19, with the build of a rugby forward and the good looks of a man lounging around in a *Men's Health* magazine. He pulled over a sack and sat near the stool. He nodded at Hypatia, who continued:

"I have a request to make of you. It's the reason you're all here." She looked at me and then Håkan as she said this, holding our eyes long enough for slight shivers to go up and down my spine.

"Our Library must be saved – or at least the most important books within it. We owe it to the future, to the generations to come, when the pall of great darkness begins to lift once more."

Again she looked at me, and smiled slightly.

"These days have been foreseen. A Sibylline prophecy in our

care, and known to your fathers –" this to Nysa and the other two girls – "has already begun to be fulfilled. The sword that long protected the most important histories of mankind has been taken, and today we know the lady in the goatskin will arrive. That marks the moment of maximum danger, but also a moment of great opportunity. For the prophecy goes on that the advent of the desert woman will mark the time when doors long sealed will once more open, and those who have not seen fifteen summers may enter once again, if their hearts be pure and their purpose honest."

She looked around the small group sitting at her feet. *Goodness, she means us!* My heart sank. Brave acts against the mob were not really my thing.

"Yes, my young friends, I do mean you. For you are the ones here now. You are the initiated who can penetrate the labyrinth or negotiate the coils of time. Between you, you can save teachings beyond price for those generations yet to come in far-off times."

Crone in a Goatskin

"She's here," said Nysa's father from the door.

"I will slip further into the shadows," said Hypatia. "I'm too well known. But you should all see and remember this day, for it will be a day of both infamy and hope."

The gradual crescendo of noise outside suggested we were drawing closer and closer to a pop concert. A murmuring rumbled around the harbour, accompanied by whistling and high-pitched yelps of delight. It had sounded much the same the day Juliette and I had gone to Hammerford Park to hear the girl band, the Fridays or the Tomorrows or whatever they were called. We stood in the shadows under the yellow awning like a bunch of kids suffering from jaundice.

People on the wharf craned to see who approached from the East. Some had crosses of ash on their foreheads, but many were sullen and shifted around as though uncertain whether to stay or flee. Behind them, craft of all sizes moved across the harbour as though this was a normal day. It clearly wasn't, though. A woman with tanned bandy legs strode towards us, like one of those marathon walkers. Others had to jog a little to keep up. She carried a knobbly dark rod of wood, with a cross piece lashed to it, making a cross as well as a cudgel. Holding it with both hands she swept it back and forth in front of her, like a drum majorette who had forgotten to toss her pole in the air. Some watchers cheered.

"Elizabeth," they murmured. "Elizabeth."

She wore an animal skin that only just protected her modesty. The legs of this long-deceased beast bobbled around her knees. Her shoeless feet slapped against the flag stones on the wharf. As she drew closer to where we stood at the mouth of the warehouse, she started to look about her, and slowed her rhythm. She studied the faces of those near the wharf. Some offered gormless grins; many dropped their eyes and looked intently at their sandals. Her eyes raked our side of things. She fixed on me and slowed some more. Fever chills went right through my body. The words rose up inside, like marsh gas in a dark swamp, *'Ah. There you are.'* Puzzlement spread over Elizabeth's face. The crone moved on, her eyes now intent on something on the far side of the harbour.

I sat down on a convenient stool. Hard. I could only gulp breath with difficulty, as though I'd received a punch in the solar plexus. When she'd looked at me I saw and experienced again the mad red-headed priestess I'd fought with in the old Egyptian temple, the one where Shoshan was nearly sacrificed. At the same time I registered the stout woman from that night in the Coliseum, the one with the green brooch. We had gone to see a ballet after Christmas, and this lady had searched for me. Myrna's look-alike Shelley, had warned me to sneak out a back exit. Somehow she'd found me here. I felt as though I'd been picked out by a form of psychic radar.

Soft hands settled on my shoulders. I looked up to see Hypatia now standing behind me. She didn't speak out loud.

'The forces of Set are powerful. It's best just to let them go. They will have their day for a while. But they will never, ever win.'

A warmth spread from her hands, through my shoulders and down to my abdomen. I could breathe once more.

'Stand and watch. It's important this abomination is witnessed.'

I must have been seated for longer than I thought, for the minxy desert lady had nearly crossed the long causeway that ran from the mainland to the island with the huge Lighthouse. Crowds followed her, but kept a distance, in case her waving cross delivered them an unwelcome whack. Near the Lighthouse, and to its left, stood a rather impressive temple.

"The Temple of Isis," Nysa murmured as though following my thoughts, as indeed she probably was.

An elderly priestess stood halfway down the steps that ran the whole length of the temple's entrance. Gathered at the top were a group of ten or twelve priestesses, trying to keep their dignity in the face of the approaching mob. A man galloped across the causeway, forcing Elizabeth's followers to press themselves against the low walls. One bystander nearly tumbled into the sea and was hauled back by his fellows, who hooted with mirth.

"Peter. Peter the Reader," said Nysa.

"The man on the pale horse" whispered Devorah, "just like the prophecy."

His horse, chunky, rather than like a racehorse, towered above the watchers; its flanks were the colour of old chewing gum, with dark-brown socks as though it had just waded through mud or worse. Nysa jabbed me in the ribs.

The crone had reached the bottom of the temple steps. The elderly priestess, the mother superior I assumed, approached her with her hands spread in welcome or supplication. Elizabeth spun her body with surprising speed and swished her cudgel straight at the other old woman. The priestess went down like washing falling from a washing line. The vicious crone danced about waving her stick. The crosspiece had flown off. The other priestesses fled inside. A trumpet sounded off to our right. A group of soldiers, wearing dark-blue cloaks and helmets with dark-blue plumes, ran in unison along the wharf. The trumpet sounded again, and someone screamed.

"The Governor's men." Nysa's father's face had a crumpled look but a flicker of hope showed in his eyes as the soldiers went past.

The temple now had a sea of people all around. Peter, the rider on the pale horse, appeared to be shouting orders, although the half-mile between him and us meant his words didn't carry over the commotion. Another scream from close by, and a woman with a grubby brown tunic pointed at the temple and made a strange wobbling movement at the same time. A flame appeared at a window. Then another flame sprang out. Men outside ran past holding firebrands. The shouting woman collapsed. Angelos ran over to her.

"Are they burning them alive, Father?"

"No, Nysa. I think the priestesses long decided to offer themselves as a sacrifice if this day came. For to allow their temple to be desecrated would be more than any of them could bear."

The soldiers had by now reached the far side and the crowd began to return. Of Elizabeth there was no sign. Peter, on his horse, was talking to one of the soldiers. They didn't seem disposed to arrest him. We went back inside the warehouse. I threw up in a corner. Hypatia had left. She'd slipped off during the worst of the crisis.

I kicked a sack.

"What can we do," I said. "That is so horrible."

'First you can remember you are mute.' This came from Myrna.

Angelos sat where his mistress had been just an hour or so earlier. He told us what we could now do to help. We all agreed, even though it sounded both unpleasant and dangerous.

Entering the Labyrinth

The oars dipped rhythmically into the water. They'd been painted black, matching the midnight shade of our craft which bumped over the choppy waters of the harbour. We were dressed in dark-grey tunics with matching cloaks, like so many young Ninjas. My face itched where it had been smeared with burnt cork. We sat low in the boat and drops of seawater frequently spattered over us. We'd set off twenty minutes earlier, from the wharf in front of the warehouse.

After the attack on the temple, the mob led by the Desert Vixen had stomped off elsewhere in Alexandria, and no one had paid much heed to five teens and their young companion Angelos, setting out in a long rowing boat. Nysa pointed to the large ship that lay between us and where we were headed, noisy with sailors carrying lights about the deck.

'Father arranged that as a distraction.' Nysa nodded towards the ship, her eyes glittering with reflected firelight, contrasting with her blackened face. I blinked as salt water stung my eyes. I kept glancing towards the glowing remains of the Temple of Isis. The occasional flame and shower of sparks still jetted out of the rubble. A tear or drop of seawater, tickled its way down my cheek. I sniffed. Whatever they wanted us to do, I would now do it, if only for the way those brave women had faced the mob.

We kept the Lighthouse to our left and approached the dark mass of the palace where Håkan and I'd arrived only a few days back. On the harbour side someone juggled with firebrands. Nysa touched my arm and pointed at the performer.

'Look. As arranged. He's distracting the guards.'

I could make out a group of young men standing around the harbour edge holding long poles. We could just hear them chatting and laughing, above the slapping of the waves against the tiny jetty. Light from the firebrands reflected on metal, suggesting armour and swords. They were only the length of a cricket pitch away. Luckily, their backs were to us as they watched the juggler and we disembarked in silence, making our way up to the garden outside the palace. The boatmen who had brought us over, pushed off straight away and rowed on silently, quickly disappearing into the murk.

We walked slowly in single file round the edges of the garden. Above us the palms swayed with quiet majesty, hiding and revealing sparkling stars as we moved. Angelos took the lead, followed by Håkan and then Anastasia. I came next, with Nysa and Devorah behind. The weak light from lamps along the harbour gave us just enough illumination to separate out the back of the person in front from a pillar or a bush. We eased our way up the steps and approached the great doors. They stood slightly ajar. Angelos stopped just outside them, his hand half raised and we all froze where we were. He remained entirely motionless for enough time to allow an egg to become hard boiled. The muscles in my leg ached and knotted. I half-bent down to rub my calf and prevent complete cramp setting in. When I straightened up Angelos, Håkan and Anastasia had vanished. I looked around in panic and Nysa grinned and pointed to the door now opened wider. I entered the darkness of the palace room and careered straight into Anastasia's back.

She caught my arm and squeezed it none too gently. Nysa came up next to her and Anastasia whispered something. I caught a vision of legs, and frowned. It made no sense.

'The guard. He's been knocked out or worse. Angelos tripped over his legs. The guard's been gagged.' Nysa provided the commentary.

'We're not alone,' she continued.

'Are we going back?' I formulated the words with care in my mind, with a mixture of relief and disappointment rising up inside me. Nysa shook her head which I sensed rather than saw.

'We can't. The boat is meeting us by the hidden door. We have to go on.'

Probably the adrenaline would have kicked in at that point anyway, but the sound of shouting ahead of us produced that effect in spades. We took each other's hands and walked across the pale mosaic floor, heading towards the dim rectangle of less black darkness that suggested the side doors. The freshness of the sea cleared my head as we emerged onto the colonnade. Nysa still clutched my hand in hers and I felt reluctant to let go. We were heading straight towards where the shouts came from.

'We must go through the labyrinth. It's the only way out.'

I squeezed her hand in response. They'd told me in the warehouse that we would have to make our way through the maze of the Labyrinth Library. Apparently Nysa would lead the way as she'd recently passed through it and no changes had been made. We approached. Above the door two twisted copper clips showed where the sword had been displayed only a few days ago.

We could hear at least two voices quite close by. This area had lamplight. Nysa's eyes sparkled once more and her mouth had a compressed look I associated with someone about to run a competitive sprint. She released my hand and whispered very quietly in Angelos's ears. He nodded and drew a long dagger from the folds of his charcoal grey cloak. He beckoned Nysa forward. She took my hand once more and looked across at Håkan, standing by Anastasia.

'They have entered the labyrinth and are lost. We're going to slip through. Even if they see us, if we are swift we will outrun them. If they catch us Angelos will deal with them. Our job is to keep on moving forward.'

She waited to ensure we all understood. Perhaps the other girls could follow her thoughts or maybe they already knew the plan. Holding Nysa's hand, I reached back for Håkan. We slipped past a picture of some pale-faced god surrounded by voluptuous women, and entered the curving rows of storage slots. I looked around desperately for the books we were meant to be saving and then remembered that in this era writing was on scrolls, which must be what was stuffed into these giant cubby holes. Nysa hardly paused. We padded silently, first in one direction and then another. At one point we could hear our fellow library visitors just on the other side of the high shelving. The tone of their voices and the tinge of panic in them suggested they realised coming in here hadn't been such a good idea. The light danced on the ceiling far above from the flaming torches they carried. I think they balked at the idea of setting alight their own funeral pyre.

At a gap between one circle of storage and a more inner one, Nysa paused. She pointed out a hieroglyph of a feather, near the floor. A wave of terror swept through me. A sense of despair quickly followed, much like I'd felt with the vision of my own dad begging in some horrible Hammerford future. Nysa took a deep breath and pulled me through the gap. The feelings left instantly. Moments later we stood near a giant cow with a sun between its horns.

'A bull,' corrected Nysa, a little smile of triumph on her face. I nodded, had a closer peek and concluded she was correct. We stood at the centre. *Now what?*

Nysa let go of my hand and led the way down a passage towards a stone chamber glowing with lamplight, some metres ahead of us.

Angelos spoke. Out loud. My heart hammered itself almost out of my chest. Was he an idiot? The older boy grinned at us as he tugged on a long chain hanging near the door to the chamber. It moved silently but a distant soft rasping noise answered as he pulled. Nysa looked at both Håkan and me.

'The library is now closed and will hold its quarry. The only way out is now through this room. And that way has its own perils.' Nysa's teeth flashed another smile.

"Will they die?"

We entered the room with a large pillar in the middle. All the walls had paintings. Angelos led us to look at the right-hand wall and studied the picture there. I recognised Anubis, the jackal-headed god, and my favourite, the Lady with the feather on her head. Nysa and Angelos stared at some smaller pictures, nodded to each other and then had us stand in the far left corner of the room.

Angelos pointed to a rectangular stone that stood out, literally, from the back wall, and had a face of some type of anteater on it. He said something and I got we were absolutely not to touch this. He and Nysa pushed on other pictures and they depressed inwards. Moments later, by the other back corner, a huge slab of the floor slid under the wall, making a dull grinding noise. The young men stuck in the labyrinth shouted, fear and anger colouring their words. The girls descended into this new hole, with Anastasia leading Håkan.

Angelos beckoned to me. He knelt down by my knees and grasped my legs. He was really strong. He stood up, lifting me high towards the lamps over our heads.

'Swing.'

I got the message and pushed the lamp. It swung on the chains that went high up to the ceiling in the total murk above. We repeated the exercise with the other lamp, producing a weird effect on the pictures in the room. They almost came alive and didn't now have a very friendly disposition. Angelos shouted something rude, judging by the disturbing anatomical image that arose in my mind, and we ducked down the stone stairs to the room below the chamber. We could hear feet flapping about somewhere above us. Angelos spoke slowly in his own language.

'Now they will easily find the Apis Bull and the chamber. But it will be their sarcophagus unless and until the librarians decide to let them out. Let's hope there are librarians still left alive tomorrow to do so.'

He grinned without any mirth in his eyes. He pulled a lever and a rasping noise accompanied the stone ceiling juddering back into place above us.

'Come. We've a task to do.'

For some hours we worked in a blur of activity. In these rooms below the library other scrolls were stored, along with strange chimney-shaped pillars of pale clay, full of writing I couldn't begin to fathom. We carried our precious parchments, scrolls and tubes of ancient wisdom across a large room decorated with lovely frescoes that I didn't have time to study. Sweat dripped into my eyes and the regular blast of sea air became a welcome respite when we made it outside to where the boat had been docked. The ceremonial room, as Nysa called it, had a further stairway going down. After descending this and following a corridor, we came to a doorway leading to a vestibule and a further door. Both stood open. We emerged onto a hidden outer area behind high rocks. We descended a few more stairs and reached a tiny wharf hidden behind an outcrop of rocks further out to sea. Here our boat bobbed up and down. Strong hands took our precious cargo and stowed it with great care. Above us stars twinkled. On this side of the island we could hear nothing of the harbour life and could just make out the top of the great Pharos Lighthouse. The boatmen didn't come inside and seemed a little nervous of what they were handling with such gentle concern.

"We're finished." Nysa smiled, her teeth brilliantly white against her charcoal-dark face. "Come," she murmured, "something you must see."

We followed her back to the room under the painted chamber with its clever trick wall. One set of stairs ascended, to end in the ceiling made by the huge slab of stone that had returned to its original position. On the other side of the room, away from the door we had been passing in and out of like pack animals, a narrower stairway rose up much higher. I followed Nysa up and she pointed out a hollow area in the wall. Pressing my face into that I could look through a peephole into the chamber beyond the labyrinth. The paintings in the room still swayed like a crazy ship at sea, as the lamps continued to swing. Two young men paced up and down the wobbling room. They held smoking torches in their hands. The air now had a haze and one of them coughed. Their eyes darted about this way and that and despite their tans they were very pale.

I descended the stairs and let Håkan have a look.

'Will they die?"

"No, I don't think so," Nysa smiled a tight smile at me. "It's important they respect the Library and now they will. I don't think any of their friends will come this way anytime soon. I'm sure the Lady, Hypatia, will see they get released. Eventually."

'We must go." This from Angelos.

Some few minutes later we were far out into the harbour once more, gliding through the darkness, this time with Maimonides' ship giving its distracting display on our left.

"Now we become slaves." Nysa rubbed my arm and grinned up at me. "It's going to be quite an adventure."

I'd a horrible suspicion she might be right!

A Smelly Ride

Our smelly cart crunched and bumped its way over the uneven road. We lay or sat on the soft straw, watching the Nile to one side of us and the cultivated fields on the other change hour by hour and remain essentially the same. The upright poles of our mobile prison were made from thick bamboo. A crosspiece of stout planking, extending all round these poles and lashed to them, had cooking pans and water sacks attached. Over our heads a torn canvas covering protected us from the relentless sun. A flap of the same stained material could be unrolled on the outside of either side of our contraption, meaning fair-skinned slaves like me would not end up lobster red.

Four substantial horses pulled us along. Angelos sat outside with the driver, his hair now oiled, a dagger at his belt and the black lines around his eyes giving him the look of a young slaver. Our driver, as big as two all-in wrestlers rolled into one, gave me great confidence we were not about to be sold to some Nubian potentate for his amusement. We were being driven by Magnus, the man mountain who'd saved me more than once already.

'We're halfway there.'

'Oh, good,' I responded to Nysa. *'I'll miss the smell when we finally get out of this cart.'*

She smiled. Nysa had a grubby cloth pulled over her head, and wore an old dress from one of her servants. Anastasia wore gaudy clothes with her bare tummy just showing. She had a circlet of silver coins around her forehead. Her hair, which she kept rearranging this way and that, hung loose and had taken on a dusty quality. Håkan sat close by, dressed like me in a simple tunic with a thin blanket to keep him warm at night. Devorah had fallen asleep with her head in Nysa's lap. One of her sandals had slipped off a rather grimy foot. To be honest, I hardly noticed the smell any more, designed to keep the curious at a distance.

It had been Myrna's idea when we set off from the warehouse in the early hours of dawn, the same night we'd taken the scrolls from the library. The straw covering the bottom of the cart had a sweet smell and proved to be surprisingly soft as we walked over it. Myrna had taken a phial from her satchel and dribbled a gooey liquid around the edges of the cart. Aroma de cat pee mixed with fragrance of foot rot. Goodness only knows how she'd made it. We all protested, but she pointed out in her own silent way, that it would keep us safe by disguising us. We could remain the sweet-smelling children of merchants that most of us actually were.

We'd left Alexandria through the southern gate. It had taken a good thirty minutes to weave through the streets even at that early hour. Although most of the rioters seemed to have gone to their beds, market traders were abroad and our cart became involved in more than one argument. The conflict resolved swiftly once Magnus stood up. Just outside the city gates, stall-holders were setting up their wares by lamplight. Various people milled around waiting for the bell that would indicate strangers could enter the city. I saw the black twins at the same moment they spotted our cart. One leaned close to the other. I pretended to be dozing, sitting leaning against the struts of our new home, and tuned into their talk.

'Is that them?'

'Dunno. They look filthy, not the highborn and the son of kings at all.'

'Disguised?'

'Could be. It's our best bet. We've watched here for two days. The prophecy said they'll move to the south towards the palaces of Sothis.'

'The Pyramids, you mean.'

'Just so. Come. Let's tell Simoneas. We'll easily catch them.'

Once Alexandria had passed out of sight I told – inwardly – what I'd heard to Nysa and Håkan. Nysa told Angelos, using more conventional means of communication. Magnus as usual didn't comment. Angelos looked over to me, chewing his lip. He murmured something in Magnus's ear and Magnus nodded. About half an hour later we came to a crossroads of sorts, with a track leading west away from the Nile that flowed by relentlessly on our left. Magnus eased the horses onto this track and behind a significant clump of palm trees. We took this side road for about fifteen minutes and then he stopped. The man mountain came round and opened the door at the back of our cage. Angelos suggested we stretch our legs. A quick interchange took place between Angelos and Nysa. She pointed at me.

'Go with him. You can hear best at a distance, better than me. We'll see if we're being followed.'

Under Angelos's direction, I wrapped a clean square cloth around my head, giving myself an air of eastern mystery and keeping the sun off. The heat pressed down on me as we climbed a significant dune behind the trees.

'Keep low,' Angelos whispered and gestured at the same time. When we made the crest of our little sandy hill, without stepping on any scorpions or seeing any asps, we surveyed the road we'd followed stretching back several miles. In front of us the Nile glittered in muddy glory. One boat made its way upstream, with its sail flapping in the strong breeze. I wiped sweat from my eyes, and squinted at the road behind us shimmering in the dazzling sunlight. It moved away from the river for a bit, passing through cultivated land on both sides. Rocky outcrops and sandy slopes broke up the view even from our higher vantage point. Anyone following us could not be sure if we were ahead or not.

Angelos poked me. He pointed back towards Alexandria. Dust rose from the road and reflected light flashed from a chariot pulled by two horses. Behind rode three or four men on camels. They would be level with us in about fifteen minutes, I judged.

I turned to ask Angelos a question but already he was loping down the hill in slithering strides of sand and dust. I followed and arrived back at the cart streaming with sweat. Angelos went with Håkan back the way our cart had taken, carrying two brushes.

"To hide our tracks," Anastasia murmured in my direction. I figured as much and studied Anastasia watching Håkan jog alongside Angelos. A little while later they returned and we all drank deeply from our water flasks. We refilled them at the well near the palm trees. I splashed cool water on my face and enjoyed the sensation of drops trickling down my sweaty back. *Oh for a shower.*

Angelos, Håkan and I climbed back to the lookout point. The party following us, assuming they were, had drawn much closer. They'd stopped a few hundred metres away and we could hear snatches of sound as they talked to each other. I'd not noticed, but the track had divided at that point and they were having to decide which way to go. After studying the ground for a bit they settled on the route we'd taken.

"Sugar! I couldn't hear what they were saying. A jumble. They all spoke at once."

Angelos stared at me. I remembered he didn't speak twenty-first century English. He smiled.

"No, it's all right,' said Angelos. 'We need them in front of us."

They passed us by five minutes later, never appearing to notice the track to our little wadi. Or perhaps Magnus or Angelos had other powers that misdirected people. The fact was that after that point we didn't see them again. *Maybe they're not following us after all.* But I knew that to be a vain hope. The man standing in the chariot had been Simoneas, with one of his coal-black companions. He'd been looking for me the night I'd arrived. I expected the hunt remained in play, with me as the quarry.

'Yes. Halfway there. Another two days and you'll see the pyramids.' Nysa winked at me and I stopped ruminating.

Yes. That would indeed be mega cool. Then we could get rid

of our precious cargo and finally I could go home. I wasn't sure how that would be accomplished, but I'd not given much thought to the possibility that the rest of my life would be spent in Egypt, watching the Roman Empire collapse from a ringside seat.

The scrolls and teachings bumped along just below us. Our cart had a very large false floor. Under this sprung wood floor that held our greying straw, the precious writings had been wrapped in oiled cloths and carefully stowed. Maimonides and Hypatia had watched over that, offering advice. They'd been the ones to decide which scrolls would have to be left behind in the warehouse, for there was not quite room for all those we'd rescued. Angelos appeared to know where our priceless consignment would end up. I wondered if it might be below one of the pyramids.

The next morning, when we'd put a few miles under our belts, Devorah stood and pointed. There, across a dusty plain, with the Nile glittering nearby, lay the pyramids. They dazzled. Pictures I'd seen at school suggested they were built of a reddish stone, but these three pyramids were white and shone on the horizon, as the sun caught their eastern slopes. We pulled into the shade of some high rocks in order to make breakfast. Angelos and Magnus went off to collect brushwood and fill water flasks. Håkan and I sat as the girls bustled around organising honey cakes and a rather tasty omelette. Anastasia threw Håkan an orange. I coughed but she didn't seem to hear.

"Hey, Anastasia, what about me?"

But she paid me no heed at all. She entirely concentrated on the three men on camels who approached on the road in front of us. I elbowed Håkan and we looked behind. The two black twins sat on a rock looking down on us. One was cleaning his nails with the tip of his dagger. The other flashed us the friendliest grin and opened his arms wide.

Entombed Alive?

The distant Sphinx watched us with its sightless eyes. As we trundled towards it we really were captured slaves this time. Behind the bland features of whichever pharaoh had stamped his face on the stone beast, the Great Pyramid rose in stunning glory, much, much higher than I'd imagined. Knowing you're about to be sacrificed in some grim ritual takes the edge off being a tourist. I hardly looked. My tummy rumbled, complaining about lack of breakfast.

Our captors had bundled us quickly into the cart, not giving us time to eat. Magnus and Angelos had disappeared and were out there somewhere in the desert. At least I hoped so. Simoneas, the wavy-haired leader of the group who looked like a rather exotic Roman centurion, gave the orders. All I could pick up was 'quickly' and 'pyramids'. He trotted on ahead and we were left to the tender mercies of the twins. Four swarthy soldiers on camels rode point. One had filed teeth, which he used to amuse the girls, only they didn't seem to get the joke.

We joggled along for quite some time in sullen silence. Once our identical drivers had lost interest in goading us for a bit, Nysa nudged me with her foot.

'Are you all right?' (Nysa)

'Yes. Hungry though. We never had breakfast.' (Me)

'Sorry, Rhory, I should have shared my orange.' (Håkan)

'Can you pick up what they are saying?' (Nysa)

Nysa nodded towards our drivers, who were talking quietly to each other. I tuned in and realised I'd been receiving impressions all along. I formed these into ideas slowly in my mind. Nysa and Håkan watched me intently.

'There's going to be some sort of ceremony. They – the twins – want to watch but may not be allowed. It'll be underground. It's to call forth

some great spirit, some master. They've waited years to see him. Someone lost in an early Dynasty. Simoneas told them the prophecy about this man. He's a great magician … or some such thing.'

I found it weird. As they talked, I kept getting impressions of the longhaired priest I'd come up against before. A few months earlier, the hidden sanctuary, dedicated to a Roman god and buried deep beneath the Hammerford Bandstand, had provided a portal to the past. I'd slipped back temporarily to Ancient Egypt and found myself with friends, in a foul temple. This man, with long hair and dark designs, had tried to sacrifice my Egyptian priestess friend Shoshan, by shutting her in a pen with a huge wild boar. We had escaped. Just.

Was this the dude trapped way back when, in time? I certainly didn't want to invite him into the here and now.

'What'll happen to us?' (Devorah)

I shook my head. The images that floated by as the twins spoke were too horrible to put into words, even words I wouldn't speak. I assumed they didn't really know what would happen to us, which is why they wanted to watch. Their imaginations were the stuff of the horror films I shouldn't have watched, but had … with Juliette. Ugh!

I flicked my eyes around my friends.

'They need something from us. We have a power they want.' (Me)

Anastasia nodded. *'If we can just see how, we have an advantage.'*

Nysa hugged her knees and shuddered. Håkan stared out at the Nile. A hawk circled lazily high above, a silhouette against the deep blue dome of the sky.

'We have to try and escape. We must get our books and scrolls to wherever they need to go.' (Me)

'They have no idea why we are really here, do they?' (Nysa)

'We must look for a chance to do something really bold. I've not come all this way to end up as a burnt offering to some disgusting god.' (Håkan)

We both looked at him. He'd put into words what we'd both

imagined. It didn't help quell the sensations of panic spreading through me.

The hawk drifted off towards the top of the pyramids.

The Sphinx passed by on our left, its face as yet unblemished by some stupid Napoleonic gunner's cannon ball. The setting sun bathed its worn flanks in a reddish hue. My stomach complained about lack of food once more. *Condemned prisoners don't need feeding.* We rode on for another minute or so, heading in the direction of the pyramids. We stopped abruptly by an excavation in the ground.

Even not speaking Egyptian, Greek, North African or whatever the twins were shouting at us, I understood we were meant to get out. A few metres away, at the bottom of a stone stairway, a large grave-shaped hole stared at us with a rectangular black eye. It didn't add to my sense of longevity. One of the twins, notable by a gold tooth in his otherwise pristine pearlies, pointed to the hole and indicated we should climb in. The soldiers, whose camels had settled in the sand with a relieved rocking movement, drew their swords and approached us. Goldtooth hissed to these ruffians:

'Not to be hurt. Make them go down.'

Well at least we weren't going to be executed immediately. Two stout poles, planted in the sand about half a metre away, tilted over the opening. From these poles hung a fairly substantial rope ladder. It disappeared into the utter darkness below.

A tomb with no view?

Green Brooch Lady Returns

Devorah, holding her head high, marched straight to the hole and looked down. She spoke and I gathered there were lights shining down below. The twin with perfect teeth descended first whilst Gold-tooth stood at the top. Devorah followed Mr Perfect Teeth down, her face full of defiance. I went next. Not for the first time I found myself going underground, and unwelcome memories came back of being trapped in the dark Hammerford well. The rectangular hole had stone sides forming a sort of chimney. This continued for at least three metres, and then my head cleared the ceiling of a large underground chamber. The roof had flaking paint decorations showing stars made of five points. The ginormous room extended into darkness in one direction. Light came from four huge torches blazing in sockets about two and a half metres up the walls of the subterranean room. Sand drifted down from the hole over my head.

Up above me, Håkan leant over the hole holding one of the poles, his head and shoulders a dark silhouette against the evening sky. He nodded at me. The ladder swung alarmingly as I made my way down from the high ceiling. Perfect Teeth had let go of the end and stood behind Devorah. He pushed her towards a niche in the end part of the room, furthest away from where the space disappeared into total darkness. As I descended the final two or three metres I noted her hands were now tied behind her back. As I jumped down Devorah tripped and sat on the sand-strewn floor, before wiggling herself back on her feet and stepping up into the niche.

Way above me Håkan began to descend, and long before Perfect Teeth had my wrists tied behind my back Håkan stood next to me. Even in the evanescent torchlight I could see the ferocity in my Swedish friend's eyes.

A few minutes later we were all standing in the niche.

Between us and the end of the rope ladder lay a huge rectangular block of stone, twice as long as it was high or wide. A dark stain blemished the centre with streaks down one of the sides. On our left, another much shallower niche, set higher in the wall, had a large hieroglyph showing two arms held up, like a bad guy surrendering to the local sheriff, only the picture had no head, just raised arms.

'The Ka sign. We believe the spirit of a man can pass through a doorway like that.' Nysa offered me a tight smile. *'I think that's what this is all about. Getting back the magician through that doorway.'*

'That's never going to happen.' Håkan showed me his hands and returned them behind him. Devorah, at my back, started doing something to the rope that bit into my wrists.

A sound suggestive of a ghost being strangled came from the darkness far beyond the rope ladder. The glow in the rectangular slot in the roof, noticeable only a few minutes earlier, had almost vanished. Night had arrived swiftly up there. Down here night remained permanent. A drum started throbbing, joined by a second. The ghost shrieks, produced by some thin reed pipes, I guessed, became more insistent. Multiple tiny lights bobbed and wove their way towards us out of the deep gloom. A procession approached.

My hands were untied.

'Keep them behind you, Rhory.' Nysa banged her shoulder against my arm. *'They mustn't know we're free.'*

Devorah wiggled her way in front of me and the sharp shard of pottery in her hands explained how we'd been liberated. She worked swiftly on Anastasia's rope shackle.

For some moments, Perfect Teeth had been staring transfixed towards the procession coming his way. Now, without so much as a fare-thee-well, he shinned up the rope ladder at the sort of speed that gets you into the Guinness Book of Records. Keeping his arms hidden from the approaching wailers and drummers,

Håkan faced us. He outlined a plan, silently, image by image. Nysa nodded and spoke the same points softly to Anastasia and Devorah. We all nodded. It was better than nothing. Better than just allowing some zombie magician to pass through a stone wall from the distant past. I thought the chance of it working was marginally less than zilch, but as I didn't have a better idea I kept my counsel. I only hoped Håkan's gymnastic skills were up to it and that the girls were in good voice.

As the lead figures in the procession came close enough to be brushed by the lamplight, the girls started crying. I know girls can turn tears on and off like a soda fountain in a café, but the display proved pretty awesome. By sympathetic magic I found myself sniffing and my legs attaining the consistency of one of those trick rubber pencils. Håkan rocked back and forth on his feet with the fervour of a Sami shaman. He stared at the approaching ghouls.

My bowels nearly took on a life of their own when I realised the lead priestess on the left, dressed in a robe of deep green, had red hair. My nemesis. Green Brooch Lady. What on earth was she doing here?

Next to her, looking like Miss World wearing a disguise from the local party-clothes shop on Halloween, was the blonde woman I'd last seen at Sebastian's and Jolyon's party in Hammerford: Victoria, their supposed aunt. She may indeed have been their aunt, but I knew she could travel to dark realms and do dark deeds. I'd seen her at it.

Behind, other men and women followed. Maybe the light played tricks but the two leaders – the witch ladies – had fuzzy edges. I imagined I could see the others through them. The procession had been walking two by two, like primary school children; now they fanned out to form a three-quarter circle around the big stone that became more and more like a sacrificial altar. Victoria and the redheaded Green Brooch woman fully threw back their cowls letting their loose hair stream free. I didn't doubt their reality any more, nor the sharpness of the sickle-shaped blade held by Victoria. The music, played by others further back in the gloom, crashed and bashed its discordant way, the sounds bouncing off all the walls and making thought just about impossible.

Then total silence.

Green Brooch Lady lowered her arm. She surveyed her guests with the diligence and care of a crocodile choosing lunch. She muttered some words under her breath, and inside my mind a huge centipede rose out of muck, with fangs of dark fire and beady eyes full of malice.

As though on some hidden signal the celebrants turned to face the upraised arms in the stone niche. Victoria called out a name and as she did so, the longhaired priest appeared as though standing inside my mind. Unexpectedly, he had a black cigarette in his mouth. Hard to see the funny side when facing imminent and painful demise, but I think I giggled. I'd remembered once seeing the stub of a cigarette just like that outside Hammerford's museum. Someone had been following me. He must be the man that managed to get himself stuck in the wrong time period. Well, we weren't going to be the ones who let him back into our time.

Håkan, Torch Bearer

The girls, sobs extinguished, all screamed in unison – a noise so piercing and high my eardrums nearly gave up the will to live. Flapping their arms around, they jumped down spinning and dipping onto the sandy floor and ducked under the arms of the taper-carrying procession. Anastasia sprang onto the stone altar, followed by Devorah and then Nysa, at the same time as Håkan raced towards the nearest flaming torch. I leapt, shouting something that would make Mum blush, and barged through, sending Victoria into an inglorious heap on the ground, her taper falling and sputtering out, her blade clanging as it hit the paving stones. She felt about as substantial as candyfloss. Candyfloss made of sharp ice.

Håkan reached the wall at speed and leapt up, tipping backwards at the same time and taking two paces high up the stonework. He grabbed the torch, somersaulted backward, landed on his feet and raced towards the other side, using the flaming torch as a Viking might have used a double-handed sword. In the near darkness, the flames flared into huge snake shapes, which the robed ritualists dived to the floor to avoid. Their tapers went out one by one as they waved their arms around wildly, surrounded by the girls' glass-shattering screams. The sand that over years had fallen into this subterranean hall had gathered deepest near the edges. Snuffing out the torch there, Håkan loped to the opposite side and repeated his trick. So audacious did it appear that we all stood watching with our mouths open as he ran up the wall again, plucked the torch from its holder and span backwards to land cat-like with complete control.

Nysa shouted at me to keep moving. I woke up and used my best soccer skills to bash into a man of some size and make it over to the rope ladder. Simoneas yelled something unpleasant at me as he tripped on his fancy robe and fell. So far the plan had worked as intended.

The girls, whose dance skills enabled them to pivot and spin, leapt once more off the altar. Anastasia and Devorah weaved over to me, and jumped with great agility onto the ladder, climbing up towards the night sky above. Simoneas had moved with greater speed than I thought credible and held Nysa by the wrist. As Håkan dowsed the third flaming brand and reduced the room to almost complete gloom, Nysa jumped up, catching his nose with the back of her head and, sticking her legs straight out in front, descended fast, to land rump first on the feet of the slaver. He shouted in pain. Her arm now free, she rolled sideways and skittered across to me. Håkan had the final torch and shouted, "Climb, Rhory, now!"

I did. Victoria shouted, "Catch his feet!" But I guess the Greeks and Egyptians didn't speak English and were perhaps now spooked by the speed at which they were being entombed in the dark. No one got near my feet except Håkan. When almost level with my waist, he lit the rope ladder below us with the final torch. Flames licked up in our direction, adding to my motivation – already pretty strong – to climb. In a couple of athletic movements, Håkan overtook me and disappeared into the rectangular hole above. The bottom third of the ladder fell away in a cascade of sparks. We were safe.

Then I remembered the camel-riding soldiers waiting at reception level above. I paused. The smouldering end of the ladder cast a little light. Robed figures groped their way towards the utter blackness. Someone stepped onto a dropped drum, tripped and cursed. Pinpoints of taper flame gave firefly illumination.

'Come on, Rhory!' This from Nysa, above.

I emerged into the cool night air. Angelos pulled me safely onto the sand around the hole. Of the camels there was no sign. The soldiers sat trussed and gagged at the top of the steps, lit by a huge torch Magnus held high above his head. He smiled slightly in my direction.

'Angelos has explained. There's no time to lose. We must ride on into the desert, just you, me and Håkan. We're the only ones who can find the Hall of Records. That's our job,' Nysa beamed into my mind.

'Why can't they help?' I'm not sure if inner speech can sound petulant but I fancied keeping Magnus on our team after our recent adventure.

'Has to be us. They're too old.' Nysa pointed to Angelos and Magnus. *'And they're not Seeds of Life.'* She nodded towards Anastasia and Devorah.

"I'll drive," said Håkan to me, in Swedish. "You and Nysa sit and watch. We're looking for flames that will appear in the desert."

He flicked the reins and the horses pulled to get the cart moving. In the distance we heard a shout. A few of our recent captors had made it out to the surface. In the dark I guessed they were about the distance of a cricket ground away. They didn't sound happy. I checked to see how Magnus had reacted, but of him, Angelos and the girls I could see nothing.

The horses surged forward with enthusiasm, and I bumped my back against the unyielding bamboo struts of our erstwhile prison. Night had settled in, with only a smudge of a memory of pale green over on our left to suggest where the sun had set. Stars sparkled in the blackness above, with all the clarity I'd seen in the snowy wastes of a Swedish winter. We rumbled towards murky darkness across a gritty terrain. Nysa stood, holding onto one of the bamboo upright poles of the cart and leaning out to the side, grasping the final torch which flared bright as the breeze caught it. I could see nothing ahead and had no idea where Håkan was heading, nor how he'd chosen our course.

Shouting from over to our right sounded alarmingly close. Some of our pursuers were on horseback and riding in such a way as to cut us off in less than a minute.

"Douse the flame!" I shouted at Nysa. "They can see us."

Nysa didn't speak Swedish so I repeated the demand in English, louder and more slowly. She must've picked up my meaning somehow and threw the torch in a great arc. It disappeared beyond a low dune behind us. The thrumming of horse-hooves on sand drew closer. Håkan flicked the reins and shouted the Swedish version of giddy-up. Once more I banged into the struts behind me, nearly losing my balance entirely. When I righted myself, the robe-wearing horse riders were closing in on us like the wraiths of some ancient Klu Klux Klan posse. The flames in front appeared without preamble or warning, illuminating two great doors at the end of a long slope descending gradually ahead of us. They stood partially open.

We approached down the sandy roadway. High banks of sand rose on either side. Håkan pulled sharply on the reins, slowing the horses right down. He put a finger to his lips. The riders appeared above us with their horses scuffling and skittering. As we passed quietly below them they looked for us in vain.

"Where've they gone?"

"One moment they were just ahead and then they vanished."

"Did they fall into this wadi?"

"Where did this gully come from? I've never seen it before."

"Perhaps an old tomb has caved in."

"Might be treasure. We'll come back in the morning. If they tumbled down there they won't get out."

We slipped between the doors and left them to their speculation.

Hall of Records

The hallway we entered had a floor that continued to slope down. More torches just inside the doorway gave enough light for us to make our way steadily forward. The walls on either side of us carried no decoration except for occasional panels of hieroglyphic writing. Ahead of us a soft glow revealed two pillars bearing a crosspiece, set across the breadth of the wide passageway.

"Where are we?"

"We're in the Hall of Records," Håkan responded softly in Swedish. Our lowered voices still echoed around the huge room we were entering. Its walls emanated a glow that gave ample illumination. Håkan had a bad cut on his face. Nysa nursed her wrist and rubbed a deep bruise on her forearm.

'What happened to your face?' Nysa looked over at me.

'I don't know.' I touched my cheek and it stung.

'You're all grazed.'

I remembered careering into Victoria, or at least into some version of Victoria, and the sensation of being dragged past multiple frozen thorns.

'You can leave the cart here.'

Two bald-headed men stood over to one side of the room, near a doorway, with a winged sun painted above. They were identical in every way, from their merry faces to their priestly clothing. Their ears protruded from almost completely spherical faces.

"Thank you," I said, my voice booming around the chamber as though I'd spoken through a loud hailer.

Both men flapped their hands at me, shaking their heads and apparently wiggling their ears all at the same time.

'We can talk quite nicely like this.'

'We invite you to do so too.'

'Better for our nerves.'

I'd no idea which twin had said what, but nodded and just managed to avoid saying, "I'm sorry," out loud.

'Apology accepted.'

'Gratefully.'

'We don't have much time.'

The twin on the right turned to his brother and smiled, nodding.

'But we have to hurry.'

'What we mean is that you don't have much time.'

'We have all the time in the universe.'

A sensation like fizzy water going up my nose happened instead somewhere inside my chest. They were giggling. Håkan and Nysa joined them. We all grinned at each other like something delightfully funny had happened. Which in a way it had.

'Come.' This came from the twin on the left, who led us into the room behind him. *'There's someone you must all meet.'*

This room had relief carvings all around, some picked out in colour. They were arranged in distinct panels, exquisite in their delicacy and fine detail. The closer I looked the more detail I could see. Although the style had every appearance of being Egyptian, the clothing did not. One panel showed a group of people on skis; another revealed reindeer. Further on, a girl stood in front of a bull with a sun between its horns. I studied her face.

'Nysa!'

Nysa crossed the room as though I'd shouted at her. She peered at the wall and then half-frowned and half-smiled.

'It's me. How we rescued the books is recorded over there. And Håkan and the firebrands in the tomb or whatever it was, is shown there.' She pointed to the wall to our right.

'But look.' She took my hand and led me to the far wall opposite the entrance. Here, to one side of a further doorway, a fresco showed a circular building, where the roof stood

supported by statues of Greek goddesses. Walking towards it were two figures, shown only in profile. One, slightly taller, could only be me, and the other, shorter with broader shoulders, quite clearly revealed Håkan.

'But that hasn't happened,' I thought.

'No,' thought Nysa, *'but I know exactly where that palladium is in Alexandria.'*

Håkan, who had entered the next room, stuck his head back out and looked at us.

'Someone wants to meet you.'

We entered. In the middle of the room, a little bit behind Håkan, a girl stood with her dark hair beaded and falling to her shoulders. Over to the left, a woman with iron-grey hair sat on a rather grand armchair made of carved wood. The girl spoke inside our minds.

'We have long awaited this moment. Welcome, my brothers and sister.' She opened her arms. *'Welcome back, Red King and High-Born Son. And to you who bring a New Beginning –'* she nodded to Nysa – *'a special welcome.'*

Shoshan, the Egyptian priestess I'd first seen reflected in the cabinet glass in the British Museum, walked over to Nysa and held both her hands. Then they embraced.

Tears streamed down Nysa's face.

'I've always known you. Always.'

'And I you,' responded Shoshan. *'We just had to remember.'*

Shoshan came over to me and laid her hand on my shoulder. We held each other's gaze. Her features remained those of the young teenager I remembered, but her eyes, in the soft light that flowed around us, appeared beyond age and deep beyond measurement. She nodded and smiled, and looked thirteen once again.

'Red King, you saved me once, and now you've served our blessed Order again with your journey, bringing these priceless treasures to this sanctuary. We will meet once more before this adventure is

complete. Now I must greet my new brother and you must take what little time remains with someone who has waited long for this moment.'

She gently pushed me towards the seated lady, and crossed over to speak with Håkan. The woman wore a simple saffron-coloured robe, gathered above her waist. She beckoned me to a second chair, next to her own. The feet of this chair were formed from tiny carved lion's paws. I sat and turned to the woman. For a moment she remained a stranger, a woman of middle years with some grey in her hair, handsome and with penetrating but kind eyes. Then she became Great Aunt Bridget. Her features fuddled and dissolved into fogginess as my eyes filled with tears. She took my hands.

'I'm so proud of you, Rhory. What the three of you have accomplished is no small thing. You have played your part to the full and I'm pleased I am able to be here to welcome you at the end, well, nearly the end of this venture.'

I took back one hand and wiped the tears from my eyes.

'Does this mean…?' My thoughts trailed off. I didn't know how to give my question the right words.

'Does this mean I'm not dead? Bridget said inwardly. The much younger Bridget than the aunt I'd seen shortly before she died in hospital, smiled.

'We never really die, Rhory. All births and deaths are stepping through a new doorway. Our Nysa's name means New Beginning and that's there at every great change. We go on, adopting first this form and then that, always following our chosen destiny, sometimes well, sometimes less well, but doing what only we can do.'

She put her hands up to my face.

'You saw a vision of how things could be if you and the other Life Seeds had ignored the inner prompting that brought you here. For there are consequences that reach to the very end of time, for all we choose to do or not do. But you acted with courage, even if you took a cold bath in the process.'

I remembered my involuntary exploration of the water

beneath the frozen lake in Sweden. We talked for a bit more. She seemed to know about Dad, Mum and Juliette, but wanted to hear my version. She asked me about meeting Paracelsus and the Sami sisters. For some time we sat in stillness. She squeezed my hands.

'Now you must go. For time passes even while we talk in this space slightly outside time.'

She stood and pointed me towards a painting on the wall behind her chair. One of the wiggly-eared twins pressed on the fresco of a boat travelling down a stylised river; the stone wall pivoted. It opened onto a dimly lit tunnel. The priest beckoned and with me leading the way, Håkan, Nysa and I entered.

Nile Cruise

I eased the soft flesh off a small ripe apricot, using my teeth to extract the pit. I'd become pretty good at this over the last two days. Apricot juice filled my mouth. With considerable skill, I expelled the stone with a whoosh and it hit the rail of the barge, before cannoning into the fast flowing river. I awarded myself ten points and reached for another fruit.

I settled back into the soft cushions of the sofa and contemplated the cook at the end of the Governor's barge beginning preparations for lunch. This was truly the Life of Riley, whoever Riley might be. Last night we'd slept in a palace, the night before in a marquee fit for a pharaoh. On the shore, villagers lined up to watch us go past. They neither waved nor jeered, but stood utterly still as the barge soared by, propelled by the current and the ten oarsmen.

Anastasia, standing on the starboard side (or maybe the port), anyway the side on the right looking forward, called out in her own language. The image of the crocodile in Peter Pan came unbidden to my mind. I eased my way out of my comfort zone and crossed to join her and Nysa at the rail. About fifty metres away a crocodile could be seen lazily swimming down the river. Its tail flipped the water and it had to be at least three metres long. The captain, standing near the front of our craft, where the golden prow rose in curving grandeur, laughed and made jaw-gnashing movements with both his arms, in a passable imitation of a croc eating a schoolboy. I leaned a little over the side, enjoying the manner in which the yellowish water swirled its muddy way past us. The outside of the barge had been painted in yellow and blue designs that matched the canopies, the sail and the storage room at the back of our boat. The steersman, dressed with just enough cotton cloth to be decent, skilfully deployed the great paddle. Our cook, squatting in front of him, put more chicken bits on sticks, on to roast. Yummy.

The wind rustled my hair and I touched my swollen cheek. Brushing against vile Victoria had not been good news for me. My cheek had come up with a welt that stung slightly all the time.

Once we'd left the Hall of Records we emerged through a nondescript cleft in the rocks in sight of the Nile. Angelos sat on a convenient rock with a tiny oil lamp casting enough light for us to find our way to him. When I looked back I could see the craggy hillside and a few stunted palm trees, but I could no longer make out the gap we'd just passed through. He held his fingers to his lips and pointed to a track leading towards the great river. We followed it down. My legs and arms and head ached and I couldn't believe my eyes when, approaching the riverbank, we saw a huge barge drawn up at a small jetty.

Hypatia had arranged through her friend and student, the Governor of Alexandria, to have his barge waiting for us. Goodness only knows what explanation she'd offered him, but grubby, with torn clothes, and looking like the escaped slaves we were, we were greeted by the captain as passing royalty. For most of the first day we all crashed out under the blue and gold canopy, snuggling into the padded seats and sleeping the day away. That night we stopped just outside a small village on the eastern bank, and found a huge marquee kept there for when the Governor wanted to get away from it all. The girls even slept in the Governor's bed! Håkan and I bathed in scented water, dried ourselves with the softest towels this side of Harrods, and dressed like minor pashas in the silky clothes provided. We entered the Riley period.

With ears all around us, however in awe of who they'd been told we were, we didn't share our thoughts on what had happened until we reached the palace the following evening. Built entirely of wood, it stood next to a small damaged stone temple. We spent the late afternoon in even greater luxury, in rooms with exquisite paintings on the walls and wonderful views over the gardens. Later, Nysa, Håkan and I sat together in the back garden enjoying the fragrance of the plants and the spectacular sunset over the Nile. Anastasia and Devorah were playing a board game with Angelos.

'Did Angelos betray us?' (Me)

'No. I don't think so. Leaving us like that had been planned.' (Nysa)

'Been nice if we'd been told.' (Me)

'Would it have helped to know we were the planned human sacrifice?' (Håkan)

We all pondered on that one.

'I'm not sure they were going to sacrifice us, just use us and our connection with time to get back the person they had lost.' (Me)

I told again the story of how the Greek boy Dimitris, along with Shoshan and I, had travelled back in time and thwarted some awful ritual that a tall longhaired priest and the redheaded Green Brooch Lady had planned. The longhaired man had been stuck back in that past. Or at least that's what I guessed. Green Brooch Lady had not, because I didn't think she'd ever been completely there.

'Like this time. The two women at the front of the procession, they weren't quite real … sort of icy projections or something. I think that's why my cheek has gone all funny.'

Nysa bit her lip and then giggled.

'Well you do look funny with that bandage going all round your head.'

I had a poultice on my cheek held on by a bandage. It gave some relief and had been prepared by the housekeeper in the palace.

We congratulated Håkan once more on his remarkable gymnastic skills. He shrugged with some modesty and went off to watch Anastasia playing.

'Do you think we have finished our task now?'

'It looks like it.'

'I wonder how Håkan and I will get back to … to our homes.'

"I think Hypatia will have a way to help. She has this remarkable shape, a mathematical knot. She calls it the Time Knot, as it somehow resembles the way time flows in spirals. We brought you here safely using that with sunlight projected through it. Now the Knot is in Devorah's home, in that big room.'

I remembered the shape we'd seen shrouded in cloth. I nodded, not totally convinced, but calm enough that we would get back … somehow.

Up in Flames

Håkan nudged me out of my daydreaming.

"Look. A boat is approaching and I think that's Myrna aboard."

A small craft had left the western shore and followed a collision course with us. A woman, looking very much like Myrna (or indeed my one-time friend Shelley) stood in the prow. The captain shouted an order and our oarsmen stopped rowing. He shouted again and two of the oarsmen quickly took down the yellow and blue sail. Their colleagues did something clever with their oars so we became motionless with the river racing by.

Myrna came on board. The captain watched with increasing puzzlement as she sat with Nysa, holding her hand, and looking into her eyes in complete silence. Nysa stood. She spoke rapidly to Angelos and the other two girls. I only caught odd images of rampaging crowds and a surreal inner picture of the black twins looking at me through binoculars.

'We must now travel separately.' Nysa indicated. *'Somehow, Simoneas and his companions returned to Alexandria before us. Maybe they travelled through the night while we slept. Anyway, they've persuaded one of the bishops to arrest us on our return. They know we are on this barge. But Myrna and Hypatia have arranged a way to thwart them.'*

Nysa explained the plan to us as the captain and crew watched in bafflement at three kids standing staring at each other in total silence, with all sorts of emotions playing over their faces. One or two of the crew clutched at amulets hanging from their throats, others made strange hand signals.

After brief farewells, with Anastasia brusquely wiping away a tear as she shook Håkan's hand, Nysa, Håkan and I stepped down into Myrna's boat. I slipped and fell knees first into an inch of bilge water. My Life-of-Riley days were officially concluded.

We sailed with a lot of other small craft carrying fruit piled high, into a canal that gave off one of the numerous arms of the lotus flower delta of the Nile. This led to a huge freshwater lake called Mareotis. It sat just south of Alexandria. We could see the Governor's barge way off to the east, on the same lake. It would come closer to land and then anchor while still offshore, making it hard for even a bishop to arrest anyone. That would give Nysa, Håkan and me a chance to slip into the Mediterranean Sea unnoticed, using another canal. By the time said bishop realised we were not there we would have landed at Nysa's father's wharf. Soon after, we planned to be safe in Maimonides's house, or better still in my case, back in Hammerford.

All this had taken time. Night was setting in, giving us useful cover. Nysa dug her nails into my arm.

"Ow!"

She pointed to the approaching shore. I twisted around to see a building on fire, the flames, whipped bright and high by the brisk wind, flaring over the water.

'That is where the canal entrance is.'

'You mean right by the fire?'

I contorted once more as flames dipped and licked right to the water's edge. Something collapsed and sparks jetted skywards.

'We'll have to land near the South Gate and make our way on foot.'

Nysa grimaced. This hadn't been part of the plan at all, and would mean walking right through the City, with the bishop's men and goodness only knows who else looking for us.

I glanced over at Myrna, and she nodded. Nysa spoke to the man in charge of our little boat. He tacked and headed towards the shore somewhat east of the canal entrance. Håkan had adopted his dour expression once more. I felt my stomach sinking past my scraped and damp knees. My comfortable cotton tunic, with embroidered shirt, now had stains. I no longer looked like a minor prince of the East. Once more I ached everywhere and my cheek felt like I'd just been massaged there with coarse sand paper.

We wove, with some skill, through rows of boats moored to buoys close to a little harbour. Unlike the main harbour on the other side of the city, this one had scant illumination. That didn't give our sailor pause, and he steered by his own radar, narrowly missing dark boats and occasionally nudging one slightly aside, to slip closer to the shore. We were so focused on his nautical weaving skills that the shouting took time to register.

"There's a riot going on," said Håkan.

Moored boats with furled sails hid parts of the harbour. Behind them the darkness flowed with opaque motion. Here and there a face, lit by a fiery torch carried high, shouted silent words. Faint screams reached us until the wind altered and beat against our faces, accompanied by shouts of terror or ferocity, and maybe both. The boatman looked at Myrna and she indicated he should continue in.

'I foresaw this in a dream.'

Myrna leant close to us even though her mute mouth remained firmly closed. *'You must seek the garden with the Palladium. That is your salvation.'*

'I agree, I saw it too, in the Hall of Records.' Nysa squeezed my arm.

'How do we find it?'

This from me, being practical as well as doing a passable impression of abject terror. Myrna touched my undamaged cheek, her eyes full of warmth.

'We'll lead you. The confusion will hide you and is your friend. Just keep close. Our advantage is we don't have to talk or shout to find each other.'

Myrna pulled the belt of her robe tighter and slipped a hood over her dark hair.

The boat bumped against a small sloping jetty. Our boatman jumped out holding the painter and shouted at us to be heard over the hubbub. We scrambled onto the slippery jetty. I skidded, just avoiding another damp tumble, and then we were swept into the crowd. Panic, fear, excitement, anger surrounded us, as did fire. Young men shouted as they carried flaming brands. Even with all these voices and all the emotions I could pick out the shared idea.

'They are going to burn the Great Library.'

Nysa and Myrna nodded. Håkan beat his fist into his palm. We put our heads down and forced our way through to the low warehouses at the back of the narrow wharf. Moments later we'd slipped down a tight little alley, disturbing cats and what might've been a fat rat, and we'd made it into the back streets of Alexandria. Myrna led us up weaving lanes and tiny passageways. She seemed to know this obscure back part of the city really well. We reached a medium-sized temple by the edge of a small square. Here a strange silence reigned, as though the building held its breath. We pressed close into its shadows. Myrna stopped by a small studded door. She ran her hands over it to find something. Drawing a key from the folds of her cloak, she slipped it into a large keyhole; moments later we were in the relative quiet of an atrium.

'This belongs to our Sisterhood. We should be safe here. The mob has its sights set on much bigger prizes than this obscure temple to Maat.'

She led us further in and we mounted some stairs towards the back. We came out on a flat roof that had a view across the city and to the top of the Pharos Lighthouse rising up above the rooftops. We could make out the main streets running from East to West. They all flickered with torchlight.

Women standing on the roof started keening. They swayed against each other. A mournful, groaning sadness arose in me. Nysa held my hand and I held Håkan's. Myrna stood behind us with her arms across our shoulders. Watching history happen is not the joy it should be, whatever the History Channel claims. We moved to the edge of the roof, beside the priestesses. Nysa choked back a sigh.

A huge square central to the city filled with lights; maybe I'd visited this forum when about to be auctioned as a slave, the one near the statue of the bearded god. Gradually it grew brighter as hundreds of young men gathered. When the wind, swirling around, blew once more in our faces, we could hear the growling menace of hundreds, maybe thousands of men, determined to be bad.

One moment the square pulsed with light. The next, the street leading from there towards the Great Library became a flowing river of fire.

'The prophecy.' Nysa spoke slowly so we could follow her words within. *'The prophecy is being fulfilled. When a river of fire flows a great calamity will come ... something like that.'*

I pushed my knees against the cold stone of the balustrade. How could these idiots be stopped? How could these idiots be so idiotic?

A small cry came from one of the priestesses. She pointed. A tiny dart of flame arose in the darkness far to the left of the Lighthouse, whose beam watched these iniquitous events with the dispassion of a god. The first flame found its twin and then the twins had a companion. Moments later a huge blaze arose at one end of the building, picking out its vastness in eerie shimmering light. The windows of the Library glowed, as though a party of monstrous merriment was taking place inside. Scrolls, books, learning, priceless thoughts from the previous thousand years, or maybe much longer, vanished within seconds. Manuscripts that had taken days to copy were gone in a twinkling: one moment luminous ideas and the next, glowing ashes. The priestesses hung onto each other, wailing. Myrna held us closer. The paving shivered under our feet. I felt drunk. The rooftop moved like the boat we'd just been on when it sideswiped another craft. I put my foot back to keep balance and hit Myrna's shin. Nysa fell over.

'An earthquake.'

It had finished by the time we'd helped Nysa back on her feet; but the landscape had changed. The fire in the Library, raging through such flammable wisdom, had weakened the building enough that the earthquake had brought down one of its walls. The flames now leapt so high we could make out the details of nearby Alexandria as though in daylight.

Two priestesses came closer. The shorter one whispered in Myrna's ear and then both gave Myrna a hug. She nodded. The short woman, in her thirties, her eyes red, looked at us steadily. She touched my good cheek, did the same to Håkan and then kissed Nysa.

'Come –' Myrna squeezed our shoulders once more – *'now is the time to go. Everyone will be watching the end of the world as they know it. We know different. The long night has begun but you, my young friends, you will all be there at the dawn.'*

She stood in front of us, at the top of the stairway, her face lit in the reddish glow of the fires that now jumped from building to building.

'And maybe so will I,' she added, and I had the distinct image of Shelley, the Irish girl who had helped me at a crucial moment, getting up from a chair in a distant cottage as though she'd seen a ghost.

"Time to go home"

A surge of distant noise swirled around us, along with glowing embers and charred scraps of documents. Smouldering cinders high above mocked the purity of the stars, crossing the sky like minute devil's comets. The streets we followed were largely empty, but easy to navigate in the reddish pall that now enveloped all of Alexandria. At one point we pressed ourselves into a dark doorway as a troop of soldiers rushed past, swords drawn, fear distorting their faces.

'The Governor's men. Not a good night for them. They're meant to protect Alexandria's treasures.'

Myrna held her arms across us as she shared her thoughts, waiting until the last rattle of buckle on breastplate had been swallowed into the distant mêlée of sound.

We crossed a square, avoiding two figures lying very still in the middle of a puddle. On the far side a building had collapsed, leaving a gap like a missing tooth. We picked our way carefully over rubble, and disappeared into a narrow lane.

'This leads to the park. The one with the Palladium.'

We froze as a growling mass of paws and jaws barked its way past us; at least twenty feral dogs intent on goodness knows what. A few minutes later we entered the comparative calm of the park. The reddish glow of the not-so-distant hell gave the trees a piebald look. We crossed a central ceremonial walkway leading towards a distant glimmering temple and could see the main harbour for the first time. The Lighthouse stood undamaged. To the right, where the palace with the Labyrinth Library stood on its own island, flames surged into the night, reflected as a gash of fire on the water as though the sea itself burned.

Myrna groaned. Nysa shouted and tore at her hair. I felt sick.

Tiny figures, silhouetted against the inferno, danced and

waved torches above their heads. Snatches of some hymn carried on the ash-strewn breeze along with frenzied shouts. A man on a pale horse galloped along the harbour's edge scattering the arsonists. He carried a banner that flapped maniacally above his head. Cheers followed him as he swerved onto the main parade that led down to the harbour from the city centre.

Håkan swore in Swedish. I shouted something that would make a football player cringe. Myrna turned to face us.

'Peter the Reader. A man sent by the devil himself.'

Behind her the sea frothed. The ground under us trembled and a low groaning passed beneath our feet. Everything wobbled and shook. Seagulls, soaring like flaming doves over our heads, screamed and screeched. The palace on the island quivered, shattered with an explosion of flame and a giant fountain of sparks, and tumbled slowly into the surging waves. Moments later the sea gushed over the harbour wall and ran, glowing like red lava, up the side streets. When it finally flowed back the harbour stood empty, its wet surface reflecting the embers that now filled the night sky. Many buildings near the harbour had fallen and new fires sprang up in their rubble.

To one side of us a great crack had opened in the soil of the park, big enough that we had to jump to cross it. Myrna pushed us further into the park, moving parallel to the harbour. The ghostly shape of Apollo's Palladium appeared between the trees. It stood on a low rise surrounded by a paved area, now cracked as though some celestial giant had dropped the whole thing from a considerable height.

'Go on. The moment is now. Now you can return.' Myrna held each of us briefly. I shook Nysa's hand, and then with historical inappropriateness, kissed her on the cheek. She put her hand to where I'd touched her.

'Now,' Myrna shooed us on with her hands. We ran towards the Palladium, where eight goddesses stood straight holding the roof high and one had half turned, as though in surprise at what

had occurred in the harbour. We entered a bandstand from a different era. Nysa and Myrna stood half hidden by trees bathed with distant firelight. Smoke or something caused my eyes to water.

Nysa nestled into Myrna as the boys ran up towards the Palladium. Her mute friend drew her close with her arm.

"Losing Rhory and Håkan is like losing two brothers."

'You'll see them again, I'm sure.' Myrna smiled at the young girl, and used her sleeve to dab at a tear. They both lurched to the side as the ground seemed to tip. Nysa screamed. A further tremor had her on her knees as a terrible crashing noise pounded her ears. Dust rose from the Palladium, glowing red with the flames of ancient learning. Nysa scrambled to her feet and pounded her way to where the boys might be trapped under the fallen masonry.

A groaning, formless cry came from behind her.

'Careful, careful.'

Hovering on the first of the three steps that led up to Apollo's circular sanctuary, Nysa surveyed the stonework and damaged floor. Dust still flowed like toxic fog. Myrna came up next to her, limping. Firmly gripping her shoulder to keep Nysa standing outside the broken building, Myrna mounted the next two steps and entered. She crossed the floor to the far side and then circled around back to the entrance. She took Nysa's face in her hands.

'They've gone.'

Nysa wailed. "You mean they're..." She couldn't say it.

'No. I mean they've gone. Returned. They're not here.'

It took time for the meaning of Myrna's thoughts to seep into her soul. Nysa smiled. Turning again to the Palladium she could now make out all the floor. In the middle lay a single stone, the size of a pear. She crossed over to it and picked it up. Its edge felt sticky against her palm. The smudge on her hand, illumined by distant firelight, looked like blood. It mixed with the abrasions on her palm.

"Now we are truly brother and sister," she whispered.

Myrna smiled. *'Time to go home.'*

Hospital

England – about now

The nurse checked the monitor in the corner of the room and the level of the clear fluid held high by a stand and connected to the sleeping patient's arm. All remained as it should. The patient's breathing rose and fell steadily. The nurse made some notes on the chart at the bottom of the bed. As she turned to leave a movement of the hand on the white cover on the bed alerted her.

"Oh. You're awake. Just rest easy. I'll get the doctor."

The patient managed a wan smile.

Outside the private room in St. Bart's Hospital sat a man with an expensive suit and silvery hair. He carried a bunch of flowers and a rather small, expensive basket of fruit, crinkly with stiff cellophane.

"Are you in charge?" The man smiled a nurse-winning smile.

"No," said the nurse, smiling back in spite of herself. "I need to get the doctor."

"May I go in? I'm a relative," the man purred. "I've been waiting more than an hour."

Once more his eyes crinkled and once more the nurse found herself behaving not as normal.

"Of course," she answered, and bustled off to find the doctor.

Victoria used the button to raise the back of her bed to a better angle to talk to her guest. Sardius had placed the fruit on her bedside table and sat in a functional but comfortable leatherette armchair nearby. Its pale green colour matched the decor of the room.

The man's eyes glittered.

"You failed, then."

Victoria felt a wave of anger pass through her, but kept her face passive. She wriggled higher up against the pillow and pulled her light silk dressing gown closer around her bosom. A moment of light-headedness vaporised her thoughts. She took a sip of water from a little plastic cup. Her hand, despite all that had happened, remained steady.

"No. We succeeded. We arrived at the right place at exactly the right time. The brats acted like a homing signal. Emerald and I emerged in the temple and had ample time to prepare our reception for the three junior time travellers. All was proceeding really well. We'd made an energetic link with Diamond while we were still in London—

"I know, Onyx," said Sardius, his words falling onto her like sharp icicles. "I was there. Remember? We had it all set up for you. All you two had to do was the relatively easy task of dealing with these troublesome children."

"Now you mustn't tire our patient." A doctor entered the room, in jeans and a rather expensive white ribbed pullover bearing a small logo of a crocodile with a red mouth. His straight blue-black hair suggested his origin in India, and his good looks might have offered an alternative career in Bollywood. He took his stethoscope from its position as a pet snake around his shoulders and listened to Victoria's chest. He took her pulse.

"Everything is ship-shape Victoria," he said, using a level of familiarity that on other occasions would have had her spitting pure venom. "But you need to rest, my dear. Not too much stimulation."

This the doctor directed to Sardius.

"And plenty of sleep." And with a nod to the nurse, he'd gone.

"Leave us alone please," said Victoria to the nurse, with just enough chill in her voice to restore the cosmic balance.

"Please get me a tea. Be a dear." She emphasised the last word and Sardius frowned but left the room in search of the tea dispenser.

Victoria settled back into her pillow. Only a few days before all had been running just as it should. She'd reached Number 11, as the office building was titled. She travelled up by the express elevator and gained the stunning panoramic view over the City of London. Crossing the extensive Penthouse Suite she descended five floors on a private elevator, the one few people in the building even knew existed. She entered an inner space constructed precisely over the remains of a temple to some ancient Middle Eastern goddess, thoughtfully erected by the Romans when this plot of land near the Thames had briefly belonged to them. The roof of this part of the building was formed by a pyramid of thick glass, similar to the one outside the Louvre, but older by several years. Money and influence kept its form hidden even from the never-sleeping eye of Google Earth. The light streamed down to the foundations of the temple far below, because the seven floors of this building within a building were made entirely of reinforced glass. Every part calibrated, the entire structure acted as a powerful time vortex. Some of the Stones even joked about it, calling it Tardis-by-the-Thames.

"Here's your tea," said Sardius, easing himself back into the armchair. "Now tell me what happened."

Victoria did, as far as she could, although the violent ending, with the Hammerford Puppy bashing into her alternate self, causing all sorts of dangers for her, had left her memory with a few holes. When she'd finished, Sardius nodded.

"Shame. You were very, very near. Next time we'll do it. Next time we'll do it here, now, in England and with the Bruce brat under our direct control. Kids disappear all the time. He'll just be one more mystery for the Daily Express to get all riled up about."

Victoria tasted the tea and its sweetness. She never took sugar. She put it down with a sigh.

"Made a right mess of Number 11."

Victoria looked over at Sardius, her eyebrows asking the silent question.

"Two of the floors cracked right across and will need

replacing. The one where you lay and the one where Emerald lay. You were both lucky that you, and the rest of us, didn't go crashing down in a shower of crystal shards."

"No one ever said this would be easy or safe." Victoria decided she would drink the tea, sweet though it was. She needed all the energy she could muster to plan her revenge.

"You're Alive! Rhory!"

Alexandria – about now

My head felt like a dumper truck had unloaded a mound of hard-core inside my skull, and none too gently at that. As I moved so did the broken bricks, their sharp edges causing more damage. A crashed aeroplane had lodged in the ceiling leaving just its propeller showing. I knew it had crashed because the propeller remained motionless. Nearby, a huge clear weather balloon floated to ward off enemy raiders.

"I think he's awake," someone whispered in a trench far away.

I turned towards the sound, and rubble relocated itself, tumbling inside my head. My rifle must be nearby.

"He moved. I'll call the doctor."

The cloudy sky above my head solidified into a firm ceiling with a distinct crack and a small stain. The propeller remained a propeller but shrank into a ceiling fan. The weather balloon became the colostomy sack nurses use to put fluid in patients' arms. I followed the clear tube down and found it ended in the back of my hand. Of my rifle I could see no sign. The paratrooper looming over me had probably taken it.

"Rhory. Rhory. Thank goodness. OMG. You're alive. Rhory!"

The head shrank to more normal proportions.

"Natash…" My lips were not working quite as they should, owing to being twice their normal size on the right-hand side of my face.

"Wait. Rhory. Don't go anywhere." Natasha grinned and sniffed all at the same time. "I'll get your mum."

Bricks re-arranged themselves. Small outhouses were constructed. Arc lights came on. Duck boards were laid over the sticky mud oozing through my mind. I followed a thought that danced and pivoted between the bullets and reached dry ground.

"MY MUM?" I tried to sit up. All the outhouses tumbled at once. Silence spread like the brick dust. I felt sick ready to rise up from deep in a shell hole nearby. Then the thought returned. *My mum is skiing somewhere in Sweden. No, not Sweden. Switzerland. What is she doing in Alexandria?* On a table next to my bed a bottle of Lucozade had Arabic writing. The door swung open and Mum came in, followed by Natasha with a grin the size of a bulldozer, and then Dad. Something really serious must have happened. I wondered what as I fell asleep.

Natasha ate some of my grapes, popping them in her mouth four at a time. At this rate the huge bunch would last approximately ten minutes.

"Mmmm ... delish."

"I know, you've told me once. Tell me again. What happened?"

Natasha grinned. "You're blocking out the story, Rhory. Story Rhory! Ha! It rhymes. You'd gone to bed, remember? You were feeling ill. We'd gone out leaving just the housekeeper behind. You must have got up because you'd carried your clothes into the bathroom. You'd taken off your pyjamas but not yet put on your jeans or jacket. They lay neatly on the edge of the bath. You must have either fainted or slipped. You fell, hitting your forehead on the sink and somehow scraping your cheek really badly. No one knows quite how. That's how Auntie found you."

A slow smile crept back over her face. The account she had given re-arranged itself in my mind. Clothes came off but didn't go back on.

"You mean..."

Natasha nodded, her eyes looking like a contestant about to win a jackpot.

"You mean when Auntie..."

Natasha nodded like the knitters did when French nobility

mounted the slick steps to the guillotine.

"You mean I was stark…" I couldn't finish the sentence. The reality dawning in my mind had an awfulness that shouldn't be allowed. That positively did not bear thinking about. Dad coming into the hospital room helped me pretend I still did not know quite how Auntie had found me.

"Hullo, Dad," I croaked.

He held his hand up, smiling. He had something to say, but in his own time of course. I'd been awake now for three days and no longer puked every half hour or so. I'd even managed to keep down some Egyptian food. I'd only been bitten by one mosquito. Things were looking up, although apparently Juliette was seriously peeved her skiing holiday had been reduced to just one day before the family all flew back to the UK. Mum and Dad then flew on to Egypt.

Dad rattled a newspaper. *The Daily Mail.*

"I know, I know. It's all they had. And it's out of date. I found an Asterix Book like you asked for but it was all in Arabic, so I didn't get it. But listen to this, Rhory."

He rattled the paper once more to add dramatic emphasis.

"'Did the Egyptians invent the bagpipes?' That's the heading. "Bagpipes have been found in a dig in Alexandria in remarkably good condition. Professor something-or-other – a long Egyptian name – says they're definitely not from World War Two.. They've dated them way older than that. They've put them at the third or fourth century. It goes on: 'Bagpipes are characteristic of the Scots. But maybe the Egyptians or the Greeks got there first. These are the oldest ever found. And after all, the Egyptians also wore kilts.'"

Dad came over and showed me the picture. I could easily recognise Håkan's pipes lying on a table. Behind them, without any comment apparently, lay part of a drum. The drum I'd played in with the Sami way back when, with two stick figures and a bear quite clearly painted on it.

Time Sphere

A timepathway book

M.C. Morison

When a teenage priestess in Ancient Egypt connects with a schoolboy on a visit to the British Museum, they each come under threat as they search for Time's Key.

Paperback: 978-1-78279-330-4 ebook: 978-1-78279-329-8

Bird Without Wings

FAEBLES

Cally Pepper

Sixteen-year-old Scarlett has had more than her fair share of problems, but nothing prepares her for the day she discovers she's growing wings...

Paperback: 978-1-78099-902-9 ebook: 978-1-78099-901-2

Briar Blackwood's Grimmest of Fairytales

Timothy Roderick

After discovering she is the fabled Sleeping Beauty, a brooding goth-girl races against time to undo her deadly fate.

Paperback: 978-1-78279-922-1 ebook: 978-1-78279-923-8

Escape from the Past

The Duke's Wrath

Annette Oppenlander

Trying out an experimental computer game, a fifteen-year-old boy unwittingly time-travels to medieval Germany where he must not only survive but figure out a way home.

Paperback: 978-1-84694-973-9 ebook: 978-1-78535-002-3

Holding On and Letting Go

K.A. Coleman

When her little brother died, Emerson's life came crashing down around her. Now she's back home and her friends want to help, but can Emerson fight to re-enter the world she abandoned?

Paperback: 978-1-78279-577-3 ebook: 978-1-78279-576-6

Midnight Meanders

Annika Jensen

As William journeys through his own mind, revelations are made, relationships are broken and restored, and a faith that once seemed extinct is renewed.

Paperback: 978-1-78279-412-7 ebook: 978-1-78279-411-0

Reggie & Me

The First Book in the Dani Moore Trilogy

Marie Yates

The first book in the Dani Moore Trilogy, Reggie & Me explores a teenager's search for normalcy in the aftermath of rape.

Paperback: 978-1-78279-723-4 ebook: 978-1-78279-722-7

Unconditional

Kelly Lawrence

She's in love with a boy from the wrong side of town...

Paperback: 978-1-78279-394-6 ebook: 978-1-78279-393-9

Readers of ebooks can buy or view any of these bestsellers by clicking on the live link in the title. Most titles are published in paperback and as an ebook. Paperbacks are available in traditional bookshops. Both print and ebook formats are available online.

Find more titles and sign up to our readers' newsletter at www.johnhuntpublishing.com/children-and-young-adult
Follow us on Facebook at
www.facebook.com/JHPChildren
and Twitter at https://twitter.com/JHPChildren